Heart of the Hawk

Band of Bastards, Book 1

Lois Templin

ARE YOU SIGNED UP FOR DRAGONBLADE'S BLOG?

You'll get the latest news and information on exclusive giveaways, exclusive excerpts, coming releases, sales, free books, cover reveals and more.

Check out our complete list of authors, too!

No spam, no junk. That's a promise!

Sign Up Here

www.dragonbladepublishing.com

Dearest Reader;

Thank you for your support of a small press. At Dragonblade Publishing, we strive to bring you the highest quality Historical Romance from some of the best authors in the business. Without your support, there is no 'us', so we sincerely hope you adore these stories and find some new favorite authors along the way.

Happy Reading!

CEO, Dragonblade Publishing

Chapter One

Marcher lands bordering England and Wales.
Late summer 1282

"A PEACOCK? YOU want me to marry a peacock? And an old, withered one at that?"

When she became a widow, Alyce Chetwynd had not anticipated the endless stream of men who would woo her just because she was the sister to the lord of Hawkspur Castle. She certainly benefited as a result of the inheritance of Hawkspur Castle from their uncle, but this elevation in society also came with new expectations for her.

Her brother found the perfect man for her at the change of every sennight. The most recent peacock strutted past for her approval was Luc Montworth—a condescending, grating oaf of a man.

"Old?" Cynwulf spun on his heel to face his sister and scowled. "How can you think Montworth old? He is but ten and five years your senior."

Alyce Chetwynd was a woman willing to settle for nothing less than the man of her dreams, and Montworth was certainly not him. Her desirable characteristics in a husband included charm, integrity, understanding, acceptance, and loyalty above all else. He must also be contented to never have an heir, at least not from Alyce. Thus, the reason Cynwulf's suggestion to marry Montworth, a seemingly reasonable idea to him, was perfectly ludicrous to her.

"I will give you that he is not so old," Alyce admitted, watching her brother pace back and forth in front of her, "but I have no desire to marry him. He does not truly desire me but rather desires a proximity to the lord of Hawkspur Castle. He only wants to be tied to you. If I marry again, I plan to be very discerning in the man I choose."

"Alyce," her brother growled between gritted teeth. "We have been through this time and again. Your expectations are too great. You are preparing yourself for little else but disappointment by wishing and waiting for your ideal man."

"'Tis not true," Alyce said coolly, crossing her arms stubbornly in front of her. "I will not marry again."

"Ah!" Cynwulf exclaimed. "Now we get to the root of the matter. 'Tis not that you truly await the perfect man, 'tis that you never wish to remarry. Your impossible standards are nothing more than your justification to avoid that which you unreasonably fear."

Alyce cringed at the crassness of his remark, but she kept her voice steady. "Unreasonably fear?" she asked, intercepting Cynwulf in his pacing to push against his shoulder with her flattened palm. "Who are you to say I am unreasonable?"

Cynwulf sighed and held her gaze. "People die. People leave. It is a part of life we cannot change. I know you wish for it to be different, but life is constantly changing."

It was true Alyce disliked change because it rarely seemed to be for the better. Most of the changes in her life had started with someone dying. "It's more than just that, and you know it," Alyce said quietly through the lump that seemed to be swelling in her throat.

"Geoffrey was a good man."

She expected nothing less than loyalty from her brother regarding his trusted friend. Cynwulf and Geoffrey had met as young boys while training as squires for Sir Ranolf Chetwynd. Sir Chetwynd was lord of Hawkspur, brother to Alyce's father, and eventually guardian of Cynwulf and Alyce upon the death of their parents. When Uncle Ranolf died, he left Hawkspur to Cynwulf with the stipulation that Alyce would always have a home at the castle for as long as it remained in the family. Cynwulf became lord of Hawkspur, she became chatelaine, and Geoffrey served as Cynwulf's commander of arms until he was killed in a rebel ambush just over a year prior.

Cynwulf tilted his head to the side and spoke in a soft, chiding voice. "He loved you, and he was a good husband; one indiscretion does not change how he felt about you."

A sudden chill froze the blood in Alyce's veins. She dropped her hands to her side, her shoulders drooping as a heavy, familiar weight settled upon them. In many marriages, a husband having trysts or taking a mistress did not constitute a major indiscretion, but she and Geoffrey had the rare privilege of marrying for love— or at least, she'd thought they had married for love. Her uncle could have forced her into a political marriage, but he vowed to let her choose her own path. Had her marriage to Geoffrey been arranged for political strategy and devoid of love she mayhap could understand, even tolerate, her husband taking another woman to his bed, but to her, it had been a humiliation.

"Mayhap for him it did not change how he felt, but for me, it changed everything." The pit of her stomach hardened as shame balled in her belly.

"Nothing changed," Cynwulf said. "He was your husband. You had a life together, and you can be a wife again."

His authoritative voice might work with his men, but to her, he was brother, not lord, especially within the privacy of the family chambers. If anything, his attempts to dictate to her only angered her more. Her spine stiffened and she leveled a cold stare at him. "Nothing changed? How can you say such a thing? Everything changed and I have a constant reminder of it every day."

Cynwulf's eyes rolled in exasperation. "At your word, I will send her and the boy away. Why do you insist they stay?"

"Where will they go? A maid and her bastard son? My husband's bastard son." Alyce shook her head with determination. "I will not make an innocent child suffer for deeds that were not his doing. As for her...." Alyce did not know what she wanted. Janet flaunted her shapely form in front of every man in the castle. It sickened her to look upon the kitchen maid at times and saddened her to see the little boy clinging to her skirts as she served the men in the great hall, flirting all the while. The woman had given her husband the one thing she could not, and thus broke her heart.

"No, the boy and his mother will stay." She hated that her voice still shook when she spoke of them. The woman kept the pain alive in Alyce. Janet served as a constant reminder that it mattered not how much she tried, she could never give a man the heir required and eventually he would break her heart because of it.

"Why do you torture yourself in this manner, Alyce? You have seen her with your own eyes, you know what she is like, and you know the wiles she uses to lure a man."

Alyce wanted to scream with rage, but it would accomplish nothing. Cynwulf did not intentionally hurt her and because of that, she would control her seething temper. "If he loved me the way I loved him, she would not have been a temptation. I alone would have been enough for him."

Cynwulf shook his head slowly from side to side, as he always did when they had this discussion.

"Geoffrey suffered as you did. He felt terrible after, and he realized he had been a fool because he did love you and nearly lost you." He pointed a commanding finger at her, a gesture Alyce had found irritating since they were children. "That is more than most marriages. Many wives are forced to put up with constant mistresses. Geoffrey made one drunken mistake that he regretted for the rest of his time with you. Do not let one incident spoil the memory of the five years you shared."

"I have not let it spoil all memories of him. I knew Geoffrey almost as long as you did, and I loved him until the day he died. How could I not?" Alyce fisted her hands and dug her nails into her palms, determined to force back the tears welling in her eyes. She turned away from her brother, pacing quickly back and forth in front of the hearth. Why must he be so obstinate about her finding another husband?

"I have many fond memories of Geoffrey and our time to-gether. I learned a lesson, however, about trust, and the way love changes once trust is lost. I will not be the wife who sits idly by while her husband takes mistresses to his bed, pretending not to notice because it is what is expected of me. I cannot give a man the heir he requires to continue his legacy and he will have no choice but to eventually set me aside." She stopped her pacing to stand in front of her brother again. "The humiliation would kill me. I want more, Cynwulf, or nothing at all. And since more is impossible, I choose nothing at all."

Cynwulf looked at her with pity and impatience. Inwardly, Alyce cringed at the pleading in Cynwulf's eyes. She knew he was frustrated with her only because he wanted what he thought was best for her.

And she knew exactly what he would say next.

"If something happens to me, where will you go? I will rest easier if I know your future is secured."

"Hawkspur is as much mine as it is yours. Uncle Ranolf left it to both of us."

"And he would have left it solely to you if he didn't fear others would try to take it from you because you are a woman. You must be realistic, Alyce. If something happens to me, you will not be able to hold Hawkspur on your own. Especially amid another Welsh revolt."

Alyce threw her hands up, bored with this argument. "Don't get yourself killed and my future is secure. Unless you wish for me to leave Hawkspur." She narrowed her eyes at him, suddenly suspicious. "Is that the way of it? Are you planning to marry? You fear a wife will not be willing to share Hawkspur with me, don't you?"

"No, I have no plan to marry, and if I did, my wife would have no choice but to recognize your place here. I just want more for you than crops and ledgers."

"I am happy as chatelaine of Hawkspur. Your ledgers are well-kept, the castle well-managed, and the stores are well-filled. This is my home, Cynwulf, and the people here are my family. I want for nothing more."

"It would be one less worry if I knew you would not be alone if something were to happen to me." Cynwulf buried his hand in his hair and dragged his fingers through the dark strands. "You can manage the castle and the land as well as, or even better, than any man but none of that matters if you can't defend Hawkspur."

"Do you not feel you are deserving of Hawkspur, Cynwulf? Father raised you from a babe and never thought of you as a stepson. Neither did Uncle Ranolf."

"They both gave me more than I deserved." Cynwulf placed his hands on her shoulders, shaking her lightly as he spoke. "Uncle Ranolf built Hawkspur, and the castle belongs to the Chetwynd family. You know as well, by rights it would be yours if you were a son instead of a daughter. I am a Chetwynd by name only, not by blood as you are."

"But no one knows that, and Father never treated you as anything different than his own. Nor did Uncle Ranolf. Nor have I." It puzzled her that Cynwulf still felt he did not belong despite being raised by her father from the day he was born to their mother.

Cynwulf lowered his head to look her in the eye. "I must know that you will be taken care of if something happens to me. I must know that you will be safe. If I am gone, the people of the village cannot protect you."

Cynwulf's tone troubled her, frightened her even. Her brother was not a man to worry needlessly. So why was he being so obstinate and repeating himself, as if he wouldn't be satisfied until she agreed with him?

"Why now? Why suddenly is this so important?" Her heart started to pound in her chest as Cynwulf's tongue remained still, but Alyce could see the tension in his eyes.

She jumped as a knock thudded on the wooden door of the solar. Cynwulf dropped his hands from her with a heavy sigh and moved to answer the summons.

A stocky man entered the room, his light brown hair clipped close to his scalp, making him appear even younger than his twenty-five years. Aelwin had been promoted into the position of captain of arms when Alyce's husband died, and he was never far from Cynwulf's side when needed. "My lord, there is a party approaching the castle bearing the banner of the king, along with another I do not recognize."

"The king? What would bring him here?" Alyce's skin prickled with dread. Did her brother know the king was coming? Was that the reason for his unusual behavior?

"It is likely contingent dispatched on behalf of the king and not the king himself," Aelwin said to Alyce, then turned his attention back to Cynwulf. "The other banner appears to be of a bird on a crimson background, one I have not seen before."

Cynwulf muttered an oath, then grabbed his sword from where it rested against the table to slide the blade into its sheath at his waist. "I suppose a proper greeting is required."

Alyce and Aelwin stepped out of his path as he brushed past them. Aelwin followed on Cynwulf's heels, but she took her time, collecting her thoughts as she crossed the hall. Stopping at the door to catch her breath, she smoothed the wrinkles of her tunic and adjusted the gold filigree belt hanging low on her hips as she tried to calm her nerves. She needed to get to the root of her brother's odd behavior, and she did not need the distraction of unexpected guests.

She tugged on the tight arms of her chemise to cover her wrists and adjusted the wide sleeves of her tunic. When she could find nothing more about her appearance to fidget and fuss over, she pushed open the heavy door of the castle and descended the narrow stairs to the bailey.

There had been no warning of a contingent from the king arriving. At least, none that she was aware of. For a fleeting moment, she suspected Cynwulf of hiding the news from her but dismissed it as foolishness. He'd never been one to hide things from her, and she knew of no reason for him to start now. With a bit of luck, the party was merely stopping on their way to another destination and would be gone before the day was over.

Then she would lock Cynwulf in the solar with her until he explained whatever had him acting so strangely.

Chapter Two

Hawk eyed the inhabitants of the small village with suspicion from atop his bulky destrier. Welsh rebels were proving pestilent, attacking Marcher holdings from one end of the border to the other, and here the villagers were as many Welsh as English. He studied the wary faces staring openly at the small army of English knights clopping along the narrow street. He harbored no doubt word had traveled this far of Daffydd ap Gruffydd's conquests in the north of Wales. The English king would not lie down while the brother of the Prince of Wales continued his path of death and destruction through the Marcher lands.

"Does the hawk come home to nest?"

Hawk lowered his brows as he flashed a curious glance at his burly companion. "What say you?"

The man tipped his head to the side and flashed his teeth in a wide grin. "And could it be his mate awaits, tugging on her jesses in anticipation?"

Hawk grunted. "Quit your attempts at wit, Red, and say what you mean."

Red shrugged a huge, fur-covered shoulder and turned his jovial gaze to meet Hawk's. "Just that the king himself dubbed you 'Hawk' because of a lucky feat on your part upon the battlefield, and now he sends you to protect a castle aptly named Hawkspur. I cannot help but think it is a sign from the gods."

Hawk scowled in feigned offense at his friend's remarks. "Lucky?" he growled, "I will have you know, had I not moved as swiftly and accurately as I did, the king would now wear the blade of a Welshman as permanent ornament through his spine."

"That you did, Sir Grogan, revered knight of the realm," Red responded, goading Hawk with mock formality not tolerated from any of his other men. "At the end of the day, naught was lost and you gained the favor of the most powerful man in the land. Thus, my question: Has the hawk come home to nest? Hawkspur is a worthy prize, and more than a coincidence in my mind. Perhaps the king believes it is time for you to have a home."

Hawk did not dare ponder such possibilities. The king spoke often of rewarding him well for his loyal service to the crown, but to aspire to be lord of his own castle was the unobtainable. He was a bastard, and though all knew his father was landed and titled, his father never acknowledged any obligation to his by-blows. And the king had never granted a man such as he with a prize meant for a man of noble birth.

"You forget Hawkspur already has a lord." Hawk continued to keep a watchful eye on the people lining the road as they approached the gated wall of Hawkspur Castle. "We will fulfill the king's command to remind the young lord of his duty. When he has proven himself trustworthy in our opinion, we will leave."

Red shrugged. "And if our host does not comply with your king's command?"

"If Lord Cynwulf does not honor his oath of loyalty, then the king will bring down the full weight of his wrath." Hawk narrowed his eyes at the man who had proved loyal to him without ever needing to mutter an oath. "Edward would not be pleased to hear you refer to him as my king and not your own. You have served him well enough and long enough to look upon him as your liege in spite of your Viking birth."

Red turned his eyes to his commander and met his stare without wavering. "'Tis you I serve and 'tis you I give my loyalty. If you choose to reward the king with your own loyalty–" he shrugged as he spoke– "then he holds my loyalty through you."

The trust and steadfast allegiance this man gave so willingly humbled Hawk, as did the unwavering commitment from the band of men riding behind him. He often felt like an impostor, unworthy of such loyalty, but he would lay down his life for every one of his men.

Men deemed by others as unworthy due to their status as by-blows Hawk deemed as the men most suited for his small army of elite soldiers. These men were entitled to nothing and knew what it meant to fight for everything they had. Like him, each one was bastard-born and forced to fight for wealth and respect, more so than most men. It was the plight of having noblemen for fathers and serving women for mothers. They were nothing more than a band of bastards. A lethal band, but still bastards, nonetheless.

They grew to manhood just out of reach of the opportunities, riches, and respect—often unearned and undeserved—given so easily to the legitimate offspring of the same men who denied any responsibility for the existence of their illegitimate offspring. Though some bastard children were raised in the same house-holds as the legitimate children of their fathers—always with the understanding they were never as good as their legitimate siblings—more were shunned and forced to grow up hungry and afraid. These were the men that Hawk recruited because he knew their worth as the best possible brothers of the shield. Respect and loyalty mattered to these men, and once given they were more steadfast than the steel in his sword.

As the small army passed through the gate of the thick castle wall and the massive keep came into view, the Viking let out a low whistle of approval. "'Tis a certainty the king will not reward you with such a prize? To my eyes, Hawkspur looks to be a castle worth fighting for."

Hawk rolled his eyes at his friend, though he could not help but admire the towering structure. He studied with approval the heavy portcullis hanging overhead, ready to drop down to barricade the entry at a moment's notice, as he rode through the gatehouse and into the open bailey. Scores of men walked the walls of the fortress, and Hawk expected more stood at the ready in each of the four towers anchoring the corners.

Highborn men were given fortresses such as Hawkspur to lord over, not bastard warriors, no matter how skilled they may be.

Hawk shifted his gaze to the Viking riding at his side. "Focus on the mission, Red. King Edward sent us here to ensure the lord does not attempt anything foolish, and to quell the Welsh rebels once and for all." Turning his gaze back to the fortress, Hawk forced himself to ignore the familiar twist in his gut when he coveted something out of his reach. "Let us make our introductions to the lord of this castle."

Without looking back, Hawk knew his soldiers rode in a perfect column behind him, the mounted knights in two straight lines, each man riding even with the horse and rider next to him. He had honed his small band of soldiers into warriors of unflappable discipline and precision, and he understood well the fear instilled by just the sight of them in formation. The Viking reined in his mount just inside the gate to stand as sentry until the entire procession of knights passed unhindered through the gatehouse to enter the inner bailey.

As the entourage moved closer to the main keep, Hawk eyed the young man who awaited them, feet apart, arms crossed and face stern in greeting. The man was taller and broader than most, but Hawk was not intimidated in the least. Next to him stood another man looking just as young, but not as tall nor as stern. Both men looked to Hawk like they were hardly beyond boyhood. Could it possibly be that these two men were the lord and first commander of Hawkspur? One looked like a snarling dog, blustering but harmless, and the other looked like a damn pup.

He turned again to the taller man with the wary look in his eyes, deciding this must be the young lord by the way he studied the small army as though they were a pack of unwanted rats invading his storerooms. Hawk was adept at intimidation and had every intention to put the arrogant youth in his place, but a flutter of movement from behind the men caught his attention.

A surprisingly tall woman scurried across the bailey in their direction, her hands holding up the hem of her gown while loose strands of auburn hair, as rich and bright as autumn leaves, blew across her face as she made her way toward the men. Even in her haste to get to them, her head kept turning from side to side, nodding in acknowledgment of the people she passed, a polite smile on her face as she spoke a few words to each one, but she never slowed her pace. The king had warned him the lord of Hawkspur had a sister who was never very far from her brother, and Hawk had no doubt this was her.

He intended to find out everything there was to know about the woman and how much she knew about her brother, but that would have to wait. The brother required his attention first.

ALYCE LIFTED THE hem of her gown just enough to allow her to trot to Cynwulf's side where he stood with Aelwin in the center of the yard, warily watching a small army that entered under the heavy portcullis. She murmured greetings and acknowledgments as she scooted past everyone in the bailey, not wanting to cause concern despite her rush to get to her brother. A deep foreboding settled over her as she studied the band of men. There were no more than twenty knights altogether, but each wore full armor with weapons and shields adorning their sides. The sight and sound of them was impressive, even intimidating, and Alyce felt a slight shiver run through her frame.

The clamor of the pounding hooves against the hard ground, the rattling armor of the riders, and the squeaking leather of the saddles settled into a quiet din as the knights halted their mounts in front of Cynwulf. A somber silence settled over the baily, punctuated only by the occasional scraping from restless horses pawing the dirt and the whispers of wary villagers.

There was nothing to be concerned about, she reminded herself. The king often sent patrols to the border castles to see with their own eyes the current situation and gather any news to report back. This was surely no different.

Yet, an uneasiness had settled over her that she could not reason away.

The king's banner and another banner of crimson snapped in the wind over the heads of the knights, but she could not recall any other of the king's army looking like this group. All the knights were clad in black from head to foot. Every bit of their armor was black, and except for the lead knight, their shields were black. Even their horses were eerily black. The only sight more ominous than the knights themselves was that of the silver blades of their swords shimmering in the morning light in heavy contrast to these warriors clad in armor dark as midnight.

It was not unusual for English knights to don full armor with their swords at the ready while riding near the Welsh border, especially considering the recent skirmishes with the armies of the Welsh prince, Llywelyn ap Gruffydd, and his marauding brother, Daffydd. She took a calming breath, reminding herself that there was no need for concern, but her heart would not stop racing and her intuition had gooseflesh rippling over her skin.

Though small in number, this band of men felt more threatening than the entirety of Cynwulf's army. Her gaze moved from one shield to the next until reaching the final shield of the man leading the group as she worked to keep her face expressionless. The last thing her brother needed was for her to appear unsettled by these men. She would perform her duty as lady and chatelaine of Hawkspur and would remain collected and poised while greeting guests of the castle, especially guests sent by their king.

She stared at the deep, garnet-red shield of the lead knight for a long moment, especially the bird painted on the expansive surface riveting. It was a hawk preparing for flight, its broad, black wings arching on either side of its body whilst its talons clung tightly to a gleaming sword. Her gaze moved over the puffed white chest of the hawk to a startling pair of black eyes of piercing intensity. As a crest, it was quite striking in its beauty; as a representation of the man who carried it, it felt very foreboding.

Pulling her gaze away, she decided it was better to look at the man than at his shield and discovered he was staring at her intently when she lifted her eyes to his. His eyes were as black and severe as the hawk's on his shield and his sharp features mimicked those of the bird, with rigid angular lines making up his nose and cheeks, jaw, and lips. Jet black hair draped over his shoulders, resembling the white-chested hawk flanked by black wings.

The hairs on the back of her neck stood up in warning. Even taking into account the armor encasing the knight, his size was daunting. But it was the candid way he stared at her that made her throat go dry.

And the dark knight would not look away from Alyce. How dare he stare so openly at her as though she were nothing more than a trinket on display? It took all of her will not to fidget with unease, but she could not stop herself from seething at his audacity. She refused to give him the satisfaction of meekly diverting her eyes and instead kept her eyes locked with the knight's. The moment seemed to drag endlessly, turning her unease into embarrassment. Finally, he looked away from her, but not before one corner of his mouth twitched with the barest of smiles.

Or was it a smirk?

The thunder of hooves pounding across the bailey turned Alyce's attention from the intriguing knight. A powerfully built, dun horse approached. On its back sat another giant of a man covered in furs with a full head of dark red hair. Two thick braids framed a rugged face, pale blue eyes, and firmly set lips. He took his place next to the leader of the band of knights, looking out of place in this group of rigid men. He nodded once to the lead knight then looked down at Cynwulf, Aelwin, and Alyce. As big as he was, he wasn't nearly as intimidating as the dark knight at his side. He looked almost jovial in comparison to the others.

"I am Sir Grogan." The gravelly voice of the black-clad lead warrior rumbled like thunder as it broke through the tense silence.

Alyce shifted slightly to watch her brother out of the corner of her vision.

"I am Cynwulf, lord of Hawkspur."

"I thought as such," the knight responded. "I am here on the behest of King Edward. We require lodging and stables for our horses."

The Marcher lords were an independent lot and this knight, so obviously used to his every word being obeyed, would please Cynwulf as much as a thorn stuck under his fingernail.

"Any man of the king's is always welcome at Hawkspur," Cynwulf stated with cool cordialness, though Alyce thought she detected a slight tick in his jawline. He raised his hand in the air in a quick gesture to the stable marshal waiting in readiness outside the stable doors. "See to your horses and join us in the hall. 'Tis unusual for guests to arrive in time to break the morning fast, but you are welcome at our table." Almost as a side he added, "We will discuss your business once you have had a chance to eat."

In unison, the knights dismounted and walked their horses past the stable boys, who hovered near and stared at the men with eager eyes wide in admiration.

Cynwulf turned on his heel and nearly collided with Alyce in his haste to return to the hall. Running to keep up, she moved to his side and said in a low voice, "These men do not look like the typical patrolling armies of the king. Why would he send these knights here?"

"I do not know," Cynwulf said through gritted teeth.

"It does not bode well that the king did not send word of their pending arrival," Alyce continued.

"It does not." Every word was a sharp beat as his strides grew longer with his frustration.

"Mayhap King Edward believes the Welsh prince's army to be headed this way," Alyce suggested, though why the king would not inform Cynwulf first made no sense.

Cynwulf gave a distracted shrug of his shoulders as they climbed the steps to the castle and pushed open the heavy door. The anticipation and tension in the hall hung in the air as thick as the smoke. Word of the king's knights arriving had spread through the castle folk quicker than the ague, and the kitchen maids were bustling with the greatest haste to accommodate the extra mouths with more platters of bread, cheese, and cold meat.

Alyce followed Cynwulf across the great room, her chest filled with a heavy foreboding. She studied her brother and wondered if the unsettling conversation they had in his solar had anything to do with the sudden appearance of the king's men. She nearly stumbled as she stepped up onto the dais while her stomach lurched with dread.

Cynwulf rarely excluded her from the business of Hawkspur, but when he did, it nearly always ended poorly. Best she stiffen her spine now and prepare to fix whatever mess Cynwulf had created.

Lord, but she dreaded the day she could not right what her brother set to wrong…and she prayed this was not that day.

Chapter Three

HAWK'S MEN FELL into step behind him to mount the stairs of the keep and walk the length of the hall toward the dais where the young lord of Hawkspur Castle awaited them. Above the fireplace nearest the back of the dais was a coat of arms depicting a hawk at rest, his wings snug against his slightly turned torso. The head of the bird was swiveled to stare boldly ahead, and behind it were two crossed swords on a field of pale blue, the same color as the English sky on a clear summer's day.

The young lord stood and motioned to a bench at the head table for Hawk to join him.

"Hunter, you and the others will stay here," Hawk said in a low voice to the knight who walked directly behind him, nodding toward an empty table directly in front of the head table on the dais. "Stay alert but do not start any trouble. Red, you will accompany me." While his men took seats at a trestle table set with loaves of dark bread and pitchers of ale, Hawk and Red stepped up onto the raised platform to sit with the Lord and Lady of Hawkspur Castle.

Hawk studied the face of Cynwulf and felt a surge of suspicion. The scent of resentment wafted from Cynwulf as clearly as the rot from a decaying beast. All was not right here; Hawk felt it in his bones. One look at Lord Cynwulf's excessively calm, yet icy expression assured him the man felt no affinity toward the contingent of the king's army invading his domain.

The question was whether his hostility came from territorial instincts…or guilt?

Hawk's gaze shifted to where the lady of the castle sat beside Lord Cynwulf. The corners of his mouth lifted slightly when he remembered the way she had reached behind her as she studied the line of knights and tugged the braid of auburn hair around her until she had the curls at the end tangled around her fingers. He doubted she was even aware of her actions, and he wondered what other telling habits she possessed that so blatantly gave away the emotions hidden behind the serene expression. Hawk was amused by the way her cheeks grew rosier with his scrutiny, and the cleft in her chin deepened as she pressed her lips tighter together.

Hawk did not know what made this woman so intriguing, but he found it difficult to look away from her. He liked the bold way she held his stare, refusing to back down despite the color flushing her face and the irritated slant to her eyes. She caught her bottom lip between her teeth in what was likely another of her nervous reactions, drawing his attention to the enticing curve of her lips.

He shook his head at his foolishness. Too long in the saddle without a woman had him fixating on this woman. He could not let himself be distracted and he needed to keep her at a proper distance, or he risked losing his ability to remain impartial. The king made very clear his mission and what hung in the balance if Hawk were to succeed. He did not need to say what the consequence would be if Hawk failed.

But Hawk could not completely disregard the sister of Lord Cynwulf. She may be a valuable source of information, and possibly a threat to his success if he underestimated her. He cocked an inquisitive eyebrow at her, enjoying the way she reacted to him as he studied her. When she boldly cocked one eyebrow back at him in response, he couldn't stop his lips from curving slightly with amusement. He didn't know what possessed him, but he winked just as he was about to look away, enjoying immensely the way her eyes widened with indignation. He wanted to laugh aloud his amusement at the woman's candor, her inability to hide exactly what she was feeling or thinking, but it would not serve his purpose to upset the lady any more than he already had.

THE ARROGANT KNIGHT had Alyce feeling off-kilter in a way she did not like.

This was not the first band of knights to pass through Hawkspur, and she was no stranger to playing hostess to all manner of men. So why did *this* man and his little band of knights arouse so much unease in her?

Sir Grogan was arrogant, imposing, and far too sure of himself—but that was no different than any other man of rank with whom she was acquainted. Still, there was something about the manner of this particular knight that ignited her irritation. He'd hardly spoken a word to her, but the way he openly studied her made her cheeks flame with indignation.

Or at least she thought it was indignation until an unexpected thrill tingled down her neck. Regardless, she would not give him the satisfaction of demurely lowering her eyes from his while he boldly studied her. If he expected her to show obeisance or swoon at his attention, he would be sorely disappointed.

Sir Grogan was likely accustomed to women fawning over his intense gaze, but she would not be one of them. He was attractive, that she could not deny, but she was no naive maiden whose heart was so easily set aflutter. And she would never be one of his conquests—of which she was sure he had many.

She stayed locked in this silly game of seeing who would look away first and again, she couldn't help but notice his appearance. His features were rigid, his nose straight, and his jawline sharp even when covered with a day's growth of dark hair. When she returned her gaze to his eyes, he cocked one dark eyebrow at her, as though asking if she liked what she saw. She arched an eyebrow back at him in response, congratulating herself on her boldness, confident he would be thrown off by her unexpected daring.

Until his lips curved upward ever so slightly, and he winked at her!

Any fascination she felt for the man melted away, quickly replaced by irritation. If he expected her to be overcome by a sly smile and a condescending wink, he would be gravely disappointed. Unlike other women, she had no desire for that sort of attention from a man. She lifted her chin and glared at him to show her displeasure.

"What brings you to Hawkspur, Sir Grogan?" Cynwulf interjected, pulling the knight's attention away from Alyce.

"Call me Hawk. I am here on the behest of His Majesty."

"Ah," Cynwulf said, his tone clipped. "The famous Hawk, savior of the king."

"Servant of Edward, merely performing my duty," Sir Grogan corrected warily.

Alyce winced at the cynical way her brother spoke to the king's knight. He could do with polishing his manners, displaying a measure of cordiality, and realizing that there were more important matters to worry about than the man's name. Sir Grogan had just revealed the king directed him to come to Hawkspur, which meant his business was with them and he was not merely passing through.

"Please, take a seat, break your fast." Cynwulf gestured to the bread and cheeses laid out on the table. "Where did you stay last night that brings you here so early this morn? Or is your business so urgent you were compelled to travel through the night?"

"We camped but a league from here," Sir Grogan said as he and his burly companion lowered themselves to the bench across from Alyce and Cynwulf.

"Why did you not continue your journey here last night?" Alyce prodded when Sir Grogan offered nothing more in explanation. "Surely another hour in the saddle on dry roads would have been far more comfortable than sleeping out in the cold."

"We did not come by the road, my lady," Sir Grogan responded.

The man was proving to be as perplexing as he was exasperating. Alyce tilted her head in question. "If not by road, then what route did you take?"

Sir Grogan's eyes stayed locked on Cynwulf as he answered Alyce's question. "We came through the forest. The people we are looking for do not tend to travel out in the open."

Alyce looked at Cynwulf, searching his face for any reaction to Sir Grogan's explanation. Her brother remained stoic and silent, his eyes not wavering from the knight. Turning her attention back to Sir Grogan, she asked, "Who do you think to find in the forests around Hawkspur other than our own patrols?"

Sir Grogan shrugged while his companion reached for a hunk of bread, breaking it in half and handing part of it to him. He took it but kept his focus on Cynwulf. "Does the rebellion in Wales spill over the border here?"

"Now and again a group of rebels will cause a ruckus and engage a handful of my soldiers in a skirmish," Cynwulf answered. He speared a piece of milky white cheese and chewed it thoughtfully before speaking again. "Really more of an irritation than a threat. Is that why you are here? If so, your efforts are better spent elsewhere. We can handle whatever comes our way."

"Is that so?" Sir Grogan's voice was eerily calm. "The king has reason to believe our efforts are very much needed here."

Cynwulf did not immediately answer, and Alyce noticed for the first time the overall quiet of the hall. Rising calmly to her feet, she said, "Perhaps, my lords, this is a conversation best continued in private."

HAWK ROSE AND followed Cynwulf and his sister to a door near the corner of the hall. He was startled to note that Lady Alyce found it necessary to duck her head to pass through the doorway; she was a tall woman, almost as tall as her brother. Hawk watched her disappear through the opening, then signaled for Red to follow him as he stepped through the small port of the door, pausing to look up the spiraling staircase before entering the door to a large solar.

"Sir Grogan, Red, please, be seated." It was not Cynwulf who made the offer, but Lady Alyce, her hand extended, inviting them to sit in the comfortably cushioned chairs beside the glowing fire facing a worn wooden table. Hawk nodded his acknowledgment of her offer but refused to sit. He preferred to stand. Intimidation was one of his favored tools, and his size allowed him to use it well. Red took his place beside Hawk, arms crossed over his chest with legs braced.

Hawk watched as Cynwulf walked around the table to sit behind it—not at all surprising. What did surprise Hawk was to see Lady Alyce also move around the table to seat herself next to her brother.

Cynwulf cleared his throat and demanded, "Explain the reason for your presence here, Sir Grogan. It's apparent you are not just looking for respite on your journey to some other destination."

"I do not understand why the king has sent you with no forewarning, Sir Grogan," the sister said, her eyes wide in what appeared genuine surprise.

"We have not requested reinforcements and have no need for any," Cynwulf added.

Hawk looked from one to the next, not sure to whom he should address his answer. Obviously, the sister was more involved in the oversight of Hawkspur than just managing the servants and seeing to the linens. Whatever her role, he liked her candor. He did not like to bother with niceties when just stating the point was much more expedient, and both Lady Alyce and her brother appeared like-minded.

"The king has heard reports of troublesome Welsh rebels along the border, and there is a rumor, Daffydd, brother to the prince of Wales, may be in this region leading the rebels. The king wishes to ensure that the Marcher lords are fortified as needed and..." he paused. No use in being evasive about his reasons for being here. In his experience, the bold truth spurred anyone with a guilty conscience to act foolishly sooner rather than later. "And to keep Hawkspur from falling into the hands of the Welsh. Someone is assisting the Welsh rebels, and he fears the rebels are coveting a Marcher castle. He has sent reinforcements to several castles along the border to defend against the Welsh attacks and to remind the Marcher lords to whom their loyalty belongs."

"Hawkspur has always been loyal to King Edward," Lady Alyce interjected sharply. "No one here would do anything to jeopardize Hawkspur or the people who live here."

Hawk wondered if the surprise on her face was well rehearsed, or if she felt truly taken aback by the suggestion. "Hawkspur is a very strategic castle, well-fortified and well-placed. Welsh rebels would like nothing more than to take it out from under Edward's rule. If you have Welsh sympathizers within your walls, Hawkspur is vulnerable."

Cynwulf's eyes sparked with anger as he planted his hands on the table and rose from his chair. "If there was a traitor here, I would know before anyone. We do not need you to protect Hawkspur. This is my castle, my men, my village; nothing happens here without my knowledge, and everyone here is loyal to me." Cynwulf took a deep, calming breath. "And loyal to England."

"I do not understand, Sir Grogan," Lady Alyce interjected before her brother could say more, rising to her feet to stand with the men. "Does the king suspect someone here is assisting the Welsh in a rebellion? Or does he wish to assist us against the rebellion? There is a marked difference in your mission if it is one over the other."

"That, my lady, depends on the situation here at Hawkspur."

Cynwulf put a hand on Alyce's shoulder but kept his eyes trained on Hawk. "I will not tolerate betrayal from anyone at Hawkspur, be they a trusted knight or the simplest of servants." Cynwulf's words were gruff, and Hawk wondered if determination or guilt sparked his vehemence.

"And the king will not tolerate betrayal from any of the Marcher lords regardless of their family history and connections." Hawk turned a pointed look to Cynwulf.

Cynwulf met his gaze, steady and strong. "You do realize the

Marcher lands are not like the rest of England. We take care of our own. We set the laws and enforce them. The king does not have sovereign rights over my castle, according to tradition and Magna Carta. As long as we keep the Welsh under our thumbs, the king is to leave us alone to govern this land. My men can handle any Welsh rebels who think to cause trouble here." He narrowed his eyes at Hawk. "I swore fealty to the king and use Hawkspur castle to serve him, but it is ours, and I am lord here. I have every right to refuse you access to Hawkspur."

Hawk studied Cynwulf for a long moment. It did not slip his notice that Cynwulf referred to the castle as *ours*. "You do have every right to tell me to leave. But you are also aware that if you do not cooperate willingly, the king will look the other way while matters here are settled. This is an enviable stronghold, a castle worth fighting for, no doubt coveted by every lord in the land." Hawk shrugged with indifference. "If King Edward does more than just quell this rebellion and decides to take the whole of Wales once and for all, the Marcher lands will no longer be necessary. All will be under English rule, and you will be no different than any other lord in the land."

Lady Alyce gasped at his words and her face paled visibly.

"Are you threatening me, Sir Grogan?" Cynwulf's voice remained steady and menacingly quiet.

This lord might be young, but he did not lack for grit.

"No. I am telling you the way of things. The Marcher lords have enjoyed very little intervention from the king. If your neighboring lords, or any others seeking a fortress such as this, sense weakness or loss of favor with the king, they will not hesitate to expand their holdings and wealth at your expense, enjoying very little intervention from the king." Hawk leaned forward, pronouncing each word with sharp clarity.

The young lord of Hawkspur did not blink or waver. Nor did he respond. His face remained stonily indifferent as he held Hawk's gaze. Hawk preferred this over some driveling idiot too afraid to stand on his own two feet in the face of uncertainty. He could even respect him for it, but he did not have to like him.

"You are wrong, Sir Grogan." Alyce's voice was as hard as her brother's now. "You will find no wrongdoings at Hawkspur, or from its lord. Our family has always been loyal to the king. Our uncle even served as knight to the king while on crusade."

"Then you have nothing to fear," Hawk said, his eyes still locked with Cynwulf's.

"And no need for your presence," Alyce said in a cool voice.

Hawk turned his attention to Alyce. He knew better than to underestimate the abilities or cunning of a woman. "Consider us a gift from the king. Edward does not wish to see any more lives lost among your loyal men. If the Welsh try to attack here, we will be proof of the king's support of Hawkspur castle and the Chetwynd family."

"I do not question the judgment of King Edward," Cynwulf said, his teeth clenched, "but I am disappointed he does not put his trust in me. Hawkspur has never been close to falling into Welsh hands. We are as strong as ever."

Hawk looked first to the sister, then to the brother. "The Plantagenets have been successful in their bid to remain in power because they trust no one, not even their loyal lords or favored knights."

Cynwulf's nostrils flared, but he calmed himself when Hawk arched a questioning eyebrow, daring him to say more. The lord of Hawkspur may be young, Hawk decided, but he was a formidable leader with more backbone than he'd expected.

"It will be in your best interest to not interfere with my mission. We will train with your men while we are here." Hawk made no pretense of phrasing it as a request. "And if there is anyone here sympathetic to the Welsh rebels, we will find him." He turned and started toward the door without requesting permission to leave, saying over his shoulder as he strode toward the door, "Or her, as the case may be."

Chapter Four

ALYCE TURNED TO her brother after the arrogant knight and his hulking accomplice left the solar. His face was pale and looked as though it had aged ten years in the last few moments. Her chest tightened, and she could not draw breath. When she tried to speak her voice was little more than a hoarse whisper. "Cynwulf, tell me everything will be all right."

Cynwulf's square jaw was set in a rigid line, the angry tick still throbbing visibly behind the dark locks of hair resting on his broad shoulders. He was unusually tall, like his sister, and they shared the same sapphire blue eyes as their mother, but where she was pale-faced with fiery auburn hair like their mother, he was darker complected with dark brown hair.

Like his sire?

"Father raised you as his own, as did Uncle Ranolf," Alyce said soothingly. "Never have you ever been known as anything other than a Chetwynd. The king cannot possibly doubt your loyalty."

Cynwulf kept his stony gaze focused on the wall in front of them, not even acknowledging Alyce's words, leaving her to wonder if he had heard her speak.

"Cynwulf?" Alyce pleaded, "What are you keeping from me?"

Her brother was the one constant person in her life. He had been her confidant since they were children, always at each other's side when needed, and her protector after their parents had died. She could not imagine what she would do if anything happened to him.

"Do you think the King is remembering the times Daffydd has been a guest a Hawkspur and is misinterpreting the purposes of those meetings? Surely he understands the necessity of the Marcher lords to maintain diplomatic communications with the Welsh princes and will not hold that against us."

"Of course, the king understands that, but he would be a fool to not be suspicious anyway."

She reached out her hand, resting it on his forearm. "Cynwulf," she said in a low voice, "No one remains who knows mother came to our father with you already in her belly. And no one knows who your father is."

"We do not know that," Cynwulf muttered. "It was the king himself who blessed the hasty marriage of my mother to your father."

"Our father," Alyce interjected. "He was never any less your father than mine."

"I know," Cynwulf agreed, "but he was not my sire. And we cannot know if the king was aware of her condition when he allowed Father to marry her."

"Even if the king did know, what does that matter now?"

Cynwulf sighed. "Mother had relatives in Wales, and she married Father immediately upon returning from an extended stay with cousins. I likely have more Welsh blood coursing through me than anything else."

"But you were raised English," Alyce argued. "And you have proven your worth as lord of Hawkspur."

"It is not so simple as that, sister." The tone of Cynwulf's voice made Alyce uneasy. What was he not telling her?

"Then what is it, Cynwulf? You know you can tell me anything."

Cynwulf finally sat down and turned to her. He studied her face for several moments, then cupped her cheek in his hand. "You need not be concerned. I will not let anything happen to you."

Before Alyce could recover from the deep dread that gripped

her with his words, Cynwulf rose and left her alone in the solar.

What did he mean that she need not be concerned? Why did he not say *we* need not be concerned? And what did he fear could possibly happen to her? It was not like Cynwulf to withhold information from her.

Alyce felt lightheaded with dread and helpless frustration.

"HAVE YOU ALREADY drawn your conclusions?" the Viking asked Hawk as they walked across the bailey to the barracks.

Hawk nodded.

"Do you plan to share them with me, or am I to guess?"

"You know my mind almost as well as I, Red, it would not be much of a guess," Hawk reminded the man who had been his friend, confidant, and right hand for most of his adult life.

"You are certain about the brother, but still unsure of the sister," Red surmised.

Hawk glanced sideways at this friend and nodded once. "Something is amiss, of that I am certain, and the lord of Hawkspur plays a part. But the sister...." Hawk furrowed his brow, uncharacteristically unsure of what to make of the woman. "Her face and mannerisms reveal her every emotion, even if she is not aware of her actions."

"Is it the seemingly genuine look of surprise when you re-vealed your suspicions of a traitor that makes you uncertain, or is it the way her eyes flash when she's angry?" Red ignored the roll of Hawk's eyes. "Or mayhap it is her lovely face or...? Well, you know what is said of red-haired maidens."

"You are a foolish romantic, and you have a soft heart for women, Red, especially red-haired women. Do not let it interfere with your judgment of her." He glared sideways at this friend as they walked. "How is it that the toughest warrior I know can be so weak when it comes to a winsome woman?"

"You did notice her beauty then." Red smiled broadly at his commander. "I know you, my friend, and your heart is not as hard as you would like everyone to believe. Besides, is it not time for you to settle down? After all you've done for the king, it is time you are rewarded with a warm hearth and a warm woman to call your own and give you little hard-hearted sons."

Hawk scoffed aloud at the notion.

Red smirked but said nothing more about the lady. "You have determined Cynwulf is guilty of something; have you discerned his intentions, then?"

"No," Hawk muttered. "But if the king's suspicion as to who his sire may be is correct, then it is not difficult to guess."

TWENTY ADDITIONAL KNIGHTS filled the barracks to the limit, leaving Cynwulf with no choice but to offer Sir Grogan and Red shelter within the castle. Propriety suggested that Cynwulf should offer the king's man and his first-in-command the comfort of the castle anyway, but Alyce suspected her brother would not have done so if the lack of space had not made it necessary.

For the remainder of the morning Alyce, her lady's maid Edna, and all the servants of the castle bustled about opening and refreshing bed chambers and assisting the kitchen in preparing extra food for the unexpected guests. Alyce focused her thoughts on the mundane tasks to keep her mind off the fact that something may be amiss at Hawkspur Castle.

"They are quite handsome, my lady," one of the maids said, with a cheeky grin.

"Gertrude," Edna admonished. "'Tis no way to talk in front of Lady Alyce, and you best be keeping your eyes and hands to yourself."

Gertrude giggled and winked at Alyce as she shook out the bedding. "You know I love you, dearest Edna, but our lady is not a woman gone blind. Men like that must catch the gaze of even a woman your age."

Edna turned a sharp eye on the younger girl, but her voice held more amusement than reproach. "I am sorry for Gertrude's rude mouth, my lady. She forgets herself and her position."

Edna had been nurse to Alyce from the time she took her first wobbly steps. She raised her as though her own when her mother died and served as her maid and mentor when she became a young woman with a new husband. She respected the woman as much as she loved her.

Alyce squeezed Edna's shoulders affectionately. "Which is precisely why I enjoy working alongside Gertrude more than any of the others. She makes the time pass quickly."

"You are too soft, my lady," Edna muttered.

Alyce grinned and whispered to the woman who knew her better than any other, "And you, Edna, are not as modest as you would like all to believe." She winked as she dropped her arm from around the older woman's shoulder. "I know some of your secrets."

"Secrets?" Gertrude's voice trilled with anticipation. "You must tell us, my lady. What secrets does Edna hide?"

"They are not for you to know, girl." Edna waggled a finger at Gertrude, but her lips twitched up at the corners.

Alyce could not keep the events of the morning from her mind despite the playful banter with the maids. The return of her somber mood seemed to permeate the room, and even Gertrude's usual high spirits plummeted.

"A band of knights from the king arriving and stories of Welsh uprisings erupting on the northern border, what does this mean for us?" Gertrude asked tentatively.

Alyce squared her shoulders and resumed a posture expected of the lady of Hawkspur. "It means we continue on as usual."

"But what of Cook, Bernard, Wart?" Gertrude hesitated before adding, "And me? What will become of us if the war comes here again?"

Alyce felt a pang of pity for the young Welsh woman. Gertrude's parents and grandparents had grown up in the village, and like Gertrude, had probably never traveled more than a day's journey from Hawkspur. "Whatever happens between King Edward's army and the Welsh rebels does not affect us. I cannot believe the people here would fight one against the other no matter which side of the border they call home." Alyce prayed her words were truthful, but how could she know for sure what the villagers would do if the uprising in the north and the occasional rebel skirmishes turned into a full war?

"But if the fighting does come here," Gertrude insisted, "what then?"

Alyce felt a twinge of uncertainty where before there had been none. Did any of the Welsh among the villagers harbor ill-will toward Cynwulf, or her, or the English? The respect and loyalty between the villagers and the lord of the castle had been strong for as long as Cynwulf had been at Hawkspur, and their uncle before him. But that did not mean that the Welsh villagers were loyal to the English king, and if war broke out, many would be forced to choose between loyalty to the Welsh prince and their ancestry or loyalty to their English lord and their livelihood.

Mumbling what she hoped sounded like reassurance to Gertrude, that all would come out right in the end, Alyce excused herself to search for her brother. There was more at stake than just Cynwulf's title and her role as his chatelaine; people's lives and livelihood depended on the safety and wellbeing of Hawkspur. Her gut told her Cynwulf was not being truthful with her, but never had he been able to keep a secret from her for long.

She must find him and force him to confide in her before he put everyone in danger.

Chapter Five

"Upon my oath, I watched the lot of them leave."

Alyce's hand stopped mid-stroke along the bulging belly of her pregnant mare. She pivoted her head in the direction of the muffled voice.

"Then make haste," a second voice hissed in command, followed by the whoosh of a stall gate swinging open upon its leather hinges.

Overcome by curiosity, Alyce stepped gingerly over the straw strewn on the floor of her mare's stall, moving closer to the gate to peer into the passageway. Sunlight streamed in through the open barn door but only the dust swirling in the beams of light was visible, and the dark silhouette of a man holding the gate while another led a horse out of the stall. Alyce pulled her head back out of sight, knowing they would have to walk directly past where she stood to get to the saddles and tack. Not wishing to be discovered, she stepped farther back into the stall, out of the view of the men.

Thieves? At the height of day?

Pressing her back into the rough planks of the wall behind her mare, Alyce held her breath and listened. The muffled thudding of hooves on the hard-packed dirt floor grew louder in unison with the beats of her heart as the men led the horse down the aisle way. Thankfully, they were too absorbed in their task to look in her mare's stall as they walked by.

The footsteps stopped just beyond the next stall. All was quiet save for the rustling of the two men and the horse. Alyce had welcomed the silence when the stable master and stable boys left for the midday meal. Cook refused to let any man, woman, or child work on an empty belly, and all who lent a hand at the castle could expect sustenance, albeit simple, in return. Now she prayed Cook would quickly shoo them from under her feet and out of the kitchens. She did not wish to confront thieves alone.

"The envoy of knights from the king does not bode well. Tell him to keep his distance." Alyce recognized the voice despite the low murmuring and her stomach lurched with dread. Why would drive Cynwulf to have a clandestine meeting in the barn with an unknown man?

"You must find out what you can from these knights. He will want to know if they are on a scouting mission and if more troops will follow?"

She did not recognize the second voice, nor did she know who the "he" was they referred to who wanted information. She wanted to believe it was just another Marcher lord being curious and cautious, but covertness would not be required if that was all it was.

"Urge him not to set foot near Hawkspur; the danger is too great. I will be of little use to him now. He must stay away."

"He will not like that, and he will not be put off so easily."

"There is nothing I can do about it," Cynwulf hissed. "You must go, now. None will question you leaving at this time of day, but I have no wish to dally long enough for anyone to see us together." The saddle groaned as the other man hoisted himself into the stirrups. "I'll take you to the side door. Ride around the backside of the training field where you are less likely to be seen."

"And if I'm questioned?"

"Tell them you brought a message from Montworth and are returning to him. Godspeed, man. I give you my trust this message will reach him in time, or all will be for naught if he comes here."

Alyce quickly ducked behind the pregnant mare. She wanted to know the identity of the other man but her fear of being seen was greater than her curiosity. As the horse plodded past, the back of the man's hooded head was all she could see.

Cynwulf could be impulsive and headstrong, but he was not foolish. She trusted he would never do anything to jeopardize Hawkspur, but at times Cynwulf's best intentions did not work in his favor. None of what she heard boded well, but she also had no idea what any of it meant. She must find out what Cynwulf was about, and she would not let him put her off again.

She waited for the creak of the heavy side door closing, then stepped from the stall into the aisle to face her brother. But she faced nothing more than the dust floating idly in the air. Cynwulf was gone.

For a fleeting second, she wondered if she had imagined it all. Could Cynwulf really be so foolish as to send a messenger to the Welsh right under the noses of the army sent by King Edward?

She shook her head. Likely as not, she misunderstood the true nature of the exchange. Cynwulf could not possibly be involved in treason. She could think of no reason for him to betray his king and country. Such an act would endanger not only their family, but everyone at Hawkspur, all the people who had looked to her uncle for protection and guidance, and now looked to her brother.

Lost in thought, Alyce returned to her pregnant charge. The mare craned her neck and nuzzled at her hand. Obediently, Alyce rubbed the soft nose and scratched under the heavy forelock, letting the soothing, warm scent of the horse's hide mixed with the scent of the fresh hay fill her lungs and calm her nerves.

"'Tis strange, Guinevere," she murmured to the horse. "Cynwulf is impetuous at times, but foolhardy is not like him. I fear what he has gotten himself into this time."

Chatter filled the air, putting an end to Alyce's musings as the stable master and his gaggle of helpers returned from their noon meal. The boys laughed and boasted, shoving at each other in their efforts to best one another. Alyce blocked out the cacophony of voices and rubbed her fingers along the back and belly of the mare in long strokes to steady her trembling hands.

"'Twill be anytime now, my lady." Bernard, the stable master, unlatched the gate and approached the mare. He grinned at Alyce, showing yellowed teeth and several black, gaping holes. When the man spoke, his grey beard twitched and moved with his face in a way that always made her smile.

"Not long now." Bernard stood beside Alyce, his balding head not quite reaching the top of her own. The scent of manure, hay, and horse permanently clung to him. She had developed the tactic of breathing as little as possible in his presence long ago, but she adored everything else about old Bernard, which made this one discomfort tolerable.

"She is restless," Alyce said. "She has no liking for being confined, but I worry about her birthing her foal in the pasture if turned out."

"Wart!" Bernard called over his shoulder. "Come, lad. Bring a lead."

A small boy of no more than six or seven summers appeared almost immediately, rope in hand. He bobbed a bow to Alyce and smiled widely. "My lady," he said with exuberance.

"Wart," Alyce addressed him, tipping her head and winking at him. The child was perpetually smudged with dirt, and his dirty blond hair seemed to be in a constant tangle, but she found him endearing, nonetheless.

Bernard took the rope from Wart and looped it around Guinevere's muzzle and neck. "The mare needs air, Wart. Take her walkin' in the grass. Keep 'er from the other horses." He handed the long end of the lead to the boy and shooed him on his way. "And don't you be runnin' 'er, even if yer legs are itchin' to go faster, or yer sure to feel the sting of that rope on yer backside when I find ye."

Alyce watched her mare, belly swaying with each step, lumber slowly toward the doors with Wart's gentle coaxing. He turned to look back at Alyce and grinned proudly when she nodded her approval. A sharp pang of regret gripped Alyce as she watched the boy, but she quickly put all thoughts of what could not be from her mind.

"I'll send word, milady, as soon as that foal shows signs of presentin' to the world," Bernard promised. "The ol' girl will be fine. She knows what to do."

"I will rest assured she will be well in your capable hands," she said, then left the stables to seek out her brother.

Ffyddlon, her loyal wolfhound, bound to greet her, then began trotting along at Alyce's side as she emerged from the stable. She rewarded the hound by rubbing her fingers into her coarse hair. The adoring look she received in return comforted Alyce, and she smiled down at the beast. "You and I, we make a good pair, do we not? I, an aging, barren widow, and you, a staunch maiden." Thomas, the kennel master, had referred to Ffyddlon as a "cold bitch" due to her refusal to mate. She would snap and growl until the male became frustrated, and the coupling would never amount to more than a scuffle. Alyce's husband had been dead less than a sennight when she discovered the hound had been turned out from the kennel and forced to fend for herself.

She had snuck the abandoned wolfhound into her bed and slept the night through with the dog curled against her. Never had a maid slept in the room when she was married, and she did not want anyone in her chamber after her husband died to hear her cry herself to sleep at night. The chamber proved less lonely with the dog for company, and perhaps wishing to return the favor for being saved from starvation, the dog escorted and guarded Alyce wherever she ventured, her faithful companion.

"Tell me, Ffyddlon, what shall we do about Cynwulf?" Alyce asked softly as she walked with her wolfhound, trying to sort out in her mind the peculiar scene she overheard in the stable. She could not bear the thought of anything happening to her brother. She trusted him above all others, but he obviously did not trust her because whatever he was up to now, he was not confiding in her.

She should withhold her judgment until she spoke with him. Mayhap she misunderstood, she rationalized, clinging to a shred of hope, but she could not stop the tight knot forming in her belly.

Cynwulf had sworn fealty to King Edward. The safety and security of every person within the castle walls and in the village fell to him. She could not believe he would get involved in anything that brought danger to those who depended on him.

But mayhap the Welsh blood of generations was more powerful than one lifetime in an English household to determine a person's heritage. The Welsh were said to be a mystical people with the blood of King Arthur running through their veins. Did Cynwulf feel a loyalty to his ancestors that he could not explain or ignore, even if he did not know exactly who they were?

She was loath to admit it, but she depended upon her brother. If anything should happen to him, she would be forced to depend on the charity of a nunnery or to find a husband. By Marcher customs, the ownership of the castle had been transferred to the new lord according to the wishes of the previous lord's will. The king did not own the castle and did not have the final say in who would be the next lord of a Marcher castle. But willing a fortress to a woman was risky, especially when the woman was made even more vulnerable by not having any living male relatives to support her.

Had the lords of any Marcher castles been traitors to the English crown? She could not recall but she wondered if the rule of the Marcher customs would still prevail if the treason scandalized the family who owned the castle.

Uncle Ranolf, never one to conform to expectations, left the castle to both Cynwulf and Alyce with the stipulation that if anything were to happen to Cynwulf before he begot an heir, Hawkspur would be hers. But she did not want that responsibility, and she could not do it alone. She knew well how to manage the day-to-day life of the castle and the village, overseeing the planting of crops, harvesting, filling of the stores, and seeing to the needs of all who resided here. What she did not know how to do well was to defend the castle and the village while navigating the political machinations of the king and the other lords, and she had no desire to learn. The bloodshed, manipulations, and flexing of muscles felt like nothing more than men needing to stroke their egos.

Women had served as castellans before, and though rare, it was not unimaginable. Everyone in the Marcher lands knew the tales of Isabella Mortimer and her iron fist rule of Oswestry Castle as she garrisoned the fortress to fight the prince of Wales. As the daughter of the powerful Lord Mortimer, her authority was not questioned, and she stood to inherit the castle when her father died. The king rarely intervened in Marcher traditions, but if he suspected treason nothing would stop him from going against Marcher tradition to demand forfeiture of Hawkspur.

If something happened to Cynwulf, would the king offer her up along with Hawkspur as a reward to one of his loyal nobles, forcing her to marry out of fear she could not hold Hawkspur alone? Or worse yet, he might forcibly remove her from her home and marry her to some landed baron seeking a bride. Was she strong enough to serve as castellan of Hawkspur if the lives and wellbeing of the villagers depended upon it? She prayed she would never have to find out.

She crossed herself quickly as a cold shudder rippled through her frame at the thought of anything happening to Cynwulf and she pushed the dreadful images from her mind. She clung to the hope nothing would change at Hawkspur and Cynwulf would remain lord of the castle for many years to come—even if it meant he continued to hound her to take a husband for the remainder of her days.

That thought brought on a scoffing snort. She desired a doddering widower to take as husband about as much as a man would desire a barren widow for a bride, no matter how young she may be.

Alyce put the idea of being forced to marry again out of her mind and instead focused on what she would say to Cynwulf. She crossed the great hall, too lost in thought to even remember entering the castle, crossing the hall, or halting in front of the door to her brother's solar. But here she was and there was no reason to delay yet another confrontation with her brother. It seemed they did more arguing than anything as of late.

With quick determination, she balled her fist and rapped her knuckles on the worn wood of the door.

HAWK WATCHED LADY Alyce cross the bailey, absently scratching the head and neck of the wolfhound at her side, too lost in thought to notice anything but what lay directly in front of her. She appeared troubled and curiosity drove him to follow her.

In a man, expressing every thought and emotion so plainly on one's face would be a flaw of the utmost severity, but in Lady Alyce, he found it to be quite intriguing. It proved her innocence in his mind. She could never be trusted to be a part of a treasonous plot—everyone would know the moment they looked at her if she was desperately trying to hide something shameful.

He followed her up the stairs of the keep, across the hall, and even ducked after her through the doorway leading to the tower stairs and Cynwulf's solar, and still, she did not notice he followed her. The hound had turned its head several times to assess Hawk but continued to trot along at the lady's side.

Alyce puffed out a loud breath and leaned her head against the solar door when her knock went unanswered. Leaning a shoulder against the door frame he just passed through, Hawk crossed his arms over his chest.

"Troubles, my lady?" he asked gently.

She nearly jumped out of her skin at the sound of his voice, but he already knew that would happen. He had a strong feeling that the woman wouldn't hear a marauding army approach when lost in her own thoughts.

When she turned to look at him, he was mesmerized by her sapphire blue eyes for a moment so that he wouldn't have noticed a marauding army either. Anger reddened her cheeks and flashed in her eyes, but it only intensified the allure of her face.

"Wh...what?" she stammered, one hand over her heart. "Where did you come from?"

Hawk shrugged nonchalantly as he continued to watch her wordlessly—a trick he had picked up as a youth. Silence intimidated people, often making them ramble under scrutiny and revealing much more than ever intended.

A slow smile crossed his face as she boldened and stared back at him, allowing the silence to linger. Her face paled slightly, but she did not back down from him, nor did she resort to nervous chattering. She gathered her composure more quickly than he expected and returned his intimidating look. Of course, she wasn't intimidating in the slightest. He cocked his head to the side as he tried to recollect any other woman standing her ground with him as Lady Alyce did now.

No, he decided, such a woman wouldn't be so easily forgotten.

"I asked you a question, my lord."

Her voice was surprisingly calm and authoritative.

Hawk pushed himself away from the door frame to stand over her, and still, she did not shrink from him. He had to admit that her unusual height meant he did not have the same towering effect over her as he did others. A worried crease formed between her brows, and she wavered slightly, but she did not retreat from him in the slightest.

Such gall deserved an answer. "I followed you from the stable," he said.

"You followed me? Why?" Her eyes opened wider, and Hawk's suspicion was aroused. She was incapable of hiding anything of great importance, of that he was sure, but something had her feeling guilty.

"Does this upset you, my lady?" He fully expected her to back down, contrite, to ease his suspicions.

"Yes, it upsets me. Why did you follow me?" Her voice rose with anger, and she surprised him by taking a step closer. "Timid" did not describe this woman. Nor the hound—it took a step forward as well and a low growl rumbled in its throat.

He did not usually explain himself to anyone, but he wasn't ready to end this conversation, and he wanted to know what had upset the lady. "I am looking for your brother, and this was the logical place to start. You happened to be walking in the same direction."

The sideways tilt of her head and her slanted lids indicated she did not believe him. He grinned at her and twitched his eyebrows once to let her know he did not care if she believed him or not. He nonchalantly reached out his hand to the dog and let it sniff at his fingers.

"Obviously, Cynwulf is not in his solar. You will have to look elsewhere," she said, lightly lifting the hem of her gown with both hands to step past him. "I will take my leave. Good day, sir. Come, Ffyddlon." She said the last through tight lips while keeping her eyes locked with his as though in challenge, and he had to admit he admired her fearlessness.

Hawk did not move out of her way. Instead, he forced her to press against him as she tried to pass by. "If you find him, Lady Alyce, tell him to come to me."

Alyce stopped mid-stride, which put her shoulder to bicep with Hawk, her face close enough that all it would take to kiss her was the slightest dip of his head. A temptation for sure, but not one he thought the lady would appreciate at this moment. The dog, however, showed more appreciation for his attention, nuzzling its head against his leg as he scratched its ears.

"Lest you forget, Cynwulf is lord of this castle," she said through gritted teeth. "I will tell him you have requested a meeting so he may bid you to come to his solar at his convenience."

Hawk should be offended by this woman for her haughty attitude, but he found himself wanting to see just how riled he could get her. Quite the change from the woman who had stood in the bailey with her hair twisted around her fingers looking up at him with uncertainty when he arrived only that morning. Aye, he'd unsettled her then, but now her hackles stood up like a she-wolf's.

"Ffyddlon!" Alyce's tone was that of a mother scolding a child who had forgotten her manners. She snapped her fingers and pointed to her side. The hound had the good sense to quickly pull away from Hawk's fingers and nudge Alyce's hand for forgiveness.

He wanted to laugh as she glared at the dog for its betrayal, but he held his mirth when Lady Alyce turned her glare to him in warning to stay away from her pet.

"What manner of name is that?" he asked, unfamiliar with the word.

She eyed him with suspicion for a long moment before answering. "Ffyddlon. It is Welsh. It means *loyal.*"

"Fitting," he said as the hound sniffed in his direction again.

"She is meant to be loyal to me, not you, sir, but she seems to have forgotten that." She tugged at Ffyddlon's ear to turn her attention away from Hawk.

"You should follow the hound's good instincts, and put your trust in me," he said with a grin, knowing it would irritate her. Alyce's gaping mouth lacked appeal, but the fire blazing in her eyes was well worth her wrath.

"And do you expect me to follow you around the yard wagging my tail and looking at you adoringly?" she said in an angry huff. "It takes more than scratching my ears to earn my loyalty, sir."

An image of exactly what he would like to do to make her appreciate his attention filled his mind, causing another slow smile to spread across his face. He knew his nearness was affecting her because her fingers started fidgeting with the cuffs of her gown.

He couldn't resist asking, "What would make your tail wag, my lady?"

Her mouth dropped open again, but she quickly snapped it shut as her cheeks heated and filled with color.

"You overstep your bounds." Each word was clipped with irritation.

"Aye, my lady, I do." He was making her uncomfortable, her renewed fidgeting gave her away, but he detected the faint aroma of lavender when she was near, and he didn't want to move away quite yet. How could the woman show every emotion, every feeling, and thought on her face and in her gestures, and still remain so beguiling?

ALYCE WANTED TO be away from Hawk, and quickly. He obviously believed his arrogance to be charming. Hawk's swagger and physique might make other women swoon at his feet, but she'd be damned if she would.

And she would not wag her tail for him!

She pushed past him and walked through the hall with as much poise as she could muster, head held high and shoulders back as though she still had a hold on her quickly shredding nerves. Even as she tried to convince herself that the man deserved nothing more than her loathing, she could not stop the flutter of excitement his presence caused in the pit of her stomach.

Everyone at Hawkspur doted upon her as though she were a child in need of consoling, and not just because her husband had died. No, the pitiful coddling had started nearly two years prior when the kitchen maid bore him the son she could not. The pity she saw in other women's eyes when they smiled at her consolingly caused more humiliation and hurt than healing. She'd learned a long time ago to harden herself to their whispers and annoying stares. Only Ffyddlon, her loyal hound, didn't look at her with sympathy or pity in her eyes.

Nor did Hawk.

Sir Grogan made her feel alive again. He didn't look at her with pity, but with lust, something which should offend her, but she found it invigorating. Granted, he said things that were beyond his liberty to say, but at least he'd evoked some reaction in her other than humiliation and hurt. He roused her anger, aye, but she felt more alive than she'd felt in a long time. It was unladylike for her to feel flattered by base remarks a man should never dare say to a lady, but it had been a long time since anyone had looked upon her as a woman and not a sad, barren widow.

It was true Sir Montworth professed a desire to marry her, but that had nothing to do with her as a person so much as it did with the political advantage he would attain in his bid to gain favor with the other lords and the king. And the look in Montworth's eyes when he raked them over her body made her flesh crawl with disgust.

Heaven help her, when Hawk did the same, she shivered with the potential and promise she saw in his eyes. She had no desire for a husband, but obviously, the desire for a man was not completely dead within her.

Alyce wanted nothing more than the privacy of her chamber, but in her haste to get away from Sir Grogan she'd flitted past him and into the hall instead of up the spiral stairs of the tower to her chamber. Hawk still stood watching her from the small doorway blocking the only access to her chamber without going outside, through the bailey, into the guards' quarters, and up onto the parapet. She didn't know which was more foolish; pretending to busy herself in the buttery until Hawk left, or taking a very long route around the castle just to sneak into her own chamber?

Still, she inspected the inventory of the buttery until she finally saw Hawk crossing the hall to take his leave. She peeked around the door of the buttery, watching until she was sure he was gone. As soon as the heavy door closed behind him, she hurried across the hall and up the stairs to her chamber.

Ffyddlon bounded into the room behind her, tail wagging and ears perked.

"'Tis not a game I play, Ffyddlon," she scolded gently. "And you deserve no rewards for your betrayal, letting yourself be seduced by that arrogant man."

Alyce plopped on her bed while Ffyddlon sat on the floor and leaned against her legs. The dog put her big head on Alyce's lap and looked up at her as if to say she, too, could not help herself. Alyce rubbed her fingers into the fur behind Ffyddlon's ears. "There is something quite alluring about him, I must admit." He may look upon her with desire now, but she must not forget that he would just as easily condemn her as bed her if he found anyone at Hawkspur was anything less than loyal to the king he served.

Alyce turned her thoughts to her brother. The fear mounting in her quickly dampened the invigorating tingle that lingered from Hawk's flirtation. What game did Cynwulf play?

"Cynwulf had better not do anything foolish," she muttered to Ffyddlon. "If he's fallen in love with a Welsh woman and lost all sense of reason, we could all be in trouble."

Chapter Six

THE GREAT HALL came alive in the evenings with knights, ladies, townsmen, and serving women, talking and laughing. Alyce leaned forward slightly to peer down the length of the head table trying to catch a glimpse of Aelwin, Cynwulf's right-hand man. She wondered if he knew what had Cynwulf sending messengers off secretly during the day and acting so strangely. She sighed and leaned back again when all she could see was the back of his head as he spoke with the woman seated to his other side.

She would make herself addlebrained if she continued to speculate about each and every person under the command of her brother, suspicious they were all part of some secret she knew nothing about.

Three rows of tables ran parallel to each other down the length of the hall at right angles to the raised dais where Alyce sat. Hawk's men filled more than half the seats along the table directly in front of where Hawk and the burly Viking sat, at the opposite end of her table. Alyce knew Cynwulf would never be so discourteous as to seat a favored knight of the king at a lower table, but he did have the gall to seat Hawk and his companion on the far end of the table with Alyce, several middling lords and ladies, and the residing priest separating them from the lord of Hawkspur.

"You are unusually quiet tonight, sister."

Cynwulf's words startled Alyce, pulling her from her thoughts. She stabbed her dirk into another piece of eel soaked in a savory sauce as she smiled stiffly at her brother. "There is enough chatter without mine added to the din."

She was finding it difficult to keep her jittering nerves calm, and she did not want to cause a scene with so many others around. If she spoke, she was afraid she might start yelling at Cynwulf in her frustration, like a raging beast ready to pounce. He had managed to avoid her since the king's knight arrived, being in her presence only when surrounded by others. She took a deep breath and reminded herself not to overreact to Cynwulf's evasiveness.

Cynwulf relaxed back in his chair as though nothing was amiss at Hawkspur. "You have that expression you get when you are thinking too hard. What is churning in that head of yours?"

Alyce slowly chewed her food, stalling for time. The dining hall was not the place to discuss delicate situations, but she must talk to her brother soon about what was really on her mind. For the moment, she hedged. "I am just thinking about all that needs to be done. Autumn will be upon us before we know it. I must start preparing the stores for the coming winter."

Cynwulf cocked a questioning eyebrow. "You are concerned we will not have enough to see us through?"

"I have concerns. Let us meet in the morning and I can discuss the progress and the plan with you," Alyce suggested, thinking she had found an excuse to get her brother alone. And then she would make him explain what he'd been doing in the stables.

"Let us discuss it now," Cynwulf responded. "I cannot seem to find a moment to spare during the day."

"Now? Very well. Shall we retire to your solar?" Alyce pushed her chair back, but he grabbed her wrist and motioned for her to stay seated.

"It will be rude if the lord of the castle leaves the table before others have had a chance to finish their meal. We can discuss it here." Cynwulf looked around the room with a half-smile on his lips. "Besides, everyone here is more interested in their drink than talk of harvests."

"I am merely concerned that if we do not plan accordingly, we may find ourselves in a dire situation come winter." She lowered her voice and turned her face away from the main tables. "What happens if we do not have enough men available to work the fields and bring in the crops? Conflict will bring more hardship to the village, yet King Edward seems bent on war with the Prince of Wales." She darted a glance at Cynwulf as she said the last, looking for a reaction.

Her worry of being shorthanded in the fields was real, even if overshadowed by her concern about the secrets Cynwulf kept from her. As the lady of the manor, she'd proved even more adept at inventories and planning than her uncle. Calculating, tallying, and forecasting seemed second nature to her.

"Do I worry overly much? Is all this talk of war exaggerated?" Alyce asked when Cynwulf did not react to her statement of the hardships of war. "We do not want to be caught unaware and unable to sustain Hawkspur through the winter."

"I would venture a guess your worries have more to do with the king's knight sitting at the end of the table than with your duties as chatelaine."

Alyce darted a quick glance to the far end of the table. "Tell me why he is here, Cynwulf. The presence of Sir Grogan and his knights will only serve to unsettle everyone at Hawkspur. Do you think the king really believes someone here is plotting against us to take Hawkspur Castle and give it to the Welsh rebels?"

"Do not concern yourself. Everything will be fine. Sir Grogan will tire of his search when there is nothing to find and leave soon enough," Cynwulf muttered.

"Do you really believe this, Cynwulf? The king does not send his enforcers unannounced without good reason." Alyce eyed her brother carefully, looking for any sign of uneasiness.

Cynwulf stiffened, then patted Alyce's hand. "You need a diversion, sister."

There. He was at it again, changing the topic. Always had he known how to soothe her ruffled feathers through distraction. Not this time. She narrowed her eyes at Cynwulf and demanded,

"Tell me now what it is you hide from me."

Cynwulf sighed and brought his cup close to his lips, effectively hiding his mouth while he spoke. "I hide nothing from you, but I will admit the king's men make for additional stress."

"Cynwulf," Alyce chided in a low voice, holding her own cup to hover in front of her face. "None know you better than I, and I know there is more to it than what you say. I heard you in the barn just this morn whispering to someone. Since then I have been imagining conspiracies around every corner."

She reached out her hand to lay it over her brother's where it rested against the arm of his chair. His face remained impassive, but she saw his eyes narrow ever so slightly as his brow furrowed. It was a familiar expression; one he had made since he was a boy. It was the look of guilt mixed with the hope that he could still hide whatever he had done.

"Tell me true," she pleaded in a whisper as she grabbed his hand in both of hers, "is it all a misunderstanding, and I am finding treachery where there is nothing?"

"Not now, not here," Cynwulf said through tight lips, a false smile plastered on his face. He turned his hand to grab hers and relaxed the muscles in his face. "Please, dear sister! Your overactive imagination will gain you nothing but frustration. You need not worry about me; it is I who should be worried about you. You have become obstinate and cannot even begin to see the merits of taking another husband. You are young and beautiful, and any man would be a fool to not want you."

Alyce released her brother's hand and sat back in her chair. She would let him have his way for now, allowing him to change the topic. "You, dear brother, are touting the finer qualities of every eligible bachelor you meet as a potential husband when you know I have no desire to marry. You cannot convince me that a barren widow can make a prized bride no matter my young age. Tell me, why is it so important to you that I take a husband?"

"You cannot possibly be contented with your duties as chatelaine being all you have for the rest of your life," Cynwulf reasoned. "Do you not want something more?"

Alyce hated it when he avoided her questions by asking his

own. "I tire of this topic. If this is another one of your attempts to marry me to some aging lord with a brood of children, you had best put it out of your head."

"Luc Montworth has requested to enter formal negotiations for your hand, and he is neither old nor decrepit," Cynwulf chided. "And I know of no brood to his credit. He is also widowed and already has his heir from his first marriage. He has proven himself worthy once more in the eyes of the other lords and I believe his lordship is to be restored soon by the king."

"Montworth may have his own sons already, but he is too boisterous for my taste. If you honestly believe there is anything about him I would find appealing then you do not know me well." Alyce turned to Cynwulf. "Can you tell me in all seriousness you find him to be a likable man?"

Cynwulf gave a small snort of laughter. "In truth, I do not care for him overly much, but he has wealth to provide for you and strength to protect you.'

"I do not need those things. I have Hawkspur and I have you, dear brother. I never want to leave Hawkspur, and I never want to be without you."

"A brother is not the same as a husband. Don't you want someone to grow old with?"

Alice sighed. "I will grow old contentedly as auntie to your children."

"You need a husband, Alyce."

Alyce shot an annoyed glance at her brother. "I had one, and I am through discussing this with you."

"But you are so alone, and time is running out to find a husband and still make a family."

Alyce's eyes widened before she quickly looked away to hide the pain inflicted by his uncharacteristically cruel words.

"I am unable to have a family, Cynwulf. You know this," she said in a hoarse whisper.

"Perhaps with another man and more time, you will prove fertile."

Alyce turned her gaze to her brother again. His sharp blue eyes showed only concern, but he could hurt her more easily than anyone. He loved her enough to push her, for her own good he always claimed, but she was tired of it. Cynwulf's refusal to accept that she was barren was misguided if he thought to help her, and it would be truly unfair of him to betroth her to any man of title, or with a potential for title. Men needed heirs and the duty of a wife was to provide many; she could not fulfill that duty.

"The proof of the truth is in front of us every day," Alyce said evenly.

Cynwulf's head turned to look out over the great hall, and Alyce knew he was looking at the small boy playing with a wooden block by the buttery door as his mother sauntered along the tables filling cups with ale. Alyce need not follow his gaze to see the familiar white-blond hair of the toddler.

Or the green of his eyes.

Or the dimple in his chin.

"Geoffrey was with her one foolish time, and he regretted it for the rest of his days. She may say the child is his, but the likelihood is just as great that he belongs to any one of the men in this hall, including me."

"Your vulgar insinuations may be true, but I care not to hear them." A familiar lump of humiliation caught in Alyce's throat.

"Vulgar or not, I speak the truth. I've sampled her myself. The child could even be mine."

Alyce scrunched her face in disgust. "That may be so, but five years of marriage did not produce a child for me, and one night with her produced a child nine months later with his same green eyes and dimpled chin."

"Other men have green eyes and dimples, and his features look similar to half the men in my regiment." Cynwulf turned to Alyce and gently captured her chin between his thumb and forefinger to make her look at him. "Geoffrey loved you, Alyce, and I know you loved him. You can find contentment again."

The muscles in Alyce's neck went rigid as unbidden anger filled her face with heat. "As what? A mistress? Or a wife to an old man? A barren woman cannot provide an heir and cannot provide a husband with what he needs most. Any man in his prime—

including Montworth, who believes making you his brother-in-law will give him the respect he lacks—will tire of me as soon as he realizes I cannot provide him with more heirs and will deem me useless. I will be forced to endure the humiliation of more mistresses bearing my husband's bastards."

"A man can still love his wife while ridding himself of his baser needs elsewhere. You will be hard-pressed to find a man willing to forgo the services of another just because he has wed." Cynwulf tilted his head to the side and gave her a weak smile. "Do as the others do, Alyce, and look the other way. Many women are content and happy in their marriages. It just takes the willingness to be tolerant. A man's indiscretions do not indicate a lack of care for his wife. Men are different creatures from women, with different needs."

"If that is what you truly believe, I pity the woman you marry." Alyce took a deep breath to calm herself. "I tire of this conversation, brother. It seems to be the only topic we discuss these days."

She entwined her hands together tightly on her lap as a hollowness enveloped her chest. She would never be content as a tolerant wife. Once, her love for Geoffrey had felt boundless, and she felt loved in return. She trusted him and felt safe with him…until he betrayed her trust and broke her heart. She knew he had loved her, that he had regretted immensely his indiscretion, and though she could forgive, she could not forget all the promises broken by that one act. She could not go through the humiliation and hurt again. And she could not be as tolerant a wife as Cynwulf described.

"I want more," she whispered, her eyes meeting Cynwulf's. "And I hope you can give the woman you marry more than what you have just described to me."

She rose to her feet, unable to say another word, not even a courteous "good night", as she walked the length of the raised dais and took her leave of the hall.

HAWK WATCHED LADY Alyce deep in discussion with her brother, the emotions on her face changing quicker than the sky over a roiling sea with each passing moment. She went from concerned to pleading to frustrated to complacent and back to concerned, then dejected, and finally angry as she rose from her seat and walked briskly across the dais and through the door leading to the spiral staircase and the chambers above.

Hawk wanted to follow her, to offer her—what? Solace? Reassurance? She would not want them from him, and he had no good reason to be the one to offer anything to her. He pushed the lady from his mind and turned his attention back to her brother.

Cynwulf played a dangerous game—whatever that may be—and Hawk did not want to see the gentle woman hurt by her brother's actions. He could not be certain exactly what Cynwulf planned, but he felt in his bones the man was up to something that would not bode well for Hawkspur or his sister.

Hawk determined that Cynwulf was either very daring or very careless. Only a man with incredible cunning or a complete idiot would dare ignore the demands of a king and treat his envoy as nothing more than a nuisance. For that is what the Lord of Hawkspur did when he seated Hawk and Red at the far end of the great table after avoiding him for the entirety of the day. Avoidance was the tactic of a coward and a fool, as far as Hawk was concerned.

He picked up the silver cup of wine before him and took a long, slow drink as he contemplated his next move. His gut told him Cynwulf planned something ominous, and likely traitorous. Now all that remained was to learn what he plotted and who was foolish enough to assist him.

The king had confided in Hawk that Cynwulf and Alyce had the same mother but not the same father, though the old lord Chetwynd raised him as his own blood. The rumor among those close to the family was that Cynwulf's mother had married Lord Chetwynd immediately upon returning from an extended stay in Wales, and Cynwulf was born less than six months later.

Which meant the lord of Hawkspur likely had Welsh blood running through his veins.

Hawk locked eyes on his prey at the other end of the table. Cynwulf sat quietly now, his watchful gaze moving slowly over the people drinking and laughing at the long tables before the dais. He pondered what could possibly make a man of his moderate but comfortable wealth and position get involved in something that would jeopardize his role as lord of Hawkspur. Even if Cynwulf had Welsh blood, he had been raised since a babe by an English family loyal to King Edward. He had inherited a castle from his uncle, who was one of King Edward's most trusted noblemen in the Welsh Marches. His loyalty to his adopted family and the king they served had to run deeper than any affinity he felt for the country of a father he probably did not even know.

Cynwulf did not have to fight for Hawkspur, nor did he have to prove his worth to the king to become lord of Hawkspur. He was given Hawkspur because it was his family's castle. Marcher castle lords were not merely stewards of their castles because of the grace of the king; they owned their castles and could bequeath them to their families as they wished. It would take something as treacherous as an act of treason to lose ownership, and Hawk could not imagine Cynwulf would be so foolish as to jeopardize his family's castle.

If Hawk was lord of a castle such as this, he would do all in his power to keep it. He would use it to train knights to serve the king, thus fulfilling his duty to his king to provide an elite fighting force while having a soft bed to sleep in every night.

He shook his head before his imagination could get carried away with foolish thoughts. Hawkspur was not his, and he was not destined to be lord of anything more than a sword and a steed. He was the bastard son of a nobleman with no hope of gaining either land or fortune of any magnitude. He earned his way from the bite of his blade and not from the comfort of a fortress as a lord with a family at his side.

Best to focus on the task at hand and complete his mission, give the king what he wanted, then leave Hawkspur Castle and the Lady Alyce behind when his work was done.

It should not matter to him what happened to the lady after

he left, but an unfamiliar twinge of regret niggled at him. He cringed, thinking of the harm it would cause to her reputation and what her future would look like if he proved her brother a traitor.

For tonight, he would let Cynwulf and his sister dismiss his presence, and on the morrow he would take command of the situation—something he should have done already but he had wanted to watch how the lord of Hawkspur reacted to his arrival. The tactic had paid off since Cynwulf did just as Hawk expected. It had only taken a few short hours for Cynwulf to arrange a covert meeting in the stable and send a messenger out through the postern gate, riding hard for the Welsh border.

The king had warned him Cynwulf was not above suspicion, and guilt had radiated off the man from the moment Hawk set eyes upon him. Cynwulf was also smart and calculating, and Hawk knew better than to underestimate him. Perhaps on the morrow he will have some answers. His best tracker, Hunter, had followed the messenger from Cynwulf's clandestine meeting in the stables earlier in the day with instructions to find out where he went and the names of everyone he spoke to or met along the way.

Cynwulf's loyalty to the king might be in question, but Hawk harbored no doubt that Lady Alyce and her brother were loyal to each other. Despite Lady Alyce leaving the hall earlier in an obvious state of agitation, brother and sister were close. The question was, were they close enough for Cynwulf to confide in Alyce? The woman seemed incapable of doing anything underhanded herself, but that did not mean she was not in her brother's confidence and aware of at least the broad details of his intentions.

"What is the plan?" Red asked in a low voice, interrupting Hawk's thoughts. He followed Hawk's gaze to where it rested on Cynwulf.

"To further ruffle the feathers of Lady Alyce," Hawk replied. "I believe he will protect his sister. Her agitation will add pressure to Cynwulf and propel him into action."

"And you think whatever action he takes will damn him

further?"

"Aye, I do."

Finally, Cynwulf turned to look down the length of the table at Hawk. They locked eyes like two stags taking measure of each other, neither willing to be the first to blink or back down.

"He is a man not easily intimidated," Red observed, "and not one likely to act without thought first."

Cynwulf was forced to look away when another man approached him, clapping him jovially on the shoulder to capture his attention.

"I agree," Hawk said thoughtfully. "If it was only him, he would not buckle easily, but I believe he will not want to see his sister in distress."

Red pinched his bushy red eyebrows together and shot a warning glance at Hawk. "What is it you intend to do?"

Hawk turned to face his old friend. "You know I will not harm a woman. I intend to do nothing more than force my company upon her. The lady's nerves seem to be set on edge by my very presence, and the woman is horrible at hiding her thoughts and emotions. If she knows anything, Cynwulf will not want her near me."

"And if she knows naught?"

"Then she will be saved from her brother's fate." He felt a pang of guilt as he thought about what her future would be as the sister of a disgraced lord of the realm. But he could not think about that now.

Red raised his mug to salute Hawk. "To the mission."

"To the mission."

He knocked his cup of wine against Red's mug of ale, sloshing liquid onto the table, then took a large gulp.

"And what of the Lady Alyce?" Red asked.

"Lady Alyce's future will be the king's to decide if this mission ends as I suspect it will, and we will be gone, never to look back."

Red flashed a grin. "I wouldn't wager on that."

Chapter Seven

WHEN SHE COULD not leave the confines of Hawkspur to escape into the forest alone, Alyce walked the high castle walls, as she did this morning. Rarely did she encounter anyone other than the soldiers on patrol in the early morning hours as the sun rose, so it surprised her to see an unmistakably tall figure looking out over the wall, his profile sharp in the dawning light.

She contemplated turning around before he noticed her presence but thought better of it. The king's knight and his army had been at Hawkspur for nearly a sennight, and she had spent the whole of that time busying herself with every possible mundane task of maintaining the castle to avoid the dark knight who unsettled her composure every time he was near. In truth, she'd expected him and his army to be gone by now. But since that was not the case, better to know what Hawk was doing and what conclusions he was drawing if she wanted to protect Cynwulf—though from what exactly, she did not yet know. He seemed to be avoiding her as much as she was avoiding Hawk. Mayhap it had nothing to do with the treason suspected by the king, but until she uncovered Cynwulf's secrets, she would do what she could to divert Hawk away from him.

Moving quietly, she walked nearer to him, then followed the direction of his gaze. Hawk's strong features were stony with seriousness, even sharper-looking than usual as he leaned on his elbows and stretched his neck to peer down into the valley below with a perplexed expression on his face.

"You look as though you suspect treason at any moment from any one of them, Sir Grogan," Alyce said.

Hawk did not look at her when he responded. "Please, call me Hawk. And I suspect everyone to be in the wrong until they prove to be in the right."

"All right. What offense have the people of the village committed to deserve your suspicion, this early in the morning, Sir Hawk?"

"Just Hawk," he corrected again. "None, but neither have they done ought to prove above suspicion."

Alyce had hoped that the fact he took time to contemplate the villagers was a sign he was a man with an open mind. How disappointing that he insinuated innocent people should be thought suspect without reason. She gritted her teeth and forced a cordial smile. "You've yet to even meet them."

"Aye, hence, I cannot know if they are worthy of being above suspicion."

Alyce sighed heavily. "Nor can you know they are unworthy of being above suspicion."

Warriors could be stubborn she knew, and she feared nothing she said or did would make any difference to him or alter his opinion of the people of Hawkspur. In truth, it was not her nature to back down, but she did not care to argue with someone who refused to see reason. She turned on her heel to leave, then hesitated, reminding herself that more hung in the balance than her displeasure.

"Do I trespass, my lady?"

"Yes, Sir Grogan, you do." She turned to face him again, hands on hips. "You come into Hawkspur expecting my brother to do your bidding. You forget Cynwulf is lord here, and you skulk around our home suspecting everyone guilty of treason."

Alyce waited for a response, bracing herself for rebuke—but she would not be contrite. Even knights of the king needed a reminder of their station when overstepping their bounds.

He straightened to his full height, nostrils flared, and towered over her. She wished he would not stand so close, and she almost took a step back to put more space between them but stopped herself. She refused to give him reason to believe she was afraid and instead looked up at him to meet his gaze with as much confidence as she could muster.

"First, my lady," Hawk drawled, narrowing his dark eyes at her. "I am here at the king's bidding, which puts me in a station above either of you, regardless of your precious Marcher traditions. Second, Cynwulf's position as lord does not put him above suspicion and scrutiny. And third, I never *skulk*."

She wanted to laugh. He'd been more offended at the accusation of skulking than of being inconsiderate and rude. Perhaps "skulk" was not an apt description; he was larger than life and not one to lurk in the shadows. She gave him an indulgent smile and said, "You are right, you never skulk. No, you enter a room with a swagger and a puffed chest, like a stallion claiming a pasture of mares. You have too much arrogance to skulk."

His eyes widened with surprise when she imitated his strut in a circle around him, chest pushed out and elbows wide as she swung her arms. She could hardly believe she'd just gone to such efforts to insult him by mocking his annoying ways, but it was too late to take it back. She stopped when she was in front of him again and forced herself to look at his face. She did not want to lift her eyes above his chin, but she would not back down now.

She braced herself for whatever retribution he should choose to deal out. It suddenly occurred to her that he might be a man with no qualms about striking a lady and prayed he would not hit her. Never had her father, uncle, brother, or husband ever struck her, but she knew some men were prone to such behavior and a warrior like Hawk was no stranger to violence. Next time, she would think it through more carefully before she decided to throw an insult in his face.

But he did nothing.

And said nothing.

She stared at his chin for what seemed an agonizingly long time until she saw it quiver slightly. Forcing herself not to flinch in the face of the anger that caused the tick in his chin, she lifted her eyes to his. What she saw there took her completely by surprise. His eyes didn't burn with anger, they…twinkled! And he was on the verge of laughing. Her shoulders dropped with relief, but she jumped the very next second when he let out a booming hoot of amusement.

HAWK HAD NEVER seen anything like it before.

No one had ever dared mock him to his face or insult him as openly as this woman. Though, in truth, he found her comment about his swagger and puffed chest to be quite complimentary. Ah, but the Lady Alyce was a fresh change from the women with whom he usually kept company.

"First, thank you for the compliment," he said, wiping the tears of laughter from his eyes. "And second, that is the finest bit of playacting I've had the pleasure of witnessing in a very long time."

"Well, *first*," Lady Alyce drawled, mimicking him, "'twas not meant to be a compliment, and second, even the chickens in the yard can imitate your strut."

Watching the emotions play across Lady Alyce's face fascinated Hawk. She held nothing back. The look of surprise in her own eyes as she said the last was as amusing as her words. Her insolence should offend him, but he found it too entertaining to put a stop to it.

He stepped closer until their toes were nearly touching so she had no choice but to tip her head back to look at him, despite her height. She kept her eyes locked on his chin, refusing to look any higher. Her cheeks had turned red when she first began her insults, but now her entire face showed the heat of her embarrassment.

Or was it something else? He felt his own heat rising, but it had nothing to do with embarrassment and everything to do with the hundred different ways he would like to test her boldness, each one starting with her sprawled across a bed. Did she find herself as attracted to him as he was to her at this moment?

Hawk decided her heat was from embarrassment, she was

too sincere to feel anything else after the display she'd just put on.

"Thus far, lady, you've compared me to a stallion and a chicken." He put a finger under her chin and forced her to look up at him. "Any other livestock you care to compare my likeness to?"

He felt some satisfaction when her ears and throat turned as red as the rest of her face, but she did not blink or back down from him.

"No. I believe those will do." At least her words sounded contrite even if her voice did not.

She had lovely eyes fringed with dark lashes that brushed the top of her cheeks when she looked down—which she didn't do for very long. The lady had nerve if nothing else. He was just about to move his fingers from her chin to catch a loose wisp of her hair when she stepped back, putting distance between them. The intoxicating aroma of lavender, and something more subtle but equally alluring, faded as she moved away.

"Would you like to count my teeth and inspect them for soundness?" she asked, her voice a mixture of sarcasm and annoyance.

Hawk realized he had been staring at her overly long, but he had no idea what she meant. He tilted his head to the side, looking at her through narrowed eyes, furrowing his eyebrows questioningly.

"I am not a broodmare to be examined for imperfections."

Again, he had unintentionally offended her. Her face, hair, and scent had mesmerized him, and he'd forgotten for a moment they were acquaintances standing on the top of the castle wall instead of lovers sitting by the warm glow of a hearth. He may dare look his fill at a bonny lass in a tavern, but Lady Alyce was a different sort of woman. Her boldness was not flirtatious, and her confidence was not a sultry invitation. He could see no conniving in her eyes when she spoke to him, and she obviously did not desire him the way most women did. He was lost in his thoughts again and caught uncharacteristically off guard when Alyce turned away from him to leave.

"Where are you going?" He sounded gruffer than he'd intended.

She stopped and turned to face him, her posture now regal. "I do not feel it necessary to ask your leave, sir; this is my home, and you are the guest. I am leaving you to your musings, or whatever it is you were doing up here. Good day, Sir Grogan."

"Wait. Explain this to me," he said with a nod toward the village.

"What is it you look at, Sir Grogan?" Her arms were crossed in front of her, feet planted. He was hoping she'd return to his side.

"Call me Hawk. You sound angry when you call me 'Sir Grogan'."

"Mayhap I am angry," she said with a smirk, one elegant eyebrow arching enticingly.

She did look angry—and invigorated. Her lips were pursed, and she exhaled with the force of a raging bull. The luscious curve of her breasts pressed tightly against the linen of her gown with each exaggerated breath, and Hawk had to struggle to keep his eyes on her face. She seemed completely unaware of the enticing effect of her anger, and he grinned, thinking it would only anger her more if she knew he did not feel the least bit chastised, and instead was getting more uncomfortable as his growing lust strained against his breeches.

She dropped her arms in resignation and walked slowly back to his side, stopping an arm's length away. She leaned against the castle wall to look out over the village, her body stiff and tense as though she suspected he might grab her and throw her over the wall if she came too close.

He wanted to grab her all right and throw her over his shoulder to carry her to his chamber. If she had any inkling of the erotic things he wanted to do to her she would probably throw herself over the wall instead.

Alyce peered over the wall trying to discern exactly what Hawk was looking at, but she could see nothing unusual. "I ask again...Hawk." She hesitated before saying his name, the moniker feeling awkward on her lips. "What—or whom—do you study so fervently from your perch up here, high above your unsuspecting prey?"

Suddenly, his name did not seem so inappropriate.

Hawk turned his head slightly in her direction and cocked a questioning eyebrow as he looked sideways at her. "I am trying to understand the motives of the villagers. Some are English, many are Welsh, yet they work and live together despite the animosity and turmoil between the two lands."

Alyce studied his face a moment before answering, surprised to see the hard lines of his face soften, a look of genuine interest in his dark eyes. An unexpected bloom of warmth spread through her chest, and she buried her hands in the folds of her gown until the urge to touch her fingers to the curve of his cheek subsided. "Perhaps, my lord, you have spent too much time waging war and not enough time lording over a castle. Do you have a home of your own?"

He turned his entire body to face her, resting his hip against the wall and leaning on one forearm—a large forearm, at that. She didn't know what was more aggravating, the man himself, or the way her breath seemed to catch in her throat when he turned his full attention her way. He brought out the worst in her, infuriating her into saying rude things she would never dare to say, or even want to say, to anyone else. Good lord, she'd even been so flustered as to strut around him like a rutting stallion just to show him what he looked like. She could hardly blame him if he chose to throw her over the wall after the things she'd said and done.

He'd started talking, but the way he grinned—a bit lopsided and surprisingly full of boyish charm for someone who exuded nothing but masculinity and strength—made her traitorous heart skip a beat. It had been a long while since conversing with another person left her feeling so exhilarated, but she was definitely feeling that way now—invigorated—and like something other than a widow to be pitied, or a sister to be looked after.

"Will…will you repeat that?" She tried not to stammer like a foolish girl. "I was thinking of the morning duties I must attend to soon." *You are a woman married and widowed, not a naïve maiden.*

She repeated the words in her head over and over as he continued to stare at her. Hawk was a dangerous man, and she must not forget that. Not just to her sanity, but also to the future of Hawkspur.

His grin broadened with that all-knowing confidence he seemed to have in abundance, and he leaned a bit closer to her. "I said no, my lady, I do not have a home. I am a fighting man, a knight of the king. I rarely sleep in the same bed for more than a month or two if I am lucky enough to have a bed to sleep in. Most of my days are spent fighting, and my nights are spent bedded down in tents or under the stars, moving from one battle to another, quelling one uprising after another. I earn my gold by wielding my skills on the battlefield."

"Ah," she said, nodding, flustered to realize her focus was on his lips as her head filled with images of what they would feel like pressed against her own. With a quick shake of her head to clear it, she turned toward the village. Wasn't there an old saying about keeping your enemies close? Better to know what Hawk was thinking and doing than to have him roaming the castle unhindered, looking for treason in every corner, she reasoned. "Would you care for me to enlighten you about the Welsh and English villagers here at Hawkspur?"

"Please do, Lady Alyce. Enlighten me."

Alyce ignored the mocking tone of his voice. "To the villagers, the things of importance are their family, their crops, their livestock, and the weather. These things are their entire world. They work every day to feed and clothe their children and themselves, whether Welsh or English. They care not who claims dominion over their lands, or whether their present lord is loyal to the English king or the Welsh prince. As long as their lord is fair and protects them in return for a share of all they reap, they are contented."

"Ha," Hawk scoffed. "I have a hard time believing, with all due respect, my lady, that any man can willingly swear fealty to a lord not of his heritage whilst his Welsh brothers are fighting the same lord."

Alyce smiled as though indulging a child. "These people," she swept her arm out over the wall in the direction of the village, "do not have time to concern themselves with the machinations of kings, lords, and knights who see all of this as though it were a chess board, manipulating and maneuvering for more squares. While fighting men spend their days planning and battling to gain more land and wealth, the people of this village work from sunrise to sundown working the land, tending sheep, gathering eggs from chickens, repairing cottages, mending clothing, cooking meals, and praying the weather will be kind to their crops and animals and that the winters will be short and mild."

"You understand the game of chess, my lady?" Hawk asked, genuine surprise in his voice.

"Yes, but that is not the point."

Hawk nodded slowly but Alyce wondered if he truly understood or if he was merely indulging her as a naïve woman expressing soft-hearted thoughts.

"Their world extends as far as you can see," she continued, undaunted by his doubt. "Few have ever ventured over the tops of those hills in the distance, or even know what lies beyond them. What matters most is that the lord is reasonable, just, and wise in the ways of managing a castle and a village. They want nothing more than to take care of their families and live in peace."

"And the rebels, those who seem to materialize from nothing and attack quickly and fiercely before disappearing back into the wilderness, where are they from?" Hawk's face was dark and sharp, and Alyce felt like the deadly bird had focused on her as his new prey.

"I do not know where the rebels come from, but they are not of Hawkspur Castle or village," Alyce snapped more churlishly than intended. She could not believe that any of the people who lived here would betray the village.

Hawk was staring intently at her, the intensity of his dark eyes unnerving, and his face showing neither gratitude for her explanation nor anger. Alyce shifted her weight on her feet and nervously grabbed a lock of her hair, twisting the curls through her fingers. She looked down at her fidgeting digits when Hawk's eyes moved to her hands, then back to her face.

"Thank you for enlightening me, my lady. You have been most helpful."

"You are welcome," she responded, her tone more curt than intended.

"Do I make you uncomfortable, my lady?"

She let go of the strands of hair and squared her shoulders. "No, sir, you do not."

"Ah," he said, raising his eyebrows.

Alyce took a step backward in preparation to leave. "Mayhap you should visit the village one day soon."

Hawk bowed slightly. "I look forward to it, my lady."

Alyce recoiled, unsure if he expected her to escort him. "I meant only that walking among the villagers may help you to understand the motives behind their existence."

"And I am saying you are right. Will tomorrow suit you, lady, to show me the ways of your village?"

She eyed him warily. Whoever had said to keep your enemies close probably did not have an enemy who looked at them the way Hawk was looking at her now or caused shivers to ripple over their skin as they did over hers at this moment.

"Tomorrow," she agreed reluctantly, "after the morning repast."

Hawk reached for her hand and pressed his lips to her bare knuckles. Her body thrummed as the blood rushed through her veins with an exhilaration she'd not felt in a long while, especially as his warm breath curled over her hand and up her wrist. "I look forward to it, Lady Alyce."

Snatching her hand back, she nodded stiffly and hurried away. How annoying that the source of her renewed energy was none other than a dangerous knight of the king who believed treason lurked in the heart of her brother and every other living soul at Hawkspur.

Chapter Eight

ALYCE WANTED NOTHING more than to escape the castle, her brother, the king's knight, and her frayed nerves after finishing her daily duties. Her discussion with Hawk earlier that morning had left her unsettled. Changing into her sturdiest boots and simplest tunic, she picked up a small basket and headed through the outer gate to the forest that stood just beyond the fields being worked by the villagers.

She had not been able to get her brother alone to discuss the incident in the barn. He was always training with his troops, meeting with the stablemaster, or listening to grievances from the villagers. Even when she met with him to discuss the management of the castle and the progress of the planting of the fields, there were others in the solar with them, ready to carry out the directives of Alyce and Cynwulf. When the meeting was over, he'd hurry off to his next duty before she could stop him.

Even if she had been able to get a moment of Cynwulf's time, either Hawk or one of his men was lurking nearby. Hawk had made his intentions clear that as long as he was at Hawkspur; he would not allow anything to happen that would displease the king. In truth, Hawk was acting as though Cynwulf needed his approval for any action he took.

And if he did not approve, what then? Would Hawk swoop in and take over as lord of Hawkspur in Cynwulf's place?

Alyce's uncle had ruled over the strategic fortress with might and kindness, protecting his village as his family. Lordship over the castle meant much more than just possessing the stones with which it was built or reaping the benefits of the crops and livestock. Her uncle understood that. Cynwulf understood that. *She* understood that. A knight of the king, traveling from one battle to another, could never understand the skills and compassion required to keep a castle and village thriving and safe.

Ffyddlon wriggled excitedly by her side, nudging her hand to get her moving. Alyce shook her head to put an end to the frustrating thoughts in her head and scratched the hound behind the ear. They passed under the heavy portcullis of the castle gateway, through the village, and onto a trail that wound through the copse of woods at the edge of Hawkspur. She picked a few flowers, and herbs for the kitchen, placing them in her basket as she walked.

The trail soon sloped down into another valley behind the castle and her tension eased once in the protection of the trees, tall and thick with leaves that formed a canopy over the forest floor. She set down her basket next to the trunk of a mossy tree, hiked her tunic to her knees, and slanted her eyes at Ffyddlon.

"Are you ready for the chase?"

Ffyddlon crouched in a playful stance and then bounded up the trail. Alyce picked up her feet, the folds of her gown clutched in her hands and chased the dog until she could not catch her breath. When she could not run at a fast pace any longer, she slowed to an easier pace and continued to run along the path behind Ffyddlon, up another hill. The forest was tiny compared to the vast swaths of woods beyond the borders of the fields, but it felt like a hidden paradise to Alyce. Here she could let down her guard and be free.

Ffyddlon yipped excitedly but slowed her pace to allow Alyce to catch up. Even when running ahead, she constantly looked back to be sure Alyce was still in sight. Ffyddlon was tall and could be very imposing when she felt the need, and Alyce had no doubt she would protect her at any cost.

She loved Ffyddlon as much as she loved Cynwulf or Edna. Many would think her foolish, but Ffyddlon filled the hole in her heart created by an unfaithful husband and a childless marriage. When Geoffrey had died, Ffyddlon had stayed by her side and offered comfort as she'd cried herself to sleep night after night.

That Ffyddlon craved her attention and wanted to do everything at her side was perfectly acceptable to Alyce, and thus she indulged the dog by playing chasing games and exploring the forest with her. She'd soon discovered that playing and running was as beneficial for herself as it was for Ffyddlon. They would run until Alyce could not take another step, her chest heaving with every breath. It was in this state of pure freedom and exhaustion that she was able to think through more clearly the perplexing and irksome details of her life.

Ffyddlon stopped when they reached a secluded pond in the forest, much to Alyce's relief. Rarely had they encountered another person here and she had come to think of it as her own private paradise. She removed her boots and crawled up on a large rock on the edge of the little pool of water and lay back on the flat of the stone until her breathing returned to normal. Ffyddlon splashed into the pond and lapped up water, waiting for her mistress to follow.

Once the sun had warmed her into feeling drowsy, Alyce stripped down to her chemise and lowered herself into the cool water. Her skin tingled at the decadent feel of the water caressing against her nearly naked body, and as usual, she said a prayer that nobody would discover her hidden pond while she indulged herself. She wrapped her braid around her head to keep it dry and held it there as she walked in circles in the pool, Ffyddlon still splashing near her.

"Now," she said to the rocks and trees as the cool water reinvigorated her, "What am I to do about Cynwulf?"

Hawk waited nearly two hours for Alyce to emerge from the forest.

He had watched Alyce slip through a side gate of the castle after meeting with the young lord. She had a basket on her arm and Ffyddlon at her side. Curiosity got the better of him, so he returned to the parapet to see what she was about. A movement near the base of the hill caught his eye. He recognized the long copper plait hanging down the back of the woman who disappeared into the trees, so he stayed at the wall, watching. The logical conclusion was she ventured into the forest to gather berries or flowers, or whatever it was women filled their baskets with, but his suspicious nature forced him to wait and confirm her intentions.

When she did not return in a reasonable amount of time, he started to doubt she was as innocent as he first believed.

Or some misfortune had befallen her.

He was about to leave the parapet to search for her when finally the wolfhound bounded out of the forest just before Alyce emerged from the trees. Her brisk pace and carefree swinging of the basket did not ease his mind—two hours foraging in the forest should have returned more than just a light basket of spoils.

Could he have been wrong about Lady Alyce? He found it hard to believe he misjudged her, but until he was sure, he would assume her as guilty as he assumed everyone else.

Chapter Nine

AFTER CONTEMPLATING THE prospect of escorting Hawk on a tour of the village, Alyce decided she was wrong to dread the deed as she had initially. The afternoon in the forest with Ffyddlon had cleared her head, and she now believed showing Hawk the village would make him see the people of Hawkspur did not have time in their day to embroil themselves in the conflicts of kings and princes. They wished only to live comfortably in peace, and they were willing to put in the work to make that happen. He would understand then why nobody at Hawkspur would plot to conspire with the Welsh princes and bring down the wrath of the English king upon the castle and the villagers—especially Cynwulf.

Still, the fear Cynwulf hid something important from her would not go away. It had been a full sennight since she overheard her brother and the strange man in the barn, and she was questioning her memory of what truly happened. The incident had played over and over in her head so many times, she was no longer sure what was real and what she had imagined. She wanted to believe her suspicions about Cynwulf were merely a product of the chaos of the last several days, that the conversation she overheard could be explained.

She really must stop overreacting.

She tugged at the sleeves of her gown to calm her nerves and occupy her fidgeting hands as she descended the spiral staircase on her way to the great hall for dinner. Stopping at the bottom of the stairs, she ran her fingers over the cuffs embroidered with little white moons and yellow stars blazing boldly against the deep blue hue of the gown. It was her favorite, and she wore it to bolster her confidence. Tonight she would not let Hawk unsettle her and she would not let Cynwulf dodge her.

She knocked on the solar door, hoping to find Cynwulf within, but not at all surprised when there was no response. Her brother was proving more slippery than an eel, constantly avoiding her attempts to speak with him. She turned away with a sigh and ducked through the entry to the hall.

Once every fortnight, Cynwulf's hall was filled with prominent townspeople, his highest-ranking soldiers, and any others seeking an audience with Cynwulf. Tomorrow afternoon, her brother would hold an open council to resolve grievances and listen to petitions. The eve before each council was filled with as much feasting and merrymaking as it was political bargaining and scheming to sway Cynwulf to favor one side over another before the official council even began.

In the years Geoffrey had been alive, both she and her husband sat at Cynwulf's side to offer council when requested. After Geoffrey had died, she'd stopped attending; at first, she'd thought it would be for just a while, but then she'd never gone back. Cynwulf was a fair man and he resolved issues with as much compassion and common sense as her uncle had done before them. He did not need her counsel and she felt her time better spent in the planning and managing of the castle resources.

In reality, she preferred the duties that kept her away from the attention that followed Cynwulf as lord of the castle. She did not relish taking part in the gathering before tomorrow's council, but it was her duty as the lady of Hawkspur, and so she forced herself to feign pleasantness and present herself in the hall.

Hawk's imposing form immediately caught her eye from the far end of the hall, and she felt her breath catch unexpectedly. He stood nearly a head taller than everyone else in the room except for his Viking companion at his side. His straight black hair hung loose down to his shoulders, accenting the dark green of his tunic.

He crossed his arms over his broad chest as he surveyed his domain with sharp, dark eyes, ready to swoop in at the first sign of trouble. He was an intimidating figure for sure, and it galled her that she found him so appealing.

Surely the tingling that raced through her at the sight of him was due to her nerves being set on end in preparation for the agitation he was bound to ignite in her. Though she had to admit, if only to herself, that she found the bantering exhilarating. He didn't speak to her with pity, condescension, or guarded protectiveness as she had become accustomed to in the year since Geoffrey died, or in the two years since his son had been born to another woman.

He didn't treat her like a heartbroken widow. Or a conquest. Or a woman requiring shelter from the rest of the world. When they were on the castle wall earlier in the day, he conversed with her as though he had no fear that her feelings were too fragile and listened intently to her explanation of the villagers and what mattered in their lives.

More importantly, he did not chastise her nor dismiss her when she mocked him for his arrogance, comparing him to a stallion and then a chicken.

Some women swooned at fancy words and romantic gestures, but Alyce was attracted to a man who recognized her as a woman with thoughts and opinions that mattered. And when that man was built like Hawk, broad and tall enough as to make a woman of her height feel dainty, her mind turned to thoughts that were not very ladylike and urges she had not experienced since her husband had died.

Alyce tried to push that thought from her mind. She could not let herself be distracted by a handsome warrior when that same warrior was hellbent on proving her brother to be a traitor. She tried to divert her attention from his arrogant stance and possessive watch over the hall—Cynwulf's hall—but those piercing eyes settled onto hers before she could look away. Their eyes remained locked together for a long moment.

And then, he winked at her.

Flustered and irritated, Alyce broke off the gaze as a shiver rippled through her body and began searching the room for her brother. She did not have time for flirtatious games. Truth be told, she didn't even know how to play at being flirtatious. She might admire his form and height, but she would not allow herself to be distracted from the task at hand, which was to convince Hawk no traitors dwelled at Hawkspur, then send him on his way back to the king before her brother did anything more to raise suspicion.

She spotted Cynwulf leaning against the hearth on the far side of the raised dais, talking with a group of men. She started towards him but stopped when a commotion caught her attention by the entry. Another half dozen men had entered the hall, talking and laughing boisterously, and the most boisterous of the group was a familiar voice that made Alyce cringe.

It was for good reason Alyce had referred to Luc Montworth as a peacock when Cynwulf suggested him as a suitor. The man was loud and constantly preening. He had fallen from the king's graces years ago but was weaseling his way back into the ranks of nobility. He wielded his power as sheriff of the forest as though he were already named lord of a manor—which the king promised to do soon. He was an ambitious man, always greedily eying his next prize.

But Alyce was not a prize, and she had no desire to tie herself to such a self-serving and self-centered man. How her brother could even consider him as a possible suitor for her was beyond reasoning.

Montworth immediately started across the hall in Alyce's direction, eyeing her like a chest of gold. Alyce looked frantically for Cynwulf to save her, then decided escape was her best option as she turned on her heel and headed toward the buttery.

She walked briskly toward the back of the hall and slipped through the entry to the buttery where the servants stored barrels of ale and wine, ready to be decanted and served to the guests in the hall. She instantly regretted her choice to come here for refuge. An all-too-familiar buxom maiden filled jugs with ale while a small boy sat on the floor in the corner playing with a wooden horse.

The woman turned to see who entered, then cocked her head with a puzzled expression on her face. "I did not expect to see you in here, my lady. May I assist you with something?"

Alyce felt flustered for a moment at the sight of the woman with whom her husband had spent one forbidden night, but before she could say anything the little boy pushed himself to his feet and held his toy up to Alyce.

"Horsey," he said proudly of the carved wooden animal in his hand.

Alyce studied his pudgy cheeks and excited eyes, searching for definitive proof of her dead husband's features in this little boy who was the child of another woman. Was the dimple in his chin or the green of his eyes exactly the same as Geoffrey's? Or could those features be inherited from some other green-eyed man with a dimple and light hair?

"Henry," Janet chided softly, "do not bother the lady."

The little boy's face fell, and he looked about to cry, as though he'd done something wrong. Alyce did not want to distress this poor little boy who had no idea how he affected her. "It is a very majestic horse," she said, squatting down to look at him from his level. Her gown billowed around her feet and pooled on the floor, making Henry laugh and plop down on his knees next to her, trying to catch the flowing material with his fat, little fingers.

"Henry!" Janet scolded. "Do not touch. You will ruin her gown."

"It is all right," Alyce said softly, reaching out to touch Henry's hand where he patted at the gown. Did it really matter if this boy was the offspring of her husband or some other man? Even if the child was not Geoffrey's, her husband had shared the woman's bed. The sight of Janet usually caused her an instant feeling of queasiness in her stomach. Images of her naked husband lying with the woman started to fill her head, but she quickly pushed them away. Whether or not this boy was a product of her husband's drunken indiscretion, he was an innocent child. Like Alyce, Henry did not take part in what happened, yet had to suffer the consequences of the choices made by his mother and Alyce's husband.

Alyce put her hands under the little boy's arms and picked him up as she stood to lift him off her gown. Her husband, like every man, had desired a son to carry on his legacy. If this boy was her husband's son, then Geoffrey lived on. And if he was not his son, then there was nothing left of Geoffrey other than her memories. Neither was easy to live with…but perhaps Geoffrey deserved a legacy.

She smiled at the child laughing and wiggling as she held him out and set him back on the floor. She patted his head then smoothed her gown. When she looked up, Janet was staring at her fearfully.

"Carry on, Janet," Alyce said evenly, then turned to leave. To her surprise, she did not feel as sick to her stomach as usual when coming face-to-face with the evidence of Geoffrey's indiscretion.

Cynwulf had offered many times to send Janet and the boy away so that she would not have to look at them as Janet served the hall. Some days she regretted her decision of refusing the offer, but if she allowed it then she was as petty and shallow as she imagined Janet to be. Though sending her away would ease Alyce's discomfort, it would not change what happened. Besides, Janet and the boy were a constant reminder that she could never give a man the child he required from a wife. Though her brother chose to deny the importance of that fact, she must never forget it, for any marriage she entered into would sink into disappointment for her unlucky husband and a more shameful heartache for herself.

She squared her shoulders and left the buttery, nearly bumping into Luc Montworth as she stepped out into the hall.

"There you are, Lady Alyce," he said, too loudly, as though acting for the entire hall to witness. He reached for her fingers and planted a hot, moist kiss on the back of her hand.

"Sheriff," Alyce said with a nod, gently tugging her hand from his grasp. Had Sheriff Montworth always been such a small man? She realized now that she had to look down to meet his eyes. She had thought him broad and strong, but now she realized he was just thick and paunchy. She scanned the room, searching for her brother, and sighed with relief to see him walking toward her, though the look on his face did not bode well.

Sheriff Montworth started to say something to her, but he paused, and he stayed silent as something distracted his attention. His eyes widened as though in fear, then he pinched his brows together and his face contorted with anger. Alyce took a step back, unsure what had Montworth so flustered. She stopped mid-step in her retreat when she hit something solid behind her and felt a firm hand settle onto her shoulder. She did not need to look to know Hawk stood at her back. Montworth grabbed her by the arm as though to help her avoid a fall and pulled her forward. Hawk's grip on her shoulder tightened as he held her solidly in place.

"Unhand her," Hawk commanded in a low growl.

"You unhand her, sir. The lady is to be mine," Montworth boasted, tightening his grip on her arm.

Alyce felt as though she were in the middle of two dogs fighting over a juicy bit of meat, each growling and tugging at the coveted prize. But she was not a piece of meat and was about to voice her indignation at their treatment of her when Hawk suddenly placed his hand on Montworth's wrist, clamping down with such force that the sheriff immediately released her.

"I do not appreciate being treated like a bone thrown to the dogs," Alyce said through gritted teeth, glaring first at Montworth, then at Hawk. She tried to shrug Hawk's hand from her shoulder, but he would not budge.

Montworth sputtered in outrage, his face now so flushed his ears burned red, and Alyce leaned closer to Hawk to stop him from trying to grab her again.

"Sheriff," Cynwulf interjected. "I was not expecting you today, but you are welcome at my table."

Montworth appeared as though he was at a loss for words as he looked from Cynwulf to Alyce pressed up against Hawk and back to Cynwulf.

"Introductions are in order," Cynwulf continued. "Sheriff Montworth, this is Sir Grogan, trusted knight of the king and our guest." He turned to face Hawk next, gesturing with his hand toward Montworth. "And this is Luc Montworth, Sheriff of the Forest as appointed by the king."

"Soon to be lord," Montworth muttered.

Cynwulf continued to blather on about the good work Montworth did for the kingdom, hardly stopping for a breath as the other two men glared at each other. Finally, he held out his arm to Alyce, much to her relief. "And now if you will allow me to escort my sister to the dais, our supper will soon be served," Cynwulf said to Hawk, his voice cordial but cold as he looked pointedly to where Hawk's hand still rested on her shoulder.

Hawk gently pushed Alyce in the direction of her brother, and she gratefully took Cynwulf's arm.

"You have saved me," she whispered as they walked away from the other two men. She dared a quick glance over her shoulder in time to see Hawk fold his arms over his chest and brace his legs apart as he stared down at Luc Montworth with a bored expression on his face, making it quite clear he viewed him as nothing more than a nuisance hardly worthy of his time. Montworth huffed but avoided looking at Hawk, then turned to walk away.

"What was all of that about?" Alyce asked in a harsh whisper through a stiff smile lest any of the guests in the hall watched. She did not want others to think there was cause for concern regarding her brother, the sheriff, or the king's knight.

"Montworth may be under the assumption that his negotiation for your hand in marriage has been accepted," Cynwulf admitted with a sheepish grimace.

Alyce came to an abrupt halt, stopping Cynwulf in his tracks. "No!" Her response was louder than intended and she looked around the hall quickly, but only a few heads nearest them turned in their direction. She forced a smile again and said through gritted teeth, "No, Cynwulf. How dare you enter negotiations with Montworth without my consent? You promised you would never do such a thing."

Cynwulf said calmly. "I believed it was for the best at the time, Alyce. I admit now it may have been a mistake. It will not be easy to undo."

Alyce was too angry to speak. She could hardly breathe, and it took all of her will not to pounce on her brother and strangle him. But there was an equal measure of fear to match her anger. Cynwulf would never betray her confidence this way unless he was desperate. She jerked on his arm as she started walking toward the head table again. They stepped up on the dais and Cynwulf led her to the chair next to his. She obligingly sat but then pushed back to her feet when she realized her brother did not intend to sit down beside her yet.

"Where are you going? I must speak with you," she said, grabbing his arm.

Cynwulf looked like he was about to protest, but then he nodded and pulled out his chair.

Alyce angled her chair toward Cynwulf's and looked him in the eye. "Tell me now, brother, what is happening with you? And do not tell me there is nothing to worry about because I know you would never betray my trust this way unless you felt you had no other choice." She paused a moment to sigh heavily then added in a hushed tone, "And I overheard you in the barn the other day. You have secrets you are not sharing with me."

Cynwulf's face remained steady, as did his eyes, but he did not rush to deny Alyce's words and she felt like she'd been doused in icy water as cold fingers of dread slid down her spine. It was a long moment before he parted his lips to speak but then raised voices from a group of men in the center of the hall stopped him from saying anything. Montworth's small contingent of men were forcefully trying to claim the table where Hawk's men sat. Hawk's warriors all stood in unison.

"This will not be good," Cynwulf muttered, shaking his head.

Hawk's men remained in place without lifting a threatening hand, but the imposing size of the band of warriors, as they stared quietly at the pestering men had the desired effect. The sheriff's men, realizing they were outnumbered and outsized, continued to bluster but moved away and found a less formidable group of men to intimidate into giving up their table to them. Seeing the difference in how Hawk's men demonstrated their authority compared to the way Montworth's men, who bullied others into doing what they desired was one more reason the sheriff was not a man Alyce could ever respect, especially as a husband.

"Montworth and his men seem more arrogant and demanding than usual tonight," Alyce said in a near-whisper to reach Cynwulf's ears only.

Her brother sighed, then looked Alyce straight in the eyes, his mouth a grim line. "He believes he is here to propose to you."

"What?" Alyce gasped. "Tonight? You must stop him. You said you made a mistake."

As of late, Alyce realized, she felt on the verge of hysterics after every conversation with her brother. She'd prided herself in her even temperament, but she had been pushed to her limits with all that had happened in the last several days between Hawk arriving on a mission from the king to find a traitor in their midst, her brother secretly communicating with unknown messengers in the barn, and now, she discovered, arranging a betrothal for her without her consent, even if he regretted it. She cherished familiarity, routine, and predictability, yet the last few days had been anything but those things. She put her hands to her pounding temples.

"How could you betray my trust this way? Why continue to pursue such madness when you know I will never agree to marry Montworth?" she asked Cynwulf, wondering if he would tell her the truth of the matter or if he would continue to be evasive.

"I sent him a message that he should not come, and we would discuss this more later but he either did not get the message, or he willfully ignored it." Cynwulf suddenly looked very tired and defeated, and a wave of protectiveness washed through Alyce. She could help him if he would only confide in her.

The full weight of his words finally worked their way through the confusion in her mind. *He sent Montworth a message?* Her head nearly spun with dizzying relief. *Of course!* That was what she overheard in the barn and why Cynwulf was being so secretive about it. He did not want to upset Alyce nor did he want Montworth to complicate the situation while Hawk completed his investigation. This new bit of information gave her complete confidence that there was nothing untoward happening at Hawkspur. Her brother was only guilty of trying to fix his mistake and deflect a persistent suitor. She had been wrong in jumping to the conclusions she did after overhearing him in the barn. It was foolish to think he would ever do anything to harm Hawkspur, his position as lord, or the people who looked to him for protection.

She wanted to shout her relief out loud—Cynwulf was only guilty of stubbornness and stupidity, not treason!

But it was still hurtful to her. Her brother had to stop trying to arrange her life for her. Hawk would soon be gone, and she could go back to managing the daily affairs of Hawkspur at her brother's side. If fortune was good, her brother would marry and have an heir to become lord of Hawkspur in his place one day. And when he did have children, she would be sure to spoil them endlessly so they, too, would never want her to leave Hawkspur.

She felt her life righting itself again and squared her shoulders. "Now I understand why you were behaving so strangely. You should not have kept this secret from me, Cynwulf." To stress the importance of what she was saying, she looked squarely into the depth of his brilliant blue eyes, so much like her own, so much like their mother's. In truth, their eyes and their height were the only resemblance each had to the other.

Their mother was carrying Cynwulf in her womb when she married Alyce's father, but she never revealed to Cynwulf the identity of his sire. Her father treated and loved Cynwulf as his own. Cynwulf and Alyce had still been children when their parents were killed during a storm by a runaway horse that pulled their wagon over the edge of a cliff. Mayhap their mother planned to reveal the truth and tell him who his father was when he was older, but she did not live to see her son grow into a man. It had been Uncle Ranolf who told Cynwulf the truth about his heritage shortly before he died.

She wondered if Cynwulf was curious about his sire, or if he ever searched for him. Did having a loving man who called him "son" make up for not knowing the man responsible for bringing him into the world? To her, he would always be her brother and nothing less. Never her "half" brother.

She grabbed his hands in hers. "Let us forget about Mont-worth and put our minds to showing the king's knight that there is no threat of treason at Hawkspur. He is to accompany me into the village tomorrow," she continued excitedly, warming to the plan. "Once he realizes the people of Hawkspur care only about the rigors of daily life and will gain nothing from war or fighting, he will understand there is no cause for concern and will return to the service of the king. Everything will be set to right, and we can return to our lives as they have always been."

"Do not be so sure," Cynwulf replied quietly. Before Alyce could question him about his puzzling answer, he pushed himself to his feet and turned his attention to the king's knight and the sheriff as they approached the dais.

She couldn't help comparing the sheriff to Hawk, who strode toward the platform with the nonchalance mastered only by men with absolute confidence in their own place in the world. Montworth nearly ran to keep up with him, darting from side to side as though trying to pass him in a race to the table. The sight of him bobbing and skipping behind the tall knight was comical, and Alyce turned her attention back to Hawk to stop herself from laughing aloud at the puny man's futile attempts to assert himself over the king's most revered knight.

Looking at Hawk, an unexpected warmth came over her as she recalled the way he had stood behind her when Montworth first approached earlier. It was a protective gesture she was unused to from anyone save her brother, a gesture she liked much more than she wanted to admit, even to herself. He had an alluring confidence, a presence that drew her to him.

Since she was being honest, even if only with herself, she also liked looking at him more than was decent for a lady. His breeches were snugly around his thighs, accentuating the ripple of his thigh muscles with each step, and she was having a difficult time tearing her eyes from the sight. The man certainly looked every bit the fierce warrior that she knew him to be, but he could also be a charmer when he wanted, flashing his boyish grin with a mischievous glint in his eyes. She'd learned that fact on the parapet during their early morning encounter.

Reminding herself that this man was here to disrupt their life at Hawkspur, she forced her gaze away from Hawk's muscular legs and was immediately mortified. Hawk was watching her with a small but knowing smile on his lips and an arrogant arch to one eyebrow.

Hardly charming! The man was arrogant, imposing, assuming, overbearing, and far too masculine. She should dislike him terribly. The way he'd situated himself behind her to intimidate Montworth earlier and force him to release her should have irritated her. She knew how to handle Montworth and would have been just fine without his interference; it was insulting for Hawk to think her incapable.

But his hand on her shoulder and the way he stood behind her didn't feel like a statement of her capabilities as much as to show that he stood with her and was there to support her if she needed him.

No! That way of thinking would only lead to trouble.

She tried to ignite her anger and force herself to dislike the knight, but what she was feeling was something altogether unexpected. God help her, but she *liked* having Hawk at her back, intent on protecting her. She was loath to admit it—she bristled any time anyone tried to coddle her—but she felt stronger having Hawk as a protector.

Cynwulf met the men as they stepped onto the dais. Montworth found his chance to finally get past Hawk and quickly edged his way around the table to get to Alyce's side before anyone else. As fortune would have it, Cynwulf interceded, calling out to Montworth and motioning him to the chair on the opposite side of his own, away from Alyce. She gave her brother a small smile of gratitude, not wanting Montworth to see her relief.

Montworth's face hardened and he openly scowled at her brother, then he quickly took up Alyce's hand again and bowed over it. "Until later, my lady. I insist after we sup that you take a stroll with me in the bailey—with your brother's permission, of course."

Montworth kissed the back of her hand again while caressing her palm with a clammy finger. Alyce forced her face to remain serene but inwardly, she cringed. She muttered something noncommittal, then turned away from him, only to freeze as she reached for her chair.

Hawk was watching the scene and his face looked as though he wanted to kill Montworth. The expression was gone before Alyce could even blink her eyes, but she had seen it clearly.

Could the mighty Hawk possibly be jealous?

Chapter Ten

HAWK NEARLY LEAPED over the table to throttle Montworth when he started slobbering over Alyce's hand. And he would have had Red not knowingly clamped down on his shoulder to stop him from the rash act. His trusted companion always knew when to support him.

Hawk watched Alyce's face intently, looking for any hint of unease; he was determined to hurt the sheriff if necessary. Alyce's stiff smile did not slip, but she turned her head slightly to the side as though not wanting to fully watch as Montworth pressed his mouth to her hand. If Hawk had his way, he would knock every tooth from that mouth before the night was over.

"Steady," Red muttered to him as they circled the table. "I've never seen you so lacking in control."

Hawk did not miss the questioning pinch of Red's brows, but he had no desire to explain himself, and he wasn't even sure he could. He clenched his fists at his side, reasoning that this sudden surge of protectiveness over Alyce was nothing more than his distaste for any man who made a woman uncomfortable with unwanted advances. He was forced to watch as a child while his mother suffered the attention of men she did not want, but whose touch she allowed as a means of survival.

Cynwulf pulled out Alyce's chair for her to sit, then motioned to the chair beside her as he looked at Hawk. "I ask you to be a companion to my sister as we sup, Sir Grogan."

Hawk eyed his host suspiciously but nodded his consent. The corners of Cynwulf's lips turned up in a cordial smile that did not reach his eyes. After the meeting they had earlier in the day, Hawk expected no less.

Cynwulf had insisted the king had no reason for concern, that the rumors of his paternity were nothing more than speculation, that Hawkspur was loyal to the crown, that he had everything under control, and that there was no need for Hawk and his men to waste their time here when there the king surely needed them elsewhere. Hawk had listened to Cynwulf's entire speech, his boredom apparent. When finally he'd stopped his one-sided argument, Hawk told Cynwulf his efforts to defend his innocence made it quite clear that he did not have everything under control at Hawkspur and Hawk's presence was most definitely required here.

He had expected vehement denial and more bluster from Cynwulf but to his surprise, his demeanor calmed. He became as focused as a wolf who had suddenly spied a fat hare, and Hawk realized he needed to be careful to not underestimate the young lord of Hawkspur. Cynwulf dared, then, to demand Hawk shield Alyce from the ugliness that would certainly accompany the Welsh rebellion when it reached Hawkspur's borders.

At that moment, Hawk wondered if he had misjudged Cynwulf. Perhaps the reason for Cynwulf's lack of cooperation was simply rooted in his desire to protect his sister from distress and not due to a guilty conscience as Hawk originally suspected.

Except Lady Alyce's disposition did not seem so frail as to need coddling or shielding from distress.

And Hawk's intuition was rarely wrong. Cynwulf wanted her protected from something other than the threat of the rebellion disturbing the peace of Hawkspur. It was obvious to Hawk that Cynwulf feared she could be in danger, but from exactly what, the man would not say, and Hawk did not know…but he would find out.

The lord of Hawkspur may have resigned himself to the inevitability of acquiescing to the presence of the king's knight embedded in his castle, but he would not bend completely. Hawk had to admit he would lose respect for any lord who readily allowed even a man of the king to displace his position of authority without some resistance.

If he were lord over Hawkspur, he would not give it up without a bloody fight.

Hawk dismissed the troublesome meeting with Cynwulf and turned his attention to Lady Alyce as he lowered himself into the chair beside her and stretched his legs out under the table. He found it amusing that she would not look at him now despite not taking her eyes off him as he walked to the dais. He'd purposefully slowed his gait to give her more time to look her fill, and to goad the little weasel scampering along behind him trying to get to Lady Alyce first.

"I believe you have an admirer in Sheriff Montworth."

Alyce flicked her hand in the air as though swatting away a pesky fly. "It is nothing," she said, still looking straight ahead.

"You may look at me, Lady Alyce," Hawk drawled, deciding she would avoid facing him for as long as possible unless he did something about it.

She turned to him, her nostrils flaring, and Hawk smiled at her in return, completely satisfied with her response. It did not take much to raise the lady's ire, and it seemed the best way to get her to engage with him was to ruffle her feathers.

"I do not need your permission, Sir Grogan," she said in a haughty tone, putting extra emphasis on his name to show her displeasure with him. "Mayhap I did not want to look at you."

"Ah, we are back to 'Sir Grogan' which can only mean I have perturbed you again." Hawk cocked one eyebrow at her, thoroughly enjoying the way her cheeks flushed with color whenever she was flustered or angry. He guessed she was both by the way her eyes widened as she pursed her lips together. "You may not want to look at me now, but you were definitely looking your fill of me a moment ago."

Lady Alyce's mouth dropped open with a gasp, and Hawk's eyes went immediately to her lips, her white teeth, and the pink cavern of her mouth. He felt a surge of lust as he thought about what he would like her to do to him with that mouth, then immediately pushed those thoughts aside.

He had to be careful when it came to Lord Cynwulf's sister. She could be a valuable tool in determining what Cynwulf was up to, but she could also prove to be a distraction if he let himself get too drawn in by her unexpected appeal. She was not the type of woman Hawk typically dallied with, but something about her honest responses and lack of courtly flirtations was refreshing. She did not play coy with him, yet he knew by the way she watched him and her nervous fidgeting when he was near that she felt unsettled by him.

"It was a rather amusing display," she said, quickly recovering her composure, "with the sheriff bobbing up and down and side to side behind you like an agitated mole."

"I took my time so I could look my fill at you, as well, my lady. Your gown matches your eyes and suits you well," Hawk admitted, surprised at his own honesty. "Goading Montworth was an added boon."

Her cheeks flushed again and watched the enticing way her breasts swelled under her gown with her indrawn breath. She held his gaze, but her hands fidgeted with the edges of her sleeves. It was no great mystery to discern what Lady Alyce was feeling at any given time; the mystery was how she could so boldly hold his gaze while nervously plucking at her cuffs at the same time. She was a confusing and alluring mix of nervous and brazen, questioning and confident.

Platters of food were placed on the tables by bustling servants, along with jugs of wine and ale.

"I am forgetting my manners, Sir Grogan—"

"Hawk," he said in reminder. He speared a piece of mutton from a platter and offered it to Alyce, placing it on her trencher when she nodded approval.

"Hawk," Alyce agreed, as a polite smile curled her lips. "I suppose I should be thanking you instead of being irritated with you for your interference when the sheriff first arrived. Had you not intervened, I would still be trying to escape his clutches."

"He is not your lover, then?" Hawk asked, more gruffly than he meant.

"Lord, no!" Alyce's face dropped at her outburst, and she looked quickly in the direction of her brother and Montworth. Hawk was sure Montworth would be making every attempt to keep his eye on Lady Alyce despite Cynwulf trying to draw him into a conversation.

"And though I do appreciate your concern," she continued in a softer tone, "you should know I am quite capable of handling myself when it comes to unwanted advances."

"I have no doubt of your abilities, my lady. I apologize if I offended you."

Her fingers settled into her lap at his apology, and she appeared to relax again. It was not that he felt her lacking, but that he believed Montworth to be untrustworthy. He merely wished her to know he was near should she need him. "Just know I am at your service should you require it."

Alyce nodded politely in acknowledgment of his offer, but her shoulders tensed again, and Hawk had to suppress a smile pulling at his lips. The woman was definitely independent and did not like to admit she ever needed anything from anyone.

But she'd leaned into him when Montworth advanced toward her a second time during the encounter. He didn't think she even realized what she had done. But he noticed.

Hawk was a protector—that's how he earned his gold. It's all he knew how to do. The only thing he knew how to do well.

The only person he hadn't been able to protect was his mother.

Hawk lifted his cup to take a long drink of the fragrant wine. He set it down, then said quietly for Alyce's ears only, "Montworth believes to have an agreement with your brother."

"Cynwulf told you that?" Alyce's cheeks flushed and she quickly diverted her gaze to her food.

"I overheard him speaking to your brother." The king may have named him Hawk because of his speed on the battlefield, but Red made the moniker stick, declaring it more fitting than even the king realized. Hawk had an uncanny sense of hearing and often eavesdropped on conversations at other tables in the same hall that sounded like nothing more than garbled mumbles to others.

Red also claimed Hawk could best an owl in seeing a mouse on the forest floor in the dead of night. Hawk attributed it to the need to hone his skills for his own survival, skills honed since the death of his mother when he'd been at the age of seven. His father had not provided for his mother or him as his bastard son, but he at least had the decency after his mother had died to arrange for Hawk to be trained in the household of a fellow knight.

"Yes," Alyce conceded, "my brother entered into negotiations with Montworth without my consent, something he swore he would never do. Something he regrets now." She turned away from him and Hawk surmised she was embarrassed by her confession.

"He is not the man you would have chosen?"

Alyce shook her head, and Hawk felt a greater relief than he had a right to feel. Of course, Alyce would not hold any esteem for a man like Montworth, but it should not matter to him what she thought about the sheriff. Or any other man, for that matter.

"I choose no man," Alyce stated firmly. She chewed slowly on a slice of the mutton from her trencher, then said, "I am contented as my brother's chatelaine and do not have the need nor the desire for a husband. I will not marry the sheriff or anyone else despite my brother's insistence." She paused a moment, a blush rising in her cheeks, then said, "Now I must ask for your forgiveness. I sometimes speak more plainly than is considered polite, reveal more than I should."

"I like your honesty," Hawk said, pressing her for more truths. "Are you truly content with a life of serving your brother and never having a family and home of your own?" He watched Alyce's face tense as she started to fidget with the sleeves of her gown again. He followed the path of her stare to a serving woman with a small child toddling after her. When he looked back at Alyce, her expression had changed to one of pained resignation.

She shook her head quickly as though clearing it. "I have everything I need here. I have a home that keeps me content, duties to fill my days, and people I care for deeply. The village has become my family, and I want for nothing." She lifted her chin as she said the last, as though daring him to question her.

He thought Alyce a most unusual woman. She was forthright, even as she tried to disguise her pain. Hawk looked to the serving maid again and wondered what the woman had to do with Alyce.

He broke off a piece of bread from a loaf placed on the table and handed Alyce a part of it before dunking his portion into the juices on his platter and taking a big bite.

"Forgive me if I do not believe you are as contented as you say." He couldn't help himself. He did not intend to poke at a raw wound, but he wanted to know more about Alyce, and she seemed to want to talk despite her reluctance.

Alyce stilled her hands in her lap, folding her long fingers together, then lifted her eyes to look directly at Hawk. "It is quite bold of you to judge my life of servitude to my brother when you are no different. You serve your king and have no home or family of your own, yet you appear content. How is that any different from the life I lead?"

This was not the response he expected, and he quickly tamped down the hollow feeling that her words wrought. He had accepted a long time ago what his role in this world entailed, and he was realistic about the bounties he could expect from such a life. His sword arm and acumen had earned him the respect of a king and an abundance of gold to live comfortably, more than he ever expected as the bastard child of a middling baron, but his status as baseborn did not give him noble blood, a title, or enough gold by which to build a home and a family.

And even if he did take a wife and sire children, they would come to resent him for always being gone to do the king's bidding, to fight the king's battles, never certain he would return alive.

He would not ever be called lord, but the gold he had earned gave him solace, as did the women who warmed his bed from time to time. He thought for a brief moment about his latest mistress Nicola but found that he did not long for her when he was away from the king's court. He should feel guilty about his easy dismissal of her, save that he knew she did not pine for him while he was away either. Hawk was not her only paramour, and she did nothing to hide the fact, though she did give him precedence over the other men in her life when he was at court.

"You seem to be at a loss for words," Alyce said to him when he didn't respond to her question about how her life of willing servitude was any different than his.

"Perhaps you and I are not so different after all," Hawk conceded. "We have both made the most of what is offered to us."

"Although your life is far more exciting than mine," Alyce said with a wistful smile.

He was pleased to see Alyce's shoulders relax and her face soften again. "Tell me of the excitement you think you lack in your life, my lady."

Chapter Eleven

ALYCE FELT LOST in the depths of his dark stare, the gold shimmering in his rich brown eyes mesmerizing. Feeling awkward for blatantly gazing into Hawk's eyes, she dropped her stare to his mouth, trying to remember his question. He had that broad grin on his face that made him look mischievous.

And startlingly handsome.

The first time she saw Hawk atop his destrier clad in armor, she thought him to be sharp, angular, and unyielding in appearance. She realized now that when Hawk let his guard down and smiled with that twinkle in his eye, all of his harshness disappeared.

Hawk cocked an eyebrow at her when she lifted her gaze from his mouth back to his eyes. To hide her embarrassment, she turned her attention to the small heap of root vegetables remaining on her trencher. She pushed the food around with the tip of her eating knife, wishing she was more daring.

But she was not a woman who knew how to flirt or be seductive.

Her husband had been a friend first, almost like family, comfortable and familiar. Their courtship was expected. She remembered being a little flirtatious with Geoffrey, but it was the playful banter of young, inexperienced love. When she became aware of the way men and women flirted with each other in the hall, she was astounded by the shocking and erotic things some of the women dared say to the men.

She wished he knew how to look Hawk square in the eye and say something seductive to him in return, but she had no idea how to even begin to know what to say, or how to say it, that would not leave her completely mortified of her own behavior. She may not desire a husband, but if she were honest with herself, she did still crave passion.

She listened to the way the maids spoke of men, and the toe-curling nights spent at the hands of their lovers, and she wanted to know what that was like. Geoffrey's lovemaking had been quite nice, and she enjoyed being in his arms, but after hearing the stories from her maids, she'd wondered if perhaps there was something missing between her and Geoffrey.

Perhaps that was why Geoffrey had strayed into the arms of Janet. Mayhap something had been lacking in their marriage, or at least, their marriage bed. Was it because both of them had been so young and inexperienced? Or perhaps they were better friends than lovers?

She stuck a length of carrot in her mouth, chewing it slowly as she diverted her attention from Hawk and watched the soldiers and other guests laughing and drinking at the tables below them. Hawk would think her a wanton woman if he knew what was going through her mind, but she knew of many widowed women taking lovers, some more discreetly than others. Since she could not bear children, she could not see herself as a wife again. But could she be a woman who took lovers?

She thought about it a moment more then decided she could not imagine herself taking lovers to her bed just for the sake of pleasure. She was incapable of separating her emotions in everything she did, a fault Cynwulf warned would only cause her more hurt than good. But she could not change who she was or how she felt. She needed to trust any man she brought to her bed and such intimacy would just lead to heartache.

She turned her attention back to Hawk, realizing she had not answered his question about the excitement lacking in her life. He still looked at her intently, but the smile on his face was even broader.

"Watching your face, Lady Alyce, is like watching a storm wash over the ocean," Hawk said in a low tone that sent shivers through Alyce. She liked his deep voice and how when he spoke to her as though he wanted only her to hear; the sound rumbled in his chest, and she felt the vibration of the words as much as she heard them.

"I've never been to the ocean. I've been told it is more vast than I can even imagine." Alyce cringed at how breathless she sounded, aware that her heart was beating faster. How could this man make her respond like a besotted maiden with just a smile and a few softly spoken words? She must stop this foolishness, for nothing good could come of it.

Hawk nodded. "The ocean is so vast, you can see a storm coming before it hits the serene waters that precede it. The wind will come first, changing the small ripples on the surface to frothing waves, then the clouds roll over and the rain beats down, whipping the ocean into a frenzy with water crashing in every direction. The storm will move on before you fully comprehend what has happened, and in its wake the sea churns and rocks until it's exhausted of emotion. Then it settles back into a gentle calm. From start to finish may only be a matter of moments, yet an entire story plays out before your eyes in that small space of time. When you are thinking, Lady Alyce, your face changes from one instant to the next in much the same way."

As he spoke, Hawk brushed the back of his fingers over the top of her hand where it rested on the arm of the chair between them. Her skin warmed with the heat of his touch then tingled as it turned to gooseflesh.

Her eyes darted around the hall now to see if anyone saw Hawk touching her, but everyone seemed to be absorbed in their own conversations, paying little attention to her, and for that she was grateful. Even if their hands were out of sight, her flushed face was proof enough of the effect Hawk had on her.

"Tell me, Lady Alyce," Hawk said in a husky whisper meant for her ears only. "Do you imagine my hands touching you as often as I do?"

"You should not speak to me that way. Someone might

hear." Her voice sounded strained and breathless, and she almost laughed out loud at her own pitiful state. Her entire body felt boneless like it had just melted into her chair. Maybe she wasn't as opposed to taking a lover as she had thought if this was her reaction to a simple touch and one seductive whisper.

He smiled at her then, devastatingly handsome, and dangerous. He stretched his long legs in front of him, settling more comfortably into his chair, but his gaze stayed locked with hers. "Everyone is too far into their cups and more interested in their own affairs to concern themselves with ours."

"We are not having an affair," Alyce said, trying to sound indignant but failing miserably. Even she could hear the seductive challenge in her tone. And if she doubted her ability to play the temptress, the sudden hitch in Hawk's breathing and the molten look in his eyes reassured her.

"Sadly, that is true," Hawk agreed, his eyes falling to her lips, then sliding slowly down her body before returning to meet her gaze. "If we were having an affair, then I would not be tormented at night by imagining what you would feel like in my bed because I'd know."

Alyce felt her breath catch in her throat, but she kept her expression bland, as though they discussed nothing more interesting than the crops in the fields and the possibility of rain. She should stop Hawk from talking to her this way, but she felt bolder than she had in a very long while.

As a matter of fact, she had never felt this bold.

Or this desired.

Or this empowered.

She let her eyes drift away from his, pretending her heart wasn't racing, and resisted the sudden urge to wet her lips with her tongue. "Have you considered counting, Sir Grogan? Perhaps you would not feel so tormented in your bed at night if you occupied your mind with the mundane."

She looked at him from the corner of her eyes when he did not reply. He stared at her with an unblinking intensity. Heat spread from her core, up her neck, and into her cheeks. She cursed her body for betraying her as his eyes dropped to the flushed skin exposed at her neckline then slowly raked over her throat, her lips, her cheeks, and back to her eyes.

"I prefer to imagine unlacing the ties of your gown and pushing it over your shoulders." The words were spoken so softly that Alyce was forced to focus on his lips as he formed each word. She turned to face him completely but said nothing. She opened her mouth to reply but she could not find her voice.

"You blush just as prettily in my dreams." He said each word slowly, deliberately. "Your nipples are the same dusky color as your lips—"

She inhaled sharply. "Stop!" It was a hushed command.

"Is that really what you want?"

She pressed her lips into a straight line and turned her attention to the tables at the foot of the dais. Just as Hawk had said, everyone was too wrapped up in their own conversations to notice theirs.

Hawk shifted in his seat so that he leaned closer to her, close enough for her to feel his breath as he spoke. "Once I had you freed from your gown, I'd kiss the soft skin of your neck, working my way down to your shoulders, and lower still until I had one of those beautiful nipples in my mouth."

Alyce's heart raced in her chest as it rose and fell. She couldn't catch her breath and her skin itched to be touched. Alyce's mouth opened then closed, unable to form words.

"If you have trouble getting that image from your mind when you are alone in your bed tonight, try counting," Hawk said with a mischievous grin. "It's said to help calm the mind." He shrugged as he leaned back in his chair. "And if that doesn't work, you know where to find me."

She sat there a long moment, waiting for her senses to return. *Curse him!* Her nights had been tormented already with thoughts of Hawk kissing her, but now she would never get any sleep thinking of the wickedness he described doing to her naked body with his lips.

"Tell me, Hawk," she said, her mind racing to find a topic to turn the conversation, "is it not rude to ignore Red? He has no one to converse with on his end of the table."

"I am fine, my lady."

Alyce was startled to hear Red respond, for she was quite certain she had said the words in a hushed tone.

Hawk did not acknowledge the man's response, keeping his eyes locked on hers.

The realization that the Viking had likely heard every word Hawk had said to her brought a new flush of embarrassment to her cheeks. Still, it was far safer to include Red in the conversation than to allow Hawk to continue to fill her head with erotic images that should not be there.

"I do not like for any of the guests at Hawkspur to be excluded. Please, push your chair back so your man can be part of our conversation." She gave Hawk a look to remind him she was Lady of Hawkspur, and the topic was not up for debate.

The sound of Hawk's chuckle rumbled in his chest, and then he said in his deep voice, "If it pleases you, my lady, then it is my pleasure."

His tone was not at all one of a man acquiescing to a lady's request but instead, that of a man trying to seduce a woman, and the now familiar chill shivered down her spine once more. He pushed his chair back, extended his long legs again, and turned to his friend just as Cynwulf's voice rose, probably louder than Alyce expected he meant to use.

"We will discuss the matter later!" he declared.

The room hushed as chatter fell from its loud roar to a hushed buzz.

"The sheriff is displeased by our host," he said to Red.

Montworth's chair scraped the floor as he suddenly pushed to his feet and stepped around Cynwulf and moved toward Alyce. She felt her stomach falling to her feet and her blood rushing to her face as all eyes focused on her and the sheriff.

"My lady, may I request your company for a walk in the bailey?" Montworth held out his hand to Alyce, a strained smile on his lips that did not reach his eyes.

"Only if my brother may accompany us," Alyce said, panic filling her. She had no desire to be alone with the sheriff, but she also did not wish to cause a scene or embarrass the sheriff any more than he had been already this eve. "Though I must admit to being unusually fatigued and was about to excuse myself for the night. Perhaps another time, Sheriff Montworth."

A crimson hue crept over his cheeks, and his red-rimmed, bloodshot eyes bulged slightly. "I really must insist you accompany me, Alyce, and surely your brother will trust us to be alone for a short time. You are no longer a chaste maiden whose virtue must be protected at all costs. No one will begrudge a widow some privacy with her betrothed."

Alyce gasped at the sheriff's audacity and his insinuation they were to be married. Before she could respond, both Cynwulf—and Hawk—had pushed to their feet.

"You will step away from my sister." Cynwulf spoke with such force that Alyce sunk lower in her chair. Hawk and her brother both glared at Montworth, and Alyce felt like a trapped hare with the three men towering around her.

Montworth's face was filled with hatred as he glared at Cynwulf. "You will regret this, *my lord*," he hissed, the last words filled with so much venom that they sent a chill down Alyce's spine.

With that, Montworth turned on his heel and stalked away from them. The room had gone silent when the commotion started at the head table, and now all eyes were on them. The sheriff's men stood to follow their commander as he stormed toward the door at the far end of the hall.

Montworth pulled the heavy door with such vehemence as he left that it nearly broke the hinges. She almost found humor in the fact that, in his haste, the sheriff slammed the door in the faces of his own men. They stood in an uncertain huddle by the door for a moment, then one of them carefully opened the door and peered out before exiting with the rest of the men behind him.

Alyce stood and turned to her brother. "What was that all about?"

"Against my better judgment, I told Montworth I would not honor the agreement, that there would be no betrothal." Cynwulf breathed a shuddering sigh, then pulled her into a hug. "What am I to do with you, Alyce?" he muttered into her hair.

When Cynwulf pulled away, she thought she saw a flash of desperation in his eyes, desperation that went beyond her stubborn refusal to take a husband. It was time to stop acting the naive fool and face the truth, whatever that truth may be, and however much it might hurt her.

Alyce pulled away from Cynwulf and took his hands in hers. "You are to trust me, dear brother, that is what you are to do." Her voice was low, meant for his ears only, but she chose her words carefully with Hawk and Red so near.

"I've always trusted you. You've been a better sister to me than I deserve." Cynwulf cupped her cheek in his palm as he spoke, looking at her with…what, Alyce could not quite discern. It wasn't frustration, it wasn't quite pity, but it was unsettling.

"Come to my solar in the morning," Cynwulf said, his voice no longer lowered. "I wish to go over the ledgers with you." His face was once again the mask of indifference that she had become accustomed to since the arrival of Hawk and his men.

"Of course," Alyce said with a nod.

She turned to face the knight and his Viking friend. "If you will excuse me," she said with a quick bob of her head, "I will take my leave and bid you goodnight."

As she stepped away from the men, Ffyddlon rose from her place by the hearth and trotted to her side. Alyce scratched her faithful companion behind her ear and muttered, "I think some fresh air is in order, Ffyddlon."

After the commotion of the evening, she wanted nothing more than to get away from people and to be alone with her thoughts and her hound.

HAWK WAS TOO agitated to return to this seat. He watched Alyce disappear through the doorway at the back of the hall. He did not like the idea of her being alone but took some comfort in the fact that her loyal hound accompanied her. The dog would not let anyone near her. He picked up his cup of wine and moved to lean against the hearth where he could keep a watch on the door to the stairway and anyone who may try to follow her.

The sound of a deep chuckle drew Hawk's attention. Sparing Red a glance, he asked, "What do you find so amusing?"

"You, my friend." The skin around the Viking's eyes crinkled as he grinned merrily.

Hawk raised his brows in question.

"The stew keeps getting thicker."

"What are you talking about now?" His first-in-command could be damned irritating at times.

"The lady, the betrothal, the conniving sheriff."

Hawk gave a noncommittal shrug. "My only concern is discovering what game Cynwulf plays."

Red did not respond, but Hawk could feel his eyes boring into him. He would not give Red the satisfaction of acknowledging him, and he did not care to see the smirk he knew adorned the Viking's face.

"I need some air," Hawk muttered, pushing away from the hearth.

"The parapets have fresh air," Red offered cheerfully. "And pretty company."

Chapter Twelve

ALYCE RAN UP the spiral stairs with such speed, her head began
to spin. The leather of her shoes scuffed softly against the
stones of the spiraling staircase as she climbed them with
Ffyddlon at her heels. Circling higher, she passed the passageway
to the bedchambers and continued upward until she reached the
small door leading to the parapet. She craved fresh air and the
freedom of the wide view from the wall walk to clear her head.

Cynwulf had come to her rescue in the end, but it still galled
her that he'd arranged a betrothal to Montworth without her
knowledge or consent to begin with. "How could you, you daft
horse's butt?" She bit out the words in frustration as she stomped
along the castle wall walk, eliciting a soft whimper of concern
from Ffyddlon. She sighed and patted the top of the dog's head.
"In truth, I wanted to call him much worse, Ffyddlon." The
hound watched her attentively, trotting along at her side as Alyce
paced briskly back and forth along the wall trying to sort out the
thoughts pounding in her head.

Mayhap Cynwulf wanted her away from Hawkspur. Had he
chosen a wife and not told her? He might fear a new wife would
not take kindly to the presence of another woman as chatelaine of
his castle. Alyce tried to remember if he had mentioned a
woman's name lately or hinted in any way that he was finally
willing to stop cavorting with tavern and scullery maids and settle
down. What would she do if he meant to take a bride? She had

not thought until now how his eventual wife might perceive her as a threat or intrusion.

A tugging at her heart told her she was still giving Cynwulf the benefit of the doubt when all the signs were clear that he was playing a much more precarious game than matchmaking, one which she did not understand.

Cynwulf had Welsh blood running through his veins, but could that possibly be stronger than the bond of the only family he'd known all of his life? He'd loved her father as his own, of that she had no doubt. As far as she knew, he'd never learned the identity of his father. And even if he *did* discover the name of his sire, would he be willing to give up everything—his life at Hawkspur, the loyalty of the people who lived here, his loving sister—for someone who had never been a part of his life?

She couldn't imagine Cynwulf ever betraying his position or the king just because his father was Welsh. But she *could* believe that he might lose the will to fight the Welsh rebels, never knowing if perhaps he killed a kinsman. That in itself could be construed as defying the English king and a traitorous act.

Her head was beginning to pound and her stomach to churn. She leaned against the cool, damp stones of the parapet. Though the night sky was clear, it must have rained during dinner. Alyce took a deep breath, and the sweet, fresh scent of the trees and the earthy scent of the nearby forest filled her nostrils and soothed her nerves. Even from this distance, she could hear the summer-time songs of the frogs in the ponds in the woods just beyond the village walls.

The creak of the door to the spiral staircase opening turned her attention. For a brief heartbeat, she dreaded Montworth had returned and discovered her secret hiding place. Or—hopefully— her brother had come after her and she would finally wring the truth from him. While she waited for the person to come into view, she looked down to confirm Ffyddlon was at her side. The dog had not growled at the intruder or given any warning of another's presence. She was glad Ffyddlon was at her side in case she needed protection, although her wagging tail and wriggling body did not bode well that she had any plans to defend her mistress.

Alyce lifted her head then, her breath catching at the sight of Hawk's large frame walking toward her. She was annoyed with herself that she felt a thrill run through her at his appearance, and even more annoyed with Ffyddlon that she seemed to be just as smitten with the man.

"Traitor," she muttered to Ffyddlon. She meant to sound stern, but the accusation sounded more like sympathetic understanding than a reprimand.

Hawk closed the distance between them in long, smooth strides then stood looking down at her for several long breaths. "I thought I would find you here. Are you all right?"

She remembered how Montworth had paled in comparison while standing near Hawk. Montworth looked like a strutting peacock in his bright colors and padded, puffed-up clothing which did nothing to hide his paunchiness, or the lack of chest and shoulder muscles, the kind that came from hard work or warrior training, or the pitiful weak form of a man used to being pampered and having others do for him. In comparison, Hawk, attired in his simple tunic fitted snugly over the expanse of his broad frame looked every bit a man of unquestionable authority. The bulge of his muscled arms and legs could not be hidden by any amount of clothing, nor could the brawn in his shoulders and chest. He exuded strength, power, and control without even trying, and Alyce found herself inexplicably drawn to his commanding presence—when it was not being wielded over her.

"You shouldn't be here." She had not meant to sound so abrupt, but every nerve was on end and her stomach fluttered uncontrollably. It was an affliction she really must get under control.

"Do you mean up here with you? Or do you mean at Hawkspur?" The deep timbre of his voice sent a shiver down her spine, and she cringed at the immediate heated response of her body. Had she ever felt this consumed by attraction when she was Geoffrey? In truth, she prided herself in being beyond such silliness, and it seemed like girlish foolishness the way Hawk made her feel each time he came near. She'd enjoyed their flirtation in the hall, but it was folly to let a little seductive banter consume her imagination.

"Both," she answered honestly. His presence at Hawkspur made it difficult for her to get Cynwulf alone to get a straight answer from him. But the bigger threat was the fact that she spent far too much of her time thinking about this dangerous knight.

He was standing very near to her now, so near that she could feel the heat radiating from his body. He stared down at her, and though she could not see his eyes clearly in the darkness, she was sure she felt the smoldering intensity of them.

Good Lord, he was going to kiss her!

If she let that happen, it would be a disaster. She turned quickly from him to look out over the castle wall. "If you are expecting to catch me plotting against the king, you will be disappointed." She did not attempt to hide the sarcasm in her voice and immediately felt a little guilty for the petty response, but she could think of no other way to stop herself from doing something she would only regret.

"You know that is not why I am here."

Hawk leaned on his forearms against the castle wall next to her, following her gaze over the muted horizon lit by a sliver of a moon. Ffyddlon wriggled between the two of them and sat on her back haunches. Alyce was not fooled for a moment; Ffyddlon's actions had nothing to do with being a protective barrier for Alyce and everything to do with her wanting to be next to Hawk.

She closed her eyes for a moment, cursing herself for wanting to be close to Hawk as much as her dog.

"Hawk," she said with a sigh. "You are making things diffi-cult."

Hawk dropped one hand to his side to scratch the top of the hound's head as he spoke. "If you desire me to leave, say the word, my lady."

She had come to the parapet seeking solitude, but in truth, she did not want Hawk to leave. Of late, she found herself alone too often, even if by choice. She enjoyed visiting the merchants in the village or the occasional gossip with the maids who assisted her in the castle, but she had withdrawn more and more into herself since becoming a widow. She was afraid to let anyone else get close to her because they, too, might die and rip her heart to shreds. Just as her parents had done. Just as Uncle Ranolf had done. Just as Geoffrey had done. She had been contented with Cynwulf and Ffyddlon as her only close confidants and had not felt the need for more.

Until now.

Of late, when she closed her eyes images of one man seducing her consumed her. He had chiseled features, long, dark hair, and a devilish grin. She did not try to think about Hawk kissing her, but he filled her with thoughts unbidden of him, doing wonderfully erotic things to her. An affair with Hawk would only lead to more heartbreak when it was over, and she'd had enough pain to last a lifetime. She did not want more.

But as much as she tried to deny it, she did not want to be alone anymore.

Still, she reminded herself, Hawk was here on a mission from the king, a mission that could change all their lives if he judged Cynwulf's behavior questionable enough to report to the king. It would be foolish to let an impulsive attraction that could never amount to anything more than heartache cloud her judgment and possibly condemn her brother. She stiffened and pushed the thoughts from her mind.

"I desire to be alone."

Hawk preferred the melodic lilt of Alyce's voice when she was relaxed—smooth, rich, and intoxicating. But her guard was up again, and he was not oblivious to her dismissive tone. She'd straightened to her full height when she spoke. He pushed away from the wall, hiding his amusement, and watched her head slowly tilt back as he rose to his own full, towering height. Alyce may be taller than any woman he'd known and many men, but she still had to look up at him to meet his eyes.

"I do not believe you truly want to be alone right now."

He tried to tell himself his attraction to Alyce was strategic, that she was a means of getting closer to Cynwulf and learning the secrets of Hawkspur, but he knew it was a lie. Alyce was a refreshing change from the women he knew at court. She was honest to a fault, and she couldn't be calculating or manipulative if she tried. Her face revealed her every emotion, every thought. She was kind-hearted and caring, and it would kill him to ever hurt her.

His chest tightened with guilt. If Cynwulf was the traitor the king suspected him of being, then what he had to do would hurt Alyce terribly. And if Cynwulf was innocent, it would save him from tearing her world apart, but he would still be unworthy of a woman like her.

He was a bastard, a man who made his way in the world as a hired sword, a trained killer for the king. Men like him did not marry ladies and become lords, despite the king's promises. He'd been rewarded generously for his duty to the king, but it was not enough to build a fortress-like Hawkspur. Even if it was, the lords of England would never accept him as one of their own, no matter how much they may respect him. He was a threat to their way of life, to the sanctity of the almighty heir, of a first-born son bred on a pure wife of high standing.

If a bastard born from a dalliance with a maid, willing or unwilling, could garner the same riches and rewards as those with noble blood, it would tilt the distribution of power and throw the hierarchy of society and the church into disarray. Hawk knew his place in this world, and he'd come to accept it, which meant he also had to accept that Lady Alyce was not for him.

So why could he not stop thinking about pulling her into his arms and kissing her senseless every time she was near? Society and a traitorous brother be damned, he *wanted* Alyce. She wasn't an innocent maiden oblivious to the ways of men or the mutual satisfaction of intimate encounters.

He reached for her hand, then hesitated to give her time to withdraw from his advance. When she didn't move, he lifted her hand in his and gently caressed the long curl of hair entwined in her fingers. She'd tugged the tail of her plait around her body and wrapped it in her fingers when she'd said she desired to be alone. She was completely oblivious of her action, or how telling it was about her distress.

She looked down at their intertwined hands and the lock of hair trapped between their fingers.

"Nothing good can come from this," Alyce said hoarsely.

"Tell me why?" Hawk knew it to be true, but he wanted to hear her reasons. He also wanted to unwind the braid, let her hair fall loose, and sink his hands into the silky strands.

"Because you believe everyone's heart to be wrong until proven right, and I believe everyone's heart right until proven wrong. You are convinced Cynwulf's actions and words are part of a greater plot, and me to be his accomplice."

Hawk shook his head. "I think you incapable of plotting against anyone, or of having anything but the best of intentions. You, I hold above suspicion of being wrong."

"Why?" she asked sincerely, then shook her head. "I want to believe—however naively—your attentiveness to me is sincere and not just a means to an end for your mission."

Hawk inwardly cringed, an unfamiliar pang of guilt stabbing his chest, because she was right in her judgment of him. Her eyes were full of trust, as though she could never suspect him of lying to her, believing that he would have no reason but to give her a truthful answer.

He wanted her in his bed, naked with her hair splayed across his blankets. But he also realized the best way to get to Cynwulf was through Alyce.

"There is too much good in you, and you trust others to be good," Hawk said flatly, wishing Alyce were anyone but Cynwulf's sister. "But it is always the good people who get hurt the worst because of men like me, like your brother."

Hawk continued to hold her hand in his, unwilling to let it go for fear that it would be the last time he would touch her. Knowing it should be the last time he touched her.

She placed her other hand on his forearm and pleaded, "You must believe me when I say Cynwulf is not plotting against anyone. He has nothing but the best of intentions for Hawkspur."

He wished he could believe her, but his instincts were rarely wrong. Hunter had not yet returned from following the messenger dispatched by Cynwulf, but his gut told him the messenger was dispatched out of fear. However right Cynwulf thought his intentions to be, they did not bode well for Hawkspur.

Hawk may understand the ways of men when it came to self-preservation, greed, and power, but Alyce's brother still baffled him. He did not doubt Cynwulf's devotion to his sister, so why would he put her in danger?

Chapter Thirteen

ALYCE HELD ONTO the hope that Hawk would consider her words and give up in his pursuit to prove Cynwulf guilty, but in her heart, she knew it wouldn't happen. Hawk, like the predatory bird for which he was named, would be relentless in his pursuit, certain of his prey.

She must convince him he was coming to the wrong conclusions of Cynwulf.

"The only secret my brother is hiding is one from me. He should never have entered into betrothal negotiations with Montworth without my knowledge. He tried to put a stop to it after he realized his mistake, even sent a messenger to tell Montworth not to come here tonight."

She searched his face for any sign that he was considering her words, but he remained silent. A look of skepticism narrowed his eyes and a small crease appeared between his brows for only a moment, then it disappeared.

"And what of your secrets?" Hawk reached up to her face and wound a stray curl around his finger.

"I have no secrets." Alyce winced at the breathless sound of her words. "And now you know Cynwulf's only secret."

He arched a dark brow at her. "You have secrets."

She should get herself away from this man as quickly as possible instead of allowing him the liberty of holding her hand and toying with her hair. Hawk was nothing but danger. Danger to

Cynwulf because he suspected the worst in him. Danger to her because she wanted him near, wanted him to keep talking to her, to keep brushing his hand against her cheek as he ran his fingers over the strands of hair around her face.

"When you are nervous," he said, stepping even closer to her as he held up her hand in his, "you reach for the end of your braid and wrap the curl there around your fingers."

Alyce looked down at her hand in Hawk's and at the tail of her braid. He rubbed his thumb gently over her fingers and the hair entwined in them, sending shivers through her entire being. She struggled to make sense of what he was telling her amid the distraction of how he was making her feel. How was it she had never realized she fidgeted with her hair when she was unsettled?

"You have another secret." His face was so close to hers now, she could feel his breath against her cheek. "Every time I am near, you reach for your braid." He lifted her hand to his lips, placing a light kiss on the strands of hair wound around her fingers. "Tell me to leave and I will stop," he said, slanting his eyes at her over the top of her knuckles.

Alyce's breath caught in her throat. It had been a long time since anyone had touched her so intimately. And even longer since her body had reacted to being near a man. What was the advice of old warriors? *Know thy enemy.* She may regret letting Hawk near, but it was time to change her tactic.

"Do not underestimate me," she said in her best imitation of a sultry voice, "I am no timid maiden."

"Thank God for that," he said softly, lifting her chin with a thumb and leaning his face close before pressing a kiss to the corner of her lips. He barely pulled his mouth away, his lips hovering so close as he skimmed them along hers. "A timid maiden would blush—" he kissed the other corner of her mouth—"at the thoughts I'm having about you." He tipped his head to the side then pressed his lips to a sensitive spot just below her ear.

How did he know kissing that particular spot would make her eyelids flutter?

"Tell me of these thoughts," she said with a satisfied sigh.

"Are you sure you won't blush?" He nipped her below her ear.

"Yes." She laughed softly as his tongue traced the lower lobe of her ear. She meant to sound confident, worldly, like a woman who was not woefully deprived of passion, but she was having a hard time concentrating while his lips and tongue played with her neck and ear.

He chuckled deeply. "I don't believe you." He sunk both of his hands into her hair and tipped her head back to trail kisses across her throat until he reached the other ear. "But I'm going to tell you anyway." He pulled this earlobe into his mouth, scraping it with his teeth. "I'm thinking about whether or not the freckles on your neck—" he released his hold on her hair to trace his fingers down her neck until he reached the neckline of her gown, looping a finger over the material—"are also sprinkled across the rest of you." His lips followed the path his fingers had taken as he spoke.

She was thankful when he pulled his other hand from her hair and wrapped it around her waist to hold her steady. Her knees were beginning to wobble, and she feared she would not be able to stand on her own two feet if he kept this up.

"I'm thinking they are." He pressed his lips to the exposed skin just above where he tugged at her neckline. "And I want to spend hours kissing every freckle on your body."

Alyce inhaled sharply and her head started to spin. She felt lightheaded as his arms wrapped around her, pulling her tightly against the length of his body. He released her just long enough to lift her arms to encircle his neck, then crushed her against him again.

Not able to wait another heartbeat for him to claim her mouth with his own, she pressed her lips to his and slid her tongue across his lower lip. She wanted to know the taste of him, the texture of his lips.

A low growl from the back of his throat reached her ears, and she felt a moment of satisfaction to know she could still stir desire in a man. His tongue swept against hers and she became lost in the heat of his mouth, melting her body into his, unable to get close enough to him.

Suddenly Alyce pulled back out of his arms, gasping. Her body tingled with the heat of his touch, but her head swirled with confusion.

"This is foolishness, Hawk." Alyce breathed deeply to settle her hammering heart.

Hawk cursed under his breath, but he did not stop her from stepping out of his arms.

"I can never be a temptress. My heart is not made for that." She had not meant to tell Hawk the truth, but the words came out of her mouth before she could stop them. She sighed, then continued, "As tempting as you are, I cannot play at being lovers. I thought I could do it, but I cannot deceive myself, and I won't lead you on." She folded her arms in front of her chest to shield herself and put more space between them.

Hawk was silent for a long moment, but then his lips twitched. "Your heart is too tender for us to be just lovers?"

"Laugh if you must, but it is who I am. I will do nearly anything to convince you my brother is not a bad person, but I cannot stoop to toying with your heart or mine. Sir Grogan. You will either believe us or you won't." She did not know what else to say.

He laughed then. "I know you are serious since you are calling me by my surname again."

"You do not appear to be taking me seriously. And now that I have made myself look foolish, I will take my leave. Let us forget this ever happened." Alyce dropped her arms to her sides to turn away from Hawk, but he stepped closer to her before she could move. He did not touch her, but he was close enough that she could feel the heat radiating from his body and smell the faint scent of leather, hay, and forest that still clung to him.

"I am not worthy of a woman like you, but if you should change your mind, Lady Alyce, I am willing to risk my heart to show you what it means to be just lovers." He said the last two words in an exaggerated whisper. "All you need do is ask, and I will promise to bring you nothing but pleasure."

His seductive words made her skin shiver with gooseflesh.

Alyce tried to shake her head in refusal, but she couldn't seem to move.

"Mind-numbing pleasures to make you forget everything but the way I'm touching you," he continued, his deep voice a soft rumble. He dropped his face until his lips hovered just above hers again. "I'd touch every part of you, every freckle, with my lips and tongue, from your tender earlobe down to the delicate arch of your foot and everything between. I'll caress your every curve until you can think of nothing but how your body feels."

Alyce swallowed hard before she managed to say in a hoarse whisper, "You shouldn't be speaking to me this way."

"You are right, I should not," he said, his voice a rough rasp.

Alyce shook her head feebly, but she couldn't take her eyes from his lips. Kissing each other did not mean they were lovers, and surely another would be harmless.

"I'm going to kiss you again, Alyce." He didn't wrap his arms around her or step any closer. No part of him touched her except for his lips, even as he deepened the kiss, sweeping his tongue inside her mouth. She closed her eyes and surrendered to his possessive exploration.

She tried to remember if Geoffrey had ever made her heart beat out of control while also taking her breath away. Her experiences with Geoffrey had been pleasurable…but never the mind-numbing pleasure Hawk described. Just when she was about to put her arms around Hawk's neck again and boldly suggest he prove his ability to provide such pleasure, his lips left hers.

She opened her eyes to see him staring at her, his eyes narrowed and his expression disgruntled. She stepped back and turned away from him. How dare he look at her as if she'd just forced herself on him when he was the one who kissed her again?

"Goodnight, Lady Alyce." His boots scuffed softly on the wood planking of the walkway as he retreated from her. The door to the stairwell opened then closed and Hawk was gone, leaving her with an emptiness in her chest that sucked the breath out of her.

"Damn you, Hawk," she gasped into the darkness.

HAWK STOMPED DOWN the spiral staircase to the narrow hall that led to his chamber on the top floor of the keep. Red had been sleeping in the first chamber on the floor, but Hawk doubted the Viking had retired for the night. He shoved the door open to his own chamber then slammed it shut and locked it. He stood still in the middle of the room for a moment, then reached for his sword where it rested against a chest, dug out the whetstone from a satchel, and proceeded to sharpen the blade with fierce concentration.

"Hell," he muttered after he'd worked up a sweat that did little to soothe his sour mood.

Hawk didn't believe in love.

What he was feeling for Lady Alyce definitely was not love, but it was something. Otherwise, he wouldn't be feeling wracked with guilt and uncertainty—two emotions he knew little about.

He never should have said those words to Lady Alyce or kissed her that last time. True, he'd thought to seduce her. They were both adults, she was no longer a protected maiden, so why should they not find pleasure together?

But what he hadn't expected was the one word that had flitted through his mind, leaving him as dizzy as a blow to the head, all of his nerves on alert. It wasn't danger he sensed, but rather a sudden surge of possessiveness toward Alyce.

Mine.

But she wasn't his.

He didn't want her to be his.

At least not for longer than the mission required him to be at Hawkspur. Women were a distraction from the realities of his life. They were comfort, pleasure, challenge, and satisfaction…and then they were gone from his life. What they were not was constant, a priority, a commitment. And never were they kept.

Women were a liability to a warrior. Once a warrior's heart grew soft, he was worthless, easily distracted, thinking about what he left behind instead of the fight in front of him.

Mine.

No! Once he thought of any woman as his, that would be the end of him.

Even so, Red constantly pushed him to find a home and settle down. Hawk suspected it was his way of letting his commander know he was getting old. He might not be as quick as he'd once been, but he wasn't ready for a quieter life. The king had promised him a small manor house and a bride of means once this mission was complete; Hawk was sure it would be the death of him.

Who was he if he was not fighting? He tried to imagine himself growing fat, sitting by his hearth with a wife, no longer having to sleep on the ground or fear for his life. A shudder ran through him. The boredom would kill him, but it would be a long, slow, torturous death.

His arms tingled at the memory of holding Alyce's body against his own, and he wondered if he would ever tire of the taste of her lips. Why did she confess she could never take him as a lover without involving her heart? And why did he care if she risked her heart when there was pleasure to be had?

He'd treated her as he did the woman of King Edward's court, as just another conquest. He may be callous toward love, but he was never disrespectful of women. He chose the women he did for good reason – they had no expectations of him beyond pleasure. They were wealthy, also widows, with no desire to be constrained by a man, but a strong desire to be pleasured by one, and he was more than happy to oblige.

Hawk and his band of bastards were created to fight and kill, not to love and be loved.

His men preferred to bed down with the women who served in the great hall or local taverns. They wanted women willing to slack a man's lust with no expectations of anything more than the right amount of coin or the pleasures of an experienced man. Barmaids and serving women held no illusions that a tryst would last beyond a night or two and did not cry of broken hearts when he and his men moved on.

No matter who or what class the woman, though, Hawk

always insisted his men treated her well and paid her well in return for her favors. His own mother had been a serving maid in the hall of a castle, but she had not been given a choice when it came to the lord's lustful desires. He'd forced himself on her, leaving a babe in her belly and giving her nothing in return. She'd been ruined and no man would have her once it was apparent she carried the lord's bastard child. telling his mother to leave serving in the hall when he thought her too fat and to not come back until her belly was flat.

His mother had to wash clothes in the river until after Hawk was born. It had been difficult work when not pregnant, and absolutely backbreaking when with child, with all of the hunching over while scrubbing clothes on rocks that ripped at already cracked hands. Eventually, of course, his mother did return to the hall to work again, but not out of a desire to subject herself to more humiliation and degradation, but out of desperation to feed herself and her child.

The lord of the castle never acknowledged her, or Hawk.

No woman deserved to be treated that way, left with a burden too great to bear alone. He could not bed a barmaid or a castle serving women without thinking of his mother; hence, the reason he preferred willing, wealthy widows from the king's court who willingly sought his favors, not for coin but to fulfill their own lustful desires. These women used him for the same reasons he used them.

Lady Nicola, his most recent mistress, liked to cause a stir when he was at court, by choosing him as her escort. He was the king's favored knight, a dangerous man from the court's viewpoint, which always caused a thrill for well-protected women of means. The arrangement suited him just fine, and when he wasn't at court he gave her as little thought as she gave him. He did not have the inclination to fall in love, nor would he be so selfish as to expect a woman to love him back when his first loyalty was to the king and his sword.

But damn it all, the kiss tonight with Alyce had stirred something unfamiliar inside him. When she'd wrapped her arms around his neck and kissed him so boldly, he didn't expect to like it so much. There was a passion in her that he'd felt igniting with an intensity that seemed to unsettle her as much as it unsettled him. The lady claimed she had no desire to marry again, and that her heart was too tender for her to be a man's mistress, but did that mean she planned to stay chaste for the rest of her life?

He found that notion hard to believe. When they'd kissed, she had been as much on fire for him as he was for her; he could feel it. Could she really live the entirety of her life denying herself the pleasures to be had in a shared bed?

No. She would find a man to marry, someone with titles and wealth, and that man would get to ignite her passion and burn with her.

A vision of Montworth came unbidden to his mind. If Cynwulf had his way, his sister would marry the weak popinjay and be doomed to a life devoid of passion. The thought of a woman like Alyce saddled with a pompous bore for a husband who would never be enough to stir the passion he knew burned within her felt like a punch to his gut.

But soon it would be none of his concern who ignited her passion. When the mission was completed, he and his army would ride away from Hawkspur Castle to embark on the next assignment from the king.

Hawk would not take advantage of Lady Alyce and then leave. Nor could he, as a bastard son likely to die by the sword, offer her anything. He was a man whose only legacy would be the battles he fought for the king. Even the small manor promised by the monarch would never be enough to content a woman used to presiding as mistress over a fortress such as Hawkspur.

⸙ Chapter Fourteen ⸙

Chapter Fourteen

ALYCE AWOKE IRRITATED from a night of fitful sleep and dreams of a raven-haired man gliding over her body with his hands and lips, piercing her with those dark eyes, watching her, teasing her, daring her to tell him to stop. Now, frustrated, and restless, she was consumed with worry about the meeting with Cynwulf.

She'd tried to get him to tell her everything would be all right last night at dinner, that there was no reason to worry about the presence of Hawk and his men. Montworth had interrupted their discussion, but not before Cynwulf had said the words that still gnawed at her when she pressed him to agree all was right at Hawkspur: *Do not be so sure.*

The low flames in the hearth flickered softly against the walls as she rose out of bed and pulled a fresh chemise from the wooden chest at the foot of her bed. She studied the tunics hanging from a row of pegs in the wall, knowing she should choose something practical to accommodate the duties of her day, which included spending time inventorying the storerooms. But first, she would seek out her brother. She was determined to get to the bottom of whatever had him acting so strangely.

Her other obligation today was to give Hawk a tour of the village, and a small part of her wanted to choose something more flattering. She reached for a burgundy tunic with flowers embroidered along the neckline and sleeves but stayed her hand

and chided herself for vanity. Hawk had made his position clear last night when he broke off their kiss and left her standing on the parapet. He had stung her pride at the time, but now she was grateful for his rude behavior. He was a complication she did not need.

If she was honest with herself, he was also a complication she could not handle. Her judgment became clouded when she was with Hawk. She spent far too much time thinking about his lips and the feel of his arms when he trapped her against his chest; she should be thinking about how to convince him Cynwulf was not guilty of anything treasonous.

But what happens if he is?

The thought came to her unbidden, like a punch to the stomach. She shook her head, refusing to believe Cynwulf would do anything to put Hawkspur in danger. But, she had to admit, the problem with her brother was that he sometimes created trouble unintentionally by making promises he could not keep.

In his first year as lord of Hawkspur, he sold the entirety of their excess grain inventory to a neighboring lord who offered a very tempting amount of gold. Cynwulf didn't question why the man was buying more grain than he needed for his small estate; he only thought about how much easier it would be to sell it all in one transaction and be done with it. As a result, other lords who relied on trading for the grain in exchange for items needed at Hawkspur were left with no other option but to buy the grain at an exorbitant cost from the man who held it all in his greedy hands. And Cynwulf was forced to pay more gold than planned for the supplies they needed to get through the winter ahead.

Shortly after that debacle, he'd appointed Alyce as his chatelaine to manage the business of Hawkspur castle while he managed the protection. Even if Cynwulf's good intentions did not always have positive outcomes, together they had always been able to correct the damage.

Had he finally done something irreparable? Her mind started to turn over all of the possibilities of what Cynwulf may be doing that Hawk could misconstrue as a threat.

"Stop!" she commanded out loud to herself.

With that, she took a blue tunic from one of the pegs and pulled it over her head. It was plain, with no embroidery anywhere. Even with a leather belt cinching in the waist to give her a little shape, she did not feel at all alluring in it, which would serve her purpose perfectly. Her focus needed to be on Cynwulf and Hawkspur, not on Hawk, and the way his kisses made her want to forget the inevitable heartache.

Alyce pulled the fur back from the windowpane to see the sun beginning to rise on the horizon. Ffyddlon whined in protest as she stretched by the fire, then started beating her tail against the floor planks.

"Up, girl," Alyce coaxed, scratching the wolfhound behind her ears when she rose and leaned against Alyce's legs in greeting.

She slipped out of her room into the corridor with Ffyddlon at her side, dim morning light shining through the narrow openings on the outer wall to guide their way. Her knock at Cynwulf's bedchamber door went unanswered, so she proceeded down the stairs to the solar. Alyce breathed a sigh of relief at the soft glow flickering beneath the door. She knocked, then let herself in.

Cynwulf was seated behind the table, a single candle standing over the parchment he had spread open before him. His expression stiffened at the sight of her, and he gestured toward a chair for her to sit.

"I finally get you to myself," Alyce said, sliding into the seat facing her brother while Ffyddlon curled up near the fire. Her shoulders relaxed with relief now that she had a chance to talk to him, but her stomach roiled with the fear of what she may hear.

Cynwulf nodded, but his eyes did not meet hers. "I said I would meet with you this morning."

"You did." Alyce waited for him to say more, but he returned his attention to the vellum spread on the table and rubbed at his temples. "Cynwulf?"

He looked up at her and sighed.

"Tell me," she prodded. "Share your burdens with me so we can carry the load together."

"Not this time, Alyce."

A chill curled up her spine, but it was quickly replaced with a surge of anger. "Do not shut me out!" She took a deep breath to calm her ire, forcing herself to lower her voice. "Hawkspur is as much my responsibility as it is yours. If there is a threat to Hawkspur, I should be made aware."

"It is my job to protect Hawkspur." He scrubbed his hands through his hair. "And you. You have to trust me in this."

She'd seen Cynwulf angry, frustrated, and impatient, but never had she seen him this way. His eyes had lost their luster and his expression was flat with defeat. She scooted out of the chair and stepped around the table, grabbing his hands in hers. "It is you who must trust me. You can tell me anything, Cynwulf, you know this. We've always been truthful with each other."

He rose to his feet and pulled her into his arms, squeezing her as though he feared losing her. Alyce squeezed him back. "Please, Cynwulf." The words were muffled against his chest, but she knew he heard her from his heavy sigh.

"Everything will be fine in the end," Cynwulf said in a hoarse whisper. "But until then, you are safer if I tell you nothing."

Alyce tried to pull out of his arms, her lips forming a protest, but he would not release his iron grip on her.

"Alyce, I have never asked you for anything like this before. I am begging you to trust me."

Alyce felt like a knife had been stabbed into her heart. Helplessness constricted her lungs until she could hardly breathe. She loved her brother, and she would do nearly anything for him…but this was too much to ask. She could not stand by and do nothing if he was troubled or in trouble.

"I'm afraid," she said against his chest.

He released his grip on her and brushed a soothing hand over her hair. She lifted her face and peered up until he dropped his head to look her in the eye. "Don't be afraid. It will all be fine in the end."

He smiled then, and some of the sparks returned to his eyes, but it did nothing to calm her nerves. She stared at him, trying to find the right words to say, desperate to believe him.

A loud knock sounded against the door causing her to nearly

jump out of her skin. Cynwulf steadied her as Aelwin requested permission to enter.

"Come in," Cynwulf called out. He squeezed her arm in a reassuring gesture before he let her go and turned his attention to his first in command as he entered the office. She retreated to stand by the hearth and Ffyddlon moved to her side to nudge her hand, sensing her distress.

The men began discussing training schedules and weapon repairs. Alyce tuned out the words and focused on Cynwulf, willing him to look at her, but he did not.

"Let us be on our way," he said finally, putting an end to the conversation with his men. Alyce noticed he picked up the vellum from the table as he looked to the door and gestured with his other hand for Aelwin, Alyce, and Ffyddlon to precede him from the solar.

She glanced over her shoulder when he seemed to hesitate and saw the flames leaping higher in the hearth as though something had been tossed into them. He closed the door behind him and locked it before touching her lightly on the arm and following Aelwin through the entry into the great hall leaving her behind.

Alyce stood motionless for a moment, watching them leave, staring intently at Cynwulf's hands swinging easily at his sides...the parchment was gone.

Chapter Fifteen

ALYCE DIDN'T KNOW why she was even making her way to the gate. Hawk wouldn't be there; of that she was certain. Not after last night. Not after the way he'd looked at her when he broke off their kiss, as though she'd accosted him when he'd been the one to kiss her. He'd probably forgotten about asking her to show him the village and tell him about the people who called Hawkspur home.

He wouldn't be there.

The worst part of it all was she couldn't stop thinking about the previous night and how much she'd liked being kissed by him. She'd felt embarrassed and disappointed when he suddenly withdrew from her and stomped away. She'd finally given in to her desires and convinced herself that she had nothing to be ashamed of and deserved to enjoy some passion in her life. That she could quit pouting about her tender heart and start to do the things that pleased her. Who would tell a barren widow nay? Who in their right mind would expect her to live a chaste life for decades to come?

Hawk told her nay, not with words but by his actions. He'd left her standing on the parapet without even a "Goodnight, my lady." Last night she'd felt ashamed, but today she felt indignant. If he didn't like the kiss, if he'd thought it was a mistake, he only had himself to blame. He'd kissed her first.

And licked her neck.

And bit her ear.

And described exactly what he wanted to do to the rest of her.

And, God help her, but she wanted him to do it all, and would have let him if he hadn't stomped away. Her face heated at the memory, remembering that she didn't care who saw them at that moment as long as he didn't stop touching her. She would have willingly let him ruin her reputation. Wasn't that one of the privileges of being a widow? She could do as she pleased, and others could do nothing more than shake their heads at her behavior.

But then Hawk had stepped away from her and looked at her like he was appalled by their kiss. Perhaps she was nothing more than a fool for thinking that she could be anything like the confident, sultry women she envied who so easily seduced men and bent them to their desires.

She was chatelaine of the castle, mistress of Hawkspur, quick with numbers, and more adept than any man at managing the provisions required to keep the population of the castle and village thriving. She was good at the practical, yet so very bad at seduction.

After her meeting with Cynwulf, she'd busied herself with inventorying supplies and tidying the storeroom to better evaluate what was needed to ready for them for the winter. They had six months yet to prepare, but with some good weather and good fortune, Hawkspur's storerooms would be filled to the walls and ceilings with reserves enough for everyone in the village by autumn's end.

She had managed to push the conversation with Cynwulf from her head while she worked, but it was creeping back into her thoughts now that her hands and mind were free. When she was convinced there was nothing amiss for Hawk to discover at Hawkspur, she could dally with his flirtations. But now she did not know what to think or do. Did she continue with her days as though nothing had changed? Or did she need to put a buffer between Hawk and her brother until she could discover what Cynwulf was keeping from her?

After her leaving the solar and the troublesome encounter with her brother, she had nearly gone mad with worry, but the more she focused on her work and preparing Hawkspur for the future months, the more she started to question what he'd really said and how she had interpreted the meaning.

Her brother had always been truthful with her, and she with him, but did that mean they had to tell each other everything? Mayhap Cynwulf was falling in love, and he just was not ready to speak of it. Or perhaps he was negotiating alliances and did not want the king or his knights to interfere.

The Welsh Marcher lords were an independent lot who railed against anyone trying to dictate to them. Yes, they were subjects of the king, but not in the same way as other lords. Most of them had built their border fortresses with their own gold and silver. They were committed to defending the English border and keeping the Welsh as tamed as possible in return for being left to their own devices. The king tolerated the unconventional ways of the semi-autonomous region because the Marcher lords were more help to him than hindrance.

She would drive herself mad trying to work it all out in her head. Until given something tangible she could do to help resolve Cynwulf's issues or convince Hawk that Hawkspur—the castle and the village—stood with the king, she would focus on only that which was in front of her.

She emerged from the darkness of the great hall into the bright August sunshine. As she descended the stairs into the bailey, she looked to the gate to confirm her suspicion that Hawk was not there, already planning her escape into the woods with Ffyddlon so she could clear her head and think.

He was there.

Her heart stopped for a beat, as did her feet. Ffyddlon nudged her hand and propelled her forward again. *Pull yourself together!* she chided herself. She had to quit thinking like a besotted maiden and start acting like a widow, wise to the ways of men and women.

Looking at Hawk as he leaned a shoulder against the stone arch of the gate, Alyce felt her resolve flitting away like a bird on the horizon. Her eye immediately went to the muscular arms crossed in front of his chest, remembering how wonderful it felt to have those arms wrapped around her body. Her heart started pounding.

I am useless. One look at Hawk and all of her good intentions went up in smoke. She took stock of his entire body as she walked across the bailey, starting with the length of his muscular legs encased in dark hose. He wore a black, tunic-length shirt, cinched tight at his waist with a leather belt, accentuating the broadening expanse of his chest. She moved her gaze up his torso. He looked like he'd just come from the practice field with his sleeves rolled up above his forearms and the laces loose at the neck of his shirt exposing a dusting of dark hair. What would it be like to pull that shirt off him and trace the line of his hair to where she imagined it tapered at his belt?

She felt the heat rise in her cheeks when she realized that she'd just taken a deep, shaky breath at the thought.

Had she ever been this besotted with Geoffrey?

She took a deep, calming breath as she approached Hawk. He is the enemy, she reminded herself, and she had a duty to uphold. If she was not strong enough to keep her wits about her while in Hawk's presence, then she did not deserve to be mistress of Hawkspur.

He was looking directly at her, watching her approach with that arrogant smirk on his face, his eyes sparking with what looked like amusement. Ffyddlon bolted ahead, running directly to Hawk to nuzzle his hand, her tail wagging as she wiggled in circles around him, begging for his attention. Alyce wanted to be angry with Ffyddlon for her unabashed display of adoration, but she didn't want to be hypocritical.

She slowed her pace and stopped several paces away from Hawk, remembering the encounter with him the first day he'd arrived outside of Cynwulf's solar when she'd told him then she wouldn't be following him around like an adoring dog, and he'd asked her what it would take to make her tail wag.

Damn. She was no better than Ffyddlon.

Hawk pushed away from the wall and extended a hand in her

direction, palm up in invitation. "My lady, I am ready for your tutelage on the ways and worries of the villager."

Alyce ignored his outstretched hand. If she focused on his annoyingly over-confident and cocky demeanor, perhaps she could convince herself to be repulsed by him. *She* would not be wagging her tail for the arrogant man today.

She turned to the guard standing watch at the castle gate. "I am wishing for an escort. Are there any guards available?"

"No, my lady."

When the guard offered nothing more, Alyce asked, "Will one return soon?"

"No, my lady. All men not specifically assigned to a post have been commanded to report to the fields for training."

"Of course." Alyce ignored the feigned expression of surprise from Hawk.

"Do you wish to travel far?" the guard inquired.

"No. I am to show Sir Grogan about the village."

"With the men training all about and a knight of the king as an escort, and Ffyddlon—" he pointed to the dog—"no harm will befall you, my lady." The guard's face lit up with the satisfaction of having solved her predicament.

"'Tis a matter of propriety more than safety," Alyce murmured in explanation to the daft guard.

Hawk bowed, quirked a grin at her, and extended an arm in the direction of the village. The playfulness of his grin did not extend to his eyes, which were...wary? Resigned? Hawk obviously still regretted his actions of the previous night. The knowledge of that, more than her own conflicted emotions, settled into her stomach like a rock.

HAWK DIDN'T KNOW when he'd ever felt this unsettled. He was a knight of the king, deadly in battle, admired by many, and feared by most. He had nerves of steel and a hardened heart. So why did he feel like a besotted lad in the presence of Lady Alyce?

He wanted her—that, he could not deny. Yet he'd spent the

night in thought if not at rest and he'd determined that once he'd had her, the infatuation would be over. But it was folly to seduce the sister of the man he suspected of treason. Whatever happened, it would end with her resenting him at best or hating him with a fierce passion at worst. And if he pursued her now, even for a dalliance, she would think he seduced her only to glean information about Cynwulf. He'd never treated a woman so badly as to deceive her to gain information, then disregard her as though she were nothing more than another conquest.

No, he would not seduce her. He would afford her the respect due to a woman of her standing and keep his head about him.

That didn't stop him from admiring her, and that he did as she walked ahead of him through the gate, Ffyddlon trotting at her side. He noticed that today she wore a wimple to cover her hair, but the curling end of a long plait swung and danced at the curve of her waist. She'd been bareheaded until today. A married woman covered her hair to avoid undesired attention, but a maiden left hers to hang free to show her beauty to its fullest. As a young widow, Alyce could follow any standard she desired regarding her modesty, but until today he'd not seen her with her hair covered. Was she trying to convey a message to him?

Lengthening his stride to catch up to her, he was amazed again at how near in height she was to him.

"This, sir," she said, extending her arm in a wide circle, "is the village of Hawkspur."

Hawk reluctantly tore his eyes away from Alyce to look at the village sprawled before him. Breathing deeply, the first thing he observed was the smell of the village. Or rather, the lack of smell. Many years had passed since he'd spent any time outside a camp filled with sweaty men, horses, and pungent privy trenches, or a town bustling with people and stinking of waste, rot, and unwashed bodies.

A stone could be thrown from one end of the village of Hawkspur to the other, and he could count the number of people in the streets, unlike the cities Hawk resided in when not fighting. Built on the crest of a hill—albeit lower than the crest the castle was perched on—a breeze blew steadily through the village, clearing away the typical odors that stacked one on top of the other when people lived so close together. He took another deep, lingering breath, and this time he noticed the hot, metallic smell of a blacksmith's kiln and the faint aroma of meat cooking in herbs. A stout man emerged from the door of an ale house, wiping greasy hands on his stained tunic before raising a plump hand in greeting.

"Good day to you, John," Alyce called. "You must tell me someday what you use to season your roasts. My mouth waters every time I pass by."

"'Tis a closely guarded secret, my lady, but if anyone can get it out of me, 'twill be you," he said with a wink.

All the features of Alyce's face softened, and Hawk saw true joy on her face. Her eyes sparkled, her cheeks plumped from a broad smile, and her laugh rippled melodically on the air. He found watching her much more fascinating than the village and he did not want to take his eyes off her. Still, he listened politely as Alyce pointed out the various shops and services lining the main lane of the village while she greeted everyone by name.

He hardly noticed his surroundings, preferring to watch the spark in her eye and the joyful glow of her cheeks. It was an unusual woman who took such selfless delight in making others feel important. She truly cared for these people; she did not lord herself over them as their mistress and demand their respect, but rather, she treated them as equals.

Hawk had known many ladies of rank in his life, bedded some of the most beautiful, and had taken as mistress one of the more wealthy and powerful ladies of King Edward's court. His feelings of lust, desire, and sometimes even respect for them were often strong, but never had he let his feelings weaken to the point of feeling tenderness for any of them. He purposely chose independent, hard-hearted women as his bed companions for good reason. He had no desire to hurt a woman or make her feel used any more than she used him, thus he'd learned to limit his dalliances to those women who were as self-serving in their reasons for being with him as he was for being with them.

But Alyce sparked a warmth in his chest that was unfamiliar and unsettling. She had an enchanting sweetness beneath her wary exterior that drew him to her, just as the people of the village seemed to be drawn to her, wanting to bask in the glow of her attention. It was more than lust he was feeling—though lust was definitely part of it.

He forced himself to look away from her lest his resolve of not seducing the lady be forgotten. 'Twas nothing more than an infatuation easily quashed by a little self-discipline, but even as that thought crossed his mind he realized he was staring at her lips, remembering how they'd felt pressed against his and imagining the soft curves and crevices of all the other places on her body where he wanted to put *his* lips.

Alyce inquired after children, received progress updates on the planting of the crops, and inspected the work of the cobbler, promising to return soon for another pair of shoes. "I will need them to be as thick-soled as those you made for me last summer," she instructed.

"I know no other lady who goes through sturdy shoes as quickly as you," the cobbler said with a laugh. "I swear I make them as thick as a man's, yet you wear them thin. Does that hound of yours use them when you do not?"

"It must be the way I walk," Alyce mumbled, but Hawk's curiosity had been piqued. He remembered her sojourn into the woods when she'd returned with a nearly empty basket after several hours. It seemed Lady Alyce did have secrets of her own in need of uncovering. Hawk waited for her to say more, but she did not. Instead, she walked farther down the lane to the door of a small stone chapel and pushed it open. The scent of burning wax and incense met his nostrils as he followed her into the dark building, allowing his eyes to adjust before moving further into the sanctuary.

A light flickered at the far end of the little room and Hawk could see clearly the form of an altar with a heavy candle placed prominently on top of it. Alyce picked a small taper out of a wooden box on the floor, then held it to the flame of the larger candle to light it. Then, she circled the altar and placed the candle in an iron candelabra standing near the back wall. For a moment she did not move, standing silently with her head bowed. Then she placed a coin on the altar, before exiting the church just as quickly as she had entered. He followed her, not asking for an explanation, coming to the most logical assumption one can make when a widow lights a candle in prayer. Instead, he asked about the parish priest.

"We are at the mercy of the priests who travel throughout the area, stopping by the village if their journey brings them near."

"Is that not unusual to have a castle and village of this size and no priest in residence?"

"Not in these parts," she said matter-of-factly as she led him along a path winding around the hill. "The Marcher lands are not an easy place to live, and often the priests find the frustration of saving the stubborn Welsh and the independent Marcher lords too much for them."

Hawk gave a derisive snort. "Is that not what the priests are meant to do, save the unsavable?"

"You think us beyond saving, Sir Grogan?"

The words were clipped. He had irked her again. "I am not fit to judge, my lady. I am among the unsavable myself."

"Have you no faith left inside you, Hawk? Has perpetual battle turned your heart to stone?" She did not look at him as she asked the question, preoccupied with rubbing Ffyddlon's ears.

When she said his name now, it felt like a whisper of air rustling his senses. "If you mean faith in God, I cannot say. Battles and blood leave little room for faith or emotion." He contemplated for a moment. "'Tis better to have a shriveled and hardened heart when one's life is to defend a king and kill at his command."

"Surely you must have faith in something, or why go on? Do you not have faith in that which you fight for?"

"I fight for my king."

"Then you must have faith in the king." She turned her brilliant blue eyes to him.

"I have faith in the coin he pays me." Such sentiment sounded harsh even in his own ears, but he admitted only what was true.

He amounted to little more than a paid mercenary.

"Then would you have faith in another king if he paid you better coin?"

Before Hawk could answer, Ffyddlon let out a sharp bark. Hawk spun immediately to see what captured the dog's attention, his hand moving reflexively to the knife tucked in his belt. A herd of sheep was running as quickly as their stiff legs would carry them in the opposite direction from the boy who tended them.

"Ffyddlon," Alyce scolded, snapping her fingers and pointing to her side. The dog reluctantly circled her and then stood in an alert position next to her leg. "I am so sorry, Griffin. I did not mean to allow her to scare your sheep," she called out to the herder.

"'Tis all right, my lady," the boy called over his shoulder, racing to head off the flock of pudgy, stiff-legged animals with a long stick and slow them to a walk.

Beyond the boy, men were cutting a field of early oats with a small, curved blade, placing the sheaves in piles behind them for the women to tie into bundles and stack on wooden carts. Hawk had grown up on the grounds of a castle, spending his days with the horses and shadowing the stable master to make his way. Since then, he'd either lived in the king's court or camped in the forest with warriors. Never before had he given attention to all that was required to provide for a castle—or in this case, a castle and a village.

He had enough to worry about fighting to earn his own way to give it any thought. As a bastard-born son, the only fortune he could expect was that which he made for himself, and he had little time to worry about anything else. But these people did the same thing day after day, and they would never gain fortune or title, only enough to get them through another day, another season.

It seemed a very mundane life.

All the more reason to believe the people here would fight to better their positions if the opportunity arose, even if that meant fighting against their liege lord.

Alyce stood talking to the young lad tending the sheep,

Ffyddlon sitting obediently at her side. A small child had toddled up to the older boy and wrapped his arms around one of the boy's skinny legs.

As Hawk drew near he overheard Alyce asking incredulously, "He just wanders with no one to watch him? Where is his mother?" Her lips were tight with disapproval as she spoke.

"I think she is still resting." The boy shrugged his shoulders, his eyes trained on his sheep while he laid a hand on the child's head.

Hawk recognized the protective gesture of the young sheepherder toward the little boy. It was the way of children who grew up together, fending for themselves. They looked out for one another and taught each other the skills necessary to survive.

"We all keep an eye on him, my lady. We won't let anything bad happen to him," the young sheepherder assured Alyce.

Alyce's face was red with anger now as she turned from side to side as though looking for someone.

"Does the boy have a family?" Hawk asked.

Alyce nodded. "Yes. His mother tends the hall in the evenings and seems to be sleeping the day away while her baby wanders the village alone. How can she be so careless with the child? He could get trampled by horses or wander into the forest and never be found."

"We all keep an eye on him," the sheepherder repeated. Hawk couldn't be sure of the lad's age but guessed him to be a few years shy of manhood. He stood no higher than Hawk's chest with spindly limbs and a smooth face.

"I am of a mind to go to her cottage now and let her know that this child deserves better than to be left alone," Alyce said, her eyes blazing.

Hawk studied her face. Her eyebrows were creased in consternation, and there was a vehemence in her tone he'd never heard before. This was a side to Lady Alyce he'd not yet witnessed, and he wondered what was at the root of it.

She leaned down and picked up the toddler. "How dare she be so selfish and careless?" Her tone was harsh while she bounced the boy in her arms so vigorously that the toddler was beginning to look afraid. Hawk expected that Alyce didn't even realize what she was doing, so he took the little boy from her arms and tucked him into the crook of his elbow.

Alyce looked taken aback; he wondered if the shock was because he took the child from her or because she expected him to know nothing about the care of children. It had been a long while since he'd spent any amount of time with a toddler, but he'd had a lot of practice when he was growing up with the other orphans in the streets.

"Who is his mother?" Hawk asked while the little boy tipped his head back in an attempt to look up at him, tentatively reaching a pudgy hand toward his face. Hawk smiled down at the grimy little scamp and placed a finger in his outstretched hand. He guessed the baby to be no more than two years of age.

Alyce's jaw hung open for a moment, then she shook her head slightly and snapped it shut. "It's Janet," she finally said, seeming to recall his question. "She is a serving woman in the hall. You probably saw her bringing ale around to your men last night. She spends as much time flirting shamelessly as she does serving ale."

There was an uncharacteristic bitterness to Alyce's voice, and he surmised there was more to the situation than Alyce's disapproval of the woman's behavior. "Ah, I do recall seeing her. I take it she has no husband to share in the upbringing of this child."

Alyce's face paled, and she shook her head, her throat and jaw flexing as she swallowed uncomfortably. She reached for the end of the long braid dangling down her back and started twisting the ends through her fingers. Hawk looked down at the child again, then back at Alyce wondering what the connection was between her and the boy cradled in his arm.

ALYCE WANTED TO run. She didn't like the uncomfortable lump lodged in her throat or the anger that settled like a rock in her stomach over Janet's carelessness, or the way Hawk looked at her as though she had just grown another head. No matter how she felt about the boy's mother, she couldn't leave the child to fend for himself with no one to look after him. Again.

"We must go find Janet and tell her she cannot let this child wander the village alone. He could get hurt, or worse."

The sheepherder piped up again, his eyes still watching his flock. "Janet does not mean to let it happen, my lady. Henry does not like to nap, and he sneaks away as soon as his mother falls asleep. She is very tired from being up most of the night. All of us in the village watch over the boy until she awakens and comes to search for him."

"Why is she up most of the night?" Alyce asked. She and her brother never demanded the servers stay all night serving when guests could help themselves to the ale in the buttery during the later hours of the evening. "She can leave the hall any time after the meal has been served. She knows that."

The boy would not meet her eyes, keeping his face turned to his sheep. Alyce could see the embarrassment coloring his cheeks.

"You best catch up with your flock," Hawk suggested, nodding toward the wandering sheep. When the boy had gone, he turned his attention back to Alyce while he poked at Henry's belly, making him laugh.

The sight of Hawk playing with the baby and the joy beaming from the little boy's chubby cheeks as he smiled tugged at Alyce's heart, making her feel very empty and alone. Tears stung the back of her eyes, and she bit the inside of her cheek to stop these foolish emotions.

"Let us find Janet's cottage and return him to his mother," she suggested, her voice sounding very flat even to her own ears.

Hawk looked to where the sun tried to blaze through a patch of grey clouds in the sky. "'Tis still early. Is there any harm in letting her sleep? Come, I will buy a meat pie from the baker, and we can share it with this little urchin." He smiled as he spoke, but it did little to ease the sadness that had settled over her, darker and heavier than the clouds above.

"I do not think—" She started to say, but Hawk cut her off.

"The pies smell delicious," he said, turning to trace their steps back down the lane toward the baker's shop, "and my stomach is grumbling like an angry boar."

Alyce reluctantly followed in his wake, wishing she could find a way to escape to the privacy of her own room. When they reached the door of the shop where the sweet smell of freshly baked bread overwhelmed her senses, her own stomach started to growl loudly.

Hawk gave the baker the coin for a meat pie then led the way along the lane until he found a grassy patch where they could sit. He placed Henry on the ground between his outstretched legs and broke off a soft piece from the shell of the pie. He held the tiny piece of crust out to Henry who eagerly took it in his fat fingers and stuffed it in his mouth.

"My mother was an ale server in a hall much like this one," Hawk said quietly as he broke off a larger piece of the pie and held it out to Alyce. She was startled by his soft-spoken confession but took the offering of the pie, bringing it to her lips for a small bite. She contemplated how to respond when Hawk spoke again.

"It is not an easy life and can be very demeaning. She often came home with bruises, and she always looked tired."

The little bit of pie in Alyce's mouth suddenly felt like a heap of dry dirt, too difficult to chew, but she managed to choke it down after a moment. "I am sorry for what your mother had to go through," she said, uncertain how else she should respond, though what she really wanted to know was why these women continued to flirt with the men if they were treated so poorly.

"I am not telling you this to get your sympathy. I am telling you so you might have some empathy for Janet." Hawk took a big bite of the pie in his hand, then pulled some shredded meat from the remaining piece and held it out to Henry. The boy stuffed it in his mouth, then bounced on his bottom with his hands held out, demanding more.

Alyce's head pounded and she could hear the blood rushing through her body with every thud of her heart. She sympathized with the plight of Hawk's mother, but she could not do the same for Janet. "For reasons I do not care to discuss, I cannot condone Janet's actions."

Hawk looked at her for a long moment, then nodded his head. "They have very little choice about what they do, these women and their children have no choice. And often, to earn enough coin to feed the children they are saddled with, they must do more than just serve ale to the men in the hall."

Alyce looked down at her hands. She held the uneaten chunk of pie between two fingers, her appetite gone. She sat cross-legged with the length of her gown wrapped around her knees and tucked under her feet. The finer material and rich blue color of what she considered to be one of her plainer tunics made her feel shameful of her good fortune. Did others in the village struggle while she wanted for nothing?

Despite her struggles, how could she make Hawk or anyone else understand that Janet had something so much more valuable than fine clothing, something Alyce could never have? And worse, she didn't appear to care about it at all. Alyce looked from the corner of her eyes at the little boy as he leaned toward Hawk, stretching his arms toward the pie, fingers splayed wide as he smacked his lips together in an eating motion. She wanted to scoop up the little boy and hug him tight to her chest, to inhale the sweet smell of him and nuzzle his soft hair, but she would make matters worse with such a foolishly impulsive action.

And Hawk would think she lost her mind.

In truth, she probably *was* losing her mind. What other reason could there be than madness for her to be pining for this baby who belonged to her husband and another woman? It didn't matter whether Geoffrey had been with Janet only once or if it was a hundred times; her heart had broken into a thousand pieces for more reasons than she could ever explain to Geoffrey, and she definitely did not want to explain it to Hawk.

"Henry?" a voice called. "Henry!"

Alyce looked up to see Janet rushing down the lane toward them, her eyes wide and her disheveled hair a mass of tangles on her shoulders.

"He is safe," Hawk said to her as she drew near. "He is eating a meat pie with us."

Janet stopped several steps away from Hawk, hesitant and

unsure. Alyce watched her, wondering why she didn't just take Henry in her arms. The woman's face was wary, but there was a weariness there as well. Her skin was pale and dark smudges rimmed her eyes.

"I am sorry he troubled you, my lord." She shot a nervous glance at Alyce and added, "My lady."

"He is no trouble," Hawk said before he fed another bite of the pie to the toddler, then picked him up and placed him on his feet, gently nudging him in the direction of his mother.

"I see him in the hall when you are serving there," Alyce said quietly. "Do you not have anyone to assist you with him?" She meant it as an honest question, but from the look on Janet's face, the woman took the comment as the beginning of a disapproving chastisement.

"I will not bring him to the hall again, my lady," Janet said, her voice tight with what sounded like resentment as she picked up the little boy.

Alyce quickly shook her head. "I did not mean it that way. He is no trouble when he is with you in the hall. I truly inquired only out of curiosity, but I see now that it was rude of me. Please accept my apology." She gulped as she said the last, shocked by her own words. Never did she imagine she would apologize to this woman. If anyone apologized, it should be Janet to her.

Rising to her feet and shaking the folds of her skirt, she said, "Henry is always welcome in the hall." Then she bowed to Hawk, and added, "I've duties to attend to and must take my leave." With that, she turned on her heel before Hawk could see the cacophony of emotions welling in her eyes. She signaled to Ffyddlon to come, and walked briskly toward the castle, desperate for the solitude of her chamber.

Chapter Sixteen

"IT IS TIME to forgive."

Alyce felt emotionally drained from her time with Hawk in the village. After leaving him, she had gone to the stables to check on Guinevere and clear her mind. The mare had been more restless than usual, and the stable master predicted the foal would present itself to the world within hours.

Alyce stayed with Guinevere until she delivered a feisty colt. He was a fine foal and was soon on his feet, suckling greedily from Guinevere's teats despite his wobbling knees. It was late when Alyce finally left the mare and her baby alone for the night and returned to her chamber.

Edna had brought her a platter of food from the kitchen and ordered a bath. After describing every detail of the foal's birth and Guinevere's wonderful maternal instincts, Alyce settled back in the bath and closed her eyes. The excitement of witnessing the birth of the little colt had been a welcome distraction, but then her mind drifted back to thoughts of Hawk and the events of the day.

"You look sad, my pet," Edna said in a careful tone.

Alyce sighed, sinking deeper into the soothing water. "I am feeling very out of sorts today."

"Is it because of a certain dark-haired knight?"

Her breath caught in her throat at Edna's question. Was she so obvious? "Even if he is the cause, I must put him out of my mind."

"Why must you?"

Alyce was too tired to discuss all the reasons why she could not be with Hawk. "You know why," she said in a strained whisper.

That's when Edna proclaimed, "It is time to forgive."

"I do not think Hawk requires my forgiveness."

Edna clucked her tongue. "You've always had a feisty side to you, and it comes out when you feel backed into a corner."

Alyce stood up quickly, water splashing over the edge of the wooden tub from her sudden movement. She reached for the towel Edna held out to her, then stepped out onto a rug to dry herself.

Edna helped slip a night rail over Alyce's head then pushed her down on a stool by the fireplace to brush the snarls out of her wet hair.

"You know I am not speaking of Hawk," Edna said in her most motherly voice.

Alyce knew very well to whom Edna referred, but she did not want to have this conversation. She stared into the dancing flames of the fire and said nothing, hoping Edna would not press her. Edna kept up the soothing rhythmic strokes of the brush through her hair, but she would not give Alyce the peace she longed for.

"It is time to forgive Geoffrey."

Alyce stiffened. "What is left to forgive? He is dead. He is not here to forgive." She was grateful Edna stood behind her, unable to see her face. She was too tired to mask her pain—pain that felt fresh again after spending the day with a man who did not want her while watching him play with a baby who belonged to her husband but was not hers.

The entire day had turned into a constant reminder that the people she loved the most were also the people who could hurt her the worst. Cynwulf had shut her out, refusing to trust her to help him. She'd been forced to look more closely at the life of the woman whose son was a constant reminder of her husband's betrayal. And now Edna, whom she loved like a mother, who had always been there to soothe her when she needed to feel loved, was asking her to open her raw heart and forgive.

"Why must I be the one to forgive? I did not betray my husband by sleeping with someone else while he was home worried sick that I was dying in a ditch somewhere. I'm not the one who keeps secrets from Cynwulf. I do not make Janet give herself to the men in the hall."

Edna moved to stand in front of Alyce, her eyes wide as she looked down at her. "Where did all of that come from? I was speaking only of Geoffrey and your stubborn insistence to hold his betrayal close to your heart, blowing on it whenever the embers of your hurt start to cool."

Alyce felt the sting of indignant tears as she blinked to hold them back. "You think I purposely bring this pain on myself?"

Edna cupped Alyce's cheek in her hand and nodded. "Aye, I do. And before you disagree with me, listen to what I have to say."

Alyce pursed her lips together, but she remained quiet.

"My dear child, you think you have nothing to give another man, which is nothing but folly. Any man would be fortunate to have you in his life, children or no, but you are too afraid of being hurt again, so you hide behind the pain you know."

She wanted to disagree with Edna, tell her she did not understand, but the woman knew her better than anybody in her life…and she was completely right.

"If you do not forgive, you cannot move on. You cannot love again," Edna continued.

Alyce could hardly lift her voice above a whisper. "I just never want to feel this much pain again."

"Alyce. Look at me."

She lifted her eyes reluctantly to Edna's face.

"Geoffrey is dead. Geoffrey made a mistake. Geoffrey hurt you." She stroked a hand over Alyce's hair as she spoke. "But Geoffrey loved you, and we hurt the people we love whether we mean to or not."

"What he did changed everything for me," Alyce said, hating that she sounded like a whining child.

"Tell me, Alyce. Tell me how it changed everything."

"It changed everything because he made our marriage into a sham." Alyce closed her eyes and leaned into Edna's hand, seeking the warm comfort of her touch against her cheek.

Edna kissed Alyce's forehead, then released her to pick up a second stool and set it near Alyce's. She took both of Alyce's hands in her own and looked her squarely in the eye. "It is only a sham if you allow that one incident to define the whole of your marriage."

"I cannot stop thinking about how he touched her in ways that he was only supposed to touch me. I keep imagining him with her, losing himself to her, and the way she made him feel. How could I ever live up to that?" She had never spoken to anyone about the true depth of her hurt from Geoffrey's betrayal. Tears spilled down her cheeks and anguish cracked her voice. "I trusted him with my life, with my heart. When he slept with her, I lost all confidence in myself, in who we were together. I never stopped loving him despite how betrayed I felt, but my heart was shattered." Her words were riding on the edges of her sobs, the pain as fresh as the day she discovered the affair. "I cannot go through that again."

Edna stroked Alyce's hair, cradling her head as though she were a child again. "Whenever we love, we take a risk. You cannot live your life being angry forever, or else you will never find the joy in loving again. You are too young to be alone and most importantly, you are worthy of love, despite what you might think."

Alyce wanted to believe that she was worthy, but she knew her worth was not equal to that of other women's because she was barren. "She had his baby. She gave him the child I could not. No amount of love can overcome my lacking, and I can never provide the heir that every husband desires."

"Look at me, Alyce." Alyce did as she was told, startled by the firm edge to Edna's voice. "People speak of God's will and the need to be worthy of His grace to conceive but let me tell you something: I have brought many a babe into this world in every possible circumstance and it seems to have very little to do with the will of God or the worth of the person. I refuse to believe that good people are unable to have children because God deemed them unworthy. And not every man will feel your worth is to be measured by the number of sons you produce."

Alyce's eyes grew wide at this speech coming from the same woman who had taught her how to pray. The church would consider her words blasphemy and condemn her for speaking the devil's thoughts. But this was the same woman who'd encouraged Alyce to think for herself and question everything others tried to tell her; it should come as no surprise that she had her own opinions about the teachings of the Church.

Alyce had never met a woman stronger than Edna, and she was lucky to have her in her life. "I am not making you very proud at this moment, am I?"

"Never say that!"

"You did not raise me to wallow in self-pity, yet that seems to be what I have been doing for a long time."

The older woman harrumphed. "We all need to wallow at times. Then we need someone to come along and tell us when it is time to stop wallowing. Consider this me telling you."

A small laugh escaped Alyce's lips, and she suddenly felt lighter than she had for a very long time.

"I suggest you say to Geoffrey what you said to me—" she pointed toward the heavens as she said the words—"then tell him you forgive him. After that, the matter must be done."

"And if I forget and start to wallow again?"

"Give yourself a good pinch and say, 'No more.' Then think about what you can do to make yourself happy. Do not deny yourself what you desire."

"But what if what I desire will only lead to heartache?"

"You do not know where anything will lead, and you cannot avoid feeling pain for the rest of your life. But I promise you there will be more pleasure and happiness than pain and heartache." Edna touched her finger to the tip of Alyce's nose in an affectional gesture, then winked at her. "I suggest you start with allowing yourself more pleasure in your life."

❦ — •❀• — ❧

Chapter Seventeen

A LYCE HAD SPENT the last two days pushing her way through the crowded market streets of Shrewsbury, squeezing through the throngs of people to get to the stalls displaying the wares she needed. The markets in Shrewsbury were the largest in the region. People came from the far reaches of Wales and England to trade, barter, and buy the supplies needed to prepare for the busy autumn weeks of harvesting. Vendor stalls were filled with everything from the practical to the frivolous, and the atmosphere was filled with laughter and enthusiastic greetings as friends greeted one another. Three wagons, weighed down with supplies purchased, were already on their way back to Hawkspur under the watchful eye of Aelwin, four of Cynwulf's soldiers, and six of Hawk's soldiers.

When Hawk realized that Cynwulf would be escorting Alyce, he offered himself and eight more of his men to accompany the party to the market as guards. Alyce suspected the real reason for Hawk's offer was to stay close to Cynwulf. To be fair, it was less an offer and more a statement from Hawk that he and his men would be attending the market with them.

The market was the ideal location for clandestine meetings with nearly as many Welsh as English attending the market. Crowds of people everywhere were the perfect environment for inconspicuous encounters or unnoticed exchanges of information. Alyce had watched Cynwulf's every movement nearly as closely as Hawk did, and much to her relief, Cynwulf did not do anything that would raise suspicion.

She, on the other hand, had been doing her best to hide from Hawk since the day she showed him the village. She couldn't actually stay out of his sight, but she kept her attention focused on anything but him. She needed distance from him to sort out the tumult of emotions that had her stomach in knots since their kiss on the parapet.

Alyce had seen very little of Hawk since arriving at the market the morning before as she and Cynwulf spent the previous day and the whole of the current morning concentrating on securing tools, fabrics, spices, grains, chickens, and other provisions for Hawkspur castle and village.

Now that the wagons were packed and already on the way to Hawkspur under the watchful eye of Aelwin and a contingent of guards, Alyce had a glorious hour, maybe two, to look for the items she wanted from the market. Since they finished buying the necessary supplies with plenty of daylight left for the return journey to Hawkspur, Cynwulf had agreed to escort her to the market stalls for her to find some bone needles and a few other items.

"I promise to be quick, brother," Alyce said looping her arm through Cynwulf's. "I already know which merchants have the items I want."

Before Cynwulf could answer, a messenger appeared in the yard of the inn. "Lord Cynwulf," he said, waving as he jogged toward the stables where they stood. "I beg your pardon, sir, but the sheriff has requested your counsel immediately."

Cynwulf sighed and turned to Alyce. "I am sorry to disappoint, but I best do as the sheriff requests."

"Why does he seek your counsel now?" Alyce asked.

Cynwulf shrugged. "There is a disagreement brewing between one of our townsfolk and a Shrewsbury merchant."

Alyce was perplexed, sure she would have known if there were such a disagreement. "I don't recall—"

"It is nothing to worry yourself over. It will be resolved in no time." Cynwulf turned to Hawk. "May I request that you be so kind as to escort my sister to the market while I attend to the sheriff and settle this trifling nuisance?"

Hawk narrowed his eyes with what looked like suspicion at Cynwulf, then extended his hand to Alyce with a nod. "My lady."

The hairs on the back of Alyce's neck seemed to stand on end. Was Cynwulf hiding something? She reluctantly released his arm and turned her attention to Hawk. "I am sure there is no worse duty than having to follow a woman around the market. I promise to get this over with as quickly as possible."

"I'll admit, the market is not my favorite place to be, but Red cannot imagine a day better spent." He tipped his head toward the grinning Viking and another soldier of his, named Hunter. Both men had stayed behind.

Hawk certainly surrounded himself with a motley assortment of men, she decided. Hunter was a quiet man, big and brooding, the complete opposite of Red, and Alyce found him intimidating. In truth, other than Red, all of Hawk's men were intimidating with their constant watchfulness.

Still, Alyce turned to Hawk and smiled broadly as her brother quickly mounted his horse and rode across the yard and out the gate. "Then I shall request Red to escort me so the rest of you are not detained from your duties." She'd found Red to be pleasant and cordial for such a large and imposing warrior. Not only would she enjoy attending the market with him, but it would also keep her from being too close to Hawk, which was getting more difficult to endure each day.

But before she could link her arm through Red's, Hawk grabbed her hand and started toward the market in long strides. "I don't trust either of you to return before nightfall." As they passed by Hunter, busy grooming the horses, he said in a low voice, "You know what to do."

Alyce didn't like the ominous tone in Hawk's voice, and she feared he was just as suspicious as she was of the unusual summons of Cynwulf. If the matter was truly trivial, then it would have been handled during the hearings held every month at Hawkspur or Shrewsbury.

"What is Hunter to do?" Alyce asked Hawk's back as he

pulled her toward the market with determined strides.

"Ready the horses," Hawk said without hesitation or sincerity.

Hunter didn't have the physical appeal of Hawk or the charm of Red and spent most of his time scowling at everyone. She'd rarely heard him speak, but he'd always seemed to be watching. So now, Alyce suspected Hawk's command to him had nothing to do with the horses and everything to do with her brother. Even if the big oaf followed Cynwulf, he wouldn't be granted access to the meeting with the sheriff, so he had nothing to gain.

Whatever Cynwulf's business was with the sheriff, he would be finished with it soon, and then he would be anxious to start the journey back to Hawkspur. Best she turn her attention to finding the last items on her list so they could be underway as soon as possible. Putting Cynwulf, the sheriff, and Hunter out of her mind, she started toward the market stalls with Hawk and Red following in their wake.

Not many men had the ability to make Alyce feel small; she stood nearly as tall as her brother. With the Viking on one side and Hawk on the other, she felt petite, which was a rare occurrence for her. She found it humorous how a path cleared ahead of them as if by magic as they walked through the street teeming with people, animals, and wares. Miraculously, every crowded booth she approached with these two hulking warriors by her side suddenly had a space for her near the front.

"Does this happen wherever you go?"

Hawk looked genuinely puzzled. "Does what happen?"

She tipped her head in the direction of the people veering out of their path while the three of them consistently stayed true to their course.

Hawk still looked confused, and Alyce thought it doubtful he found anything unusual about the situation.

"He lives in oblivion, my lady," Red offered as an explanation. "He has no idea how much people shrink from him while he pays them no attention."

Hawk's mouth gaped as though grievously wronged. "If you think 'tis I that causes men and women alike to part like the Red

Sea, you are gravely mistaken. 'Tis that ugly smirk you call a smile and the frightful, matted braids at the side of your head that scare people away."

Alyce looked at Red, *really* looked at him. It was true; her own first impression had been that of a barbarian, a berserker, one of the bloodthirsty Norsemen who invaded England's shores with the Danes scores of years ago. But as soon as the big Viking had smiled at her, her fear had disappeared. Later, she'd found he wasn't nearly as intimidating once he started talking in his easy way, accentuating most of his remarks with a bubble of laughter or a wink. In truth, he was quite handsome.

"I think his smile to be quite appealing," she said in his defense. The frown on Hawk's face only encouraged her to continue. "And the braids keep his hair from covering his eyes, which I see now are so very blue and quite stunning."

"Enough," Hawk growled.

Red winked at Alyce before she turned her attention to Hawk. Aye, Red was pleasing to look at, but Hawk caused her body to react in ways that were new to her. She could convince herself any involvement with Hawk could only lead to heartache when she was alone, but as soon as he was near, she found herself able to think of little else than wanting him to kiss her again.

She focused on the vendors to hide the heat she felt rising in her cheeks. After purchasing the needles and fabric requested by Edna and Gertie, she perused a booth filled with swaths of leather in all colors and thicknesses. She found a length that was durable yet surprisingly pliable in a rich brown tone that would be perfect for a new pair of boots.

"I take the brown, and I'll have this one, too," she said to the merchant, lifting a luxuriously soft bit of leather that had been dyed a deep, forest green. She would sew gloves from it before the winter for Cynwulf and Edna. She paid for the leather, which Red immediately took from her hands to tuck under his arm along with her other purchases. Hawk, she noticed, was constantly scanning the crowd as though he suspected an attack at any moment.

"What else do you need?" Red asked Alyce, looking at the

wares of each stall as they walked.

"Ribbons," Alyce replied to Red, trying to ignore Hawk. "I like to have a collection of ribbons to give on special occasions or as tokens of appreciation."

Red looked over the heads of the others in the market, then pointed to a booth ahead. Alyce glanced at Hawk as they walked to the stall of ribbons, puzzled by the unsettled look on his face.

"What has him so upset?" she asked Red.

The big Viking answered without even turning to look at his friend and commander. "His gut is talking to him."

Alyce squeezed her eyebrows together, perplexed.

"He has a feeling in his belly that something is not right," Red explained, "and his gut is never wrong."

Alyce purchased the ribbon strands, tucked them in her pouch, and turned back toward the inn. She prayed that Cynwulf would already be there by the time they returned, waiting by his horse, and impatient to leave.

ALYCE, HAWK, AND Red returned to the inn to find Cynwulf's remaining two soldiers mounted on their horses and extremely agitated. And Hunter was nowhere in sight. Cynwulf had not returned from his meeting with the sheriff, sending word by messenger that he decided to ride out ahead of the group and would meet them back at Hawkspur. She wondered now if Cynwulf had deliberately chosen his two youngest and least experienced soldiers to stay behind while the others accompanied the wagons. Any of his other men would have left immediately to search for their commander upon getting such a message.

Dumbfounded at the news, Alyce said nothing when Hawk lifted her onto the back of her mare. He and Red mounted their horses without acknowledging Hunter's absence. Hawk signaled for the two young soldiers to take the lead while Red fell to the rear of the small group.

As they rode out of the village and into the countryside toward home, Alyce asked Hawk, "Where is Hunter?"

He was quiet for a long moment, his jaw tight, before he responded in a clipped tone. "Doing what he does best."

"And what is that?" Alyce braced herself for the answer. She noticed Hawk had slowed their pace, putting distance between them and Cynwulf's soldiers.

Hawk looked at her, his eyes full of...suspicion? Sympathy? "Hunt. More specifically, track."

"Is he hunting Cynwulf?" She cringed at the bitter bite to her tone.

Hawk nodded once, his eyes focused again on the road ahead. "Tracking." He shifted in his saddle, as though he felt as unsettled as Alyce, but he did not look at her.

Alyce took a deep breath to calm herself. In truth, she didn't know what irritated her more, Hawk sending his man to hunt down Cynwulf, or Cynwulf disappearing when he knew he was being watched. When had her brother become so addlebrained?

Alyce steeled herself for a fight, ready to protect her brother, no matter what folly he brought upon himself. Cynwulf was not a malicious man, and he strived to be as fair and just an overlord as Uncle Ranolf. Despite his odd behavior of late, she could not believe he was doing anything to threaten the king or kingdom.

"And what will Hunter do if he finds him anywhere other than at Hawkspur?" She lifted her chin to give Hawk a haughty glare, daring him to dismiss her with a flimsy lie.

Hawk nudged his horse closer to her so that their legs touched, then put his hand over hers, applying enough pressure on the rein to bring her horse to a halt. She was about to ask him, with an indignant huff, what he was doing, but the look on his face stopped her. His brow was furrowed, and his eyes immediately locked with hers when she lifted her face to his.

"He will not hurt him, I promise you that, Alyce." He looked as though the most important thing to him in the world at this moment was for her to believe him. "Cynwulf plays a dangerous game, and he has been for quite some time."

"How can you say that?" Alyce shook her head at him, confusion and anger welling up inside her.

"Cynwulf has been seen crossing the border alone into Wales

more often than is required of his position. No other Marcher lord ventures into hostile territory without a small army to reinforce his position, even for diplomatic missions. The king's sources say your brother routinely passes over the border unhindered since the rebellion began—and that this is the only stretch of the border not being ravished by Welsh rebels."

"That cannot be true. We are not immune to the hostilities between our two countries; my husband was killed by Welsh rebels a year ago."

"And how many of Cynwulf's soldiers have been killed since then? Or suffered injuries beyond a few scratches and bruises?"

Alyce gasped, appalled at Hawk's insinuation. "You think Cynwulf a spy because we have not suffered enough at Hawkspur? Has it not crossed your mind that his soldiers are well-trained and fulfilling their duty to protect Hawkspur?"

"I do not mean offend, my lady." He looked pained, as though he did not wish to say the next words. When he did speak, his tone was even, deliberately calm, "Every other fortress along the border is suffering casualties, their villages being ravished and burned. Even the unbreakable Roger Mortimer is losing men every month in the fight to keep the Welsh rebels contained. The relative calm that you are experiencing at Hawkspur is not in alignment with what is happening along every other segment of the border."

Alyce's chest heaved with every breath as she fought to contain her ire at the ridiculousness of Hawk's suggestions. "What are you saying? That Cynwulf has brokered some deal with the rebels? If he has, maybe the king needs to learn from him. Maybe Cynwulf should be put in command of the entire border." She tugged her hand out from under Hawk's and pressed her mount's side to put distance between them.

Hawk sighed but did not give her the space she desired, nudging his horse to stay close to hers. "It's not just that Hawkspur is insulated from the fighting and the killing. Our armies are being ambushed at every turn; the rebels seem to know exactly where to be and when to be there. Someone is feeding them the information they need to maintain the advantage. If we do not stop this soon, it won't be just the borderlands embroiled in a bloody war."

Alyce felt like her world was being turned upside down. "You do not know Cynwulf as I do. He would never do anything that would bring down the wrath of the king or endanger the kingdom. He has always been fair to the Welsh people who live near Hawkspur. They respect him as they did my uncle. That is why he can travel freely anywhere along his stretch of the border. He is a good man. You must believe me."

A flicker of sadness crossed Hawk's face and Alyce felt it like a knife to her heart. He didn't believe her. A cold wave of dread washed over her, weighing down her shoulders. She took a deep breath and a desperate sob caught in her throat. "My brother is a good man, Hawk."

Hawk lifted his hand slowly, as if she were a skittish mare, brushing his fingers lightly up her arm. She didn't pull away from his touch, letting him wrap his big, warm hand around the back of her neck as he leaned close enough to press his forehead to hers. "I believe you that he is a good man, but good men can make bad decisions," he said in a hoarse whisper. "And Cynwulf has made some very bad decisions."

Alyce felt the last reserves of her composure drain from her body when Hawk pulled her close. She wanted to sag into him, to let him be a shield against her crumbling world for a while. She closed her eyes as the threat of tears welled up in her throat. "He is my brother."

Hawk brushed his lips across her forehead. "I know," he said, his voice thick with compassion.

Alyce pushed back from Hawk, straightening her spine and wiping her eyes. "Let us be on our way. I am needed at Hawkspur."

Hawk simply nodded and picked up his reins, and for that Alyce was grateful. It was time to be strong, to take control, and Hawk's gentleness only made it more difficult for her to think straight. Her priority now was to pull the truth from Cynwulf and then figure out how to rectify whatever wrong he may have committed.

"Dear God," she prayed, "please don't let it be too late."

HUNTER SLIPPED IN behind the small group of riders as they entered Hawkspur's gates. Hawk noticed the addition to their party, but he hoped exhaustion would keep Alyce from noticing, otherwise, she would insist on hearing Hunter's report.

Hawk jumped down from his horse at the front of the castle and helped Alyce to the ground. As he'd hoped, fatigue made her pliant in his arms and she leaned into him until the strength returned to her legs. Stiffening, she pulled away from Hawk, muttering her thanks as a stableboy took the reins of her mare to lead it back to the barn.

This mission might be the death of him because it was killing him to see Alyce afraid and in pain. She was devoted to her brother, and for that, he could not fault her; Cynwulf was the only family she had left. What would happen to her when they had the proof they needed against him? When he would no longer be lord of Hawkspur, and she would no longer have a home here?

I'll protect her.

As soon as the thought shot through his brain, he pushed it away. She would want nothing to do with him once he completed the king's mission. The king would find another lord to marry her, one deserving of a fortress like Hawkspur.

When he thought about someone else with Alyce, his stomach lurched as though he'd been punched, and he wanted to rip the heart out of any man who touched her. He wanted her for himself, but it could never be. Hawk had little doubt of how all of this would end once he found the evidence to prove Cynwulf's guilt, and Alyce would hate him for it—which was for the best. Even if he did not ruin her life, he could never give her all that she deserved.

Hawk watched Alyce ascend the castle stairs and disappear through the heavy door before he led his own horse in the direction of the stable. He had been seething from the moment they'd returned to find Cynwulf gone from Shrewsbury. He'd expected Cynwulf to do something foolish while they were there, but he didn't expect him to be so blatant. Nor did he expect him to abandon his sister to the care of men he hardly knew.

He did not speak to Hunter until the horses had been groomed, fed, and turned out. Hawk raised a questioning brow as he and Red met up with him in the bailey. Hunter gave a single nod in response. Hawk felt a moment of triumph and an unfamiliar pang of regret. The king rewarded him well because his gut was never wrong, and he always delivered what the king wanted. Up until now, he'd taken pride in his victories, but this one was beginning to taste bitter.

"What happened?" asked Hawk.

"'Twas brief," Hunter said in a low voice. "He met his man in a forester's hut on the Welsh side of the border."

"And?" He knew he need not ask Hunter if Cynwulf suspected he had been followed.

"It was the same man who left here the day we arrived, riding for the border like he had a band of demons on his tail."

"Did you discover his identity?"

Hunter shook his head. "Cynwulf argued with the man for a while, warning him to stay away from Hawkspur." Hunter's expression grew dark, and he hesitated.

"Out with it, man," Hawk urged.

"He reminded Cynwulf they knew his sister's habits, and it would not be difficult to get to her if he did not cooperate."

Hawk's blood turned to ice in his veins at the mention of a threat toward Alyce. He didn't like the way both Red and Hunter were studying him for his reaction, but he also knew they understood him better than anyone and were well aware of his weakness for the lady.

He had to work hard to control the rage in his voice. "What did Cynwulf say?" he bit out through gritted teeth.

"Everything," Hunter said, his voice dripping with disdain. "He told him exactly which castles the king has commanded to be seized in the south, and which commanders will be leading the armies in the attacks."

Hawk's hands clenched into tight fists. He wanted to kill Cynwulf for his treachery! Then he remembered the fear in Alyce's eyes that harm would come to her brother. "God's blood! The cowardly fool!"

"Seemed like he was trying to hold back information, just giving scant details, but then the other man would mention another part of Alyce's routine and how easy it would be to get to her. He said they could kill her as easily as they killed her husband."

Realization dawned and Hawk let out a loud sigh. "So the only casualty at Hawkspur wasn't a random skirmish with Welsh rebels. It was a message to Cynwulf."

"When he finally took his leave," Hunter continued, "he didn't look good. Had the look of a man about to hang in the gallows."

Hawk had hoped, for Alyce's sake, that it wasn't too late to save her brother from the gallows, but it seemed his fate was sealed. "Where is Cynwulf now?"

"Expect he's here," Hunter said with a shrug of his shoulder. "He went straight to the main road and turned this way. Kept my distance, but I know he didn't leave the road again."

"Good work, Hunter." Hawk clapped the big man on the back in appreciation.

Hunter grunted, then took his leave. Hawk and Red turned toward the castle.

"Do not let her out of your sight, Red," Hawk said in a low voice as they started up the narrow stairs to the castle door.

"You don't want that job?" Red raised a questioning brow at his friend and commander.

Hawk shook his head. "For her sake, I will keep my distance from her."

And for his sake, he could not afford to let any attachment to the lady cloud his judgment. He had a duty to the king, which must be fulfilled, even if it ruined Lady Alyce's life.

Chapter Eighteen

"HE GROWS STRONG."

Alyce turned at the sound of her brother's voice. "Aye, that he does." She rested her arms on the fence and peered out over the lush pasture.

The colt had thrived and was prancing around his mother in the pasture, leaping and playing on gangly legs with the vigor of youth while Guinevere grazed quietly. Ffyddlon wagged her tail excitedly at the antics of the colt, trying to climb through the opening in the fence to get to him until Alyce snapped a finger at the wolfhound and forced her to lay at her feet. She'd pouted, with her back to her mistress for a long while, then lay down in the sun and dozed.

The energetic colt and tending to Guinevere had kept Alyce occupied for the past two days, but that didn't stop her from constantly thinking about the events that unfolded at the market and Hawk's accusation. She found it hard to believe that Cynwulf was crossing into Wales as a spy and not as Lord of Hawkspur Castle, sworn liege to King Edward, as Hawk suspected. But even she deemed Cynwulf's recent behavior suspicious. She'd been trying to work up the courage to confront him, knowing that things would never be the same once she did—not for Cynwulf, not for all the people who called Hawkspur home, and especially not for her.

She fretted over Cynwulf every waking moment, but when

she closed her eyes, it was Hawk who filled her mind, despite her best efforts to push him away. He was the enemy, the man tasked by the king to prove her brother a traitor to the crown. She should want nothing to do with him.

But there was no one else she could turn to in this maelstrom of secrets, covert meetings, and suspicion. Cynwulf was hiding truths from her, and she dared not discuss it with anyone else for fear they were either in on the deception with him, or they were completely unaware, and she was exposing his deception to them. Hawk was the only person who seemed to have any idea what was happening.

And the only person sympathetic to the fear was tearing at her insides.

He had not been to the hall for his meals since they returned from Shrewsbury after being abandoned by Cynwulf. She'd not spoken to him and saw him only from afar as he stalked across the bailey, trained with his men in the field, or huddled with Red and Hunter in earnest discussions.

Cynwulf had not been to the hall in the time they returned from the market either. It was as though everyone was avoiding a dreaded confrontation.

Alyce eyed her brother now that she finally had him to herself. His defenses were up, she could see it in his posture. Deciding a straightforward attack was the best approach, she led with a bold question. "Why did you leave me at the market with two of your least-experienced soldiers as escort?"

"You had Hawk and his men to protect you," Cynwulf said with a shrug.

Alyce sighed in frustration. "That doesn't excuse your behavior. And I thought you did not like Hawk, so why did you trust him with me?"

"I resent Hawk's presence here, but by all accounts, he is a man of honor."

"High praise, indeed! I should hope you consider him honorable since you left the well-being of your only sister in his hands." When had Cynwulf become so cold and uncaring?

"He's taken a liking to you; he would never harm you."

When Alyce said nothing in response, he continued, "I am sorry, dear sister, if I misjudged. Just say the word and I will ensure you are never in his presence again."

Alyce shot her brother a sharp look through slitted eyes. "What do you mean by that?"

"No need to look at me that way. I'm not going to have him killed. I just mean that I will tell him to stay away from you if that is your preference."

"And what makes you think he will do as you ask?" she scoffed. In truth, her tone had more to do with her fear of not seeing Hawk again than it did her skepticism of him obeying a command from Cynwulf.

"I do know a bit about Sir Grogan and his band of bastards."

"His what?" Alyce exclaimed, appalled that Cynwulf would refer to Hawk and his men that way.

Cynwulf held up his hands defensively. "It is what they are called, even by themselves. I did not make up the name. Besides, in this case, it is *because* they are bastards that they are honorable."

"Now you are talking nonsense." Alyce felt her frustration growing as her brother talked in circles, avoiding her questions.

"Hawk and his men are all base born. Each one of them has a sad story of being an outcast forced to witness the harsh treatment of his mother and a resulting sympathy toward women. The rumor is they take their oath of chivalry very seriously. Hawk will not tolerate any man in his guard mistreating a woman."

"You are saying they swear not to touch women?" Alyce stared at her brother in disbelief.

"No," Cynwulf said with a smirk, shaking his head, "they swear not to mistreat women. That does not mean they are monks."

Alyce waved her hand in the air dismissively. "That is not what I want to discuss. Something has changed," she said carefully, staring at him intently, trying to read his response to her. "You are changed; I don't recognize you. You've never shut me out, lied to me, treated me as though I were just another one of your vassals. What has happened to you?"

Cynwulf leaned against the fence and looked at her. The softness had returned to his eyes, and he looked at her with a warmth she realized had been missing for some time. Alyce felt like she'd won a great battle. The wall had come down and his face lost the hard edge he'd had of late. "Tell me what is troubling you. I can help, whatever it is."

Cynwulf shook his head. "It is my doing; I will fix it."

"What is your doing? What must you fix?"

Cynwulf reached for her hand and cupped it between both of his own as though to protect it.

"Do you remember that Aelwin was a witness when Uncle Ranolf was on his deathbed? He can testify our uncle's desire was for Hawkspur to stay in the Chetwynd family, and that it goes to you if I could no longer be lord for any reason. He nearly broke himself building this place. It belongs to us, and if anything happens to me, it belongs to you."

Alyce felt a cold shiver creep down her spine that had nothing to do with the cool breeze rustling the turning leaves overhead. "What do you think is going to happen to you?"

"I found my father," he said after a long moment. "Or rather, he found me."

"How?" Alyce was grateful he had her anchored in his as she felt herself sway at the impact of his words. "When?"

Cynwulf released her hand and pulled at the leather thong hanging around his neck, freeing it from beneath his shirt, and revealing a delicate ring of gold adorned with a small sapphire. "This was my mother's, given to me when I left home to train under Uncle Ranolf. She told me to keep it safe and that she would one day tell me why it was special to her and its significance to me, but she died before telling me anything more."

Alyce reached her fingers toward the ring, then stopped and raised an eyebrow at Cynwulf. "May I?" He nodded as he pulled the string of leather over his head and dropped the ring into her outstretched hand. She studied the delicate craftsmanship of the jewel. "I don't recall ever seeing this ring."

"I'd not seen it until Mother gave it to me. And after she died, when you came to live with Uncle Ranolf, I didn't want to show it to you."

Alyce felt a stab of jealousy and betrayal at his admission. "Why not?"

He smiled ruefully as he explained. "I was young, and I wanted something of hers that was only mine. It felt like a bond with her after she died that was mine alone."

She could not fault him for keeping it secret. If the ring had been given to her, she would have felt just as protective of the precious link to their mother.

"After she died, I put it on a strip of leather and wore it around my neck, tucked under my shirt. It made me feel less alone. I managed to keep it hidden for a long time, but when Geoffrey and I were sent to train under the tutelage of Lord de Ferrers, it came loose while practicing hand-to-hand combat on the field. One of the soldiers training us got near enough to grab the leather thong and use it as leverage to pull me off balance. He made an example of me, demonstrating the folly of wearing something that could be used against us. The training commander dismissed us immediately after that, but he asked me to stay behind. He wanted a closer look at the ring, and I feared he would take it from me. But it wasn't greed in his eyes; it was recognition."

Alyce remembered the summer Cynwulf and Geoffrey were gone, sent away to broaden their training. It had been the longest three months of her young life without them at Hawkspur.

"He wanted to know where I got it," Cynwulf continued. "When I told him it was my mother's, he demanded to know her name, wanted to know where she was. He tried to hide the pained look on his face when I said she was dead, and when I asked him if he knew her, he nodded. But then he left me standing alone in the field without saying another word."

"What did you do?"

"Nothing," Cynwulf said with a bitter laugh. "I was not yet lord of Hawkspur and was in no position to question a commander. I returned to Hawkspur shortly after that."

Alyce studied the ring in her hand. The exquisitely intricate design carved into the gold band meant this was a rare piece of jewelry, rich in value, and not just a fancy bauble given to a lover on a whim. "Who was the commander?"

"Daffydd ap Gruffydd," Cynwulf said flatly.

Alyce gasped. He was brother to the Welsh Prince Llywelyn, and the man King Edward hated more than any other man in the kingdom. Daffydd had twice abandoned his brother and Wales to swear fealty to the King of England in the vain hope of being backed in his bid to overthrow his brother and declare himself Prince of Wales. And twice he had betrayed his vow to the king to join forces with his brother again.

"Daffydd is your father?" Alyce asked in disbelief, and horror, hardly comprehending Cynwulf's nod in affirmation.

Daffydd was a charming, manipulative man who only cared about himself. At least that was what Uncle Ranolf had always said about him. He was not a man who could be trusted to keep his word to anyone, even family.

"Did Uncle Ranolf know?"

"Yes," Cynwulf replied. "And he was not happy about it. I told him what happened when I returned from training at Lord de Ferrer's, thinking he might know if there was any connection between Daffydd and our mother."

"What did he say?" Alyce sagged against the fence, feeling weak from trying to make sense of the whirlwind of information.

"He confessed that there had been whispers about our mother having an affair of the heart while visiting a cousin in Wales. He confirmed that when our mother married his brother—your father—she was already pregnant with me. Father swore Uncle Ranolf to secrecy, and they never spoke of it again. He didn't know about the ring, but he assumed, as I did when I showed it to him, that only her lover would recognize it. I can't imagine Mother giving it to me for any other reason than it once belonged to my father."

Alyce was putting the pieces together in her mind, realizing that Cynwulf had known long before he told her that they did not have the same father. "You lied to me all those years ago. You told me it was Uncle Ranolf who revealed we had different fathers, but that he did not know the name of your father. Why did you not tell me the truth then? Why hide his name from me?" Alyce's voice was strained, unable to disguise the hurt stabbing at her heart.

Cynwulf looked sheepish. "Uncle Ranolf said I should never tell anyone, that it would be dangerous if anyone else knew he was my father. He said it was fortunate that Daffydd did not acknowledge his connection to me that day on the field and warned me to stay away from him lest I be caught up in his deceptions."

"What does all of this have to do with what is happening now, if you only met him once?" Alyce asked, perplexed. "Oh!" she exclaimed as the realization dawned. "You did not meet him just once, did you?" She said it more as a statement than a question because she had no doubt as to what Cynwulf's answer would be.

Cynwulf slowly shook his head from side to side. "He became part of the nobility when he married King Edward's cousin, often attending gatherings of the Marcher Lords to represent the king's interest in the Welsh border. Uncle Ranolf and I would see him occasionally, but he never acknowledged me. Shortly after Uncle Ranolf died and I became lord of Hawkspur, Daffydd approached me at a meeting of the Marcher Lords. He wanted to know more about our mother, what her life was like, and how she'd died. I asked him then if he was my father, and he admitted he was."

Alyce closed her eyes and breathed out a heavy sigh. "Did anyone hear him tell you this?"

"Not that I know," Cynwulf said. "And he thought it best if we did not tell anyone of our relationship. He did not want to bring scandal to his family or ours."

Alyce snorted with contempt. "Scandal? I'd say he is as deep in scandal as he can get. The man betrayed the king and is destroying villages, ravishing peasants, and burning farms. The king is mobilizing every army at his disposal to destroy him."

"It is not scandal he thinks about now, but justice. He fights for what he believes is his," Cynwulf said with vehemence.

The words hit Alyce like a punch to the gut. Not because of

what was said, but because of how it was said. Cynwulf's tone held authority and conviction. "You speak as though you support what he is doing. He was the king's ally until six months ago, and then he attacked Hawarden without provocation. People are dying because of him. You cannot possibly be on his side."

"Is he wrong for wanting what should be his? What choice did he have but to take what he was promised by force? King Edward has broken his oath to Wales and to Daffydd one too many times. If Daffydd does not rebel against Edward, then Wales will be gone and it will all be England, with English laws and English ways."

Alyce's mouth gaped in shock. "He does not fight for what is best for Wales; he fights only for what is best for him. Uncle Ranolf was correct when he said the king never should have trusted Daffydd. He changes allegiances more often than the queen changes gowns. And now, he is leading the rebellion against King Edward. Your king. The king you swore fealty to as lord of Hawkspur. Tell me you are not any part of what he is doing."

"Lower your voice," Cynwulf said in a harsh whisper.

Alyce was so frustrated with the foolishness of the entire situation that she hadn't noticed her tone was getting louder with her growing exasperation. She looked around to see if anyone was near, but they were alone. In the distance, the stable boys were turning out horses to the smaller pastures to graze and stretch their legs, but Guinevere and her colt were afforded the luxury of having the larger pasture to themselves. Which also meant she and Cynwulf were alone as they leaned against the fence watching them.

"If I am understanding you correctly," Alyce said in a quieter tone, though she knew her anger was apparent in the way she bit out the words through clenched teeth, "you have given your allegiance to Daffydd. Which also means you are the spy Hawk thinks you to be."

"It was never my intent." Cynwulf's crestfallen face resembled that of a regretful, scared child. "I didn't know until it was too late that this was his plan."

Alyce closed her eyes, squeezing back the sting of tears, wishing she could make this all go away. Reluctantly, she opened them to look at her brother again. "How bad is it? Were you merely sympathetic to his complaints? Or have you been conspiring with him and betraying your king every time you ride alone into Wales, as Hawk says?"

"It's complicated, Alyce. I wanted to know the man who sired me, to find out more about who I am. I didn't know at the time that Daffydd would betray the king yet again. He is married to King Edward's cousin, for Christ's sake."

"You are a Chetwynd, my brother, lord of Hawkspur. You should be giving us the same loyalty we've given to you. Are we not enough for you?"

Cynwulf pursed his lips together, "I never meant to hurt you, or anyone else."

"Lord Cynwulf!" Aelwin called, startling them both.

"What is it?" he snapped at Aelwin as he turned away from Alyce to face his first in command walking briskly along the fence toward them.

Alyce wanted to scream her frustration. She finally knew the truth, but they had yet to determine how to fix the mess Cynwulf had created. Whatever Aelwin had to say, she prayed he'd be quick about it and then be on his way.

"We've had a messenger," Aelwin announced. "He bears the king's standard."

"What does he want?" Cynwulf asked irritably.

"He says he has a missive for you directly from the king," Aelwin said, shifting from foot to foot nervously, "and he suggests you make haste as there is not much time to prepare."

Alyce looked questioningly from Aelwin to Cynwulf, not understanding the implication of the messenger's words.

"God's blood," Cynwulf muttered, dropping his head back in defeat. "The king must be on his way here."

"Here?" Alyce asked, her voice nearly cracking with hysteria.

Aelwin nodded. "He carries a message for Hawk, as well."

Alyce's head began to pound, an affliction she suffered from often as of late. She was reaching her limits and it felt like another stone had been added to the pile already resting upon her shoulders. She looked at Cynwulf to see his reaction; his face had paled, and his jaw tightened.

"I will see the messenger immediately," he said to Aelwin. Turning back to Alyce, he put his hand on her arm in a reassuring gesture. "We will continue our discussion at a later time."

"I am coming with you," Alyce announced. She would not stand idly to the side and watch while Cynwulf, the king, Welsh rebels, and English armies tore Hawkspur apart.

This was her home, and it was time to fight for it.

Chapter Nineteen

THE KING AND his entourage were not expected until the following afternoon and already Hawkspur was brimming with people. Alyce slipped into the great hall unnoticed while everyone's attention was on a pair of men juggling empty tankards between them. She leaned against the wall near the door at the rear of the hall to watch the festivities and rest for a few moments after a long day. The room erupted into cheers each time someone guzzled down the contents of another tankard and handed it to one of the men to add to the dizzying swirl of silver cups flying in circles between them.

Alyce had spent the last two days working with the servants and cooks to ensure all was ready for the arrival of King Edward, Queen Eleanor, the king's army, and the queen's attending ladies. Word had traveled quickly about their impending arrival, hence the reason the hall was packed with the curious, the fortune seekers, and the hopeful. Everyone here wanted an audience with the king and queen for their own personal gain in one way or another; some just to be in the same room as the royal couple, some hoping to fill their purses with silver in return for their skills as entertainers, and others looking to improve their political positions.

Alyce wished she could avoid the king and queen completely and hide away in her bedchamber with Ffyddlon—whom she had banished to her room after tripping over the hound for the hundredth time in her hurry to get everything done. But now was not the time to disappear like a coward, despite the heavy stone of fear that had settled into her stomach.

She'd sat with Cynwulf alone in his solar this morning as he explained to her again how his desire to know the man who was his sire had led to getting caught up in his rebellion. He'd not meant for it to go this far, but by the time he realized Daffydd's true intent, he was in too deep. He'd told his sire that he would not participate in an insurrection against the king, but those most loyal to Daffydd explained to Cynwulf how easy it would be to implicate him if he did not continue to produce the information they requested. They even suggested that Geoffrey's death may not have been a random act, but rather a warning.

The only answer Cynwulf had when she asked what he planned to do next was a shrug of his shoulders. Alyce had mulled over the situation all day as she worked, intent on developing a list of options to discuss with her brother. But the day was nearly done, and she hadn't thought of even one idea to remedy the situation.

The jugglers were pushed beyond the limit of tankards they could successfully keep tossing between them, and the crowd burst into laughter and applause as the cups rained down on the wooden floor. Each juggler managed to end the show with one tankard in hand, which they clinked together with bravado, then bowed to the spectators with a flourish and proceeded to walk through the crowd collecting coins of appreciation.

She was about to take her leave when a large figure settled against the wall next to her. She knew without turning her head that it was Hawk and her heart started to beat faster as she breathed in the aroma of leather, sweat, and something that was wonderfully warm and uniquely him.

Was it worrisome that she could pick out Hawk from a crowd of men by his scent? She tried to remember what Geoffrey had smelled like, but she couldn't recall ever noticing a scent that was uniquely his own.

Before Hawk arrived, people had been crowded in around her, bumping her with their elbows as they drank and laughed.

With Hawk standing at her side, the crowd had edged away from them.

"It has happened again, my lord," Alyce said with a smirk, still not turning her head to look at him.

"What is that, my lady?"

Alyce felt the gooseflesh rise on her arms at the low, seductive rumble of his voice. "The crowd moving aside just because of your presence. What is it about your face that makes people scurry away from you in fear?" She said the last with a teasing smile.

He chuckled deep in his chest. "I can't tell you, but I hope it never changes. I don't like most people."

Alyce laughed and turned toward him, a witty remark about his rude behavior on her tongue, but the words froze on her lips when she looked into his eyes. He was staring down at her so intently, it took her breath away. For several heartbeats, the raucous laughter and talking in the hall faded away and it seemed there was no one else in the room but the two of them.

He leaned closer to her and said in a whisper, "But I like you, Alyce."

Her hair was pulled back into a long braid to keep it out of her way as she worked, with a square of linen held in place at the top of her head by a silver circlet, leaving her ears and neck exposed. She gulped at the sensation of his warm breath tickling against her skin.

It took her a long moment to regain her sense. "You are a dangerous man, Hawk. And if I seem to forget that fact, I expect you to do the honorable thing and remind me." Her voice had a teasing tone that she could not seem to suppress. In truth, it felt good to forget the seriousness of her life for a few moments and play the game of seduction with a handsome man.

He quirked an eyebrow. "And if I don't do the honorable thing?"

His words came out as a low growl that sent shivers down Alyce's spine. She bit her lip and steeled her nerve. Hawk was a pleasant diversion, but she must not forget he was also a complication in her current situation.

Janet emerged from the buttery carrying a tray filled with tankards of ale and cups of wine, and Alyce held up a hand to get her attention, waving her over.

"How is little Henry?" she asked, taking a tankard and cup from the tray, hoping her smile did not look as awkward as it felt.

Janet's eyes widened, and she stuttered for a flustered moment before replying, "He is well. Thank you for asking, my lady."

"Thank you for the drink," Alyce said handing the tankard to Hawk before taking a sip of the wine. Janet bobbed her head as others started to reach for the remaining drinks on her tray and she disappeared into the impatient crowd.

Alyce could feel Hawk's eyes on her, and she waited for him to say something. When a long moment passed without comment, she tipped her head and slanted her eyes at him. His only acknowledgment was to nod once and clink his tankard against her cup. She breathed out a long sigh, pleasantly surprised that some of the tension in her neck had eased.

A rich, melodic, baritone voice filled the hall, and a hush fell over the crowd. A bard had climbed atop one of the trestle tables and started to sing a familiar tune. He was a familiar face to many in the hall and a favorite of the traveling minstrels who regularly passed through Hawkspur.

Alyce had never given a second thought to the fact that the bard was Welsh and many of his ballads were about legends from his homeland. She'd always loved the tales, but on the eve of the king's arrival amid escalated fighting with the Welsh rebels, she worried his presence would not be welcome.

Tomorrow, she decided, she would ask Cynwulf to give the bard a purse of silver and send him on his way. Best not to add any more tension while the king was at Hawkspur.

Hawk angled his body toward Alyce and leaned a shoulder against the wall. "What does the bard sing about?"

Keeping her attention on the bard, she tipped her head toward Hawk. "'Tis a Welsh tale about a woman who emerges from a lake and the man who falls in love with her."

"It is a story you like?" Hawk asked, his breath tickling her ear as he spoke.

Alyce turned to face Hawk, contemplating his words. "I like stories, and I like this particular bard's voice. I had not thought much about whether I like this particular story."

"What is not to like about stories of love?" Hawk's intent gaze heated her cheeks. It felt oddly intimate to be talking of love with this man, even if only in the context of a bard's ballad.

"Love is kinder to some than to others." She held her head a little higher after she said it, feeling victorious that the admission did not fill her with bitterness or self-pity. The revelation brought a small smile to her lips. She was stronger than she realized, than she allowed herself to believe.

An unexpected surge of pride washed over her. As a girl, she had been taught to be humble, modest about accomplishments, and self-deprecating. But those were not qualities of people who were bold.

And she needed to be bold now more than ever, lest the actions of her brother and the decisions of her king determine a future for her not to her liking.

Feeling lighter, she turned back toward the bard, a genuine smile on her face. "Yes, I do like this story."

HAWK WATCHED IN fascination as Alyce's entire body seemed to come alive. He'd seen men come back from near defeat when others thought them finished. They'd rise up out of the mud and blood on a battlefield, shoulders back, head high, looming larger than before they were knocked down. It was as though something they had kept buried deep in their souls until that moment was suddenly found, and the men facing them braced themselves for a new and tormenting strength that would not be easily put down.

He had no idea what had brought about this change in Alyce, but the shift was almost palpable. Her cheeks were flushed, and there was an energy radiating from her. He felt like he'd just emerged from the darkness of a cave into the powerful heat of the sun, and he wanted more of it.

Before he realized what he was doing, he was gingerly picking up a tendril of hair hanging loosely over her shoulder. Her head turned slightly toward him when his fingers grazed the material of her gown. She was not adorned in any of her finery, but rather in a modest, dark tunic more suited for hard work. He noticed the smudge of dirt just under her jawline and had to stop himself from leaning down to kiss her there.

He trailed a finger along the sensitive skin on her neck, remembering the smell and feel of her when she'd let him kiss her on the parapet. At least a sennight had passed since then, but the memory of the scent and taste of her had plagued his thoughts every night since then. He wanted to kiss her again.

And more.

One night to satisfy his curiosity and purge her from his thoughts.

"You will cause a scandal, my lord," Alyce said in a low, sultry whisper that had Hawk thinking about throwing her over his shoulder and carrying her out of the hall to a secluded place. She turned her face toward him. "You forget your duty, sir, and the king arrives tomorrow. Should you not be fulfilling your mission instead of seducing me where anyone can see you?"

The revelers in the hall were singing along with the bard or swaying back and forth with their arms thrown over the shoulders of their companions. A few curious people turned furtive glances at the Lady of Hawkspur and Hawk. He stopped stroking the side of her neck, but he let his fingers skim lightly over the back of her arm as he lowered his hand back to his side.

"We are ready for the king. My men know what to do," Hawk said, glancing to where Red and Hunter stood with several of his other soldiers. He knew they were watching Cynwulf's every move and would not let him out of their sight. And if Alyce's brother tried to leave the castle, they would send word immediately.

Alyce turned to look in the direction of his men, then toward her brother. The tension returned to her face, and he felt an unfamiliar twisting in his gut.

Was he feeling guilty?

He pushed the thought aside. Cynwulf's troubles were of his own making, and there was nothing he or Alyce could do to save him.

She looked down at her hands as she twisted the end of her braid between her fingers. As though realizing what she was doing, she let go of her hair and stilled her nervous hands. She lifted her chin to look him in the eye. "If you think seducing me will help your mission, you will be sorely disappointed."

"If anything, it will hurt my mission," Hawk said, then sighed. "Yet here I am."

He didn't want her to think he was using her for his own gain. The truth of the matter was seducing her was more dangerous to him than it was to Cynwulf. The more time he spent with Alyce, the harder it was for him to remain objective about what he must do to complete his mission. He had wracked his brain trying to determine if there was a way to save Cynwulf, but he knew it was too late. What Hunter had heard when he followed him to his clandestine meeting in the Welsh forest was incriminating enough to get him hanged as a traitor.

Still, Hawk felt like his insides were being gnawed by rats every time he thought about what it would do to Alyce to see her brother arrested and punished.

"I have no power to hurt your mission," she said. The warrior goddess he'd seen only a few moments before was retreating, her face becoming guarded as she shrank away from him.

He wasn't ready for her to go. "That's not true. You have the power to bring me to my knees."

She didn't say anything for a long moment while she stared at him. Her expression was bland, unreadable, and Hawk feared he had offended her with his unexpected honesty. Hell, he'd even surprised himself with his honesty.

"You shouldn't say that, Hawk." Her tone was so soft he almost didn't hear her over the singing of the bard and the murmuring of the crowd. "I might believe you."

There was a vulnerability in the way her brows drew together, creating a small crease in her forehead that he wanted to soothe with his thumb. At the same time, there was a fire in her eyes that Hawk felt certain was lust.

The hall burst into applause and shouts of appreciation as the bard finished the ballad, the sound startling Alyce. She looked away from him and Hawk cursed silently, thinking he'd lost her.

She pushed away from the wall to step around him in the direction of the doorway, but as she passed by him, the back of her hand brushed against his in what felt like a lingering caress. Hawk felt the blood rush through him, just as it did when he was about to claim victory on the battlefield.

The thought crossed his mind that the touch wasn't intended, a misjudgment when she passed by him. But as he watched her leave, she paused in the doorway and looked back over her shoulder at him before disappearing.

Victory.

There was no misreading the sultry slant to her eyes or the seductive curve of the barely-there smile on her lips. At that moment, he couldn't think of anything sexier or more alluring than shy Lady Alyce giving in to her desires.

Hawk slipped out behind her while the crowd was distracted by the bard as he bowed from his place on top of the table and held out his cap to catch the offerings of tossed coins.

The small corridor to the solar was lit only by the light from the hall, and he could clearly see it was empty. He turned his head to look up the spiraling staircase, and there she was, standing on the second stair, waiting for him.

She continued up the stairs and he followed her until they were out of sight of any prying eyes below. He nearly toppled over when she stopped suddenly, turning into him to wrap her arms around his neck and press her lips to his. She stood one step above him, and Hawk had to tip his head back slightly to deepen the kiss, which he did eagerly.

She pulled back to look into his eyes. "I want just a little while of not thinking about kings, missions, or rebellions. Can you give me that?"

"No, my lady." He kissed her hard to chase away the crestfallen expression on her face. He smiled against her lips, pulled her body against his, and growled, "A little while will not do. I want all night."

Chapter Twenty

ALYCE PULLED ON Hawk's hand and shook her head when he started to lead her down the corridor to his chamber. For a fleeting moment, he thought she had changed her mind and a cold wave of disappointment washed over him. She half-turned back to the spiraling stairs and tipped her head in the direction of the rooms above.

He obliged, leading her up the stairs to his own chamber. Whatever her reasons, if the lady did not want to bring him to her bed, he would bring her to his. The room was dark when they entered, but he found the thick candle resting on the small table by his bed and brought it to the torch in the corridor to light the wick before replacing it on the table. He closed the door behind them, dropped the wooden slat into the brackets to secure the door, then turned his attention back to Alyce.

She stood facing him, her fingers flexing with nervous energy, looking anywhere but at the bed or at him while she took deep breaths. He stepped closer and placed a finger under her chin to lift her face until her eyes were on him.

"Why are you skittish?" he asked gently.

A nervous ripple of laughter escaped her lips, and her shoulders visibly relaxed. "Is it that apparent?"

He nodded. He wanted to pull her close to him again, reignite the fire in her he felt on the stairs, but his intuition told him to move slowly lest he overwhelm her.

She released a shaky breath. "I have not been alone with a man like this since…Geoffrey." She winced as she said the name of her dead husband, but she did not pull away from Hawk.

"Ah," Hawk said. *Of course.* The widows Hawk knew at court relished the freedom allowed by their status to discretely take lovers who satisfied their desires and whims. But Lady Alyce was not like the women with whom he typically kept company.

Her words from the first time he'd kissed her on the parapet came back to him and he repeated them. "Because your heart is too tender."

She caught his hand as he let it drop from where he touched her chin, folding it in both of hers. "Forget I said that."

He stepped close enough for their bodies to skim against each other and leaned his forehead to hers. "I can do that, but can you?"

"Yes, Hawk." Her eyes were locked with his as she spoke, and he couldn't look away. "I do not want to think about tomorrow, or the day after, or any of the days after. Right now, I only want you to touch me."

A shiver of anticipation rippled down his spine, and before he could think too much about what that meant, he let his hand glide down her sides to the curve of her hips to pull her close. "Ah, my sweet, I plan to touch you in every way possible."

ALYCE FELT HER body becoming less rigid and more pliant with each kiss Hawk placed on her neck, her ears, her face. He lifted the circlet from her hair, the pins and linen scarf coming with it, and tossed it out of the way. Moving behind her, he pulled her hair free of the leather thong tied at the bottom of her braid and ran his fingers through the long strands until they hung loose down her back.

She closed her eyes as he pulled her into him, her back pressed against the solid comfort of his chest as his arms closed around her protectively. He buried his face in her hair, then pushed it aside to run his tongue along the edge of her earlobe.

Lord, she wanted this, wanted to forget about everything else but being a woman in a man's arms. Her head fell back against his shoulder as he kissed and licked and tasted his way down the length of her exposed neck.

He turned her to face him, then slid his hands over her ribs to her arms, which he lifted to his shoulders. She responded by draping them around his neck and pressing the length of her body closer to him, wanting more of his warmth.

Of him.

He groaned, turning his face into her hair. "God, I want you," he murmured.

She felt his hands pulling on the ties of her tunic where it was laced at her sides, then pulled the garment over her head, leaving her in just her thin chemise. Running her hands down his chest to the hem of his tunic, she tugged it upward. He pulled it off in one swift move, along with his shirt, revealing his bared torso. She stood mesmerized for a long moment, running her fingers down the slope of his shoulders to the bulging muscles of his chest, reveling in the softness of his skin when everything underneath it was rock solid.

He inhaled sharply as her fingers skimmed over him, and she looked up at him with a satisfied smile, then returned to her exploration. The dark hair covering his upper chest like a shield was fascinating to her and she fanned her hands over it, surprised by the wonderfully crisp texture. She trailed her fingers down the path of hair to where it tapered over his stomach, enjoying the way gooseflesh rose under her fingers, quivering at her touch.

His hands caught hers before she could loosen his breeches. "Tonight is about you," he said in a low voice that sent shivers over her skin as he walked her backward until her legs bumped against the bed.

He pushed her down to sit on the edge of the bed and then kneeled on the floor in front of her. Alyce tilted her head and quirked an eyebrow at him, which he answered with a devilish grin that set her heart to racing.

He sat back on his heels, pulled her foot into his lap to re-move her shoe, then did the same with the other. With both of her feet resting on his bent legs, he slid his fingers over her ankles to circle her calves, then higher until his hands were hooked behind her knees.

She swallowed hard as her skin reacted to his touch, the quivering sensations sending pulses of warmth and pleasure to her core. He pushed her chemise up over her knees, then cupped his hands on the back of her thighs to gently ease them apart, coming to his knees as he pressed his body between her legs and wrapped his arms around her waist.

She slid her hands around to his back to pull him into her, wanting him close to her, his body solid against hers, to keep her from thinking about anything else. She inhaled the musky scent of his skin and grazed her lips over the sharp edge of his collarbone, her tongue tasting the tang of sweat and linen and something that was uniquely Hawk.

The cool air of the room touched the skin at her shoulders, and she realized he had undone the ties at the back of her chemise and was gently pushing it down her arms. He stopped, looking at her intently as though seeking her permission before he undressed her further.

That he would care enough to gain her approval sent a jolt of adrenaline rushing through her. She nodded eagerly, reaching for his breeches, desperate for every part of their bodies to be unhindered and pressed together.

Again, he caught her hands, a deep laugh rumbling through her chest. "I said tonight was for you and I meant it." He freed her arms from her chemise then placed her hands back on his shoulders as he wrapped an arm around her waist and splayed the fingers of his other hand over her stomach. He buried his face in the crook of her neck, scorching her skin as his lips traced a path down her neck.

His thumb brushed the undersides of her breasts, and they swelled in anticipation, wanting more of his touch. He nipped at a sensitive spot at the base of her throat, driving her mad, teasing her when she wanted more. She felt restless, her hands moving anxiously against his shoulders and neck, unable to receive without giving something back in return.

Her breath caught as his hand finally closed over her breast, the callouses on his warm fingers and palm causing friction against her nipple that was unexpectedly intense. Before she could fully analyze the way her body was reacting to his touch, his mouth closed over her other breast, his tongue brushing against her in a wonderfully erotic pattern.

"Oh," was all she could manage to say, arching into him for more. Heat swirled through her body like liquid gold, pooling at her core until she ached with her want of him. Her hands stroked up his neck into his hair and she tugged at his head until he relented and brought his mouth to hers.

A soft moan escaped her lips as she sighed into the kiss, and he rewarded her with a lustful growl of his own. She tried to scoot back on the bed, pulling him with her, but he stopped her with another growl and a shake of his head.

"You—" he whispered into her ear—"need to learn—" he kissed her just behind her jaw, lingering there until she squirmed—"to let others—" he skimmed his lips down her throat while he pushed her back into the bedding—"give you pleasure—" he nuzzled her between the mounds of her breasts, then circled his tongue around one taught nipple—"while you do nothing—" he kissed a path down her stomach then dipped his tongue into her navel—"but enjoy it."

Relinquishing control made her feel vulnerable and…guilty? She was a pleaser and a giver in all areas of her life. She didn't know how to let others do for her.

"We can enjoy each other together," she said breathlessly, watching as he sat back on his heels again to shimmy the chemise over her hips and down her legs until it could be tossed to the side, leaving her completely bared to him.

"No," he said in gentle rebuke.

"No?" Alyce asked pushing up on her elbows. She tried to calm her erratic breathing, but her nerves would not settle. She was splayed out before him with every part of her exposed to his gaze.

He grabbed her leg by the ankle and lifted it to his shoulder, turning to trail kisses along the side of her knee. "Not in the way you are suggesting." He grabbed her other ankle and lifted that leg to his shoulder, placing hot kisses on the sensitive skin just above her knee on the inside of her thigh.

"You are going to enjoy receiving pleasure," he murmured, his kisses trailing up the inside of her leg.

Alyce felt the heat rush to her face, and she tried to squirm as he moved closer to the apex of her thighs. His hands slid along the outside of her legs until he reached her hips, which he grasped to hold her still.

"And I—" he nuzzled the soft curls between her legs with his nose—"will enjoy giving you that pleasure."

"You will?" Alyce squeaked, swallowing hard.

"Oh, yes."

He kept his wicked gleam focused on her face, watching her as he licked, long and slow, along her wet folds. Her eyes fluttered and her core pulsed at the glorious sensation. He kept his gaze locked with hers as he repeated the motion, but it was too intense for her, too intimate to have her eyes locked with his while he made her feel so wickedly wonderful.

"That's it, love," he praised as she dropped her head back onto the bed and buried her hands in her hair. His tongue found the sensitive bud nestled below the curls and he proceeded to torment her there, tongue spiraling, teeth nipping, mouth sucking, until she was gasping. She arched against him, her hands grabbing the bedding at her sides, and begged him not to stop.

"Not a chance," Hawk said, releasing her hips with one hand to bring his thumb to the sensitive spot where his tongue had just been, continuing to rub slow circles while he pressed his tongue deep inside her. His hand applied pressure to her mons as his tongue caressed deeper and she felt her core start to quiver with the exquisite pressure building inside her.

It was the most amazing feeling Alyce had ever experienced in her life and she didn't want it to ever stop. She buried her hands in Hawk's hair, holding him to her as he pushed her over the edge, and she exploded into a thousand shards of shimmering light.

Even then, Hawk didn't stop pleasuring her. He licked and

caressed until the last ripple of rapture was complete.

When it was over and she could breathe again, Alyce lay panting and dazed, but once she was able to catch her breath, she started to laugh. Hawk let her legs slide down from his shoulders, then sat up on his knees so that he could lean over her on the bed with his elbows resting on either side of her body. He kissed her stomach where it still vibrated and quivered from her erratic breathing. "I hope that is a good laugh or my pride will never recover."

She smiled down at him. "I understand now what Gertie and Edna mean when they talk about their toes curling."

Hawk's lips moved into an arrogant smirk of satisfaction as he playfully nipped her side, eliciting a small squeal from her. "My pride is restored." He laid his cheek against her stomach and Alyce brushed a hand through his hair as he closed his eyes, resting against her.

She was relieved he wasn't looking at her because she needed a moment to clear her head. This had been, unexpectedly, the most wonderous night of her life—not just because of the way her body responded to Hawk, but because of the intensity of her response. Every time he looked into her eyes while he was touching her body, bringing her pleasure, she felt like she was losing another part of herself to him.

She had wanted this, wanted to forget everything else happening around her. She had thought herself capable of taking her pleasure and then putting it behind her as nothing more than an enjoyable diversion and a pleasant memory. The pounding of her heart and the intense emotion clogging her throat were proof that she was capable of no such thing. She'd lied to Hawk and to herself when she said her heart wasn't too tender.

Just as she was wracking her brain for an excuse to get out from under Hawk and leave while she still had some hold on her breaking heart, a loud pounding rattled the door to the chamber.

Chapter Twenty-One

HAWK PUSHED TO his feet at the first knock on the door, already reaching for his sword when he heard Red call his name.

"Aye," Hawk called, relaxing his stance, turning back to Alyce. She was already picking her chemise off the floor and shaking it out to pull over her head. He felt a moment of loss as the material covered the golden glow of her naked body in the candlelight.

He lifted the slat from the door and opened it wide enough to slip through, ignoring Red's unspoken suspicion in his eyes as he emerged shirtless, quickly closing the door behind him. Fortunately for Red, he was wise enough to say nothing.

"What is it?" Hawk grumbled.

"He's left the castle."

"Fuck," Hawk muttered. "Hunter is on his trail?"

Red nodded. "He left through the postern gate and disappeared into the woods, but we saw which direction he went. Hunter will have him in sight before he clears the first hill."

"Meet me at the postern gate. I'll be there shortly," Hawk said, his hand already on the door handle.

Red looked him up and down with a smirk then turned on his heel, the sound of his laughter echoing against the stones of the corridor.

Hawk returned to the chamber to find Alyce pulling the laces of her tunic tight and tying them at her waist. He found his shirt and tunic in a wad on the floor and hastily pulled them on. Parting with a woman after an intimate encounter was always awkward, but he was finding this one particularly so: first because he was leaving her to track down her brother and likely arrest him; second because he needed time away from her to focus on something other than the way her scent and the feel of her overwhelmed him in a way wholly unfamiliar to him.

But he wasn't so callous as to leave her without acknowledging what they'd just shared. He looped his belt around his waist, the scabbard hanging empty at his side, then turned to Alyce, trying to find the right words to say.

She sat on the bed pulling on her shoes, then stood and faced him. "What did Red come to tell you?" she asked, her voice tight.

"I think you know already." He spoke gently, knowing his words would hit hard. He stepped closer to her and put his hands on her arms, dipping his head to look her in the eye. She met his gaze, and he could see the fear and sadness in the set of her brows and mouth.

"Stay here. Let me take care of this," he urged.

When she said nothing in response, her eyes darting to the side, he put a finger under her chin and nudged her face toward him, forcing her to meet his gaze. "Alyce, it's not safe for you to leave here. Promise me you will go straight to your chamber and stay there until I return."

She jerked her head away from his hand as she nodded, but he didn't trust that she would do as she agreed.

"I need to know you will be safe." There was a desperation in his voice he had not intended, but it was sincere. He could not concentrate on what he had to do if he thought she was in any danger. He put a finger under her chin and gently turned her toward him again. When she didn't resist, he lowered his mouth to hers and kissed her. Her lips softened at his touch, making his body hot with desire for her, but her body was strung tighter than a bow.

When he reluctantly pulled away, Alyce held his gaze for a breath, then swallowed hard. "I'm not yours to keep safe. We called a truce for a short interlude, but it is over, and now we go back to the way we were."

Her words hit him like a punch to the gut.

She was right.

They weren't on the same side when it came to her brother. His job was to hunt Cynwulf down and bring him and the evidence before the king for judgment. When his job was complete, she would hate him for an outcome that was not his making.

Frustrated, he turned away from her, picked up his sword and sheathed it at his side, then held the door open for her. He could feel the anger radiating from her as she left the chamber, her feet moving in fast strides down the corridor. He was close behind her as she trotted quickly down the stairs, close enough to grab her arm and escort her to her chamber himself if need be.

To his surprise, she stepped out of the spiraling stairwell and walked briskly to her chamber, opening the door, slipping inside, and closing it without once looking back at him. He stood on the step, watching her door until he heard the wood slat sliding into the brackets to secure the door against intruders.

He doubted it would do little to keep her from leaving the moment she thought he was gone. His only comfort was the knowledge she likely lacked the tracking skills necessary to follow him. With a little bit of luck, they would be long gone by the time she found her way out of the castle.

The hall was packed with bodies wrapped in cloaks and stretched out on the floor, on benches, and even on the trestle tables. The torches had nearly burned out, and Hawk had to be careful not to step on anyone as he picked his way across the room. Once outside, he found his way to the kitchens, which stood no more than thirty paces from the keep.

The moon was still high enough overhead to provide some light in the deserted yard of the keep. Hawk peered up at the castle wall, but the guards there were looking outward, not inward, and took no notice of him as he crossed to the squat brick building belonging to the cook. Once there, he slipped into the shadows, ignoring the rumble of his stomach as the lingering aroma created by years of roasting meats and boiling stews floated to his nose.

Behind the kitchens was a secluded stretch of the stone wall, overgrown with foliage, but he and his men had discovered the concealed gate within two days of coming to Hawkspur. He worked his fingers along the wall beneath the vines until he felt smooth, flat wood among the rough stones. The curtain of vines pushed easily to the side, and he pulled on a leather strap looped through holes bored in the wood, opening the small postern door with hardly a squeak.

Red was already on the other side of the gate, his back pressed to the stones of the outer wall, waiting for him. He closed the gate behind him and followed Red as he hunched over to blend with the slope and began making his way quietly to the forest edge. Once among the trees, both men stretched to their full height and picked up the pace, following the markers Hunter left behind as he'd followed Cynwulf.

Even without the purposefully bent branches Hunter had left in his wake, Hawk and Red would have little difficulty finding Cynwulf's trail. In the moonlight, they could see where a trail was worn into the forest floor, narrow enough to be mistaken for nothing more than a deer path.

After some time, they crossed over a narrow stream and Hawk noticed the terrain getting rockier, the forest more dense. They followed the trail as it descended between two stony hills on either side. The temperature seemed to drop as the wind picked up speed, rustling the leaves overhead. Hawk slowed his pace, holding a hand up to Red to be alert. He stopped, letting his eyes adjust as more of the moonlight was blocked out by the proximity of the hill and the thickening canopy of the trees.

Hunter slowly emerged from the brush to stand on the trail a short distance in front of him, then disappeared back into the cover of the forest. Hawk and Red left the trail to slip quietly through the trees, stopping only when Hunter did.

"He waits below an outcropping at the base of the hill," Hunter relayed. "He's waiting for someone."

"Does he have anything with him?" Hawk asked. "Is this a

rendezvous, or is he trying to escape?"

"Doesn't look like he's planning to go anywhere, unless who-ever he's waiting for has what he needs."

There might be time to save him.

Hawk shook his head to rid it of the lunacy circling around in his mind. Thoughts like these were why men who lived their lives by the sword did not let any one woman occupy their minds. He should have been thinking about doing the job the king asked him to do, of finding the traitor and bringing him to justice. Not about whether he could intervene before Cynwulf completed his rendezvous and incriminated himself further. Thwarting him served Alyce and nobody else. She would be spared pain, but who would be hurt in the ambushes and battles caused by her brother's disloyalty?

The only option was to catch Cynwulf in the act of betraying the crown and bring him back to face the king. They already had enough evidence to prove Cynwulf's guilt with the messages they'd intercepted, and the meeting Hunter witnessed on the return from Shrewsbury.

The bigger concern, Hawk decided, was the fact that Alyce was influencing his own actions, which meant it might be too late for him. He was more worried about protecting her feelings than he was about protecting his own hide. If the king got wind that Hawk did anything to interfere with the mission, especially for a woman, the punishment would be harsh and undoubtedly painful.

"Fuck," he muttered to himself as the realization came to him that he would be willing to take the punishment if it meant sparing Alyce from seeing her brother hanged as a traitor.

Both Red and Hunter looked at him warily. The men had been his top commanders and closest confidants through years of battles, missions, and tavern brawls. They knew him better than anyone, and Hawk could tell from their expressions they could see that he was tormented. Red, of course, knew why.

He sighed, then gave his directives. "We will wait and listen, find out what he knows and who he meets, then we take Cynwulf and whoever he's meeting. We capture or we kill, but no one escapes."

"I'll take Cynwulf," Red offered, and Hawk knew he did it to prevent him from having to kill Alyce's brother, should things go wrong. But it would make no difference to her—if Cynwulf tried to escape and was killed in the melee, whether it was at the hands of Red or Hawk wouldn't change the outcome.

"Let's avoid bloodshed if we can," Hawk said. "I'd rather bring the king talking prisoners than silent corpses. Lead the way, Hunter."

Hunter pointed straight ahead. "The outcrop is there, Cynwulf is below it. We can jump down from there to the ground, surrounding them when the time is right." He smirked and shrugged. "As long as there aren't too many."

If Cynwulf were joining up with a large group, he would be going to them instead of waiting for them to come to him. This appeared to be a pre-arranged meeting to exchange information, and for the sake of covertness, the fewer people involved meant less chance of being caught. Hawk expected two or three men at the most.

They followed Hunter through the trees until he motioned for them to drop to the ground and crawl the distance to the edge of the outcropping. The underbrush extended nearly as far as the outcropping, providing cover from anyone looking up from the trail below. As they neared the edge, they could clearly hear tense voices rising from lower down. There was a small clearing extending beyond the shadow of the outcropping where the moon was able to shine through, revealing the men below.

"I sent a messenger the moment I knew the king was coming to Hawkspur." Cynwulf was trying to keep his voice low, but his anger was apparent.

"He never arrived," the other man snapped. He was hidden by the shadow of the overhang, but by his voice, Hawk guessed him to be an older man. "Daffydd heard the news from a traveler."

"I didn't know that until your messenger arrived today— which was stupid of you. Are you trying to get us all killed?"

"Watch your tone with me," the older man said, his voice

harsh with rebuke.

Hawk knew about the messenger dispatched by Cynwulf because his men had intercepted him. The boy was given enough gold to hop a boat to Ireland and a warning, to stay out of sight and with his mouth shut.

"Cynwulf?"

Hawk felt the blood in his veins turn to ice.

"What is this?" a woman asked.

Hawk groaned inwardly at the sound of Alyce's voice. How the hell had she found them?

He pushed to his feet as he heard the sounds of a scuffle below and jumped over the edge of the outcropping before he had time to think of a plan.

He heard a snarl as he landed on the ground with his sword drawn and a scream tore through the night. A man had emerged from the trees behind Alyce, knife in hand. Ffyddlon jumped at him, gnashing her teeth, but the older man had thrown his knife, catching the hound in her shoulder as she charged headlong at the threat to her mistress.

Ffyddlon fell to the ground with a yelp as a burly man grabbed Alyce from behind and pushed a knife to her throat. He had a puckered scar running over the socket where his right eye should have been. The scar was wide enough to see clearly in the moonlight where it slashed through an eyebrow and disappeared under the hair hanging over his forehead. His functioning eye and the top half of his face were visible over the top of Alyce's head. He was a tall man, but Hawk assessed him to be slow, his excessive bulk too cumbersome for swift movement.

Red dropped to the ground next to Hawk, axe in hand, and moved to Cynwulf's side, ready to pounce should anyone try to escape. Hawk nudged the tip of his sword into the back of the older man. "Let her go," he said to Scar, "or I'll skewer your friend."

He kept his focus on the man behind Alyce, knowing he would lose his ability to think if he looked at her and saw the fear on her face. Out of the corner of his eyes, he could see the dog in a lifeless heap at Alyce's feet, and worse, he could hear her devastated sobs as she squirmed to break free from the man's hold, desperate to get to Ffyddlon.

"I'm in control here, not you, mate," the scarred man sneered, "and if I don't like what's happening, you'll watch her bleed."

"She has nothing to do with this," Cynwulf said, stepping toward his sister. "Let her go."

Red clapped a heavy hand down on his shoulder to stop him from getting too far out of reach. With his other hand, he held his axe ready to strike the older man, now pinned between the lingering blade of the axe and the point of Hawk's sword.

"If you hurt her, I will tell you nothing," Cynwulf continued. "And Daffydd will want to hear what I have to say."

Hawk was mildly impressed at the calm command in Cynwulf's voice while his sister was in danger. Though it was taking every bit of restraint to keep from charging the man and killing him on the spot for touching Alyce, he let Cynwulf continue his efforts at negotiating. Her brother knew these men, which meant he had the best chance of gaining their cooperation in releasing her.

"Let them both go," the scarred man said to Hawk, pressing the knife tighter to Alyce's throat. A trickle of blood dripped down her neck. "You will come with us, Cynwulf."

Hawk gritted his teeth and glared at the dark, glistening trail sliding slowly down Alyce's neck and staining the edge of her mantel. The man would not live to see the morning light.

"You have nothing to gain by hurting her," Cynwulf said. He shrugged Red's hand off his shoulder and took a small step forward. Red looked to Hawk, and he gave a swift nod, indicating he should let Cynwulf continue.

"Come now, don't do this," Cynwulf said, holding up his hands to show he meant no harm. "Let her go and leave."

A movement behind Alyce and Scar caught Hawk's attention, but he kept his eyes intent on them. Hunter was creeping through the trees towards the man's back, no more than ten paces from his target. They just needed to keep Scar focused on what was in front of him until Hunter could bury his blade in the man's back. Hawk would have preferred to kill the man himself, but getting Alyce away from him was more important than his need to avenge her. Barely.

Another movement deeper in the forest drew Hawk's focus. A form emerged out of the darkness from behind the thick trunk of a tree, and the outline of a bow aimed at Hunter was clear in the moonlight.

"Down!" Hawk bellowed, but Hunter had already sensed the danger and dropped into the cover of the underbrush.

Red dropped to one knee, ducking his head while keeping his axe poised, ready to strike. Scar loosened his grip on Alyce, looking left to right, trying to see what was happening behind him. A loud thwack cut through the air as an arrow hit the trunk of the tree where Hunter had been standing just a heartbeat before.

Taking advantage of the chaos, Hawk dropped his sword, pulling the knife from his belt as he closed the distance between him and Scar in two bounding strides. Scar turned his head from side to side, trying to make sense of the movement all around him. Alyce squirmed in his arms and Scar turned his attention back to her just in time for Hawk's deadly grimace to fill his view as the moonlight glinted off the blade in his upraised hand. He brought the knife down hard, sinking the steel into the depths of the brute's distorted eye socket.

Hawk shoved Alyce out of the man's grip as he screamed in pain and crumpled to the ground; he followed him down, twisting the blade, driving it deeper.

Alyce kneeled over Ffyddlon, seemingly oblivious to the melee around her. Hawk pushed her completely to the ground and crouched over her as another arrow whistled by. It struck the stony face of the hill, splintering into pieces mere feet from Cynwulf.

"Stop, Bran!" Cynwulf yelled over the chaotic din of the fighting. Red and the other man were already on the ground behind him. "Stop!" he yelled again.

Hawk waited for the next arrow to bury itself in Cynwulf's chest, but it never came. Everything was still.

The silence dragged on for several long breaths.

"Claudius?" a voice called from a short distance away, Hawk presumed from Bran. "Did you get what you needed?"

"No," the older man on the ground next to Red called back.

"Stand up, Claudius," another voice called from the forest. "And walk toward us. You, too, Cynwulf."

Hawk saw Red lay his axe on the man's back and heard him mutter. "You're not going anywhere."

He scanned the terrain near him, looking for a downed tree, or anything else that would serve as cover for Alyce. Bowmen had the advantage of distance; their swords were useless unless they could get close.

Meanwhile, Alyce was trying to pull herself free from his grip. He assumed she was trying to get to Cynwulf in some misguided attempt to protect him. He tightened his grip and growled, "Stay down."

Her response was a single word in a strangled whisper. "Ffyddlon."

The desperate sound of that one word cut through him like a knife to the chest, but he couldn't do anything about it at the moment. A glance at the hound lying on the ground with a knife protruding from her shoulder, slick with blood, told Hawk it was already too late.

He released his hold on Alyce anyway so she could stretch her arms over Ffyddlon, but he stayed crouched over her. She put an arm around the dog's chest and pulled her close enough to bury her face in the fur at her neck.

"Claudius!" the voice called again. "Move away from them."

"No!" Cynwulf commanded. "You need me, but I won't come to you until you let my sister go."

"We don't need him," Bran sneered. His voice was closer to them now and Hawk suspected he was looking for Hunter.

"Aye, you do." The muffled words came from Claudius, still pinned to the ground by the threat of Red's axe.

"You'll let them go, or you'll have nothing," Cynwulf said through gritted teeth, and Hawk felt a pang of regret that Cynwulf had been such a fool. He was a traitor to the crown, but he was proving to be braver than expected. "I have information about the king's army that Daffydd needs. Let them leave and take me to him."

Bran emerged into the small clearing by the outcrop, but he was smart enough to keep some distance to retain the advantage. "It's common knowledge that the king is on his way to Hawkspur, so you've got nothing."

"Aye, but I also know the size of his army, where he's going next, and the tactics used by his commanders. I've got my informants and know who along both sides of the border for a fifty-mile range is sympathetic to Daffydd's cause. And I know who will claim to be his ally in this region but will cut him down the moment he turns his back."

The man was either much more resourceful than Hawk gave him credit for, or he was a very good liar. Either way, Hawk just might owe him his life before the night was over.

Alyce lifted her face from Ffyddlon's fur. "No, Cynwulf," she pleaded. "Don't do it."

Her brother didn't look at her but continued his bargaining. Hawk hated to see the disbelief on her face at being ignored, but he knew Cynwulf did it because he loved his sister. If he looked at her and saw the anguish on her face as she held her beloved pet dead in her arms, it would break him.

A small movement in the underbrush by Hawk's feet revealed Hunter lying flat on his stomach, hidden from the view of everyone except him. It never ceased to astonish him that a man as big as Hunter could move through a forest without snapping a twig or rustling a branch.

Hunter held up two fingers and pointed to a spot about halfway up the hill behind Bran, then held up one finger and pointed into the forest behind him. Hawk gave a quick nod, then clenched his teeth in frustration, disliking the odds of getting out of the predicament alive.

Hawk and his men were elite warriors, trained killers who did not back down in the face of adversity. But once a bowman had his target within sight, his arrow aimed and ready, there was little that could be done. In any other situation, the three of them could take down five men in a matter of moments. Any sudden movement now, and they would feel the deadly sting of an arrow.

He had done the worst possible thing a warrior could do and let his heart instead of his head dictate his actions. His men would likely die this night because of his failings. If he had any self-restraint, had thought it through before he jumped down from the outcropping the instant he'd heard Alyce's voice, they wouldn't be in this situation.

His mission was to serve the king, to intercept the flow of intelligence being leaked to Daffydd, and to bring the traitor before the crown for judgment. It had all been at his fingertips, and he'd chosen to protect a woman instead of his king.

He chided himself for wallowing. He needed to devise a plan, figure out a way to save their hides, and get them out of this situation. He turned back to Hunter, who raised a questioning eyebrow at him, waiting for direction.

He should tell Hunter to start killing the bowmen one at a time. He had the stealth to move undetected through the forest, to get behind each man, especially the two standing apart from the others, and slit their throats before they even realized he was near.

Instead, he pointed to Alyce and then pointed in the direction they'd come from, to safety.

Hunter's eyes widened slightly, and for the first time ever, he hesitated before acknowledging his commander's directive. The hesitation was no more than a blink of an eye, but Hawk saw it and felt the disappointment and uncertainty communicated in that small movement.

He also knew Hunter would die protecting Alyce once the fighting started, even if he did not agree with Hawk's decision to put a woman before the mission.

Cynwulf was talking to the bowmen, reminding them of their duty to Daffydd while trying to convince them to take him in return for his sister's life.

"I won't go with you unless I know she can return to Hawkspur safely," Cynwulf called out to the men. He was slowly maneuvering himself into a position that shielded Alyce more from Bran and the two men on the hill. "She needs these men to get her home," he said tipping his head toward Red and Hawk.

"Get the other bowman out of the trees behind us," Hawk muttered in a low tone to Cynwulf.

Red still had Claudius pinned to the ground with the threat of his axe at his back, but his eyes were on the forest beyond Hawk and Alyce, scanning for the fourth bowman.

"The four of you, including Martin—" Cynwulf pointed in the direction of the trees where the lone bowman was concealed—"will back up along the trail there until you get to the bend at the far end of the hill. I'll be right here where you can see me until my sister and her escorts are gone. They have an axe to Claudius's neck, and he will pay the price if you do not comply."

There was a long moment when no one said anything or moved. Hawk scanned the situation, assessing his options. They were completely dependent upon Cynwulf. The clearing below the outcropping was an open target for the men on the hillside, with only a smattering of underbrush for cover. Carefully Hawk shifted to block Alyce as much as possible from the danger of being shot with an arrow. "Slowly, pull your legs up behind me," he whispered to her, thankful when she complied without question.

"Martin," Cynwulf said in a tired voice, "show yourself, or have you forgotten that Claudius is Daffydd's cousin? He'll be none too happy if he doesn't return from this mission alive."

"They are witnesses, Cynwulf," Bran sneered, his arrow aimed in the direction of Red and Claudius.

Hawk saw the other man emerge from the woods behind him. "Your neck is as good as stretched if you let them go," Martin said, his arrow trained on Red.

"My days are numbered already," Cynwulf bit out angrily. "I was fool enough to think I would be the hero, the one to solidify an alliance between Daffydd and Edward, and for that, I will eventually pay with my life."

"Cynwulf, no." Alyce's whimper was full of sorrow, and the sound of it crushed Hawk harder than any boulder. He felt the air leave her lungs and her body sag deeper into the ground under the light pressure of his hand on her back.

He continued to crouch over Alyce, fully aware of the arrows trained on them by the bowmen on the hill. "Tell them to put down their bows," he growled at Cynwulf.

"Stand down," Cynwulf ordered to the bowmen. "Either you let them go and I come with you, or you return to Daffydd empty-handed."

"Just do as he says," Claudius said, the frustration evident in his voice. "Daffydd will not reward you if you come back empty-handed, or if you get us killed."

Hawk watched as the men pointed their bows toward the ground in front of them, though the arrows were still nocked, ready to aim and shoot in the blink of an eye.

"Red," Cynwulf said, not looking at him. "Pull Claudius to his feet and be at the ready. Use him as a shield and move to my side."

Hawk nodded to Red to comply. He kept the blade of the axe to the back of Claudius's neck as they both stood, then grabbed him by the cuff of his shirt and forced him to sidestep until they were both standing next to Cynwulf, creating a larger blockade in front of Alyce and Hawk.

Hawk lifted Alyce by the waist, pulling her to her feet. She protested, refusing to let go of Ffyddlon even while her eyes sought out her brother.

"Go," Hawk growled in a low voice, nudging her in the direction of the forest behind them. "Hunter will help you."

Alyce dropped again to her knees by the hound, her face hard with determination. "I will not leave her or Cynwulf behind."

"She's dead," Hawk said through gritted teeth, "and you will be, too, if you don't get out of here." He grabbed her around the waist again and hauled her up, determined to carry her if she did not cooperate.

"She's not dead! I felt her breath."

Hawk hesitated, knowing Alyce would never value her own life over that of her faithful companion. "I'll come back for her. Go!"

"Wait," Alyce pleaded, digging her feet into the soft ground, and reaching her hand back toward Cynwulf. Hawk stopped, closing his eyes as he cursed. The agony in her plea was too much for him. He kept his arms clenched around her waist but turned her to face her brother.

Cynwulf finally looked at his sister and reached his hand to her. "Alyce, I never meant for this to happen, but you must go."

"You'll come back?" she asked, her voice hoarse. "Tell me you'll come back."

Cynwulf looked at her for a moment, then closed his eyes, as though the sight of her was too overwhelming. "I beg you, Hawk, take her away from here."

Hawk picked Alyce up off her feet, one arm around her waist and the other pinning her arms to her side. She bucked against him, trying to break free as her heels kicked at his legs. He bounded for the trees, trying to ignore Alyce's agonizing sobs as he dragged her away from her brother.

Chapter Twenty-Two

ALYCE COULDN'T CATCH her breath. Panic clenched at her lungs and hummed in her ears.

"Go back, Hawk. You have to save him," she begged when he set her on her feet. "Don't let Cynwulf go with them."

There was no chance of saving him if he left to go to Daffydd. If he stayed, there might be a way to convince the king nothing of consequence had happened. He could still redeem himself. Her head was spinning as she tried to right everything that had gone wrong around her.

"Oh, God—Ffyddlon!" She wrenched free of Hawk's hold and started back toward the clearing. Ffyddlon wasn't dead no matter what Hawk thought; she knew she'd felt her slow, shallow breaths beneath her cheek when she'd laid her cheek against her fur.

Hawk pulled her back, then turned her so she was facing him, digging his fingers painfully into her shoulders.

"Stay put," he commanded.

"I have to go back!" She felt a surge of rage, hot as a flame, rise up inside her. There was too much to lose and she would not let Hawk deter her.

"Don't let her escape," he said, looking over her shoulder as she squirmed to break free. She felt another set of hands clamp onto her elbows as Hawk released her and turned on his heel.

"Quiet," she heard Hunter command from behind her. He

pulled her farther into the woods and the darkness, away from Cynwulf and Ffyddlon.

"No," she heard herself repeating as he led her through the trees, one arm tight around her shoulders and the other clamped around her wrist to keep her from escaping. The fight was draining from her with each step, and she suddenly felt boneless, overwhelmed with despair and hopelessness. She didn't resist when Hunter sat her down on the trunk of a fallen tree.

He kneeled in front of her but kept a tight hold on her shoulders. "Breathe," he said. "Slow breaths."

She hadn't realized she was panting, gasping for air, until Hunter shook her slightly and told her again to breathe. Sucking in a large gulp of air, she forced herself to release it in one long breath. It helped to steady her heaving lungs, but she still felt dizzy, like the ground was moving off-kilter under her feet.

The sound of a branch cracking and feet shuffling in the dirt made her jump.

"That will be Hawk," Hunter said in a low voice.

Alyce closed her eyes and prayed Cynwulf would be with him.

And Ffyddlon.

But the image in her head of Ffyddlon lying on the ground, her shoulder slick with blood made her stomach clench. The sound of her yelp as the knife hit her had been heart-wrenching. She'd hardly had time to be frightened of the man with a knife to her throat; she couldn't stop worrying about Ffyddlon, praying the entire time that she wasn't dead.

She gasped with relief when Hawk appeared over Hunter's shoulder, with Ffyddlon draped in his arms. He set her carefully on the ground at her feet and she dropped to her knees, cradling the hound's head in her hands. In the moonlight, she could see the hilt of the knife sticking out of her shoulder and her gut clenched with fear.

"Ffyddlon," she said, stroking the dog's face. There was blood caked on her side, but a hand on her chest confirmed she was still breathing.

Hawk took out his knife and cut a swath of cloth from the

bottom of his tunic, then squatted. "Hold her head and keep talking to her." In a quick movement, he pulled the blade out and then placed the cloth over the wound, applying pressure to stop the bleeding.

Ffyddlon flinched and whimpered as the knife was removed, but Alyce kept stroking the long, coarse fur on the dog's muzzle to soothe her. She was relieved to see the knife was relatively small as Hawk wiped the flat of the blade against his pants. If the wounds weren't too deep, then Ffyddlon stood a better chance of surviving until they could get her home and have her tended to properly.

"How did you know to come here, Alyce?" Hawk asked. His voice sounded calm as he kept his attention focused on staunching the bleeding from the dog's shoulder, but Alyce sensed his anger in the measured words.

"It is where Cynwulf would bring his paramours when he wanted to be discrete."

Hawk snorted. "And how do you know about it?"

Alyce hesitated. "Geoffrey brought me here."

She shouldn't feel ashamed—Geoffrey had become her husband and it was long ago—but for some inexplicable reason, Hawk seemed incensed by her admission.

"Red," Hawk said in a low voice. "Carry the dog, and let's go."

Alyce reluctantly released Ffyddlon and Red picked the dog up to cradle her in his arms. The cloth Hawk held pressed against the wound didn't look too saturated, and for that, Alyce said a quick prayer of thanks.

Ffyddlon opened her eyes and squirmed in Red's hold, but quickly settled when the movement seemed to hurt her. He had her cradled on her back with her side pressed into his chest so that he could keep pressure on the wound as they walked. Alyce touched her cheek to Ffyddlon's muzzle and stroked her belly as she murmured encouraging words to the dog before Hawk coaxed her away.

Red started through the woods in the direction of Hawkspur, and Hunter nudged her to follow, but she couldn't get her feet to move.

"Cynwulf?" she asked, feeling her throat close around her words. "Where is he?"

"He went with the bowmen," Hawk said in a low voice. "We must go in case any of them circle back."

"He is alive? You didn't hurt him?" She looked intently into Hawk's face, trying to discern if he told her the truth, but it was impossible to see anything other than the outline of his features in the darkness.

"I didn't hurt him," he confirmed, putting a hand on her elbow, guiding her forward.

"Will they hurt him?"

"No," Hawk said. "He is too valuable to them."

Alyce felt relief wash over her, releasing some of the tension in her shoulders and neck. She told herself that if Cynwulf was worth keeping alive, then she would see him again. He would find a way to get back to her, or at least send her word of where he was and how he fared.

She had to believe that was true, or she would not be able to go on.

She took a few unsteady steps before she realized Hawk was no longer at her side. She started to turn, but Hunter stopped her with a firm hand on her arm.

"Hawk!" she called over her shoulder. He was nearly out of sight as his dark form slipped between the trees in the opposite direction.

Hunter tried to urge her forward. "We will get you home safely."

"Where is he going?" she demanded.

When Hunter muttered some nonsense about him coming back soon, she turned, yanking hard on her arm to break free, but his grip was solid.

"Hawk," she cried over her shoulder in desperation. "Hawk! Come back!" He had disappeared into the trees, but she refused to be quiet, despite Hunter's insistence she lower her voice.

Uncontrollable hysteria threatened to choke her, and she couldn't stop herself from screaming. "No! Don't do it, Hawk!"

She pushed against Hunter, desperate to go after Hawk. She had to stop him. He was going to kill her brother, she was certain of it. "Please, Hawk," she begged as she struggled and pulled, but the words were drowned out by her gasping sobs.

Through the blur of tears, she thought she saw a shape take form in the trees where Hawk had disappeared only moments before. She blinked her eyes to clear them, sure she was imagining it, but the shape was still there.

"Hawk," she said, her voice hardly above a whisper.

And then he was there, taking her into his arms and holding her against his chest. She hit his chest with her balled fists even as she pressed her cheek against the solid warmth of him.

"Please, don't kill him," she said as tears streaked down her face. "Let him go. Don't go after him." She was grasping handfuls of his tunic in her hands, looking up into his face now, wanting to hold him close, to deter him from leaving. "I couldn't bear it if you killed him."

She heard him sigh, the force of it rustling her hair. "You're going to be the death of me," he murmured as he tightened one arm around her back and cupped the back of her head with his other hand, pressing her against his shoulder.

"Were you going to kill him? Is that why you were going back?"

"Yes," he admitted, the truth cutting through her heart. She wanted to push away from his, but his arms were suddenly like steel bands, preventing her from putting any space between them.

The memory of the horrible squelching sound of Hawk's knife being stabbed into the man's face flooded her memory. His head was near her ear, and the spray of blood had spurted past her face, splattering against her cheek and neck, feeling like hot embers against her cool skin. Hawk's face looked demonic as he'd pounced on the man.

Then he was crouched over her, the sickening, coppery smell of blood still on his hands, but he was protecting her body with his own as she'd clung to Ffyddlon.

And he was here now, protecting her again.

But it did not banish the memory of the huge man lying in a pool of his own blood with the hilt of a knife protruding from his face. Nausea took hold of her, twisting her gut and forcing the blood to her head in a dizzying rush.

This time when she shoved against Hawk's chest, he released her just enough for her to duck her head to the side and empty the contents of her stomach onto the ground. She stayed bent over, waiting for her stomach to stop heaving, vaguely aware that Hawk had one steadying hand under her shoulder to keep her from pitching forward. With his other hand, he grabbed the curtain of her hair and held it out of the way.

She felt cold once her stomach calmed and the heaving subsided. Her body started to tremble with shivers, and she crossed her arms over herself for warmth. As she stood, Hawk put his hands on her shoulders and dipped his head to look into her face.

"Are you all right?"

Her eyes felt heavy, but she lifted them to look at him. The shivers were increasing, her teeth started to chatter, and her jaw felt too tight to speak. Even if she could open her mouth to say something, she couldn't think of any words. The sound of a whimper filled her ears and for a moment she thought Ffyddlon was crying out for her.

Large hands closed over her shoulders, and she was pulled against the hard wall of Hawk's body. His arms came around her, crushing her to his chest as the pathetic noise from Ffyddlon grew louder.

Only it wasn't Ffyddlon.

She squeezed her eyes shut as her body wracked with tremors and the keening sound grew louder. Vaguely, from far away, she heard a deep murmuring, steady and soothing, the sound enveloping her like a shroud of warm mist.

"You're safe, now."

She felt the words more than she heard them, the sound vibrating against her cheek and ear where they were pressed against Hawk's chest. Slowly, she felt him breaking through the haze that had taken hold of her. She could hardly breathe, he had her cocooned so tightly against him, but she didn't want him to let go. The solid mass of his body against hers and the press of his arms on her back was the protection from the outside world that she needed now more than anything else.

At least until she could calm her mind and put the pieces of her shattering heart back together.

The shaking was starting to subside. Hawk's hold on her loosened slightly, but she wasn't ready for him to let go of her. She curled her arms into her body, turned deeper into his body, and pressed her forehead to his chest. Seeming to sense what she needed, he slid one arm up to circle her shoulders, the other around her waist, holding her to him, giving her his warmth.

"Are you back?" he asked, resting his chin against the top of her head.

"Did I go somewhere?" she asked. She couldn't think of what else to say.

"Aye, you did," he said against her hair.

"I don't know what happened." She sighed heavily. "I've seen blood before, sewn up men wounded in battle. Why was this so hard?"

He stroked a hand over her hair. "Because you've not seen the men get wounded, only after."

She shuddered. "I felt his blood splatter against my face," she said, lifting her hand to wipe at her cheeks.

He released her shoulders and gently pulled her hand away from her face. "I didn't want to kill him until you were well away, but he left me no choice."

"Sir, I'm awaiting your command," Hunter's low voice interrupted. "I need to go now if I am to catch them."

Alyce stiffened in Hawk's embrace, looking up at him, her face felt tight with fear. She desperately wanted Cynwulf to come home, but the reality of his situation was becoming clearer. She would rather her brother escape into Wales than be caught and forced to face the king. She could not bear to see him humiliated and…worse.

She held Hawk's gaze in earnest, watching the muscles of his jaw ripple as his lips tightened into a straight line. She expected him to give the command and felt her heart turning to ice as fear gripped her.

"We return to Hawkspur," he finally said, still looking down at her, and Alyce felt her breath leave her in a rush of relief.

"You know what this means." Red's words were carefully spoken, the gravity of them evident in his tone.

Alyce turned to see him leaning against a tree trunk, her dog still cradled in his arms. Weak as she was, Ffyddlon was gently licking his bearded chin, and he had to keep moving his head to dodge her affectionate tongue.

"Aye, Red," Hawk said angrily. He dropped his arms from Alyce, holding her elbows until she felt steady on her feet.

Hunter, standing near Red, thrust his hand through his hair and turned away.

"It is my order," Hawk growled.

He pulled his tunic over his head, leaving him with only a thin shirt as protection against the night air. The autumn days were still warm, but the night air had become chilled, though not yet cold enough to turn their breath into white puffs of steam.

Alyce started to protest as he slipped the tunic over her head and pulled it down her shoulders, but she could feel the tension coiled in his deliberate, jerky movements, and acquiesced. Then he grabbed her hand and pulled her along behind him as he strode toward Red and Hunter.

He stopped when he was even with his men and leveled his gaze at them. "And my order, alone," he said through gritted teeth. "Your duty is to follow my commands, and the king expects nothing less. Neither of you will be expected to answer for my folly."

Alyce was overwhelmed with relief that Hunter would not track down her brother and bring him back to face the king. But it pained her to see how difficult it was for them to fail in their mission, to know they would be embarrassed in front of their king.

Still, it was a small price to pay, in her mind, for the life of her brother.

✦

Chapter Twenty-Three

"THIS IS MY decision, Hawk, not yours," Alyce insisted, straightening her shoulders. "I will not slip in through a side gate and try to slink to my chamber undetected. I plan to walk through the front gate as Lady of Hawkspur."

The bedraggled group stood at the crest of the final hill, looking down at Hawkspur Castle, its high walls, heavy towers, and sharp corners silhouetted by the first rays of sunlight breaking over the horizon.

Hawk touched his finger cautiously to her neck where the skin had been split by the sharp blade of the brute's knife. "You look a fright, love."

Her face warmed at the endearment that seemed to fall so freely from his lips, especially in earshot of his men. Was it meant only to offer comfort in the wake of a perilous night? Or did he truly feel something for her?

The bigger question was, did she want him to love her? She decided now was not the time to ponder what it all meant when she had only just survived a night with more emotional upheaval than one should ever have to endure in the span of a handful of hours.

"Word will get out that Cynwulf is gone, and when it does, it will be pandemonium." She looked from the castle in the distance to the man standing at her side. The connection between Cynwulf's unease since the arrival of Hawk, his confession of discovering his father's identity, and his desperate actions of the last several days had become clear in the light of the disastrous rendezvous in the forest. "Better that I forestall the rumors that are bound to spread quicker than fire."

"'Tis noble," Hawk said with a slow nod, "but it will not be easy. You are exhausted and blood splattered. Aelwin and his men will want answers, demand to know who did this to you and why. They will be looking for decisive leadership, assurance all will be fine without Cynwulf to lead them."

She breathed in a deep, fortifying breath. How could she explain all the thoughts and decisions that had been swirling in her head during the trek back to Hawkspur? Her whole world had been turned upside down since the last time the sun set over the village and her home. She could either return to the castle and wait meekly for others to determine what happened next or, she could plant her feet, square her shoulders, and lean into the storm that was about to descend upon her home.

Her home.

She had the rule of the Marcher laws to back her claim to Hawkspur, and Isabella Mortimer of Oswestry Castle to hold up as proof a woman could hold a fortress through times of strife. The gossips reveled in telling of Lady Isabella's antics and the bards sang joyfully of her successes in garrisoning her castle and thwarting the Welsh rebels who'd assumed her a weak target.

"In truth," she said, swallowing hard to suppress the impulse to ignore her failings—but she must face them to have any chance of following in the path of Isabella Mortimer. "I am ashamed of how I behaved this night, and how I responded to everything that happened. You witnessed me at my weakest, but I am more than that, and it will not happen again."

"You are loyal to your brother, and you fought to protect him," Hawk said evenly. "There is no shame in fighting to save those you love, even when they are beyond saving. You had a knife to your throat, your life in peril, and the moment you were free, you went to Ffyddlon. You are selfless to the point of being reckless, but you are not weak."

Hawk lifted his hand to smooth over her hair, but she stepped out of his reach to stop him from comforting her. If he touched her, it would be too easy to let him wrap his arms around her and shield her from her challenges while he murmured soothing words into her ear.

She had to boldly face whatever came her way, or forever be at the mercy of the decisions others made for her. Burying her face in Hawk's chest and hiding in the shelter of his arms whenever life became difficult would yield nothing—unless she was willing to be content with floating through life as an aimless vessel, always at the mercy of those who would steer her where they saw fit.

Hawk stood stone still, his arms at his side, looking down at her. There was a flash of something unreadable on his face when she stepped out of his reach before he masked it with a look of indifference as he listened to her. Was it anger? Hurt? Perhaps he was disappointed or thought her foolhardy. She would not try to analyze what he was feeling now; as callous as it felt, her focus had to be solely on what she intended to do.

"Hawkspur is the only home I have left, and those people—" she lifted her chin in the direction of the village sprawled before the castle—"are the only family I have remaining. By rights, Hawkspur belongs to me, and I intend to do whatever it takes to keep it."

Ffyddlon let out a restless whine in Red's arms. All three men had taken it in turns to carry her on the journey home, but she seemed to have a special fondness for the Viking. She ruffled the fur on the dog's side and gave Red an appreciative smile. He had a grin on his face, and Alyce dared to hope he did not think her way of thinking daft.

The small gesture bolstered Alyce's confidence. She turned to see Hunter's reaction, but he was warily scanning the forest behind them. The odd, broody man had been gentle and kind when he tried to calm her after they escaped, but after the terse discussion with Hawk, and his commander's refusal to give him leave to follow Cynwulf, Hunter had hardly looked at her or spoken to her.

She turned to face Hawk again, expecting him to argue

against her decision, but it would not deter her.

He surprised her when he nodded at her once, held out his arm, and said, "Lead the way, my lady."

HAWK, RED, AND Hunter walked side by side behind Alyce as she approached the gate of Hawkspur. He didn't think Alyce had any idea how much strength she would need in order to face the next few days, but he would stand behind her. Not only would she have to convince Aelwin and his men to acknowledge her as their liege with Cynwulf gone, but she also had a king to contend with—a king with a legendary temper.

He followed silently behind her with his men, the message clear. She called to the guard, demanding entrance, and the heavy gate was lifted moments later. As she passed into the courtyard, she ordered one of the guards to find Aelwin and bring him to the barracks, along with any other soldiers not standing guard on the high wall.

Men gawked and openly stared at her as she stated her commands. With leaves and dirt adorning her disheveled hair, a cut along her throat the length of a blade, and dried blood on her face and neck, she looked like a Viking berserker who had defied death and was ready to take on the world.

It was little wonder Red couldn't stop grinning at her.

"Quit mooning at her," Hawk grumbled as men closed in around Alyce, demanding to know what had happened to her and where Cynwulf was. She did not let them deter her from her course, walking with steady determined strides toward the barracks.

"If you don't keep her, I will," the damned Viking said, his tone more cheerful than Hawk liked.

"Are you willing to pay the price in my place for her?" He hadn't meant to snarl at his friend, but his defenses were up. The king would be at Hawkspur Castle by afternoon, and it was only a matter of time before he would have to confess his failings of the last night.

King Edward was not one to brook insubordination lightly, especially from his most trusted knight. His only hope was that saving Edward's life on the battlefield would buy him enough sympathy to keep him from being completely destroyed.

Red cringed. "Thor's thunder, but I do not relish your situation," he said with a shake of his head, his tone serious. After a few more strides, he asked in a low voice, "Do you regret your actions?"

"No," Hawk said with a short, bitter laugh. "But I may be tougher to say the same once Edward is finished with me."

Hunter surprised him by laying his hand on his shoulder. "She best be worth it." He squeezed Hawk's shoulder once, then released it to move to Red's side. "Give me the dog. I'll bring her to the kennel master to be stitched."

"Tell the kennel master to bring her to Alyce's chamber when he's finished," Hawk said, knowing Alyce would never agree to her pet being kept with the other hounds.

Hunter nodded as he took Ffyddlon from Red and started toward the keep.

Aelwin was crossing the bailey in their direction with long quick, strides as the messenger struggled to keep pace with him. When he reached Alyce, she turned to him with a look of relief on her face and placed her hand on his arm. Hawk felt an unfamiliar jab of jealousy in his gut, and he stepped closer to her in a protective gesture that did not go unnoticed by Aelwin.

"I would like to speak with you first," Alyce said, her voice steady, "before I address your men." She gestured toward the side of the barracks building. Cynwulf's second-in-command looked at her suspiciously but complied without question.

"Hawk, please accompany us," she added.

Once they were out of earshot of the other men, with Red glaring threateningly at anyone who tried to come close, Alyce said to Aelwin, "Cynwulf will not be coming back to Hawkspur. You and I must do all we can to protect the castle and the village."

Hawk had not expected her to cut straight to the heart of the matter so abruptly, but he admired her candor.

"Hawk can attest to all that I say." Alyce took a deep, calming breath before she continued. "Cynwulf left with Welsh rebels during the night."

Aelwin looked like someone had struck him on the head with an iron cask. His eyes were bulging and blinking at the same time, as though he couldn't focus on what was happening. Based on this genuine shock, Hawk concluded Aelwin was not privy to the actions of his lord and commander.

"I cannot believe that he would willingly leave with Welsh rebels," Aelwin said with bewilderment. "He must have been forced. We must dispatch a patrol of our fastest and best to retrieve him."

Hawk could see in Aelwin's face as he went from disbelief to determination, his mind working to find solutions.

"It is my opinion," Hawk interjected, "that Cynwulf went with them to keep the rebels from coming to Hawkspur. From what he has told Alyce and what we witnessed tonight, your commander did not intend to betray anyone, but he exercised poor judgment and lost control of the situation."

"We do not have time to discuss details," Alyce said evenly, but Hawk could hear the despair in her voice. "The king will be here in a matter of hours, and we must be prepared. I will answer your questions at a later time. For now, what you must know is that Cynwulf..." she paused, swallowed hard, then continued, "has developed a sympathy for Daffydd, Prince Llywelyn's brother, and was coerced into sharing information with the Welsh rebels that he should not have. If he returns to Hawkspur now, he will face the wrath of the king, and cast suspicion upon us all." She swiped harshly at a tear rolling down her cheek and cleared her throat. "I am now Lady of Hawkspur. I will ask you and your men to swear fealty to me. We will do what we must to protect the castle and the people of Hawkspur from the rebels. But first, we must convince the king of our continued loyalty to the crown."

Aelwin contemplated this new information for a long moment, then lifted his face and looked at both of them with sharp, clear eyes. "This is highly unusual, my lady," Aelwin said, his voice shaky. "But Cynwulf has long praised your abilities. He trusted you, and I will do the same."

Alyce released a huff of air and Hawk saw some of the tension release from her shoulders. She had cleared the first obstacle.

They returned to the men gathered in front of the barracks. Alyce walked directly to a bench along the outer wall of the building, studying it as though trying to discern how she could climb atop. Hawk went to her, turned her by her shoulders, then placed both hands on her waist and lifted her to stand on the heavy plank of wood. She tried to smooth her clothing once she was steady on her feet, brushing her hands over the front of her gown. Hawk smiled inwardly at her wasted gesture—there was no saving her clothing.

She stood tall before the men in a filthy gown that could not be smoothed into place, draped in his oversized tunic with the swath cut from the hem for Ffyddlon, and smeared in blood and dirt. She looked more like a London street peasant than a lady of a castle, but Hawk still thought her beautiful.

He forced himself to look away from Alyce and turn toward the gathered men before any of them took notice of the way he stared at her. At least a hundred men stood in the yard before them, their voices growing louder as they became more alarmed by Alyce's state and Cynwulf's absence.

Aelwin raised his hand in a fist and the men reluctantly quieted, turning their attention to him. He still looked too green to be the lead of Cynwulf's army, but Hawk had to admit that his control over his men was admirable. It was the kind of control that came from being respected.

"An incident has occurred resulting in Cynwulf taking his leave of Hawkspur Castle," Alyce said loudly, a slight tremor to her voice.

"Where is he?" someone yelled from the middle of the gathered soldiers.

"Is he alive?" another called out.

Alyce held up her hands to call for silence, and Hawk turned a hard glare on the crowd, his height giving him the advantage of being visible to most of the men. Some of them were looking at

Alyce, but those who were watching Hawk started nudging the others around them and soon the crowd was quiet again.

"Cynwulf is alive," Alyce called out, then dropped her chin to look at the ground. Hawk could see her repeatedly balling and flexing her hands in an attempt to regain her composure. He wanted to reach out to her and encourage her to stay strong, but he would not diminish her authority in that way. His pride in her grew as she sucked in a deep breath, then lifted her head to face the crowd with a look of absolute resolve.

"Cynwulf is alive," she repeated. "He made decisions that he cannot undo, and now he has done what he must to give all of us a chance to prove Hawkspur is still loyal to the crown."

The men broke out in yells of disbelief and denial.

"I have witnesses," Alyce yelled at the top of her voice to the crowd. When the clamor of their voices was reduced to a steady hum of mumbled words, she continued. "I assure you, none of you love and respect my brother more than I, and it is breaking my heart to admit his betrayal, but it is true."

The men appeared stunned, and Hawk could see the gravity of her words sinking in.

"We will continue as we always have," Alyce said, her voice steadier. "We will protect Hawkspur and the village from rebels, and we will protect the border in the name of King Edward. Nothing about your service to Hawkspur or our duty as a Marcher castle has changed, save that Aelwin is now your commander, and you will answer to him." She paused to scan the crowd, meeting the gazes of the men to ensure she had their full attention. "And Aelwin will answer to me as Lady of Hawkspur."

Men started to shift uncomfortably, darting glances at Aelwin to gauge his reaction to the announcement. Hawk balled his fists at his side, ready to beat them all into submission with his bare hands if they did not comply.

"I will remind you," Alyce said loudly, steadying her gaze at the men before her, "I have served as steward of this castle since the day my brother became lord at the passing of our uncle. Cynwulf consulted me in nearly everything, and he depended upon my expertise to manage the stores, oversee the planting and harvesting, negotiate trades, and see to the wellbeing of the villagers. I know all of you, and you know me."

Hawk watched as nigh on all of the men nodded their heads, even if reluctantly. The scales were beginning to tip in her favor, and the esteem they held for the lady might be the key to buying herself the time she needed to prove herself.

Pressing her advantage, Alyce continued, "I know as well as all of you that I am lacking in the art of swordsmanship, the finer points of castle defense, or the strategies of war. For that, I will build a council of trusted advisors, one of whom will be Aelwin."

Murmurs of approval rippled through the crowd.

"Cynwulf relinquished himself to save us. If we stand together, we can protect Hawkspur, your families, and our homes. It is what Cynwulf expects us to do; let us prove his faith in us is well placed."

Hawk turned to look at her as she said the last. He felt a swell of admiration for the lady, standing with her shoulders squared and hands folded clasped in front of her, and thought her as regal and poised as a queen. Her insides were likely churning as she anxiously awaited their response, but on the outside, she was cool and collected.

Aelwin broke the silence. "We are stronger united."

He turned to stand in front of Alyce in her elevated position on the bench and took her hand in both of his to kiss the back of it. Then he knelt to the ground and swore his fealty to her as Lady of Hawkspur, as his liege.

Slowly the men followed their commander's lead, kneeling in a wave that started at the front of the gathered men and continued until the only man left standing was Red, who was watching the whole event from the back of the crowd with that stupid grin on his face. He met Hawk's gaze and nodded his approval.

"Rise," Alyce commanded in a clear voice that carried over the kneeling men. When they stood, facing her again, she added, "Let us not forget in our hearts the good in Cynwulf, but now we must prove Hawkspur is unwavering in its loyalty to England. We will protect the castle and border against the Welsh rebels. We will also protect those of you here who are Welsh and who have sworn your loyalty to Hawkspur, to me, and thus to the crown. Hawkspur is as much your home as ours."

She stood looking over the men for a long moment, then nodded her head once, seemingly finished with her remarks. She reached out her hand, and Hawk took it, ready to assist her to the ground, but she hesitated, then stretched to her full height again.

"Aelwin," she said in a voice loud enough for his men to hear her.

He turned to her immediately. "Aye, my lady?"

"Prepare for the arrival of the King of England."

Chapter Twenty-Four

'TWAS NOT THE flourish of fanfare Alyce expected when King Edward arrived.

Granted, he traveled with an army on the path to war, which did not deter his queen from accompanying him, but the man appeared much less regal in his attire than she expected. Though, his visage left no doubt as to his power and authority.

She'd met the king and queen when her mother was still alive, but that had been many years ago. and she had little recollection of either of them. Whenever Uncle Ranolf was summoned to King Edward's court, Alyce had stayed behind. If different circumstances had brought the king and queen to Hawkspur now, she would have been elated by the honor of meeting them and would have reveled in all the pomp and finery of their court. Instead, her heart was in her throat, and she regarded the king and queen with wary eyes.

King Edward stood nearly a head taller than the men who flanked him as they entered the great hall, his lion's mane of golden hair fluttering over his shoulders as he walked with quick, determined strides. A long, straight nose and high forehead gave his face a narrower appearance than was usual, and he had a slight droop to his left eyelid, but neither detracted from the regal elegance of his handsomeness. The worn hilt of a well-made sword protruded from a scabbard hanging on a thick leather belt at his waist. His tunic and hose were of dark, sturdy material, his boots practical. This was not a king to give orders from afar or to use royal privilege to avoid the fray of battle.

The queen, by contrast, was dressed exquisitely in a long, crimson tunic of fine wool, trimmed in dark sable at the shoulders and adorned with pearls sewn at the neckline. The linen chemise under the tunic was dyed a rich golden-yellow, with the sleeves laced tight, accentuating her long, slender arms. The queen was taller than her attending women, and her features were delicate and graceful. She had a stunningly beautiful face with skin like honey, dark lashes, and high cheekbones that defied her age. After nearly thirty years of marriage, birthing a dozen children, and burying six of them, Queen Eleanor was a force in her own right.

No less than ten ladies hovered behind the king and queen, along with scores of knights standing alert behind the royal pair. The queen was known for staying at her husband's side in all things, but Alyce wondered if the ladies would follow the king and his knights all the way to the front lines of the battle in their fine dresses and elegant jewels, or if the ladies planned to remain at Hawkspur, forcing her to keep them entertained.

Hawk had expressed admiration for King Edward of England, and after a short time in his presence, Alyce understood why. This was a man who commanded respect, and those around him seemed to give it to him freely. The men who surrounded him were watching his every move, awaiting even the smallest of his dictates. All stood proudly attentive and protective of their leader, like a pack of wolfhounds unconditionally loyal to their beloved master.

Alyce stood on the dais, her knees quaking beneath her tunic and chemise as the king and queen approached. The heavy chairs from Cynwulf's solar had been placed in the center of the platform on a thick rug. Hawk stood in front of the dais, stepping forward to guide the king and queen to their seats. The king waited for the queen to sit comfortably, then turned to face the hall with Hawk at his side, standing nearly as tall as his sovereign. As regal as the king appeared, he paled in her eyes when next to Hawk—despite the deep lines of tension in his forehead.

She wondered if Hawk felt as she did: jittering from lack of sleep, overwhelmed with the desire to have this day over, and dreading the king's response to the news Cynwulf defected across the border to join Daffydd.

When Hawk motioned her to come forward, she moved to stand directly in front of the king and queen, then dropped into a deep curtsy, bowing her head low. Unaccustomed to wearing a full wimple and veil, which pinched against her throat and jaw from being wound tightly around her head and neck, she winced as the silk scraped across the tender scab on her neck as her head bowed. Edna had insisted propriety called for her to wear it, and despite loathing the confinement, she was grateful for the concealment of the bruises and cuts she had sustained during the night.

"Rise, Lady Alyce." The deep timbre of the king's voice resonated with authority in spite of a slight lisp that made the end of her name sound more like a hiss.

Alyce rose and lifted her gaze to the king, hands clasped in front of her. When the king did not speak immediately, she stole a glance at Hawk for guidance. He looked haggard with dark circles under his eyes, and she longed to touch him to soothe away his troubles. She suspected she looked just as haggard and exhausted as he.

"I knew Lord Chetwynd, the elder. He was a fine man, well-respected." The king's deep voice brought her attention back to him.

Alyce nodded. "Thank you, Sire. My uncle held you in the highest regard."

"You are a widow." The king made it sound more like a statement than a question.

"Aye," she responded, keeping her voice as neutral as the king's had been. "More than a year hence."

"Our deepest condolences for your loss, Lady Alyce."

"Thank you, Sire," Alyce said, affecting another curtsy to show her gratitude for his concern.

"I understand Cynwulf is not in residence at Hawkspur."

Alyce did not know how to respond or how much to say with so many people gathered in the hall. She nodded once and lowered her gaze to the floor in front of the king's boots.

"Hawk has yet to give me the details," the king continued, a hint of irritation in his voice, "but he assures me all will be explained once we are settled."

She had passed a line of royal servants carrying an abundance of trunks up the winding tower stairs. Edna and Gertie had prepared Cynwulf's chamber for the royal couple, with the expectation that the queen's maids would occupy Alyce's chamber. Red had been kind enough to surrender his room on the upper floor to Alyce, and Ffyddlon was promptly moved to the chamber along with her belongings.

"I will instruct the kitchen to bring wine and something to eat while you wait, Sire," Alyce said remembering her obligation as host, and lady of the castle.

"Do not trouble yourself, Lady Alyce."

Alyce looked to Queen Eleanor, surprised by the sweet tenor of her voice.

"My kitchen staff travels with us, and they will be here shortly with refreshments. If you will be so kind as to allow us an hour of respite in your hall while we wait for the chambers above to be prepared to my liking, I would be so very grateful."

"Of course, Your Majesty," Alyce said with another curtsy. It occurred to her that she didn't know if she should curtsy every time she addressed the queen, or only when she entered or left the king and queen's presence.

"You may leave us now," Queen Eleanor said, not unkindly. "But we do insist you join us for the evening meal." She tipped her head slightly to the side and narrowed her eyes at Alyce. "I knew your dear mother well. You resemble her. It will gladden my heart for us to have a visit and be reminded of her."

"Of course, Your Majesty." Alyce was beginning to feel foolish with all of the bobbing up and down, but she didn't know what else to do. She curtsied to the king, again to the queen, and backed away until she could step down from the dais.

She exited the hall through the back, eager to escape to her chamber. She started up the spiral staircase, then stopped and turned back to stand in front of the door to Cynwulf's solar.

"'Tis mine now," she corrected herself in a quiet voice as she pushed open the wooden door to the empty chamber, the realization that nothing was Cynwulf's anymore cutting through her and taking her breath away.

HAWK FOUND HER in the solar a short while later. He knocked lightly on the door and then pushed it open to reveal Alyce sitting by the hearth, staring so intently at the fire that she did not hear him enter.

His instinct was to go to her, lift her out of the chair, then gather her in his arms to cradle her on his lap while he soothed the tension from her shoulders. Had it really been only yestereve that she lay across his bed, her soft curves in his hands, the taste of her on his lips and tongue? He wanted to taste her again.

He cleared his throat instead, not wanting to startle her, but she jumped to her feet at the sound anyway.

"The king has requested the use of the solar," he told her.

"Of course." She looked around the room. More chairs had been brought down from the upper chambers to replace the two largest that had been moved to the hall for the king and queen. She started toward the door, then stopped just before the threshold.

Turning to look at him she asked, "I am to leave, correct?"

"Aye," Hawk said, trying to keep the strain from his voice, but she cocked her head slightly to the side in question.

"Are you to stay?" she asked tentatively.

"Aye," he said again, not wanting to elaborate.

"Will you tell him of Cynwulf?"

He nodded. He would not lie to the king; he would tell him everything as it happened, and the part he played in letting Cynwulf escape.

"Then should I not stay? This is as much my problem as it is yours." She looked at him so earnestly that Hawk felt his resolve slipping.

He shook his head at her. "Not for this, my lady. He will

summon you when he is ready."

She crossed to him and placed her hand gently on his arm. "Will he punish us for what Cynwulf has done?"

He cupped her cheek in his hand and shook his head. He would give his life if that's what it took to ensure no harm came to Alyce. "He will not punish you or anyone at Hawkspur. Cynwulf acted alone; I will make the king understand that."

"I so wish none of this had happened, that everything could go back to the way it was." She pressed her cheek harder into the palm of his hand. "But I am grateful it is you the king sent, and I will forever be indebted to you for your kindness and mercy."

Hawk had never been known for kindness and mercy. It was why the king favored him above all others. He always fulfilled his mission, killed, or captured his prey, and ensured the king got whatever he wanted. He had his moral limits, but they were few and rarely posed a problem when it came to the men he was hired to bring to justice.

Kindness and mercy were the downfall of men like him.

He should hate Alyce for muddling his judgment, resent her for cutting him low with the way she looked at him so intently and openly. She made him want to peel open his chest and give her his heart and soul. The worst of it was, he didn't realize it was happening until it was too late, and he had done something irrevocable because it spared her from some measure of distress.

To keep her from being in any more pain than she already was, he allowed her brother, a traitor to his king, to escape.

He only had himself to blame for letting his guard down and falling victim to a curse as old as time: the desire for a lady—a lady not meant for a man like him. He was base born, a warrior, destined to die by the sword.

He looked down into her eyes, so full of tenderness, and the curve of her lips within reach of his. It was more than he could resist. He wanted to taste her again, to lose himself in her sweetness one last time before the king dismissed him from his failed mission at Hawkspur.

One more time before Alyce realized she was now a lady of importance and sought a man of equal importance.

He bent his head to hers, hesitating for a breath to allow her to pull away from him if she did not want his kiss. To his relief, she tilted her face up and gently touched her lips to his. It was like succor from a tempest as he cradled her face, deepened the kiss, and breathed the essence of her into his soul.

He wanted to pull her into him, feel the press of her body against his, and lose himself in her, but he stopped before he lost control.

"Edward will be here soon," he said with a sigh, resting his forehead on hers. "I need you to go."

"Let me stay," she said, her brilliant blue eyes boring through him. "I can explain that it wasn't your fault Cynwulf left. It was mine."

Hawk lifted his head from hers, meeting her earnest gaze as he held her face cradled between his hands. "No. I will do this alone. I ask you to trust me in this and take your leave before the king gets here."

She nodded reluctantly as he kissed her forehead, released her, and nudged her toward the door.

He had no desire for her to be witness to his humiliation.

Chapter Twenty-Five

ALYCE EMERGED FROM the squat stone building that served as the kitchen for the fortress and saw Hawk crossing the bailey with a stern look on his face. The king walked before him. Red and Hunter walked on either side of him and a contingent of the king's guardsmen behind them. Hawk's men fell into place to follow the procession as they crossed the courtyard in the direction of the training field.

She had much to do and a castle to prepare for the winter, but she followed behind the men, uneasy and curious as to what was happening.

As they reached the field, the king stopped near a sturdy fence separating training areas. Alyce stopped in the shadow of a tree, watching perplexedly as Hawk stripped his tunic and shirt from his torso and stepped up to put his hands on the top rung of the fence. Two of the guards bound his hands to the plank of wood while another man emerged, carrying a switch made up of several stripped willow branches tied together at the base. Red, Hunter, and the rest of Hawk's elite force stood in formation on the other side of the fence, facing him.

She realized with horror what was about to take place and her knees weakened while her stomach dropped. "No!" Alyce gasped, taking several quick steps toward him, but then stopped in her tracks, unsure what to do.

This couldn't be what it looked like. Hawk was the king's

most favored knight, a warrior of unparalleled legend, and commander of an elite army. The king couldn't possibly mean to do something this brutal to him.

The king had swiveled at her exclamation and saw her standing a mere stone's throw away. He raised an eyebrow and then crooked one finger at her in command to come near.

Her legs felt numb, her feet like they were mired in mud, but somehow she managed to obey the king's command, walking to him on shaky legs.

"Lady Alyce," the king said in a commanding tone once she stood facing him. "Sir Grogan has explained what transpired with Cynwulf this past night."

Alyce said nothing as she dug her fingernails into her palms to keep her focus.

"Cynwulf betrayed the crown, and when he is caught, he will be punished." The king's face was stern, and he spoke matter-of-factly. "I have been told you proclaim yourself Lady of Hawkspur in his place."

"Yes, Sire," Alyce said. Her voice shook along with her nerve, but she did not shrink away from the king. She swallowed hard, and added as an explanation, "Hawkspur was built by my father's brother. I am the last of his kin, and heir after my brother."

It took every bit of her strength to face the king while doubt was suffocating her. She thought about Aelwin, Edna, Gertie, and the people in the village who were counting on her. What would happen to them if she failed?

"By Marcher customs," the king said, the disdain in his voice evident as he studied her, "Hawkspur can pass from your brother to you as the next heir in line."

Alyce raised her eyes slightly and nodded, knowing more was to come.

"I am faced with a predicament, Lady Alyce. 'Tis a dangerous time for Hawkspur to be without a strong lord to deter Welsh rebels. Cynwulf has turned traitor and, according to English law, forfeited his castle." He rubbed his short red beard, contemplating. "I cannot countenance his actions by rewarding you with the castle until I have proof of your loyalty and ability. Marcher customs will not stop me from protecting England, and your brother has proven a threat and jeopardized the safety of every life at Hawkspur."

Alyce could not stop herself from jerking her head up with indignation, mouth open to protest. Her uncle had served at the king's side in the Crusades; surely he did not doubt his loyalty. She started to say so but snapped her mouth shut before she angered him further.

Edward held his hand up to stop her from saying more. "Only a fool would allow the family of a traitor to the crown to hold a marcher castle without taking measures to ensure its stability."

"I am your servant, my lord," Alyce said with resignation, "and will abide by your wishes."

"And do you wish to keep Hawkspur as your own?"

Alyce thought over her words carefully before replying. "I love the people of Hawkspur; I feel an obligation to them and want only what is in their best interest, Sire. That being said, I believe there is no one else who will protect and fight for Hawkspur and all who reside here as fiercely as I."

"I do not doubt you are well-loved here." The king considered her for a long moment. "But make no mistake, I will not hesitate to invoke the law of war and claim Hawkspur for one of my nobles if I sense you are failing. Protecting the crown is the priority, above all else. Your brother is still alive…as far as we know," the king said with a shrug. "If I hear even the quietest whisper of a rumor that treason is underfoot at Hawkspur, I will cut you down myself."

"I understand, Sire," Alyce said, fear prickling down her spine.

"Then kneel before me."

Alyce felt the blood rush from her head, unsure of his intentions. Slowly, she knelt before the king, her knees sinking into the sun-warmed grass beneath her. The king reached for the sword at his hip and pulled it from the scabbard.

Alyce looked at the long blade of shimmering steel, a shiver running through her with the knowledge her life was about to change. She would either be acknowledged as the king's liege and Lady of Hawkspur, or she would have her head separated from her neck as a penalty for her audacity and the misdeeds of her brother.

She tried to see what was happening to Hawk, but the looming figure of the king blocked out everything else, and the soldiers behind him went silent. Alyce could see only the king and hear only her own rapid breaths; no one else existed at this moment but them.

"Do you know what you must do, Lady Alyce?" the king asked.

Alyce gulped, nodding her head as the king planted the tip of the sword in the ground in front of her. She clasped her hands around the worn grip of the sword and bowed her head.

The king placed his hands over hers, commanding, "Give me your oath."

"I swear by Almighty God to promise on my faith," she said, her voice shaking noticeably, "to bear true allegiance to King Edward of England." The strength in her voice increased with each word. She took a deep breath and focused on the big, fatherly hands wrapped around her own on the sword. "I swear the allegiance of Hawkspur Castle and all who serve me, to you and none other. We will be faithful in our service to the crown of England. We will defend you and your kingdom in good faith and without deceit."

When she was finished, she stayed where she was, her head bowed, and relief flowing soothingly through her entire being. The king knew the details of Cynwulf, yet he was still willing to take her oath. She sighed deeply, beginning to believe all would be well.

She said a quick, silent prayer that Cynwulf, too, would be well in the end, that she might see him again. The benevolence of the king gave her a spark of hope that it might actually come to fruition.

"Rise, Lady Alyce, liege lord of Hawkspur, and loyal vessel to the crown of England." The king lifted his hold on her hands over the sword grip, then extended his arm to assist her to stand.

Alyce looked at the king with overwhelming admiration and gratitude. It would be her honor to serve a man such as him, and she vowed to keep every word of her oath.

"I will install another as lord here in a single beat of your heart if you fail me, Lady Alyce," King Edward said with a stiff smile on his lips. Taking her by the arm, the king turned and led her toward the field and the men standing around Hawk, still stripped to the waist and bound to the fence.

Surely the king would release him. He couldn't follow through with this madness. Hawk was loyal to his king and had done nothing to deserve this.

"Now, Lady Alyce," King Edward said in a fatherly tone, "let me instruct you regarding an important lesson in leadership."

Alyce hesitated, but the king's grip on her arm was strong, and he did not let her falter.

"Loyalty is of utmost importance," he continued. "If you allow disobedience to go unrecognized and unpunished, you will lose the respect of those who serve you. It will be perceived as a weakness, and the vultures will descend, sensing your demise."

"He was not disloyal to you, I swear," Alyce said in a whisper, her lungs too constricted to speak any louder. "He did not betray you." She knew it was folly to argue with the king, but she could not bear to see Hawk punished for something that was not his fault.

Dear God, but it should be her lashed to the fence, not Hawk.

"Sir Grogan is my finest knight," the king continued calmly. He had stopped a short distance from Hawk. "Do you know why he is called Hawk?"

She couldn't speak. Alyce's eyes were focused on him now, on the broad expanse of his bare back and the sharp angles of his profile, to the way his skin glistened in the late autumn sun. She wanted to run to him, to throw herself protectively over his hunched body.

"I will tell you." The king's voice sounded irritatingly conversational. He spoke directly to her, but loud enough for those around them to hear his story. "Years ago, during another Welsh rebellion, we were embroiled in a bloody battle. In the chaos of men and swords and blood, I was struck from the side and knocked off my feet." The king chuckled quietly. "'Tis not something I care to admit, that I was caught off guard that way. But by God's good grace, Sir Grogan saw what happened and sprinted toward me with such speed, dodging anyone who tried to stop him. His helm had fallen off in the battle and his black hair was hanging free. What I saw was the blur of something with dark wings flying toward me, weaving between obstacles with such speed and agility. It was beautiful, I tell you, just like seeing a hawk on the hunt."

The king fell silent for a moment, looking at Hawk as she imagined a father would look proudly at a son. It made no sense to her. How could he love someone so much, yet think of punishing him in this way?

"He killed the man whose sword was just a hand's breadth away from impaling the king of England." She saw him inhale deeply, then he turned toward her again. "He saved my life that day, and for that, I will be forever grateful."

"I don't understand, sire." Alyce's words were rapid with desperation. "How can you esteem him so greatly, and then do this?" She lifted her hand limply in the direction of Hawk.

"It is because I esteem him," the king said, a hint of sadness in his voice. "Hawk was given the order to determine Cynwulf's guilt or innocence, and if he was proven guilty, to bring him to me to face judgment. He not only defied my order, but he let your brother escape to Wales to join forces with Daffydd, a known enemy to the crown." He nearly spat out the name of the Welsh prince's brother, his loathing clear. "His duty was to detain Cynwulf or take his life if he must. He did neither."

"But it was not his fault," Alyce pleaded. "It was my fault. It was because of me that my brother escaped." She paused, her throat clogged with fear. "It should be me you punish."

The king looked at her the length of several pounding heartbeats, then said, "I commend you for your honesty, for taking your due part of the responsibility." He sighed and turned toward Hawk again. "I just explained to you that Sir Grogan is a knight of incomparable speed and agility with the focus and conviction of a deadly predator. There is only one thing that can sway a man such as him, and I fear he has fallen victim to it, as all men eventually do."

Alyce pinched her brows together, his words confusing.

"And though I cannot fault him for his weakness, for his moment of chivalry, he knows it will not go unpunished. Had he wanted to, he could have stopped your brother and his band of rebels from ever stepping foot outside of that forest alive." The king shook his head in dismay, then lifted a hand in a signal for the punishment to commence.

The punisher lifted his hand, the long willow branches of the switch swaying in the air as he held it high. She'd always loved willow trees, the way the wispy branches swayed and danced in the wind as they reached for the sky and then cascaded back toward the ground.

These branches were stripped bare, only small, hard knobs remaining where the leaves had once been. These willow branches were ugly…and then they were gone.

Alyce did not see the switch move, but she heard the snap as the whip-like branches connected with their target and the grunted whoosh of air from Hawk's lips as the thin lengths of willow bit into his flesh. His back was suddenly striped and discolored.

Nausea took swift hold of Alyce's gut, and she felt her legs giving out. The king put his arm around her, supporting her before she could crumple to the ground.

"I do not like it either, but we must both be here. It is my duty as king and your duty as the new liege of Hawkspur," King Edward said. His words were rough, and she was relieved he showed at least some evidence he did not enjoy watching what was happening.

The whip cracked again, and Alyce squeezed her eyes shut, holding her breath and willing the flogging to be over. Hawk grunted again but did not cry out as she expected a man subjected to harsh punishment would.

"If I must give an order as distasteful as this, I do not then hide while others carry it out," the king continued. "I must not shirk the difficult tasks, or I am not fit to be a leader."

Another crack.

Another grunt.

Alyce continued to squeeze her eyes closed while the king talked to her as though explaining how a horse is to be trained.

She found it difficult to reconcile the warm, protective father figure who held her hands in his own over the grip of the sword accepting her oath of allegiance to this seeming madman who did not flinch as his most revered knight was being beaten, the switch surely ripping him to shreds.

But she couldn't look.

"My dear," the king droned. "You confessed your part in what happened. If you are to be a leader—"

Crack.

Another grunt, but this one was quieter, and she feared his life was being drained from him. Alyce's eyes flew open, horrified by the thought that he might be dying, if he wasn't dead already.

"—then you must stand by your actions," the king said, tipping his head toward the bloody body hunched forward over the fence, swaying slightly on his feet, "and take responsibility for the outcomes."

Crack.

The sound Hawk emitted this time was little more than a harrumph. His knees started to buckle but he pushed himself back to standing, took a deep breath, and squared his shoulders, waiting for the next.

"You, dear lady, asked my most accomplished soldier, my most heroic soldier, to let your brother go."

Crack.

"And he did it." He sighed heavily. "I cannot fault you for your loyalty to your brother, but now you must bear the consequences of your actions just as Hawk must bear the consequences of his."

This was Hawk's punishment for choosing to honor Alyce's request to let her brother go, instead of honoring the king's command to bring Cynwulf back to face the judgment and justice of King Edward.

She stiffened, then took a small step forward, carefully shrugging out of the king's supportive embrace. She understood the situation now, the point of the king's lesson. She still thought the king a madman, but in one thing he was right: she must be strong enough to face the consequences of her actions.

The whip was raised in the air again. Alyce stood tall, shoulders straight and eyes focused on the ribbons of flayed skin and streaming blood that covered Hawk's back. If he had to endure this torture, then she would be here to suffer the agony of knowing she caused this.

The slashing of the whip as it bit through his back was horrifying, sickening, enraging. But she stopped herself from flinching, focusing instead on Hawk, this man who sacrificed all that he was, all that mattered to him because she'd asked him to.

Dear God, please let this stop!

She was not worthy of him.

The punisher's hand lifted over his head again, readying for the strike.

"Halt," the king finally called. "'Tis enough."

Red and Hunter rushed to their commander, untying the bonds while two more of his men leaped over the fence in one bound and braced themselves under his arms to bear his weight for him.

Alyce stood her ground, not moving as Hawk's men half-lifted, half-dragged him off the field, not one of them sparing her a glance. She watched them until they were out of sight, her vision blurring as she fought to keep her composure.

Her eyes burned and she wanted nothing more than to crumple into a heap on the ground and sob with frustration and anger. She looked around the field to find that everyone was gone, including the king and his soldiers. But then, she saw a figure walking toward her at a fast pace.

Aelwin.

When he got to her, he put a hand on her back to support her, then seemed to realize it was not an appropriate gesture from a commander to his liege, and quickly removed it. He swallowed audibly, and Alyce turned to him.

"My lady," he said with sympathy. "May I escort you somewhere? I can take you to the keep and send for Edna to attend to you."

She blinked back tears, dug her nails into her hands, and straightened to her full height.

"Thank you, Aelwin," she said stiffly, forcing the façade of calm collectedness. "I am appreciative of your offer. Please walk with me to the keep, but when you find Edna, send her to Sir Grogan. He will be in more need of her service than I."

Her second-in-command held out his arm to her, but she declined the gentlemanly gesture with a shake of her head and a weak smile. She preferred for Aelwin to walk at her side as she started toward the keep, just as he would have done for Cynwulf.

Chapter Twenty-Six

"TELL ME, EDNA, how does he fare?"

Alyce had gone to Hawk's chamber immediately upon returning to the keep, but Hunter stopped her from entering with a shake of his head as he stood with his arms folded over his chest in front of the chamber door.

He had allowed Edna to enter when she arrived with an armload of linens for bandages followed by several lads hauling buckets of water. When the door opened to let them pass, a litany of grunted profanities reached her ears before Hunter pulled the door closed again. When Hunter resumed his post as sentry, staring wordlessly down at Alyce, she swallowed her pride, squared her shoulders, then turned on her heel to take her leave.

She'd considered commanding him to open the door—it was her castle and her door, and she had every right to demand entry—but her gut told her Hunter would not see it the same way.

"He fares as well as can be expected under the circumstances, my lady," Edna reported. Her demeanor was more reserved than usual, and Alyce wondered if it was because of her disgust with what happened to Hawk, or because of Alyce taking Cynwulf's place as liege of the castle. Or because she was disappointed in Alyce, blaming her for Cynwulf's disappearance and Hawk's harsh treatment.

"Dearest Edna, I implore you to forego formalities when we

are alone." So much had changed in the last day, she needed some things to remain familiar. "You have been the woman closest to me since my mother passed. I need your guidance and reassurance now more than ever."

Edna stopped tidying Alyce's belongings to sit beside her on the bed and put her arms around her in a motherly embrace. The stiffness eased from her back and shoulders as she laid her head against the older woman's shoulder.

"I will always be here for you, my dear, in whatever way you need me." She stroked a soothing hand over Alyce's hair as she spoke, just as she used to when she was a little girl missing her mother.

"Edna, I..." she wanted to tell her how overwhelmed she felt, but her throat closed over the words.

"I know," Edna said, rocking her back and forth in her arms as she did when Alyce was a young girl. "No need to be anyone other than my little Alyce when we are alone."

She turned her face into Edna's shoulder as a sob escaped. From the time her parents died, Uncle Ranolf, Cynwulf, and Edna had been her family. Edna had been her mother's maid, and then her own for her entire life, but Alyce could never consider her just a servant. She loved Edna as she had loved her mother, and just as with her mother, Edna was the only person she felt fully comfortable enough with to let all of her defenses down.

"Have a good cry with me and get it over with. When you are done, you will be ready for whatever comes your way next," Edna murmured, her cheek pressed reassuringly to the top of Alyce's head. It was the permission she needed to release the pent-up emotions of the past night and day.

After the tears were spent and she could breathe normally again, she said, "I cannot imagine Cynwulf ever needing a good cry when he felt overwhelmed." She let out a short, mirthless laugh when she finally released Edna and sat up to wipe her eyes. She did feel like some of the fog had cleared from her mind, but each time she remembered Cynwulf was not coming back to Hawkspur, it was like the wind was knocked from her chest and she had to force herself to breathe again.

"Did you know of Cynwulf's past, Edna?" By now, the word had certainly spread through the whole of Hawkspur about Cynwulf and why he was gone.

The older woman let out a sigh. "I was with your mother as her maid since before either you or your brother were born, but you already knew that." She paused for a long moment, and Alyce laid a reassuring hand over the older woman's clasped hands. She rubbed a thumb over the back of Edna's fingers, noticing the dark spots and wrinkles of the thinning skin, while she waited patiently for her to continue.

"And I was with her when she went to stay with relations in Wales before she married your father. Her uncle was a baron in Wales, a skilled commander, and that summer he had several young men from prominent families living in his barracks and training with his men." Edna's eyes were focused on some distant point on the wall as she remembered the events of so many years past.

"We were both very young women," she said with a small smile, remembering, "naïve and enamored with the idea of love and chivalry. Your mother fell in love with one of the young wards of her uncle, but he could not woo her openly as his family would not approve."

"Was it Prince Llywelyn's brother?" Alyce asked in a hushed voice. No one could hear their conversation through the stone walls of the chamber, but it felt scandalous to say the words too loudly.

"She never said definitively it was him," Edna admitted. "She did not hide from me the fact that she was having a clandestine love affair, but she thought it best I not know his name until they could declare their love openly. I knew it was Daffydd, though, because I saw the way she watched him, especially when the men were in the yard or gathered in the hall. And he was constantly glancing her way, his chest puffing when he would catch her looking at him. Your mother claimed privately they spoke of a future, determined to find a way to be together. I'll never know if he loved her in return, but your mother was convinced he did…so convinced that she allowed him to seduce her. Fools that they were, they thought if he took her maidenhead, his family would have no choice but to relent and allow them to marry."

"How could they deem my mother not worthy of their son?" Everyone had loved Alyce's mother. She couldn't imagine anyone objecting to having her as a daughter-in-law.

"The Llywelyns are a powerful and ambitious family, and a match with your mother's family was not advantageous enough for their liking," Edna said, bitterness seeping through in her tone. "But, as good fortune would have it, Queen Eleanor took a liking to your mother. She often served as one of her ladies-in-waiting and returned to her again after her time in Wales. The queen is an observant and caring woman; she recognized very quickly that something had changed with your mother, and it was soon apparent she was with child. It was the queen who arranged the hasty marriage to your father."

Edna looked down at their clasped hands and patted Alyce's hand as she looked up into her face with a small smile. "Your father was a good man. He loved her well, and loved Cynwulf nearly as much as he loved you."

A warmth spread through Alyce's chest remembering the big, jolly man who swung her in circles as a little girl and allowed Cynwulf to ride on his back like a horse. Until tragedy took their parents away, they'd had a good life. Uncle Ranolf, who was so much like her father, gave them a home and comfort beyond what was required of him. Like his brother, he was a big, gentle man, but with a more commanding presence than his younger brother.

Cynwulf and Alyce were very fortunate to have the family they did. Most families were not so demonstrative of their love for each other, and even fewer would have accepted a child conceived by another man into their hearts and homes. If she found out her father was someone other than the man who raised her, would she be driven to find him?

"I can understand Cynwulf's desire to know the man who sired him. What I do not understand is why he would compromise his position as lord and endanger everyone at Hawkspur for a man he hardly knew. And why..." Alyce paused, trying to articulate the anger welling in her chest. "Why did he choose Daffydd over me? Why was the acceptance and admiration of a man who had forsaken our mother and him more important than the sister who stood by his side all these years?" She felt the tears welling up again but choked them back down. "Why am I never enough?"

She cringed at how hurt she sounded, but it felt like a betrayal. Once again, her years of love and loyalty were not enough to receive the same in return.

"I cannot say that I know the mind and heart of another person," Edna said, putting a hand to Alyce's cheek, "but I do not believe that Cynwulf meant to choose between either of you. Whatever he did, whatever choices he made, none of it was a measure of his love for you. I am convinced he never imagined it would come to this, that it would hurt you or put you in harm's way. He loves you above all else.

"And as to you not being enough, stop talking such nonsense." She held up her hands to stop Alyce from protesting. "I do not mean to sound harsh, my dear, but you must get past this idea that if someone hurts you, it means they don't love you. No one is infallible, and sometimes we forget that what we want or that the choices we make might hurt those closest to us. What Cynwulf did, and what Geoffrey did—because I know you are thinking about that again—were mistakes that were made in spite of their love for you, not because of their lack of love for you. Geoffrey was tormented greatly because of his mistake, and Cynwulf is surely plagued with regret now."

Edna lowered her lashes at Alyce and said in a gentle voice, "I think you might know something about actions having unintended consequences."

A slap in the face would not have stung as sharply as Edna's words. Every time she closed her eyes, the memory of Hawk's bared and bloody back filled her mind.

DINING WITH THE king and queen was excruciating for Alyce.

She'd not slept in nearly two days, and she was emotionally exhausted. It took all of her strength and composure to stay sitting upright, listening to the king regale the table with his litany of reasons for despising Daffydd ap Llywelyn.

Each time her eyclids drooped, he would describe another betrayal at the hands of Daffydd. It was beyond fathoming as to why King Edward thought he could trust a man who led a rebellion against his own brother to claim the title of prince for himself, twice swore fealty to the king of England when disavowed by his brother, and twice broke his oath to the king when reconciled again with his brother. In truth, she was finding it difficult to feel anything but indifference toward Edward's anger at Daffydd as it was his own folly to trust a man who was so obviously loyal only to himself.

She did feel a pang of sadness for Cynwulf. This man the king despised so fervently did not deserve even a handful of her brother's loyalty. He'd already proven he was not loyal to his family with the many times he turned his back on his own brother, the Prince of Wales. And now he was leading a rebellion because he felt he was owed even more than all that he had, once again.

This man would use Cynwulf for as long as it served his purpose, and then he would push him to the wayside. It broke her heart to think of all her brother had sacrificed for this man who cared about no one save himself. What else would Cynwulf have to sacrifice before this was over?

The king continued to drone on about things Alyce should care about, but she just couldn't bring herself to feign her interest anymore. She felt ready to fall from her chair in exhaustion, willing to curl up under the table at his feet if it meant she would be allowed to close her eyes for a while.

The scraping of trestle tables being pulled across the wooden floor captured her attention, and she breathed a sigh of relief. Mercifully, the king and queen finally rose from the table and bid Alyce goodnight to retire for the evening.

The queen took Alyce's hand in her own. "We will have a nice long sit down another time when you are not falling over tired. My husband sometimes forgets not everyone has his ability to blink their eyes a few times and call it a good night's sleep as he does." She turned an adoring eye toward the king as she spoke the last, then turned back to Alyce. "Get some sleep, my dear, and tomorrow will look better."

Alyce nodded and tried to smile gratefully at the queen through her exhaustion, though she couldn't be sure the corners of her mouth even moved.

She waited for the royal couple and their contingent of guards and ladies to ascend to the second-floor chambers before following behind them. Ever since the king and queen had taken up residence in the family's rooms above, a contingent of watchful guards hovered at the chamber doors and near the stairwell.

Continuing up the spiraling stairwell, she emerged into the narrower corridor of the uppermost floor and the smaller guest chambers. A single torch flickered in the wall sconce, the light dancing dimly over two forms seated on stools outside of Hawk's door. Both men came to their feet as Alyce stepped into view.

"My lady," they said in unison. She did not know the names of these two soldiers, but she recognized them as part of Hawk's elite force.

"How does he fare?" she asked, nodding toward his chamber door.

"He sleeps." One of the men responded. When it became apparent neither man intended to say anything more, she sighed wearily and continued to her room.

Gertie was stoking the fire as she entered. "My lady," she said, turning with a smile while Ffyddlon thumped her tail against her nest of blankets.

"At least someone is happy to see me," Alyce lamented with a tired smile at her maid. She crossed to Ffyddlon to keep her from trying to stand. Her shoulder had been stitched, but she would need to rest for it to properly heal.

"Thomas has just been to take Ffyddlon outside for a few minutes," Gertie reported. "He says she is doing splendidly and will be following in your shadow again soon."

The kennel master had developed a soft place in his heart for Ffyddlon, despite his initial rejection of her as useless. "She can't be coaxed into a proper heat," Thomas had explained to Alyce when she'd first discovered the scared, skinny hound hiding behind the kitchen, surviving on the discarded scraps, which were few.

She kneeled on the floor to rub Ffyddlon's fur and press a kiss to her muzzle, but once her head rested against the dog's warm neck, her eyelids closed, and exhaustion overwhelmed her.

"Up with you," Gertie insisted, pulling at her arm to get her off the floor. Somehow, Gertie managed to unlace her tunic and pull it over her head before she flopped onto the bed. She felt tugging at her feet as her shoes were removed and then blissful warmth and darkness as the blankets were pulled over her.

Her last coherent thought was a silent plea to the heavens for Cynwulf's safety and Hawk's pain to ease.

◆═══ · ◆◆◆◆ · ═══◆

Chapter Twenty-Seven

THE NEXT MORNING, Alyce rose to Gertie gently shaking her awake while Edna threw back the window covering to let in the light.

"My lady. Wake up, my lady."

Alyce blinked her eyes to clear her head from a deep, mercifully dreamless sleep. As the fog in her brain lifted, the events of the last days came flooding back, as well as the magnitude of her new responsibilities. She sat up, swinging her feet to the floor as she rubbed her eyes and gave her head a quick shake.

"Did I sleep late?" she asked, yawning.

"Not so late, my lady," Gertie said, briskly gathering her clothing and shaking out the garments in preparation for Alyce to dress.

"The king rose early," Edna warned her, leading her to a chair so she could brush and plait her hair. "He was up well before the dawn, and holding council in the hall since shortly after the sun came up. There have been messengers coming and going since before the morning meal was served."

"That sounds exhausting," Alyce muttered.

"Cook had tables set up in the yard to serve the morning meal to everyone who was not with the king," Edna continued. "She's fuming because the king's cook has taken over the kitchen. Even threw her pots, knives, and provisions right out the door to make room for his own. She had to bake bread over open fires in the yard to feed all of us."

"Oh my," Alyce said with a sigh, already feeling the weight of the coming day on her shoulders. "Thank the heavens the king brings his own cook and food, or our stores would be empty before the winter even started trying to feed his army. I will have to do what I can to cool her temper. Perhaps a few of Aelwin's men can help construct a shelter and create a usable kitchen for the time being."

She longed to see Hawk, to tell her how sorry she was for the part she played in bringing down the king's ire upon him, but would he see her? What could she possibly say that would make up for all that had been taken from him? He was once the king's most favored knight, and she'd reduced him to disgrace in front of his king and his men.

"Your face does not want to wake up." Edna pinched Alyce's cheeks. "But there is much to do today, and you do not want to give the king and queen the impression you choose the comfort of your bed over our duties."

"Oh, Edna," Alyce said, her voice heavy with dismay. "What have I done? Why did I think I could do this without Cynwulf?"

"Chin up!" The older woman chucked her lightly under her chin with a finger. "Staying in your room feeling sorry for your plight will not help you. The entire village has heard about what happened and the speech you gave to Aelwin and the guard upon your return. You made them believe, and now you must show them their trust has not been misplaced."

"But if I fail…" Alyce scrubbed her hands over her face. "If I fail, there are so many people who will suffer."

"Then do not fail," Edna said sternly.

"My lady," Gertie said hesitantly. "Nearly everyone in the village is ready to help you. The Chetwynd lords have been fair to us, even kind. We hear the stories; we know that not all lords are this way. If you do not succeed, we fear the alternatives."

"Aye," Edna agreed. "We will all help you because we know you, know what you have already done for Hawkspur, and know you will do your best for us."

Alyce took a deep breath to steady her nerves and stood.

She'd chosen her path and now she must go forth and keep her promises no matter how scared she felt in private. "Let us face the day, then." She started toward the door, then stopped and turned back to Edna and Gertie. "You said *nearly* everyone will help me. Are there those who do not support me as liege of Hawkspur?"

"They are not many, and most of them are old," Edna said, turning Alyce by the shoulders and gently pushing her to the door. "They cannot fathom a woman as an overlord to Hawkspur, but you will soon change their minds."

"Did you tell them about Isabella Mortimer?" Alyce asked over her shoulder.

"Everyone knows of Isabella Mortimer," Gertie confirmed, excitedly. "You must prove to them she is not the only woman in the marches who can hold a castle."

Alyce nodded with determination as she opened the chamber door, stepping into the passageway. She had no option other than to face the obstacles ahead to prove she was worthy to be Lady of Hawkspur.

Hunter stood sentry at Hawk's door and Alyce stopped to face him squarely. "How does he fare today?"

Hunter widened his stance and crossed his arms over his chest, but said nothing, only offering a quick nod.

It was futile to talk to the stubborn man and Alyce almost turned to leave until a voice in her head told her it was time to assert herself. She faced Hunter squarely and matched him by widening her stance and crossing her arms over her chest. Leveling her hardest stare at him, she said in the most authoritative voice she could muster, "I would like you to respond to me in words and I will not leave until I am satisfied with your answers. So, I ask you again, how does he fare?"

Hunter narrowed his gaze at her, but she thought she saw a small spark of admiration in his golden eyes. Returning his glare, she waited patiently for him to speak.

"He lives."

Alyce nodded. "I am glad of it. Does he eat?"

Hunter looked at her in surprise but grunted what sounded like an affirmation. Alyce arched an eyebrow at him, to which he sighed heavily and added, "Yes, he eats."

Alyce nodded once. "I would like to see him."

The irksome warrior shook his head at her, his lips clamped shut in a tight line.

"He doesn't want me to see him? Or *you* do not want me to see him?" She narrowed her eyes at him, staring him straight into his eyes, daring him to deny her.

"I do not want you to see him, my lady, but in the end, it is not my decision." His face was hard with anger.

"Then let me pass."

Again, he shook his head, and it took everything within her not to kick him.

Just then, a low groan emitted from the chamber. Alyce's eyes darted to the door and back again to Hunter.

"He will not want to see you now," Hunter said with a begrudging note to his voice. "Red is dressing his wounds."

A wave of apprehension turned Alyce's stomach as she looked at the door, but she nodded and started to turn away. She stopped mid-turn and looked back at Hunter. "I thank you, Hunter, for speaking with me. I find it preferable to your grunts."

He grunted at her in response, but Alyce thought she saw his lips twitch before she turned completely away.

THE REST OF the day was an exhausting whirlwind of making decisions, giving orders, coordinating duties, reassuring villagers, and attending to the king and queen. She still found it distasteful to be in the king's presence after what he'd done to punish Hawk, but she performed her duty and discussed the security of the castle, the loyalties of the villagers (Welsh or English), and her plans for keeping the castle out of the hands of Prince Llywelyn and his brother Daffydd.

After midday, Alyce ventured into the village for the first time since taking the lead at Hawkspur to gauge the mood. As Gertie had indicated, nearly everyone smiled, bowed in acknowledgment, and greeted her with enthusiasm. There were some who nodded stiffly or avoided her altogether. No matter, Alyce decided, not everyone approved of Cynwulf either, but he did not let that stop him.

She instructed Cook to come down to the village to request the bread baker, the tavern owner, and anyone else who was capable to make as much extra food as possible to be purchased as provisions for the castle while the kitchen was occupied by the royal cook. She stopped in each cooperating establishment to express her appreciation and offer reassurances they would be compensated for their service.

Alyce marveled at the sheer number of soldiers and servants who traveled with the king and queen. People were everywhere, filling the taverns, lingering in groups in the streets, and laying on the grassy slopes enjoying the last of the warmth from the afternoon sun.

The sound of children laughing and yelling caught Alyce's attention and she turned to see Griffin tending his sheep on the edge of the village, as usual. What was less than usual was the flock of small children squealing, giggling, and running in circles around him and the sheep.

"You have extra helpers today, Griffin," Alyce observed with a giggle of her own as she watched the five boys and girls between the ages of perhaps two and six.

Griffin bowed low to Alyce and then rose up to turn his attention back to the sheep and children. "Aye, my lady. Their mums are working extra hard with the king and queen at the castle. I'll earn a penny a day if I keep them with me during the day and put them in their beds at night. Lizzy!" he suddenly called out to one of the older girls while pointing at the ewe wandering from the herd. "Bring her back. That's the way, just push on her an' she'll turn."

Alyce watched in fascination as he made a game for the children out of keeping the sheep from wandering away. "You are a very kind and resourceful young man."

He blushed at her words, but his chest puffed, and a smile curved his lips, even as he tried to deny the praise.

"I will pay you the penny each day that you care for the children, plus one extra. Their mothers should keep their hard-earned money." She saw a little boy peek out from behind one of the sheep and then come running on his chunky, clumsy legs. When he got to Griffin, he threw his arms around his much taller legs and peered up at Alyce.

"Henry," she said, an unexpected warmth blossoming in her chest at seeing the little child again. He let go of Griffin and held his arms up to her. For a moment, she did not know how to respond, but then she reached down and picked him up to cradle him in her arms. "Hello, young man," she crooned softly. The bitter sadness that used to overwhelm her at the sight of the child was dissipating.

He reached a pudgy hand to the neckline of her tunic and traced the brightly stitched pattern of blue flowers with one of his little fingers.

"How do you feed the children during the day, Griffin?" she asked, keeping her eyes on the sweet, familiar face of the little boy in her arms.

"I go to each of their huts and find what scraps I can." His tone was easy, as though this was not an inconvenience at all for him to care for these children while also caring for himself and his sheep.

"How old are you, Griffin?" He hardly seemed old enough to be taking care of a gaggle of children. He had been orphaned several years ago and she knew John had taken him in at the tavern. He still attended the sheep, as his father did before succumbing to the flux, along with his mother. John was happy for the extra hand at the tavern and the source of fresh mutton for roasting and serving in return for providing a home to Griffin.

Griffin stood a bit taller and said with pride, "I don't really know, my lady, but I will soon be a man."

"So you will," Alyce responded with a smile. She tickled Henry's belly with her fingers as she had seen Hawk do the day they had come to the village together. Then she set him on his feet, patted his head, and gently guided him back toward Griffin.

Alyce fished a penny out of the leather pouch attached to her side and handed it to the young man. "Here is your first payment.

Come to see me when you need more. And once the king and his army have moved on, I will pay you the remaining pennies I owe you for watching these children." She arched an eyebrow at him in playful warning, "And if I hear you also took money from their mothers, I will be very disappointed in you."

Griffin shook his head eagerly. "Oh, no, my lady. I would never do that. I would never cheat them that way."

"I apologize, Griffin," Alyce said, looking down at him approvingly. "I should have known you have too much honor to ever be deceitful." She was just about to take her leave when she added, "Bring the children up to the castle each day for meals. I'll let Cook know to set food aside for you if she doesn't see you and the children at mealtime."

Griffin bobbed several bows in a row, his eyes wide. "Thank you, my lady. You are so kind, and we will all be happy for the food." He turned and called to all the children, "Lizzie, Edwin, Roger, Mary, Henry!" When all the children were standing still, their eyes focused on him for their next command he said, "Look at Lady Alyce and say, 'Thank you, my lady.' She is helping me to take care of you little scoundrels while your mothers work." He said the last with a wink and the children hid their smiles behind their hands.

All five children bobbed curtsies or bowed to her as though she were the queen, saying a chorus of thank yous, just as Griffin had instructed. She curtsied in return. "You are very welcome. Now be good and do as Griffin tells you."

She clapped a hand on Griffin's shoulder and gave it a squeeze of appreciation before taking her leave.

As Alyce entered the upper bailey of the castle, the queen and her ladies were approaching.

"My dear Lady Alyce," Queen Eleanor said, holding her hands wide. "Will you join me for a stroll around the grounds? My legs are in need of stretching."

Alyce curtsied. "I would be honored, Your Majesty." She

matched the queen's stride and they continued to walk along the stone wall with her ladies, constant companions, directly behind them.

The afternoon sun had warmed the cooler air of the late autumn morning, making for a pleasant day. She walked at the regal woman's side, finding the moment quite unbelievable: she was escorting the Queen of England around the grounds of a castle under her command. The guards they passed stood at attention, first acknowledging the queen, and then acknowledging her in the same way they used to acknowledge Cynwulf.

Perhaps it is not so foolish to think I can do this. She stood a little taller as the thought boosted her confidence.

"May I be frank with you, Lady Alyce?"

"Of course, Your Majesty." A prickling of apprehension shivered down her spine in anticipation, and her newfound pride deflated. Any conversation that started with a request to speak freely usually did not bode well for the listener.

"I think you very courageous," the queen began, looking at Alyce from the corner of her eyes as they walked, a hint of a smile on her lips. "It takes a willful woman with a backbone of steel to stand before the king and declare herself commander of her family's fortress. Very few people are willing to speak their mind to my husband—Hawk being one of those few people."

Alyce did not know if she expected a response, and she was yet unsure if the queen was scolding her or praising her. She chose to stay quiet and let the older woman direct where the conversation was to go.

"May I give you some advice?" the queen asked. They had neared the kitchens—both the actual kitchen and the hastily constructed temporary kitchen—and she stopped to watch the flurry of activity.

"I would be honored for your guidance, Ma'am." Alyce was sincere in her response. Queen Eleanor was well respected in the realm and by her husband. She was rumored to be her husband's most-valued advisor. Any advice she offered would be welcomed.

"Your strength will be in those you find to support you. Because you are a woman, you will have more obstacles than even the most incompetent man in proving you are worthy of your position. Men step into their roles as lords and commanders with the expectation they deserve to be there. They are assumed worthy until they prove otherwise. When a woman finds herself in a position of power, she is assumed *unworthy* until she proves otherwise. She will start in a position of distrust and skepticism, less revered than the worst dolt of a lord."

Luc Montworth immediately sprang to Alyce's mind. He was an arrogant braggart who relied on pomp and intimidation to build himself up as a leader of men. He garnered little respect, and the loyalty of his men was directly related to the amount of coin they could expect in return. If the spoils of his questionable tactics as sheriff dwindled, would his band of enforcers abandon him? And yet, there were those who would prefer a despicable man like Luc Montworth as lord of Hawkspur over her, just because he was a man.

Alyce let out a snort of frustration before she remembered she was in the queen's presence. "I'm sorry, my queen," she said, bringing her hand up to cover her mouth. "Please forgive my unladylike outburst."

The queen squared herself to Alyce, throwing her a stern glance. "Those in positions of authority do not apologize, especially for something so trivial. Never apologize unless you have truly wronged someone; then be humble about it but do not linger in the apology." She tilted her head slightly and softened the expression on her face. "Since I am being frank with you, I expect you to be frank with me in return. What garnered your grunt of dissatisfaction?"

Alyce straightened her spine and tried to imitate the queen's regal stance with her head held high and her gaze steady. "I was lamenting the unfairness of those who would prefer to see a man who is known for his cruel tactics and arrogance as lord of Hawkspur over me, purely because—" She was about to say something vulgar but stopped herself. The queen might demand frankness, but she would not excuse crudeness.

"Because of what dangles between his legs?" Queen Eleanor provided helpfully with a sardonic smirk.

"Yes, my lady," Alyce blurted in surprise.

"Fear is a powerful motivator, and men fear that a woman will not be strong enough to protect them against those who would seek to take advantage of any perceived weakness. That is why you must win the support of men who are willing to fight for what you represent. Find men you can trust, men who will not be intimidated by you, who will stand by you because they believe in you."

Hawk. Her heart pounded a rapid beat as she admitted to herself that he was the man she wanted at her side. He was the one who made her feel she could face anything. It was because he was at her side that she had the courage to stand in front of Cynwulf's garrison and proclaim herself their commander. Yet, he gained nothing by standing at her side. And it was because of her that he nearly lost everything.

Alyce pressed her lips together and clenched her teeth to hold back the flood of despair that was about to bring her to her knees. Instead, she focused on how to move forward on her own. She must be strategic in her alliances, and she must earn the loyalty of men who loved Hawkspur as much as she did.

"You will have to make difficult decisions, Lady Alyce. As women, we want to please, to never hurt anyone. Some will tell you that you must become ruthless, and must think like a man to rule effectively. And though there is some truth in that sentiment, there is also much to be gained from showing a woman's compassion."

Alyce thought about the lack of compassion shown by the king in the punishment meted out to Hawk. She sighed and dropped her gaze to the ground in front of her, praying she would be able to do what was needed when similar, hard decisions came her way.

"The trick is knowing when to show compassion, and when what you are displaying is weakness *disguised* as compassion." The queen reached for her hand and enclosed it in both of hers, looking at her earnestly. "When given a choice that will benefit you or will benefit Hawkspur as a whole, choose to benefit the people of Hawkspur before yourself. But, for those who would disobey your orders, who would undermine your decisions, compassion will be perceived as permission."

"I could never order someone flogged," Alyce said, bile rising in her throat. She looked pleadingly into the queen's eyes, hoping she would have an answer that did not require her to dispense torture as a punishment.

"It is not the only option and in sooth it was not the only option available to Hawk, but it is the one he chose. To him, being stripped of his position, having his army disbanded, and relinquishing a good sum of his fortune was a worse punishment than what he received."

Alyce felt as though someone had punched her in the stomach, knocking the wind from her lungs. "Saints above, the man must hate me for what I've done to him."

The queen squeezed her hand, then let go to hook an arm through Alyce's, guiding her as they continued to walk, her ladies still respectfully following at a distance.

"He definitely does not hate you," the queen said with a chuckle. "I would wager it is quite the opposite."

"How can that be, Ma'am, after all he has suffered because of my selfishness?"

"Your devotion to your brother blinded you to the truth of what you were asking of Hawk."

"He told you what happened," Alyce stated flatly. "I am so ashamed of my behavior, but in my panic, I begged him to stay with me and let Cynwulf go."

"That is not exactly how he explained it," the queen said sympathetically, "but I surmised the only thing that would cause the venerable Hawk to lose his prey were tender feelings for you."

"What have I done?" Alyce said with a sigh. "I understand now why his men look at with me disdain and will not let me see him. Why does the king not punish me for ruining his most favored knight?"

"My dear, his punishment, and his lesson, was forcing you to watch as Hawk paid the price for his decision. And as far as ruining Hawk, I would argue that is not the case," the queen said slyly. "I have urged the king to find a wife for Sir Grogan for some time now. He refused, insisting Hawk would let him know when he is ready to request an arrangement, and until then, I was to refrain from distracting him with my attempts at matchmaking." She laughed elegantly, a soft trill deep in her throat, and she squeezed Alyce's arm. "Even the king agrees Hawk has given him the sign he is ready."

Alyce stopped in her tracks. "Your Majesty, if you are saying what I think you are, it would be an injustice to betroth him to me. I am barren and will never be able to give a man the heirs he seeks." It killed her to admit the words, but she could not deceive Hawk about what a future with her would look like. They would be childless, with no heirs to carry on his name or their fortune.

"Are you convinced of that truth?" the queen asked. She leaned closer and whispered conspiratorially, "They may say it is the woman who is at fault when a seed does not take root, but many women have been unable to produce a babe with one man yet go on to have many children with another."

Alyce squared her shoulders and turned to look at the children lining up under Griffin's watchful eye to receive a bowl of stew from Cook. "Do you see that little boy with his hand fisted in the hem of that young man's tunic? The one with the light hair and dimples?"

The queen turned her gaze in the direction Alyce indicated with her chin. "Aye," she said cautiously.

"My husband had those same dimples, and the same fair hair with curls. And if you get close enough to see his eyes, they are the same color of green and set at the same slant as my husband's." She turned back to the queen, her chin high. "My husband spent one regrettable, drunken night with his mother and that child was the result. Five years with me and not once did I quicken with his seed."

The queen looked at the small boy for a long while. "That does complicate matters," she said with a sigh. "Hawk has amassed a small fortune of his own and will require an heir."

Alyce tried to tamp down the heat of shame that was rising in her. She clenched her teeth together and let the anger well in her instead. Others may judge her inadequate because of her inability to grow a child in her belly, but she'd refused to let it determine her worth. She might not be able to have children of her own, but her family included everyone who lived at Hawkspur, who made the village their home, protected the castle, baked bread, tended sheep, and cared for the horses. Her family was as vast as her love and devotion for them.

"It is true I cannot bear a child of my own, and I will never be a mother as you are, Your Majesty," Alyce said, her voice full of pride and devoid of shame, "and I will not have an heir to inherit Hawkspur at my death. But until then, Hawkspur is my child, and I will protect it as fiercely as any mother protects her offspring. I will love this place—" she continued, sweeping an arm to encompass the whole of the castle and village—"fortify it, safeguard it, and lead it with the same dedication, discipline, and devotion as any mother."

Queen Eleanor studied her until Alyce shifted uncomfortably on her feet, fearful she had offended her with her impassioned speech. But then she lifted an eyebrow, and a smile graced her lips. "You are a woman of singular mettle, Lady Alyce." The queen began walking again. "But without a husband and an heir, you will be vulnerable. Even if you cultivate loyal men who are willing to serve you, with no one to inherit Hawkspur after you are gone, you will be a constant target to those who are opportunistic."

"If I marry, I will be giving up my authority over Hawkspur and allowing someone else to decide what happens here, what is best for the people that I love." Alyce realized she'd begun to grind her teeth. Before she'd started this walk with the queen, she had felt she could serve as liege to Hawkspur, that the castle and people would flourish under her rule. Now she felt as though her decision was selfish, and by not marrying, she was putting Hawkspur in danger.

"Marriages, even if for political purposes, do strengthen loyalties and bonds," the queen said, her voice coaxing, though not unkind. "Perhaps we can find you a husband who has children already. Then you would have the strength of a man behind you in your bid to keep Hawkspur, and *you* would gain an heir."

Alyce pondered the queen's words with foreboding because she recognized the measure of truth to what she said.

By this time, they had walked the perimeter of the inner yard and returned to the main entrance of the castle. "I will take your leave, Lady Alyce," Queen Eleanor said as they entered the hall. "I am feeling the urge to see my own children after our discussion. But do think upon what I have said." The words were delivered with a smile.

Alyce curtsied to the queen. "I am honored by your candor and words of advice, Your Majesty. You are an inspiration to me in all things." She hoped her voice did not sound as wooden and flat to the queen as it did in her own ears.

"You are too kind," the queen said, tipping her head and then taking her leave with her gaggle of ladies following eagerly behind her.

The seeds of doubt had been planted where once she'd felt confident and they were weighing heavily upon her. Was she being foolish by not choosing a man to stand beside her and protect Hawkspur for the sake of those who lived here?

At one time, she'd dared to believe perhaps Hawk was the man who would stand by her side. He was a man of honor, of strength, of respect. He would not put his needs above those of the people who looked to him for leadership. But even if she had not humiliated him in front of the king, the queen had dashed her hopes when she said Hawk required an heir.

And the queen was right, of course. He needed sons of his own, and Hawkspur needed an heir to continue the legacy started by her uncle. If they were bonded in marriage, neither one of them would get what was necessary to ensure the future of their individual responsibilities.

Chapter Twenty-Eight

B Y THE TIME Alyce returned to her chamber, she'd sat through another interminably long supper, met with the king and Aelwin to solidify the plan to protect the castle from rebels after the king's departure—though he gave no indication of when that would be—discussed her expectations and obligations to the king and realm, and given her heartbreaking oath that Cynwulf would never be allowed to return as lord of Hawkspur.

"You are honor bound to detain your brother and turn him over to me as a traitor to the crown," the king had reminded her sternly causing a knot of apprehension to form in her stomach. It still sat solidly in Alyce's stomach as she climbed the stairs to her chamber.

She braced herself as she emerged from the stairwell, teeth gritted and ready for another locking of horns with Hunter in order to wring even the sparest of details of Hawk's state from him. When she saw the big, red-headed Viking sitting in a chair at Hawk's door, his long legs stretched across the corridor and his head tilted back against the wall, the relief that flooded her was almost overwhelming. She truly did not have the stamina for another argument with Hunter.

As she stepped into the passageway, Red was on his feet in the blink of an eye and braced to defend his commander's door. He immediately relaxed when he saw her, a broad, teeth-baring grin covering his face.

"My dear Lady Alyce," he said with a deep bow. "How fare you?"

The jovial behemoth had a way of putting Alyce at ease. In fact, it was taking every bit of her decorum not to lean in and let him wrap her in a huge, protective hug. He was a handsome man, and she expected most women would swoon at the thought of being held in his arms, but when she looked at him, all she saw was a gentle, brotherly giant.

"I am well, Red. But I would really like to know how Hawk fares. Hunter will hardly speak to me and gives me little more than disapproving grunts when I inquire." She looked up at him beseechingly. "And do not spare me the details; I do not deserve such kind consideration."

Red arched a ginger eyebrow at her, shaking his head and clucking his tongue disapprovingly. "If you think him near dead, my lady, you underestimate him."

"I saw—" She gulped and bit the inside of her cheek to push back the hot stinging in the back of her eyes as the images of Hawk's punishment flooded her mind. "I know he will not die, but I saw what he endured."

"Aye, we all saw it," Red said, his smile tightening. "He will heal. His back aches and it's striped enough to make the most devoted flagellant monk envious."

Alyce gasped with shock at the blasphemous comparison, but it was hard to take offense when everything the Viking said was delivered with a mischievous grin. She sighed and dropped her gaze to the floor before steeling herself and facing Red to ask what was truly on her mind.

"Does he hate me?"

Red snorted. "Never."

"Will he see me?" She held her breath as she waited for the answer.

"The sight of you will be the balm he needs." He laughed then. "I don't think he finds my ministrations soothing and he has been growling like a bear every time I go near him."

He reached for the door and pushed it open slightly, then signaled with his outstretched hand for her to enter. "Just be careful with him, my lady. He's been a nightmare to keep still and his back needs time to heal. If he moves too much, it will rip open again."

Alyce blushed at Red's raised eyebrow and the unspoken insinuation that she had intentions of anything more energetic than stroking his head soothingly. She entered the chamber with her heart in her throat, the beats pounding in her head. Red pulled the door closed behind her and she stood in place as her eyes adjusted to the dimly lit room. A single candle burned on a small table situated near the door. She shivered slightly and saw that the window covering was pulled back, letting in the chilly night air.

Finally, as her eyes adjusted to the soft, flickering light, she turned her attention to the man who was her reason for being here. Hawk was sprawled across the bed on his stomach with his arms stretched out to hang over the sides of the bed. A thin linen sheet covered him from his lower back to midway down his legs, his muscular calves and bare feet sticking out at the bottom. She swallowed hard, the sight of his naked limbs stirring her more than she intended as heat coiled low in her belly.

His fingers on the hand closest to her twitched slightly, drawing her attention. His face was turned toward her, his hair tied into a club at the base of his neck. Her gaze wandered slowly over the broad curve of his shoulders, the muscles there firm even in sleep. He was a truly splendid man and in any other circumstance, she would not be able to stop herself from touching him, smoothing her hands over the hard planes of his body.

Several days ago, before the turn of events that had changed their lives irrevocably, he would have welcomed her explorations, of that she was certain. But now, she did not dare touch him, even as the memory of his hands and mouth on her, the way her body had come alive under his touch as he pleasured had her breath hitching in her throat. What she would give to go back to that night, to…what? She did not know what she could do over if given the chance, but she wanted it all to end differently than it had.

Slowly, she let her eyes move to the dark pattern of slashes crisscrossing his back. She stepped closer, her eyes adjusting to the dim light, to see the lifted welts, open wounds, and discolored bruises mottling the expanse of his back more clearly.

She drew in a sharp breath and reached a hand tentatively toward him but stopped herself before her fingers touched his skin. She closed her eyes for a moment to restore her composure, then steeled herself to look at him again, forcing herself to take in every detail of his back. This was her doing, she reminded herself as her eyes roamed slowly over the damage done to his skin and muscles. The king had said it was her punishment to witness Hawk's penance for defying the king; she would imprint this in her mind and remember that her decisions had consequences.

After a long while, she allowed her gaze to climb the length of his thick neck to the line of his jaw, dusted with stubble, looking for signs of fever as the candlelight flicked across his cheeks. Thankfully, his skin was dry and even in tone. His lips were gently parted, and his eyes were…open!

He looked at her with a steady gaze, the orbs black under his thick lashes. "Come here," he said in a low voice, lifting his hand to reach for her.

Alyce dropped to her knees next to the bed and smoothed a hand over his hair, cupping his skull in her hand. She opened her mouth to speak but then closed it to look at him, all the remorse and pain of the last days welling in her eyes and spilling down her cheeks. No words could begin to express her regret.

He touched a calloused thumb to her face, swiping at the wetness on her cheek. "'Tis nothing," he said with a sardonic grin, his voice strong and unwavering. She let out a pitiful laugh and leaned into his palm.

He started to roll to his side, and she put a hand on his shoulder to stop him. "You mustn't move."

"Then come here." He wrapped his hand around the back of her neck and pulled her closer to him. She kept her eyes open, locked on his, feeling his breath warm her face as she drew near. He touched her lips softly with his, letting out a long sigh against her mouth as she closed her eyes.

She pulled her head back and locked her eyes with his. "Can

you ever forgive me?"

He shook his head and stroked a hand over the wimple covering her hair. "I make my own decisions. This is not your doing."

She wanted to ask him why he'd done it, why he'd taken the flogging instead of telling the king it was her fault Cynwulf escaped, but she could not bring herself to say the words. She would be devastated if he said he did it for love, and equally devastated if he denied doing it for love.

Because she loved him. She'd known it the moment she looked into his eyes when she was standing in front of Hawkspur's soldiers in the morning of the day prior. When she'd felt her confidence slipping, he had looked back at her with pride in his eyes. He'd believed in her, and that was what mattered to her more than anything else at that moment, and her heart had swelled.

It was the memory she would hold close to her, to take out and cling to whenever she felt too tired to go on, too lost, or too alone in the world. It would be the warm spark in her heart that she protected and cherished in the days and years ahead when she thought of him and what their lives could have been if things were different. If she was not barren.

She must remember what the queen had told her about Hawk. He and men like him needed heirs to carry on their legacy, and she could never give that to him.

She closed her eyes as his fingers worked under the edge of her wimple, pushing it back.

"Take this off," he whispered.

She reached up to pull at the pins Edna had lodged tightly against her skull that morning, grateful to have them loosened and the irritating covering taken from her head. His eyes darkened as the thin line left by the Welshman's blade was uncovered by the scarf as it fell from her neck. She brought her fingers up to hide it from his sight.

"It is nothing, Hawk, and does not pain me. Compared to what you have endured, this is an inconsequential scratch." In truth, it was a clean, shallow cut and was healing quickly.

"His eyes narrowed. "He is lucky to already be dead," he

grumbled. His gaze moved from her neck to her hair. "Now the braid," he said, a devastatingly charming grin curving his lips, his anger seemingly gone.

She pulled the ties from the end of the long plait and started to unwind the strands. He combed his fingers through her hair, catching a loose strand and bringing it to his nose to inhale the scent of it.

Pushing slowly to her feet, she sat on the edge of the bed, leaning her back against the headboard and shifting close to him. Gently, she lifted his head to lay it on her lap. His arms closed around her waist as he clutched handfuls of her hair in his fists and laid his cheek against her thigh.

She untied the leather strip holding the club of hair at his nape and combed her fingers through the strands, her fingernails stroking soothingly over his skull.

"It does not seem enough to say thank you," she said softly, keeping her focus on the thick hair, dark as midnight, flowing through her fingers as she massaged his scalp. "I never meant for you to suffer in return for Cynwulf's life."

"It is a short reprieve on his life, I will not lie to you," Hawk said, tightening his hold around her waist. "It will not end well for him. He cannot return to England without suffering the wrath of the king, and when the king defeats Prince Llywelyn and Daffydd, Wales will not be safe for Cynwulf either."

Alyce breathed deeply and released a shaky breath. She knew it to be true, knew there were no good alternatives for Cynwulf. His only hope was to escape Britain altogether. Perhaps Ireland. Or France. Even Spain. It hurt her heart to think of her brother, her only living family, so far abroad and never seeing him again, but at least he would be alive. Mayhap there was still hope for him to live a long life and have a family.

"Let's not speak of my brother now. Tell me what I can do to ease your discomfort. Have you eaten? Can I have Edna make a poultice?" She realized heat was rising in her cheeks as her gaze followed the lines of Hawk's back where it tapered to his waist, then down the rest of his body. The sheet was doing very little to hide the very well-formed muscles of his backside and long legs.

She had to concentrate to keep her rapidly increasing breath under control as images of the last time she was in this room filled her mind. Her fingers tingled at the memory of touching his finely sculpted chest and stomach, but she'd had not time to look at the rest of them before he had pushed her back on the bed and…

"Come down here so I can look at you," he said lifting his cheek from where it rested on her thigh and loosening his hold around her middle.

"Hawk," she said, warning in her voice, "that is not a good idea." He was already pulling at her waist to slide her down next to him. "It is improper, and you should not be moving if you are to heal."

He chuckled deep in his chest, then winced slightly. "We dispensed with propriety some time ago, my lady." He lifted his face to look at her. "You can either lie down beside me and let me rest against you, or I will drag you down here and damn the healing."

Alyce huffed in mock disapproval as she resituated herself to lie next to his big, warm body, her face even with his. The chill night air coming in through the open window did nothing to diminish the heat radiating from him, yet he did not seem to suffer from fever. He draped an arm over her middle and a heavy thigh over her legs, pinning her to the mattress. She turned her head to bring their noses a mere hand's width apart and looked into his eyes while trying not to think about his fully naked body pressed up against her.

"You are Lady of Hawkspur, now." A slow smile curved his lips as he said the words, the warmth in his eyes breaking her heart. "Tomorrow, when I am on my feet, I will pay deference to you as you deserve."

"No, Hawk," she said sternly with a small shake of her head on their shared pillow. "I never want you to bow to me. You have given me so much more than you can even know; I can never repay you." She turned her body just enough under the weight of his limbs to lay her hand against the side of his face. She inhaled deeply, smelling the healing herbs of the poultice on his back, but it was not enough to cover the earthy scent of his skin that was just him.

They stayed lying together, looking into each other's eyes for a long while, both silent, so many words unspoken. Alyce did not know what to say to him because there was nothing to say that wouldn't break her heart. She loved Hawk, there was no denying that now, despite her efforts to stop it from happening. And because she loved him, she would let him go, let him find someone who could give him the sons he deserved.

She remembered the gentle way he'd had with Henry, the way the child laughed at his antics, how Hawk had looked with the boy in his arms. He would be a wonderful father, just like her father. And like her uncle would have been, had he his own children.

"Do you recall the day we went to the village together?" she said, her voice whisper-soft and her eyes locked with his.

"Aye." The lines on his face relaxed, giving Alyce encouragement to continue.

She would not hide the truth any longer. "The child you showed such kindness to is my husband's son."

HAWK HAD HEARD the rumor.

Red was worse than a gossiping old crone, gathering tantalizing tidbits of information to use against others later. But he would not use this against Lady Alyce. He would let her tell him what she needed to say. So now, as she revealed the truth of the boy's identity, he did nothing more than wait for her to say more.

"His mother is Janet, the serving maid from the hall," she continued, her voice steady and her gaze unwavering as she confided in him. "He died just over a year past, after five years of marriage, and the boy is no more than two summers." She sighed, as though steeling her nerve, but she did not look away from him. "In those five years, not once did I become with child. But Geoffrey was with her for one night, and she had Henry."

Hawk wanted to soothe her, to hold her tighter and tell her it did not matter, but he sensed that despite the hurt he could see in her eyes she was trying to hide, she wanted him to do nothing more than listen.

"Cynwulf told me time and again that there was no proof he was Geoffrey's son, that there was hope I could have children with another man." A small, sad smile curved her lips. "But I knew Geoffrey better than anyone. I knew the shape of his face, the exact color of his eyes, the way his cheeks dimpled when he smiled, how he tilted his head when he was intrigued by something, the way certain expressions shaped his face."

She slowly let her hand slide down Hawk's face to curl it in a ball under her chin. He could feel her withdrawing from him, protecting herself, and he didn't like it. She was skittish under his touch, like a mare ready to bolt, so he stayed quiet, only curving his hand a bit tighter around her side in reassurance.

"I did not know a child could be so much like his sire in mannerisms as well as looks," she said with a tight laugh, her voice still barely a whisper. "But there is no doubt. With each passing season, the resemblance becomes stronger. And as my doubt of Henry's paternity decreases, my certainty that I will never have a child of my own increases."

Hawk pressed his forehead closer to hers when she stopped speaking. "I did not mean to add to your pain when we went to the village." He had not known until after they returned what the connection was between Alyce, the child, and the child's mother. He sensed then that there was more to the situation because Alyce was never brusque toward anyone, but she was stiff and guarded with Janet.

She opened her hand enough to touch her fingers to his chin, and Hawk took that as a good sign. "You helped me that day, even if it was a painful lesson. I had only looked at the situation from my perspective. I was hurt and I blamed Janet as much as I blamed my husband for what happened. I thought her cruel for taking another woman's husband to her bed, and I resented her for lack of respect toward me."

He slid his hand up her side and over her shoulder to cup it around the back of her head when she sighed and dropped her eyes for the first time, focused on something far away. He would not let her retreat from him now.

"She likely did not think of me at all when it happened, and I do not mean that in a critical way. I mean that she had other things to think about. I put more of the blame on Geoffrey now because you made me see that women like Janet often do not have a choice. I am no longer certain she set out to seduce my husband, but rather that she feared saying *no* would make her life more difficult." She took a deep breath before continuing. "And in the end, Geoffrey got what every man wants: a child to carry on his legacy. Even if he is not here to raise him as his heir, a part of him will live on. That is something I could not give him." She lifted her eyes to meet his. "That I cannot give to any man."

Hawk could see the effort it took her to say the words, to be brave enough to admit that she could not have what she seemed to desperately want, and he felt a spike lodge in his heart, hurting him far more than any lashing. "Geoffrey was a fool," he said, startled by the hoarseness in his own voice. He wanted to kill the man for making her feel she was a failure for not giving him a child or that she was not enough of a woman.

"It doesn't matter anymore." Her whisper was barely there and hollow. "Some say I did not bear a child for my husband because I did not pray hard enough. Others say God will bless me with a family when the time is right. I do not know what to believe anymore, but I have decided my family now are the people here at Hawkspur...and Cynwulf. He will always be my family even if he cannot be here with me. And as for the family that is here with me, I will devote myself wholeheartedly to them and no one else."

Hawk could see the determination in her eyes as she spoke and felt the stiffening of her body under his leg and arm. It was as though she were fortifying herself, steeling herself against that which was lost to her. He knew she would put her entire heart, her entire being, into caring for the people she had chosen as her family.

As for her claim that she would devote herself to the people of Hawkspur and no one else, he did not care for that idea at all because that meant she did not consider *him* to be her family. She would never feel for him what he felt for her, which was.... He didn't know exactly, but because he cared for her, he would bury those feelings and help her in any way he could.

"I've lived my life being damned by men, by the church, by nobles, by those who think I have no value because I am bastard born," Hawk said, sliding his hand from the back of her head to curl his fingers around her fisted hand under her chin. "One thing I've learned is to put no merit in how others would define my value, but rather how *I* define it. If others already think you lacking, then you have nothing to lose by being bold, and demanding that which is due to you."

She closed her eyes and laughed softly. "Like a stallion claiming a pasture of mares."

"Exactly," he conceded, smiling at the memory of her chastising him for his arrogance weeks earlier on the parapets, claiming he strutted like a stallion in the company of mares. He wouldn't make the mistake of comparing her to a mare again, but the truth was she was the only one worth strutting for, the only one he needed.

His forehead was still pressed to hers, her hand clasped in his, and her body pinned by the weight of his leg. He could smell the flowery scent of her soap, reminding him of how sweet she tasted on his tongue when he'd had her sprawled across this same bed only two nights before. He wanted to taste her again, but more than that, he wanted to worship every part of her body until she believed that she was cherished, that she was more woman than most.

She pressed her warm lips to his fingers and looked at him through her lashes. "Stallion or no, you need your rest, so I will take my leave."

She started to wriggle out from under his leg and he clamped it down harder against her, tightening his grip on her hand. "Stay with me tonight."

He could see the flush of color rising in her cheeks. "I cannot. I have duties to attend to in the morning. Besides, Red has already given me his command that you are not to do anything that will jeopardize your healing. If I don't leave soon, he will come in here and haul me out, and I would prefer to avoid that humiliation."

"Forget Red. He will do as I say." He groaned in dismay as she slipped out from under his leg to stand next to the bed, her hand still folded in his. He kissed the back of her palm and inhaled the scent of her. "Enough for now," he murmured, loosening his grip on her hand.

She leaned down to kiss him softly on his forehead and it took everything in him not to lift his face to hers and claim her lips in a searing kiss, but he knew if he did that, he wouldn't stop until he had her naked and underneath him.

He watched her back away from the bed to the door, opening it and quietly disappearing as a throbbing started in his chest. He felt like his war horse was standing there, crushing his heart and taking away his breath.

He knew Alyce felt an obligation to Hawkspur, to the people here, and she rightfully felt that she was the best person to take on the role of liege. No one else would care for these people and fight for them as she would because she loved them above all others. She'd said it herself—she didn't have room for anyone else in her life. And she would never choose a man over Hawkspur if it meant relinquishing her authority to him.

"I'm a selfish bastard," he muttered to the empty room, "because I want her anyway."

Chapter Twenty-Nine

PUSHING HER DOOR closed behind her after a long day of duties, Alyce flopped on her bed in exasperation. At times, the king was like a father figure, offering advice and encouragement, and then the next he was demanding and inconsiderate of everything but his own desires. Despite her dislike of King Edward at times, he *was* the king, and she was being unreasonable for expecting anything less.

While she and Aelwin were in attendance with Edward, he had sent a messenger to find out when Hawk would be ready to resume his duties. The request had surprised her as she had assumed Hawk would be dismissed from his services after his punishment, but apparently, it was only a warning, and, in the king's eyes, Hawk's service to him would continue as before.

Which meant he would soon leave Hawkspur.

"My lady?" Gertie asked, her voice laced with concern. "Are you well?"

Alyce sat up with a huff. "Aye, Gertie, I am well."

Ffyddlon let out a whimper where she lay on the rug before the hearth, then stood to limp over to her mistress. Alyce held out her hands to the hound, cradling her head in her lap to stroke the fur on her head and back. The dog was healing well according to Thomas, but still needed to rest despite her eagerness to be at Alyce's side at all times.

"The day has been long, and I should not be complaining,"

she said to Gertie, "but this is the only place where I can shake off the propriety required of being Lady of Hawkspur and just be Alyce for a short while. Forgive me if I caused you concern."

Gertie curved a conspiratorial smile. "Anything and everything that happens within your chamber will be kept in confidence with me, my lady. Have no fear I will never tell anyone that you are anyone other than Lady Alyce."

"Thank you, Gertie." Alyce sighed and let her shoulders relax. "I cannot do this alone. Your support and companionship are cherished."

Gertie seemed to swell with pride and her smile broadened as she reached for the gown spread across the wooden chest in preparation for the evening. "Now then, let us get you dressed. As Lady of Hawkspur, you must look every bit as important as the queen. No one will dare to doubt your authority."

Alyce laughed, gave Ffyddlon a pat on the head, then gently shooed her back to her rug, and stood to allow Gertie to do her duty of dressing her. "Like a stallion…"

Gertie cocked her head to the side in question. "A stallion?"

Alyce shook her head. "It just means to go forth with confidence."

Her maid nodded at her. "Like a stallion, then."

Red was emerging from Hawk's room as she stepped into the corridor a short while later dressed in a flattering gown of midnight blue that matched her eyes and contrasted with her hair, making the strands appear an even deeper shade of auburn. Her hair hung loose around her shoulders instead of being tied into a tight braid, and it was covered with a loose wimple held in place by a simple circlet of silver.

The big Viking extended an arm. "May I escort you to the hall, my lady?"

Alyce nodded with a smile and placed her hand over his extended forearm. "How is the patient today?"

"Ungrateful and growly," he said, but his tone was light and full of humor. "More importantly, how do you fare?"

"I am faring quite well, thank you," Alyce said, lifting her head and squaring her shoulders, determined to present herself with the confidence of a leader this eve.

Red smiled down at her. "Confidence is good. Even when you are not feeling it, always show it."

"Like a stallion," she said with a nod. She was beginning to understand why men seemed to always have their chests puffed and why they walked with an air of authority, even when they did not have a reason for their cockiness. Perception meant more than reality.

"I think you to be like a lioness," Red suggested. "They are fierce, protective, and more cunning than the lions."

Alyce stopped at the top of the stairs to face him. "You have seen one?" she asked in amazement.

He nodded. "Caged, in the Holy Land. We saw both a lion and a lioness. The lioness was absolutely mesmerizing, and she scared the wits out of all of us when she bared her claws and forced the lion to back away because she did not want his attention. Not even a lion will cross a lioness."

Alyce thought for a moment, then nodded once. "I like that. Fierce and protective." She proceeded down the stairs ahead of Red. "Like a lioness."

THE HALL WAS already teeming with the king and queen's entourage, Aelwin, the lesser lords from the region, and anyone else who could fit into the stuffy hall to catch a glimpse of the king and queen.

As she stepped into the great room and walked toward the table on the raised dais, she passed by Janet, who immediately stopped, turned to her, and dipped into a quick curtsy. There was a nervous smile on her lips as she rose up.

"Good eve, Janet," Alyce said, tamping down the old, unwanted jealousy. "I thank you for your service this evening." She hesitated, then added, "And if you or any of the other women who are working in the hall in the evenings are in need of anything, please come to see me. All of you work very hard in service to Hawkspur."

"Thank you, my lady." Janet looked at her, wide-eyed, and bobbed another curtsy. Her cheeks were bright with color but a sheen of sweet glistened on her face, which was pale despite the rosy blotches on her cheekbones and the tip of her nose. She looked flushed and clammy.

"Are you well?" Alyce asked, genuinely concerned.

"Aye, my lady," Janet responded, diverting her eyes. "I must get more ale for the king's men."

"Of course," Alyce said. Janet was likely warm from the stuffy room and endlessly carrying trays of food and drink across the hall. "Please do not let me deter you from your duties."

Alyce continued to the dais as Janet rushed toward the buttery, feeling satisfied that she was doing the right thing to ensure everyone at Hawkspur, including the serving women, was cared for equally. After all, everyone's contributions were necessary for Hawkspur to thrive.

As she approached the dais, the king gestured for her to take the seat to his left, the queen already occupying the seat to his right. There was an empty seat remaining between her and Aelwin, and another to the right of the queen, but she thought little of it as each day saw a stream of noblemen and commanders coming and going to hold counsel with the king or bring updates on the destructive progress of Prince Llywelyn, Daffydd, and the Welsh rebels.

She listened intently to each report, as much to plan for fortifying Hawkspur against attack as for news of Cynwulf, but no one spoke of him. At least not in her presence. Llywelyn and Daffydd were progressing south along the border, their armies quickly descending from the northern reaches of the Marches into the central region. The latest reports put their armies near Oswestry, mere days from Hawkspur.

Which meant Cynwulf may be nearby.

Her heart leaped with hope that he may send word of his welfare, and then with fear that he may try to contact her. She ached for news that he was safe, or better yet, that he had escaped to Ireland or some other distant land out of King Edward's reach. But she prayed he would not be so foolish as to come near

Hawkspur himself and further flame the king's ire.

The king signaled for a waiting servant to fill her goblet with wine as a familiar, boisterous crowd entered the hall, sending shivers of revulsion down Alyce's spine. She closed her eyes with a long sigh, wishing she could disappear before the owner of the unmistakable nasal voice reached the head table.

"Luc Montworth will do anything to win my favor, and he has served me well because of it," the king said in a low voice, leaning close to Alyce. "He is a widower, himself. Already has two sons of his own."

Alyce cringed inwardly while keeping her face expressionless. Obviously, the queen had spoken to the king about her barrenness. Matching her to a husband who had heirs would be the ideal solution in the king's eyes. She would get a husband to compensate for her vulnerabilities and serve as liege of Hawkspur; he would get a wife, a castle, and a title.

If she were wed to Luc Montworth, he would gain everything, and she would gain nothing. In truth, she would lose much if she were to agree to become his wife, as she suspected the king wished her to do. He would expect his wife to be obedient, accepting of all of his decisions, and to succumb to his odious desires in the bedroom. Of course, she had no proof he would be a demanding and selfish husband in the privacy of their chamber, but how could he be anything different when he showed himself to be concerned only for himself in every other aspect of his life?

And how would the people of Hawkspur fare with him as lord?

She would wager not well. He would take all for himself and give very little in return if the rumors were true of how he took advantage of his role as sheriff of the forest, using his position to strongarm others into giving him what he wanted, which was more than he deserved. Obviously, he was cunning enough to appease the king in order to keep his position while detracting from those who would dare complain about him.

No. She had no desire to marry Montworth, but would the king allow her to keep her right to remain a widow as well as respect the law of the Marches while the Welsh rebels pushed closer to Hawkspur? She risked losing everything if she did not acquiesce to the king's suggestion she marry, which she knew to be a thinly disguised command that would be accompanied by consequences if ignored for too long.

"Join us," the king commanded Montworth as he finished bowing his respects and blathering on about what an honor it was to dine in the king's presence. "Take the seat next to our lovely hostess, Lady Alyce, Lady of Hawkspur." He said the last with a raising of an eyebrow and a pointed look at Montworth.

Alyce's lips curved into an uncomfortable smile that hurt her cheeks as the sheriff practically skipped and hopped around the table to the chair next to hers. She wanted to laugh at his ridiculous display of enthusiasm, thinking he looked more like a court jester than a potential lord of the realm.

"My lady," Montworth said, bowing his head to her and extending a leg with flourish as he held his hand out for hers. Reluctantly, she touched her fingers to his palm and swallowed her revulsion as she tightened his grip to pull her hand to his lips and press a disgustingly hot, wet kiss to her knuckles, lingering far longer than was polite. She thought of the way Hawk kissed her hand the night before and her gut wrenched with regret at the comparison.

As though the thought of him conjured the man, Hawk ducked through the doorway and into the hall. Her eyes flew to him, but she was too stunned to do anything else as his eyes met hers, then narrowed as they drifted to the man still holding her hand.

"Hawk," the king called out as he pushed to his feet, greeting him as a long-missed friend. "Come, sit." He stretched out an arm to indicate the chair next to the queen.

Alyce pulled her hand out of Montworth's and watched as Hawk walked toward the dais with only the slightest hint of stiffness in his back. She could see the rigid lines of his face, but she doubted others would notice the strain he worked to hide. She could only imagine the discomfort he was feeling with the shirt rubbing against his scabbed back. Montworth was saying something at her side, but her eyes were on Hawk, and she did not hear a word he said.

Lord, help her, but she could not catch her breath when Hawk was near. She wanted to go to him, to take his hand and lead him out of this hall, away from the king, from Montworth, from everything. She wanted to be lying in his bed with him again, his head on her shoulder and his leg draped over her body, the smell of him overwhelming her with each breath. She wanted to hide away in his chamber, away from this chaotic world, and soothe him. With her fingers. With her body.

And she wanted the same from him.

His eyes were locked with hers until he took his seat, putting the queen and king between them. Alyce kept her focus on the table in front of her, not wanting to look at Montworth, and unable to see Hawk without craning her neck.

This was the queen's doing, of that she was sure. Queen Eleanor had told her Hawk needed a wife who could give him heirs, and she was sending Alyce a message at this moment that could not have been clearer if she stood on the table and shouted it at her.

Hawk was not for her.

$$\diamond$$

Chapter Thirty

"ALYCE, MY SWEET," Montworth said in a manner more intimate than Alyce cared for as he leaned closer to her. "How fare you?" His face went from charming and bright to sad and sympathetic in the blink of an eye. "What is this I hear of Cynwulf abandoning you at a time like this?"

"He did not abandon me," she said through clenched teeth, refusing to look at the despicable man. She had been scanning the hall, ironically, looking for Janet. She had not seen her since their brief conversation earlier. Normally, this would not be a concern to her, but she had been gone an unusually long while and she had looked quite peaked earlier in the evening. If she was ill, who would take care of Henry?

"Oh, my dear Lady Alyce, we both know that is not true," he continued, his tone condescending. "Tell me how I can be of use to you. I am at your command." He reached for her hand again, but she snatched it away from his reach.

"Aelwin has been completely competent and trustworthy as my commander. I do not need your assistance." Her crisp tone and clipped words did nothing to dampen his sickly-sweet imitation of charm.

"You know I mean to be more than just commander of your armies, Alyce. Together, we can make Hawkspur a fortress to be envied." He tilted his head closer to her and raised a suggestive eyebrow. "Put your trust in me, and I can ensure Hawkspur is protected and prospers."

Alyce knew she needed to be practical, to consider what was best for everyone at Hawkspur, not just herself. Could she tolerate a life with Montworth if it meant safeguarding the future of the fortress and providing stability to the people here? If she did not bow to the pressures of the king, she risked losing everything. Wasn't it better to be at Hawkspur, even if only as the wife of the lord of the castle, using the extent of her influence over her husband for the good of the village? She may not be the sole decision maker, and the future of Hawkspur may not be exactly as she envisioned it to be, but she was more cunning than Montworth and could use her powers of persuasion to better the lives of those she loved if she stayed.

If she refused to marry Montworth and pushed the king's patience beyond reason, she could be taken completely from Hawkspur, leaving the people here to their own devices and at the mercy of the lord appointed by King Edward. And all indications were that would be Montworth, with or without her cooperation.

Either way, Montworth would win. The only remaining question was how much everyone else would lose in the process, and the answer depended on Alyce's level of self-serving stubbornness. If she refused to marry the sheriff outright, she lost any chance of stopping Montworth from making life miserable for those who did not bow to his will at Hawkspur; if she relented and agreed to the marriage, she could use what influence she had to keep her husband from completely destroying the villagers for his own gain.

Heaven have mercy, could she really do this? She felt the bile rising in her throat but swallowed it down. She was no less self-serving than Montworth if she refused. She took a deep breath and turned to face the man who might be gracing her bed in a matter of weeks if the king and queen had their way.

"Tell me, sheriff—" Alyce dug her fingernails into her palms to maintain her resolution to do what was right—"about your children. How old are they?"

"Please, Alyce, call me *Luc*, since we are progressing toward a more intimate relationship." He leered at her in a way that made her want to run screaming from the hall, but she dug her nails deeper into her hands as he continued his answer. "My boys are soon to be men. Alfred is thirteen and John is ten." He beamed brightly as he spoke of his sons, which Alyce decided to take as a good sign. If he had a softness for his children, perhaps there was hope that he could have compassion for others as well, including a wife.

"And are they kind boys?"

He laughed. "They are strapping lads who have no need for kindness. One look at them and the other boys know to show them respect." He put a beefy paw on her arm, "But they will adore you, don't you worry. And you will love them, all the girls do."

Alyce's head began to spin. This was a terrible mistake, but she could think of no alternative. She smiled tightly and tried not to lean away from his touch.

King Edward pushed his chair back to better see Montworth, saying, "My lady wife and I were just admiring what a handsome couple you make."

"We are honored," Montworth said, his chest visibly puffing as Alyce felt her stomach flip over, nauseating her instantly. "Do I have your blessing, Sire, to ask the lady for her hand in marriage?"

Alyce stood so suddenly that her chair nearly overturned. "I beg your pardon, Sire. I just remembered I agreed to accompany Aelwin on an inspection of the guards." She looked to her commander who was thankfully pushing his chair back from the head table, though his face showed pure confusion. "I mean no disrespect to you or the queen, but I seek your permission for my commander and me to take our leave and see to the guard. Your safety and that of the queen are of utmost importance."

The king stood and studied her for a long moment. Alyce felt her legs quivering, fear overtaking her that she had pushed the king beyond his limits. Finally, he held out his hand, which she took immediately, bending low over it and pressing a chaste kiss to the knuckles.

"Duty must prevail," King Edward said in a dismissive tone,

then flicked his hand as a signal for her to leave.

"Let us be on our way, Aelwin," Alyce said, her voice shaking. Her commander extended his arm for her to precede him, then followed her as she crossed the hall as quickly as her legs could carry her without breaking into a run.

When they were free from the confines of the hall and had stepped out into the cold night, Alyce started taking deep gulps of the fresh air, ignoring the way it burned her lungs.

"My lady?" Aelwin asked. He reached a tentative hand toward her, as though wanting to pat her on the back, then seemed to think better of it.

"I will be fine, Aelwin," she said weakly, taking a final deep breath to calm herself. "I did not mean to put you in such an awkward situation but I had to get away from everyone so I could think."

"I understand, my lady."

Alyce looked at him to see if his face was as impassive as his voice. Aelwin had been a good commander to her brother, honest and forthcoming, always at the ready to complete any command her brother gave him. He was looking at her now with the same deference and patience he always showed to Cynwulf.

"Best that we follow through with my lie lest I upset the king further," she said with a derisive smirk. "Let us inspect the guard, and I will return to my room via the parapet."

Aelwin grinned at her. "Aye, my lady," he said with a nod. "I agree an inspection is in order."

When they had made the full circle of the castle wall, greeting and speaking with each guard in turn, Aelwin accompanied Alyce to her chamber door. He nodded his head in a quick bow and bid her good night, but before he reached the stairwell to return to the parapet, he turned back to her.

"Trust takes time to build between a commander and his lo-," he stopped and smiled as he corrected himself, "his ladyship, but I wish for you to know I am at your service should you need anything."

Alyce felt a surge of emotion at the gesture of loyalty, followed by a pang of guilt. "I thank you, Aelwin, and I will do my best to be worthy of your trust." He would be disappointed in her if he knew she planned to make Montworth lord over Hawkspur. She hoped he would see the wisdom in her choice once it was made.

He nodded. "And I will do the same for you."

Alyce recalled Aelwin's wife had borne a child at the beginning of the summer. "I do not think the king wants to see us back in the hall this night. Please, go home to your family."

"Thank you, my lady," he said with a broad smile, then turned on his heel and left.

Gertie was waiting for Alyce in her chamber. She did not ask questions of her lady as she helped her to remove her gown and change into a night trail and a heavy robe. For that, Alyce was grateful. She did not have the energy to discuss her evening.

After thanking the young woman for her service and dismissing her for the night, Alyce climbed onto her bed and pulled her legs in tight to her chest, wrapping her arms around them. Ffyddlon stirred from where she was sleeping on the rug before the fire and jumped onto the bed to lie down next to her mistress.

"You're feeling better," Alyce murmured, stroking the Ffyddlon's coat as the dog wriggled close to her. They lay together on the bed for a long while as Alyce did her best to come to terms with what she must do. She may have bought herself a short reprieve with her sudden departure from dinner this evening, but it would not change the fact that she would have to marry Montworth to save Hawkspur and avoid the wrath of King Edward.

She fell asleep with Ffyddlon next to her on the bed and did not awaken until the deep hours of the night. The flames in the hearth had burned down to a warm glow and a chill was beginning to settle into the room. She rose from the bed and padded to the fire to add another log, then stood and looked at the door.

Had Hawk returned to his chamber?

She started toward the door, then stopped herself.

This is madness!

The truth was like a knife cutting through her chest. She

wanted him so badly, but she was Lady of Hawkspur, and she could not put her own desires above duty.

If she went to him, she would never be able to go through with marrying Montworth.

HAWK HAD STAYED in the hall until the king finally retired for the night and Montworth took his leave. He wanted to follow the spineless sheriff into the night and throttle him, but he would accomplish nothing by the act other than ensuring his own demise at the hands of the king.

The queen had confided in him over dinner the decision had been made that Alyce should marry Montworth. It was the only way to ensure the stability of Hawkspur, and Alyce would gain stepsons to name as her heirs since she was the last of her family line.

He wanted to protest but knew it to be futile. He had lost his status as favored knight. The king may not have stripped him of his riches or his title, but he had been stripped of his influence. Had the situation not happened with Cynwulf, the king would likely have entertained his request to marry Lady Alyce. Edward would have been shocked by Hawk's desire to finally take a wife after all the years of rebuking the queen's match-making attempts, but he would have relented and granted his blessing.

He no longer had the right to ask anything of the king. And for what? He may have let Cynwulf escape certain death at the hands of the king while his sister watched, but in the end, he would still be executed as a traitor. With any luck, he had saved Alyce from having to witness her brother's humiliation, and that, at least, was worth the pain and humiliation he'd endured.

But he was having one hell of a time swallowing the idea of Montworth marrying Alyce. He had been unable to sleep since returning to his chamber, pacing in circles like a caged lion instead.

He was driving himself mad imagining Alyce with Montworth when he heard a scratch at the door. He stopped, focusing on the sound while reaching for his sword where it rested against the bedside table. He stilled his hand when he heard a familiar whisper, recognizing Alyce's voice. Paying no heed to his state of undress, he crossed the room in two long strides, lifted the slat from its brackets, and opened the door.

He pulled her across the threshold before she could protest, shutting the door behind her and dropping the wood slat back into place.

She stood staring at him, the thin linen of a white shift visible at the neckline of the heavy robe tied at her waist. His throat went dry as he thought about how easy it would be to tug the robe loose and pull the flimsy gown over her head.

He paused to collect his thoughts, then cocked his eyebrows in question as the words she'd muttered outside his door came back to him. "Did I hear you ask, 'What am I doing here?' while you were lingering outside my door?"

Her cheeks flushed with color, and she held his steady gaze as she untied the belt at her waist and let the robe drop to the floor. The light from the fire flickered and illuminated the curve of her body through the thin material. He inhaled sharply and moved close enough to her to cup her cheek in his palm.

"Why are you here?" He knew exactly why she was here, but he wanted to hear her say it.

Covering his hand with hers, she pressed her cheek into the comforting warmth of his palm. "I do not want to carry any regrets into my uncertain future, Hawk. Even if all I can have of you is one night, I want the memory to carry me through the rest of my days."

She was dead wrong if she believed he would let her go after tonight, but he would tell her that later.

"Make love to me, Hawk."

Her whispered words were his undoing. He scooped her up in his arms, ignoring the prickling pain caused by the pressure of his exertion on the fragile scabs across his back.

"I am at your command, my lady," he growled against her mouth as he lowered her to his bed.

Chapter Thirty-One

ALYCE PROTESTED WHEN he lifted her off the floor. "Your back! Let me down, Hawk," she pleaded, but the obstinate man just shook his head at her.

The way he looked at her as he lowered her to the bed sent ribbons of heat through her limbs. She framed his face with her hands as he settled over her, not able to take her gaze from his. His eyes seemed to bore into her soul, robbing her of her breath and all sense, certain he could see clearly the impossible thoughts filling her head from her traitorous heart.

I want you! I need you! I love you!

She lifted her face to his when the intimacy of their locked eyes became too much, and she feared she would put voice to the words in her head. She licked his lower lip and then grabbed it between her teeth. He rewarded her with a growl deep in his chest that vibrated against her breasts where his body was pressed to hers, the surprisingly erotic sensation making her nipples tighten.

She wriggled beneath him and pushed on his shoulders. "I need to feel your skin against mine."

He pushed up from her so that she could sit upright and tug at her the shift that covered her from shoulders to shins. When she couldn't remove it quickly enough, he pulled her to her feet and tore the thin garment over her head to fling it into a darkened corner of the room. They were standing with the mattress pressed against the back of her knees. She stopped him with a shake of her head when he tried to push her back onto the bed.

"I want to see you," she whispered, the words barely there as her hands stroked slowly down his neck and over the expanse of his chest. Her fingers followed the trail made by her eyes as she took in every hard plane and dip in the muscles of his torso, swirling her fingers in the dark hair that covered his chest and tapered down to his abdomen.

His chest was rising and falling as she explored his body. She darted her eyes up to his when his breath hitched as her hands smoothed over the hard lines of his hip bones and a wicked smile curved her lips as she looked up at him through her lashes. She kept her hands on his hips as she lowered herself to sit on the edge of the bed, widening her knees to pull him closer to her.

He hissed when she pressed her lips to his stomach, tasting his skin and inhaling his scent. She nuzzled the crisp hairs there with her nose then tipped her head to the side to bite gently at the hard angle of his hip.

His hands circled around the back of her neck as his fingers drove into her hair. "Alyce," he growled. She wasn't sure if the one word was said in warning or worship. The growl turned into a groan as she slid her hand up his inner thigh to cup the weight of his balls and roll them between her fingers. She was mildly surprised and highly flattered by the urgency of his cockstand as it bobbed against his stomach as she nibbled at the line of his hip.

She grasped the base of his throbbing cock, circling her fingers around the impressive girth to squeeze as she ran the tip of her tongue up the hard length of him. Her confidence and boldness grew as he threw his head back.

"Fuck," he said in a deep guttural tone, pressing his hips toward her.

"Should I stop?" she asked, feeling mischievous as she raised her face to look at him.

"God, no," he pleaded as she dropped his head to look at her, his eyes dark and his breath coming in gasps.

She kept her eyes locked with his as she circled the head of his erection with her tongue. His hands tightened on the back of her head as he watched her take him into her mouth. Alyce watched the rapture that crossed his face, relishing the way his breath came quicker as her lips closed around him to slide down the length of him.

The musky scent of his skin and the heavy weight of him in her hands mixed with the salty taste as her lips stroked down his silky hardness was a headier aphrodisiac than she could have ever imagined. She moaned with pleasure in the power her hands and mouth had over this magnificent man.

"Enough," he growled, pulling her head away from him and tilting her face up to his for a ravishing kiss. His lips and tongue took her mouth possessively as he dropped to his knees in front of her. His chest was heaving when he finally tore his lips from hers.

"That was amazing, but I'm not ready for this to be over," he chuckled softly as he pressed his lips to a sensitive spot beneath her ear. "I would have been completely spent if those soft lips of yours stroked my cock one more time." He nipped her neck and then pushed her back onto the mattress.

Her body was burning with need, her skin tingling where his fingers touched as his hands skimmed down her body. She let out a soft moan as he cupped both her breasts in his hands, kneading them as she arched her back to press into him. She wanted to protest when his hands stopped their ministrations to slide over her stomach, but the words caught in her throat as he pushed her thighs farther apart and brought his mouth to her core.

There was no warning, no lingering caresses with his fingers, just his mouth on her, licking and sucking, and thank God for that! She didn't want him to be slow and sweet. She wanted him to possess her. She needed this, needed to forget about everything but him and what he was doing to her.

She brought her knees up to give him better access, crying out as laved his tongue over the sensitive nub hidden in the folds of her core. He sucked until she was panting, then he drove his tongue deep inside her and she arched against him as her hands grasped handfuls of the sheet and her head fell to the side.

"Oh, God," she panted as her vision began to blur and white-hot sparks of heat shot from her core through her languid limbs.

She threw her head back, screaming his name as her body shattered with pleasure.

Then he was over her, pressing his mouth to hers. She could taste the essence of herself on his lips as his tongue tangled with hers. Her body was arching against him, wanting more of him, all of him.

She scooted herself up the length of the bed, and he followed her, raining kisses on her neck, her breasts, and her shoulders. Wrapping her legs around his waist, she rubbed restlessly against the hard length of his cock.

"I need you inside me, Hawk," she pleaded.

He wrapped one hand under her shoulder while the other slid under her back, then drove into her in one long, delicious stroke. When he was buried inside her, right where she needed him to be, she arched her back and pushed her hands in his hair as he brought his mouth to her breast, suckling hard.

He seemed to know exactly what she wanted and gave it to her. Every part of her quivered with the need for his attention as though her entire being was calling out for his. His arms wrapped tightly around her while he lapped and sucked at her breasts as his hips pulled back then thrust deep inside her again. She needed him to touch her everywhere, to consume her, forever.

His rhythm was relentless until he had stroked her into a frenzy. When she felt the pressure building low in her belly, she squeezed her muscles around him and threw her head back. His lips moved from her breasts to her neck as he changed his motion to a slow, deep rocking and his gaze locked with hers. The intensity in his eyes made her feel cherished and beautiful, and she never wanted to let him go. She clamped her muscles around the thickness of him inside her, pulsing as the excruciating pleasure increased to a breaking point.

Hawk pushed to his hands and arched his back, putting the perfect amount of pressure against her core as he continued to stroke against her throbbing muscles. She grabbed his arms and let out a cry as her body quivered and waves of ecstasy exploded through her body.

He came with her, throwing his head back with a deep groan

before collapsing on top of her, and taking her mouth in one more searing kiss.

She could not say out loud what her heart was screaming, so instead, she kissed him as though her very life depended on her lips being pressed to his, telling him with every stroke of her tongue that she loved him.

They stayed like that until their breathing calmed, the length of his body protectively covering hers. She slipped her hands up his sides and gingerly curved her fingers over his shoulders, careful not to touch his back while she kept him pressed against her. She wasn't ready for him to move or say anything to her because her mind was a jumble of thoughts and emotions that threatened to break her, all of them centered around the fact that she could not marry Montworth after tonight.

She would rather be alone with the memory of Hawk for the rest of her life than with any other man.

Which meant she had to fight for her inheritance and prove she could protect Hawkspur without a husband to rule over her and her home.

She swallowed hard to stop the burning in her eyes. Now was not the time to feel sorry for herself. Now was the time to memorize every detail of this man so she could keep a piece of him with her even after he was gone.

Hawk pushed up onto his elbows to look down into her face. He gently brushed a strand of her hair off her cheek.

"Did you mean it?" he asked as his eyes stared searchingly into hers.

His HEART SANK when she looked at him in confusion.

She didn't remember telling him over and over again that she loved him while their bodies were intertwined, his arms holding her tight as he devoured her and possessed her. As he worshipped her body with his mouth, her fingers holding him tight against her, she was telling him with words what he was telling her with his body.

I love you, I love you, I love you…

He convinced himself that even if she didn't realize she had said the words out loud, that didn't mean she didn't feel them. But he wouldn't press her to say them now. If her head wasn't ready to admit what her heart already knew, he would wait.

"Did I mean what, Hawk?" she asked, bracing his face in her hands as she looked up at him.

He almost told her then that he loved her, but he wouldn't do that to her until he was able to back up his words with action, which meant convincing King Edward that he and the queen were wrong to think he needed an heir more than he needed Alyce.

"Nothing," he said with a small shake of his head.

"I want tonight to only be about us and nothing else." She reached her lips to his and kissed him gently. "I don't want to think about our duties or our obligations outside of this room."

"I am all for you this night, my lady," he said, nuzzling her neck. "As many times and as many ways as you desire."

She laughed as she tipped her head back, the bright, melodic sound filling the quiet of the night around them. Next to her soft moans and cries as they made love, it was the sweetest sound in the world to his ears.

They lay together on the tangled bedding, his arm and leg draped over her luscious naked body as they whispered secrets and stories from their past to each other, avoiding any talk of what the future held for either of them.

When their bodies started to ache and throb with need for each other, they made love again, slowly and sweetly. He explored every curve, every hollow, every swell of her body with his lips and his tongue. He memorized every sigh, every gasp, every cry.

One night would never be enough.

❦ — ∙⊶❖⊷∙ — ❧

Chapter Thirty-Two

A LYCE RETURNED TO her chamber before dawn after Hawk had made love to her again. Extricating her body from the tangle of his limbs, knowing she may never have another night like this with him was like ripping her heart from her chest. She had to force herself not to look at him as she found her shift and wrapped herself in her robe. Even then, he had stalked from the bed like a lion on the hunt and pressed her up against the door to brand her with another blistering kiss before letting her leave.

She returned to her chamber in a daze, dressed quickly, splashed water on her face, and tried to force her attention to the duties of the day. She touched her fingers to her lips for the hundredth time as she descended the stairs from the upper chambers. It warmed her through to the core each time she did it, a new memory from the night coming back to her like a secret.

Duty jolted her back to reality as she stepped into the small passageway next to the open solar door. The king was seated at the table and men were pouring into the room to stand along the walls, next to the hearth, behind the king, and wherever else they could fit.

"After you, my lady," Hawk said, stepping into the passageway behind her from the stairs. Aelwin and Red were directly behind him. "There has been an urgent summons from the king. Aelwin knocked on your door, but Gertie told him you had already risen for the day."

The warmth in his eyes as he looked at her made her weak in the knees. "Y-yes," she stammered, quickly averting her eyes from Hawk lest Aelwin or Red see the longing she feared was clearly visible on her face.

She stepped into the solar with the other men. Aelwin positioned himself at her side, Hawk and Red at her back. If she leaned back even slightly, her body would touch Hawk's. It took all of her concentration to focus on what the king was saying and not on the heat radiating from him so close behind her.

"Llywelyn and Daffydd are on the move," King Edward announced. "My army will be ready to deploy at first light on the morrow. We will march west and cut them off before they can lay waste to any more of my kingdom. This is not a warning to Llywelyn and his ungrateful, greedy brother," the king's voice was full of scorn as he spoke. "This is a fight to the death. I want them both, dead or alive." He paused a moment then said, "No, I will take Llywelyn dead or alive, but I want Daffydd alive. The man has crossed me one too many times and will pay the price for his treachery. He will not have the mercy of a swift death."

He looked around the room at each person, stopping for a heartbeat longer when his eyes met Alyce's. She saw a muscle ripple in his jaw before his gaze continued to roam over the men gathered in the room. "Kill any Welsh rebel who does not yield immediately. Take as hostage any English traitors who chose sympathy for the Welsh over loyalty to their king. I want this ended, once and for all."

Murmurs of assent filled the air, but Alyce felt her gut twist. The king's message was clear: if Cynwulf was among the rebels he was to be captured and brought before the king. It sickened her to think of what he would do to her brother now that she knew what a "light" punishment looked like. Cynwulf would receive far worse than a flogging and a flayed back.

"Lady Alyce."

The king's words started Alyce out of her own thoughts. She bobbed a quick curtsy. "Yes, Sire?"

"I will be leaving my lady-wife here with her guard. I expect you and your commander—" he nodded toward Aelwin—"to protect her and Hawkspur at all costs."

"Yes, Sire," Alyce agreed.

"I expect you are well aware that any Marcher castle that harbors Welsh rebels, offers them assistance, or aids them in any way will be seized, and the liege and commander will be hanged?"

She did not blink or show any outward signs of distress even as the bile rose in her throat. "Of course, Sire."

"That includes any rebels who are relations. Do not let foolishness lead you into a situation that could be perceived as disloyalty to the crown."

"I will not, Sire." Alyce felt humiliated by the king's reprimand, though she could not fault him based on the events of the last sennight.

He nodded, then said, "I will send the commander of the queen's guard to meet with your commander. The fortification of this fortress will be your responsibility, Lady Alyce. Do not fail me."

"Yes, Sire." Alyce would do everything in her power to ensure no harm came to the queen or Hawkspur. If she succeeded, it would bolster her argument that she did not need to take Montworth as husband to keep the castle secure.

She would figure out the issue regarding her lack of heirs later.

The king pushed to his feet. "Everyone—including you, Hawk—prepare your troops for departure."

Alyce felt her heart sink as the men filed out of the room. In less than a day, the man she knew she'd love forever would be leaving Hawkspur, possibly for good.

ALYCE WAS EXHAUSTED by the time she climbed the stairs to the upper chambers at the end of the day. The castle had been a hive of activity as preparations were underway for the king's army to march in the morning. She and Aelwin had doubled the guards at every point around the fortress and the perimeter of the village and fields surrounding the castle. They had met with merchants and village elders to review the emergency procedures should Hawkspur come under attack. And she had consulted with the queen to ensure her comfort and security while the king rode at the head of his army.

Queen Eleanor and her ladies were prepared to wait for as long as it took for the king to return victorious, which could be as little as a day or as long as weeks or months. For her own sanity, Alyce prayed it was a matter of days and not months. She missed the familiarity of her own chamber and her bed.

As she entered the passageway to the upper chambers, she could feel her heartbeat increasing with the possibility of seeing Hawk one more time before he left in the morning. Her skin shivered in anticipation of his touch, even as her common sense told her it was selfish to spend another night in Hawk's bed, expecting him to forsake his much-needed rest the night before going to battle.

She wanted to scream her dismay when she saw that the door to Hawk's chamber was open, revealing the room had been emptied of Hawk's few possessions. She stepped inside the room, looking for any sign he would return. Hot tears stung her eyes as she realized he had left already, and without bidding her farewell.

"I will not cry," she muttered with determination, turning on her heel to leave the room and retire to her chamber.

"Gertie," she said, swinging her door open, "I—" She stopped midsentence as she realized Gertie was not in the room. Her limbs sagged with relief and her eyes blurred at the sight of Hawk standing next to the hearth, Ffyddlon's tail thumping against the floor as he scratched her head.

His arms were around her, taking her breath away, and he had her pressed up to the door before she knew what was happening.

"I thought you had left," she said, her voice a pitiful sob as she threw her arms around his neck and buried her face against his throat.

"I had to see you before I go," he said huskily. He cupped his hand around the back of her neck, pressing with his thumb to tip her face up to his. "My men and I are to find Llywelyn's camp under cover of the night and report their activity back to the king. His spies have informed him of the Welsh rebel's destination, but the king is taking no chances that they will change their course and avoid his ambush."

"You are leaving tonight?" Her hopes of another night in his arms were dashed.

"Aye. Hunter has already departed, and we are to follow him shortly." He leaned down to touch her lips with his in a gentle kiss. "I have only time to say goodbye."

"No," she whimpered, embarrassed at how pathetic she sounded.

Hawk brushed his thumb over her cheek. "I will come back."

She took a deep breath and looked into his eyes. She would not spend their last moments together crying or begging him not to go. He had his duty to attend to, and she had hers. "Godspeed to you. You will always be welcome at Hawkspur."

"Will I always be welcome to your bed, my love?"

A thrill tickled up her neck at being called his love. She smiled, saying with sincerity, "Always."

He kissed her with renewed urgency, his tongue plundering her mouth as his hands roamed over her body, pulling at her clothing to loosen it. She kissed and touched him with matching urgency, yanking at his shirt where it was tucked into his braies and chausses, wanting to touch his body and feel the hard plains of his chest under her fingers.

She stopped and looked at him in confusion when she encountered a layer of tightly wound linen instead of the warmth of his skin.

"Sorry, love," he said with a smirk. "Red's work to keep my shirt from rubbing the scabs off my back."

"Oh, God," she said with horror, "of course!"

"That doesn't mean I don't want to see you naked," he drawled, tugging her gown and chemise over her head. "Or that I'm not going to take you right here against the door." He stepped back once she was naked and looked his fill at her.

Alyce's instinct was to cover her bare body with her arms, but she would not let the image he took of her into battle be that of her shrinking away from him. Instead, she loosened her braid to shake her hair out over her shoulders.

"My God, you are magnificent," he said, his eyes scorching her body as they roamed over her breasts and hips, down her legs, and back up to her face.

She reached for him then, tugging at the ties on his braies. He hitched her leg up over his hip and cupped his hand around the back of her thigh to hold it in place as he stroked the wet folds of her with his other hand.

"Now, Hawk," she urged, wrapping her arms around his neck and lifting her other leg to leverage herself against his hips. He lifted her with his arms around her back and pressed her into the door as he entered her in one swift thrust. He kept one arm wrapped tightly around her and with the other he pushed the hair out of her face and ravished her mouth, his tongue flicking and caressing her in the same rhythm as his cock pounding into her as she squeezed around him, pulling him deeper into her.

He kept up the rhythm until her legs quivered and she was gasping and moaning against his lips. With another powerful stroke, he shuttered against her as she continued to lick and nip at his mouth. They didn't stop kissing as he pulled his hips away from hers and lowered her legs to the floor.

When he finally lifted his mouth from hers, he rested his forehead against her saying, "If I die tonight, I will die a happy man."

"Don't say that Hawk!" She fisted her hands into his shirt and shook him once. "You have to come back to me because…" She stopped, pressing her lips together. She had almost said the words.

"Because what?" he coaxed, his eyes and face suffused with so much gentleness and adoration that it was her undoing. God forbid something did happen to him tonight, she could not let him go to his grave not knowing how she felt.

"Because I love you." The smile that broke across his face at her confession was all the assurance she needed that he felt the same. "It is foolish, and the queen told me not to do it because I cannot have you, but I love you."

"Who says you cannot have me?" He looked genuinely shocked, and she wished she had not said it.

"You need heirs, Hawk." She sighed, laying her hand over his cheek. "I love you enough that I will not hold you back from taking a wife and siring the sons you deserve."

His eyes opened wide in surprise and then narrowed at her. "You would be my mistress?"

She nodded. "Until you marry, yes."

"And then what?" His voice was gruff with anger.

"Then I will let you go and be thankful for the time I've had with you."

He stepped back from her, roughly tying his braies. "You tell me you love me, and then tell me I am to marry some other woman, and you will just let me go?"

She stepped closer to him, framing his face in her hands again and forcing him to look at her. "Let us not discuss the future, Hawk. Right now, I want to remember the feeling of your body against mine and I want you to leave here knowing that I love you. You must concentrate on your mission and come back to me so I can tell you I love you at least one more time."

Hawk sighed, then pulled her into him. "I will come back, and you will tell me you love me, more than once."

Alyce did not say that would be impossible because the queen would never allow him to marry a barren woman. Instead, she kissed him and told him she loved him again.

Chapter Thirty-Three

ALYCE'S SHOULDERS FELT especially heavy with foreboding this eve. The day had started with bad news, and something in her gut told her more was to come.

She looked at the tiny boy asleep on a pallet of blankets next to the floor with Ffyddlon lying protectively at his side.

"What am I to do with him, Edna?" Alyce asked as the older women tidied the chamber and set out Alyce's night rail and robe.

Edna stopped what was doing to look down at the sleeping form. "'Tis a sad situation, my lady," was all she had to say before she continued her duties.

Janet had died that very morning of the flux. When Alyce had seen her a week earlier in the hall, it wasn't exertion that had flushed her cheeks and put a sheen of sweat on her pale skin. The poor woman had contracted dysentery, along with several others in the village and even more in the army camps set up outside the castle wall. Janet was one of four people who had succumbed to the disease.

Now the child was left motherless, and it was up to Alyce to determine what was to happen with Henry as Janet had no family to take on the boy. In truth, Alyce was likely the closest thing to a relative Henry had. Geoffrey was dead but Henry was his son, and she was his wife, and that made Henry her stepson. She was still trying to accept the bizarre twist of fate, and she was still uncertain what she planned to do for his future, but for the time being, she would see to his wellbeing with the help of Edna and Gertie.

And Ffyddlon.

The dog seemed to sense the little boy was in need of protection and comfort, and she had refused to leave his side. For his part, Henry had latched on to Ffyddlon with equal bravado.

"Can you stay with him for a while, Edna?" Alyce asked. "The moon is high, and I need to clear my head."

"Aye, my lady," Edna responded, reaching for a cloak hanging from a peg on the wall. She helped Alyce into the warm garment, then pulled the ermine-trimmed hood up over her hair. "Do not catch a chill, dear," she warned.

Alyce pulled the heavy wool tight around her body as she stepped onto the parapets. A cold wind swirled the light dusting of snow on the stones and chilled her nose. As she had done nearly every night since Hawk had left, she walked to the stretch of the parapets that overlooked the hill and forest to the west of the castle, in the direction of Wales. It was the same hill and forest where Cynwulf had met with the rebels just a fortnight ago, though it felt more like months now.

She stood on the parapet, looking out over the castle wall toward the western road and scanning the crest of the hills on either side of the road, searching for any sign of Hawk and his men returning. Five days had passed since he'd ridden out in the middle of the night to find Llywelyn's camp.

This evening, a messenger had arrived for the queen just before supper. Llywelyn was dead, but Daffydd eluded capture. The king's army was moving to Oswestry Castle to continue the offensive, and she was to join him there. A contingent of his men would arrive on the morrow to accompany the queen and her guard for the journey.

No message had arrived from Hawk. And there was no mention of Cynwulf.

If Daffydd eluded capture, then perhaps Cynwulf still lived. But for what end? If he remained with Daffydd, the king would surely capture him and kill him; if he was fortunate, he would not be tortured before being put to death. His only chance at living a long life was if he fled Britain. She would never see him again, but he would be safer.

The foreboding from earlier had settled deep into her bones, and she could not rid herself of the fear the day was not yet done. The moon was nearly full, and it hung low in the sky, illuminating the landscape as though it were the middle of a bright summer day. The trees had shed their leaves for winter, leaving nothing but spindly branches reaching for the sky and offering little protection to the ground below. The moonlight reflected off the fresh snow blanketing the forest floor, amplifying every shadow, every movement among the trees.

If Hawk and his men returned, they would come by the west road. If Cynwulf were to be so foolish as to return, he would come by the forest. Every time a deer stepped from behind a tree to walk carefully to the shelter of the next tree, Alyce's heart leaped. Her stomach churned and she could not stand still. She paced the high castle wall back and forth, watching and waiting.

And then she saw him.

He was standing on the edge of the forest at the crest of the hill. He was nothing more than a shadow, but she knew it to be Cynwulf.

She looked to the guards standing at their posts along the parapets. They had not seen him yet, but it was only a matter of time before they noticed him.

Cynwulf started to descend the hill along the same path Alyce, Hawk, Red, and Hunter had returned the night her brother left with the Welshmen. His steps looked jerky, as though it took effort to remain on his feet.

Alyce started to run along the parapet toward the stairs to the yard, her eyes trained on Cynwulf, just as the guards called out a warning of a lone man approaching the castle. A heartbeat later, the guards started yelling more warnings and Alyce looked over her brother's shoulder to see men emerging from the woods, one on horseback and the other on foot.

Another movement caught her eye coming from the direction of the road. A group of riders was galloping toward the castle but veered off the road. Six of the riders were climbing the hill toward the men behind Cynwulf, and a lone rider was bearing down on her brother at top speed.

It was Hawk; she could recognize him as easily as she'd recognized Cynwulf.

Alyce's heart lodged in her throat, cutting off her breath and she turned to steady herself against the parapet as Hawk jumped from his horse, sword in hand, to face her brother. She fought with herself, wanting to turn away from the inevitable clash, but she reminded herself she was the Lady of Hawkspur, and the king had taught her a harsh lesson. So she pushed her hood back from her face to better see the melee erupting in front of her.

The six riders had not drawn their swords, but they were riding in circles around the men from the forest, impeding their progress toward Cynwulf. Her brother had drawn his sword and was facing off with Hawk.

She wanted time to stop, wanted all of this to be a horrible dream and not a reality unfolding in front of her eyes. Her knees went weak with fear—fear for her brother, fear for Hawk, fear her life was about to spin out of her control again.

A sharp clang broke through the night air. Cynwulf spun from the force of Hawk's sword striking against his. Lifting the hems of her cloak and gown in her hands, she ran to the guard tower and down the stairs toward the postern gate.

Guards were emerging from the barracks, clad in armor and pulling on their helms, readying themselves to face whatever danger lay beyond the castle gate. More guards were swarming across the bailey to the walls and towers, preparing for the worst.

Alyce pushed between the armored men—hampered by their heavy armor and helms—and ran as fast as she could to the small gate behind the kitchen. She had to get to Hawk and her brother before the guards entered the conflict.

She ducked through the gate and started up the hill, ignoring the calls of the guards while praying it was not too late for Cynwulf.

"YOU ARE A fool, Cynwulf," Hawk yelled, balancing his sword in front of him. "Why did you come back here? Do you want to see your sister killed?"

Cynwulf had removed his armor, facing him now in only a gambeson with a dark patch of blood soaking through the quilted material on his left shoulder. Hawk had seen him get injured in the battle with Daffydd and Llywelyn and watched as Daffydd fled to safety after Llywelyn was killed, leaving Cynwulf behind to face the English with the rest of the Welsh rebels not able to escape quickly enough. When the battle was over, and Cynwulf was nowhere to be found, Hawk feared the fool would try to make his way to Hawkspur, heedless of the danger he brought with him.

"I love my sister," Cynwulf said, his sword listing to the side as his left arm weakened from the shoulder wound. "I just want to see her one more time."

Hawk tipped his chin toward his wounded shoulder. "That will not kill you." He'd seen enough men wounded in battle to know which blows were deadly. "If it does, it will be from infection, and that death will not come quick enough to save you from King Edward."

"Then you will have to kill me," Cynwulf said. "But not before—"

Hawk had been watching his own men over Cynwulf's shoulder, gaging how much longer they could hold off Sheriff Montworth and his band of enforcers. Everyone knew there was a hefty price on Cynwulf's head if he was captured and brought to the king, including Montworth. The odious man would not care that Alyce would be forced to watch her brother tortured and hanged, as long as he collected his reward.

When Cynwulf stopped midsentence, his eyes focusing on something beyond Hawk, he knew it could only be for one of two reasons: either guards were pouring from the castle and coming in their direction, or Alyce had managed to come down from her place on the wall and was trying to get to her brother.

"You've seen Alyce," Hawk said, striking Cynwulf's blade with his own to antagonize him, goading him into lunging at him.

"You couldn't have missed her on the parapet in that white cloak. She cannot help you unless you want to see her hanging from a rope at your side."

Hawk dared a quick look behind him and saw her running toward them, her red hair billowing out behind her like a flaming banner in sharp contrast to the white of her cloak. His heart sank at the sight, but he knew it was inevitable. She would not stay away if there was a chance to see her brother.

Time was critical now. He only had a few moments to end this, or Alyce would be forced to suffer more than she already had.

"Do you love her?" Cynwulf asked, lifting his sword to point it in Hawk's direction again.

Hawk nodded once. "I do, but we both know it will mean nothing when this is over."

"Then let Montworth kill me, or one of your men."

"Montworth has no intention of killing you. He will take you alive for the reward. If you do not want your sister to see you tortured, then we must do this now." Hawk looked to where his men were skirmishing with Montworth's men, then back at Alyce. She was too close and would be to them in a matter of a few moments.

"I want to die with what dignity I have left," Cynwulf said. "I just wish she did not have to see it."

"I do this because I love her, not because I think you deserve the honor of a quick death." Hawk held his sword high with one hand. "If you want to die fighting, then take your aim now."

Cynwulf aimed his sword at Hawk's chest and lunged forward with what strength he had left. Hawk easily sidestepped the attack, as Cynwulf knew he would, and brought his sword around to cut cleanly through the tender flesh under his ribs. Cynwulf dropped his sword to the ground to clutch his side, but he did not look at Hawk. His eyes were focused on his sister, running toward him with her arms outstretched and a scream on her lips.

Hawk watched her coming closer, never taking his eyes from her as he pulled his sword back, then drove the blade through

Cynwulf's chest. The wound in his gut was a killing blow; it would take a short but agonizing time for him to die while he choked on his own blood. The blade through the chest drained the last of his life from him and put an end to his suffering.

Then Alyce was there, catching Cynwulf as he fell, her face contorted with pain as tears streamed down her face. She wrapped her brother in her arms and crumpled to the ground with him, sobbing, "No, no, no." She buried her face in her brother's hair and rocked his lifeless body as his blood soaked into her white cloak, turning it and the snow beneath them red.

Hawk felt his heart splintering in his chest and feared for the space of a heartbeat that a sword had been driven through him from behind. But it was heartbreak cutting through him with a pain, unlike anything he'd ever felt before. He wanted to go to Alyce, to take her in his arms and tell her what he'd done was the only way to save her brother from being tortured and to save her from having to witness it. He wanted to tell her he loved her and beg her to forgive him, to tell her what he could do to make it right again. But he knew none of it would matter.

She had not looked at him as she ran to her brother in those last moments, and she did not look at him now as he laid a hand over her shoulder in a gesture of pity, but he did not know what else to do.

He turned at the sound of pounding hoofbeats and men yelling. His men had abandoned the men chasing Cynwulf and circled around Hawk, Alyce, and Cynwulf protectively as Montworth and his men closed in on them.

"Grogan!" Montworth yelled from atop his horse, his men panting heavily as they ran down behind him. "What have you done?"

Hawk pushed forward to face Montworth, his dripping sword still in his hand. "I have killed a traitor in the name of the king."

"I wanted my reward," Montworth sneered at him, bringing his horse to a stop an arm's length in front of him. "You did not have to kill him!"

"Do you challenge my decision?" Hawk asked through gritted teeth, lifting his sword in front of him. His blood was pulsing through his veins, anger making him reckless. "Draw your sword and face me if you dare challenge me."

The cowardly sheriff backed his horse away from Hawk, glaring at him. "You will regret this," he'd barked, then turned and rode back up the hill, his men puffing along behind him.

Hawk turned back to see that Hawkspur's guard was nearly upon them. He went to Alyce and kneeled at her side, but she would not look at him. Still rocking her brother's body, she simply said, "Go," without lifting her head.

He did as she asked, motioning for his men to retreat as he swung up into the saddle of his stallion. He galloped to the road, then turned and watched the guards lift Cynwulf's body and escort Alyce back to the castle. When the heavy wooden gate closed behind them, he commanded his horse with a press of his heels and rode away from Hawkspur.

He'd been a fool not to tell her he loved her before he rode out of Hawkspur's gates less than a sennight before. He had thought then it was more important to make things right with the king, to first earn his trust back and then request permission to marry Alyce—if she would have him. He did not want to tell her he loved her until he could have her completely.

Now that decision filled him with regret. Had he truly believed then that he would stop loving her if the king had refused his request? He would walk through fire to get to her, with or without the king's blessing.

But it was too late. How could she feel anything but loathing for him after he killed her brother?

He would love her until he drew his last dying breath, and she would hate him until she drew hers.

✦

Chapter Thirty-Four

Six months later…

"I HAVE SOMEONE who wishes to see you, my lady," Edna said with a smile, opening the door to Alyce's solar and laughing as Henry pushed past her skirts and burst into the room.

Alyce turned her chair and held out her arms to the little boy as he ran on steady legs around the desk and into her arms. He had grown so much in the six months since becoming her ward. The chubby little toddler who was constantly falling on his butt had turned into a little boy who ran everywhere.

"Mama!" he said, throwing himself into her arms. Alyce's eyes started to burn again as a smile crossed her face. Henry had started calling her *Mama* in only the past fortnight, but each time he did, her heart swelled with joy.

She hugged the boy against her chest. "What have you been doing today, pet?"

"Horsies!" he said brightly. "Berned let me ride on a horsey."

"Bern-*ard*," she said, emphasizing the last syllable of the stablemaster's name, "is very kind to show you how to ride. And you are very brave."

Henry nodded then pushed out of her arms to run from the room, Edna fast on his heels.

"I tell Giffin now," he called over his shoulder as he disappeared through the doorway of the solar.

It still amazed her that this little boy who'd brought her so much pain just a year ago brought her so much happiness now. How ironic that the product of her husband's infidelity was the person she now loved most in the world. When she had to make difficult decisions, or when she felt too tired to carry on, she pictured little Henry and remembered why her work was important.

All of this would belong to Henry when she was gone—she had the king's blessing in writing, recognizing him as her heir.

Despite her reticence toward King Edward's ways that she perceived as cruel at times, he was a man of his word. And for reasons she never fully understood, he never again suggested she marry Montworth, or anyone else, after he'd left Hawkspur.

Her mind drifted to Hawk, as it did several times every day, and always at night. She missed him terribly. She had tried a thousand different times to send a message to him in care of the king's court but stopped herself every time. The queen had every intention of finding him an heiress to give him sons. She would not make his life or hers more difficult by dragging out an affair that would not end happily.

Another knock sounded on the door and Aelwin entered at her beckoning. "There is someone here to see you, my lady— Hunter." He said the last with raised eyebrows.

"What? Why?" Her heart leaped and then plummeted. The arrival of Hawk's man could herald good news—or bad. "What does he…?"

Aelwin shrugged and seemed as bewildered as her by the unexpected guest.

"Show him in," she said, standing.

Hunter was the last person Alyce expected to see in her solar, especially just as she'd been thinking of Hawk. Or maybe she thought about Hawk so much, it wasn't odd at all that Hunter appeared as if invoked.

Though, even when he was garrisoned at the fortress with Hawk and his army, Hunter had rarely made an appearance within the castle walls.

"My lady," he said, bowing his head, his shaggy brown hair obscuring his face with the motion.

"Hunter," Alyce responded, trying to keep her voice as even as possible while her stomach lurched with fear. She could think of a few reasons why this man would grace her with his presence unless forced to do so. "What brings you to Hawkspur?"

Hunter's eyes shifted to Aelwin, then back to her as he gave a noncommittal grunt. He was an irritating man of few words.

"Is your commander well?"

Hunter nodded. "Aye, my lady."

Alyce felt her heart plummet at the news. She was happy that Hawk was well, but that meant that he had stayed away from her by choice. She'd not seen or heard from him since the night Cynwulf died. She had been so distraught over her brother's death, she hadn't been able to look at Hawk for fear it would be too much to bear. When she thought of that horrible day, she didn't want to see Hawk's face as he killed her brother or associate him with the feel of Cynwulf dead in her arms, or with the blood that stained her cloak red and soaked the ground around them. That was why she hadn't looked at him.

She'd wanted to tell Hawk that she understood why he killed Cynwulf, that she knew he did it to protect him from inevitable torture, and to protect her from having to watch her brother die a much more horrible death. She wanted him to know she did not hold him accountable for Cynwulf's death; that was his own doing. She wanted him to understand that when she told him to go, she only meant for him to leave before Montworth spun the situation out of control and made Hawk look bad in front of the king for his own gain. She didn't have the strength or the words to tell him all the things that were swirling in her head at that moment.

When days, weeks, and then months passed without Hawk returning to her, she'd concluded the king and queen had stayed steadfast in their determination he marry a woman who could give him the heirs he needed and deserved. She had told him she loved him, but he had not said the words in return, and perhaps time away from her had dimmed his passion for her.

"My lady?" Hunter asked, his face etched with concern.

Alyce shook her head. "I am sorry, Hunter. I was distracted. Please repeat what you said."

"I request to speak to you privately."

"Of course." She nodded to Aelwin, who took his leave, then lowered herself to her seat and motioned to a chair for Hunter.

He shook his head. "I prefer to stand."

Alyce had to stop an ironic burst of laughter from escaping her lips. It was nearly one year since Hawk and Red stood in this same solar, facing her and Cynwulf, both refusing to sit because they "preferred to stand".

Alyce nodded. "What did you wish to speak to me about?"

"Do you still blame my commander for your brother's death?"

Alyce was taken aback by the abrupt question. She and Hunter had never become friendly with each other, and he irritated her more often than not with his grunted answers and judgmental looks, but she respected him because Hawk did.

Taking a deep breath, she thought about how best to answer the strange question. "He is not to blame for the decisions Cynwulf made and the results of those decisions."

Hunter stared at her for a long moment, then nodded once and turned on his heel as though to leave.

"Wait!" Alyce said, rising to her feet.

Hunter stopped at the door and turned to face her.

She dropped her head for a moment and shook it, then looked up again at the obstinate man. "You've never been one for many words, Hunter, but I will not abide you asking one question and then leaving without giving me some information in return."

Hunter looked wary as he squared his feet, crossed his arms, and waited for her to speak.

Alyce wasn't sure where to start, but she surmised her questions had best be strategic because Hunter would likely only tolerate a few inquiries before he tired of her and took his leave.

"Does Hawk still serve the king?"

A nod.

"Is he betrothed as the queen so desired?"

A slow shake of his head.

Alyce sighed, then said in a quiet, awkward voice, "Does he ever say my name?"

Hunter looked at her for the space of three heartbeats—Alyce counted them—and then shook his head.

"Thank you, Hunter," she said, feeling hollow as she sat down in her chair, lowering herself steadily before her knees gave out on her. "You may go."

When the door was closed behind him, and Alyce was alone again, she sank back in the chair and looked at the ceiling, willing the burning in the backs of her eyes to cease.

It was over. Hawk didn't love her as she loved him. He'd played her for the fool she was. How easy it must have been to convince an unworldly widow that he cared for her, that she was beautiful and desirable and worthy of love when none of it was true. Resistance from the king and time away from her was all it took for her to become just another woman he could forget.

"*Now* will you go to her?"

Hawk narrowed his eyes at Red. "What are you blathering on about now?"

His first-in-command blew out a long sigh of frustration. "Why must you make everything harder than it need be?"

"Just say what you mean, you damned Viking," Hawk grumbled, his anger rising. Red could be more irritating than a clucking old hen.

"Alyce," Hunter grunted at him from his other side.

The three men navigated the cobblestoned lanes of Shrewsbury, making their way to the castle. King Edward was celebrating his victory over the Welsh rebels, rejoicing that his most hated enemy, Daffydd ap Llywelyn, self-proclaimed Prince of Wales and traitor to the English crown was finally in his hands. Hawk and his elite force of knights had been critical to the king's success against the rebels and in ultimately capturing Daffydd.

Hawk had thought of Alyce every single day for the last six months. He'd ridden to the edge of the forest outside of Hawkspur Castle more times than he could count, waiting to catch a glimpse of her standing tall on the high castle walls. It took every bit of his strength not to burst from the shelter of the forest, crest the hill on his stallion, and ride through the gates of the castle to claim her.

But she had told him to go, and he'd done as she commanded. He loved her too much to cause her any more pain than he had already. "She is better off without me."

"She doesn't think so."

Hawk stopped in his tracks to glare at Hunter. "What makes you say that?"

"I saw her."

"When?"

"Yesterday."

"Where?" Hawk wanted to shake Hunter and demand he tell him every detail.

"Hawkspur."

"Is she all right?" If the man didn't start giving up details soon, he was going to punch him.

Hunter nodded once.

Hawk clenched his hands into fists at his side but almost hit Red instead when he let out a booming laugh.

"It's a good thing I don't have my sword, or I'd skewer you both where you stand." He narrowed his eyes at both the men, who despite their irritating ways, always had his back.

"You love her," Red said. "It's why you lurk in the shadows of the woods outside Hawkspur every chance you get."

Hawk sighed. "It is because I love her that I do not go to her. I have caused her enough pain."

"She loves you," Hunter said in a flat tone. "She couldn't stop asking about you, how you fared, if you ever asked about her."

"What did you tell her?" Hawk cringed at the excitement rising in his voice.

Hunter shrugged. "You fared well, and you never talk about her."

"*That's* what you told her?" At this moment, Hawk didn't care that Hunter was one of the most skilled men in his elite army; he was going to kill him.

"You don't speak of her," he said, seemingly shocked at Hawk's response. "That doesn't mean you don't love her."

"Did you at least tell her that?" Hawk asked sarcastically.

Hunter shook his head slowly. "Doesn't she know you love her?"

Hawk clenched his teeth and growled in frustration.

"She did say you are not to blame for killing Cynwulf. She said he made his own decisions."

Hawk snapped his attention back to Hunter. "Truthfully?"

"Aye." Hunter shifted on his feet, growing uncomfortable with the talk of love and women. "She did not sound like she hated you. She sounded like she…misses you."

"You've made me a happy man," Hawk said, clapping Hunter on the back. "Now, let's never speak of this again."

"Are you going to her?" Red asked again.

"As soon as the king dismisses me," Hawk said with a grin.

"And if he doesn't?" Hunter asked.

Red snorted. "Hawk is again the king's most favored knight. He can ask for any boon he desires. And he desires Lady Alyce."

"Ready my horse," Hawk commanded. "I ride for Hawkspur. Today!"

HAWK FOUND ALYCE leaning against the fence of the outermost pasture, watching as a young colt was put through his paces by the stablemaster. Ffyddlon was sprawled out in the afternoon sun at her feet. He stood unnoticed in the shade of a tree, watching her for a long while.

She was beautiful.

She was everything.

Ffyddlon saw him first, bolting to sit upright and thumping her tail on the ground. Alyce murmured something to the dog, but when Ffyddlon's whole body started to wriggle, she looked around for the source of the hound's excitement.

When she caught sight of him standing a stone's throw away beneath the branches of a large tree, she froze. Except for her eyes—she blinked, and then again, as though she didn't believe what she was seeing, and when Hawk took a tentative step forward, her throat bobbed as she swallowed hard several times. She watched him as he walked toward her, never taking his eyes from her face.

It broke his heart as he drew near and saw the wetness on her cheeks. She kept her spine stiff, and her head held high, but he could see her hands trembling at her sides. He stopped an arm's length away, willing himself not to reach for her yet, terrified she still could reject him. This was why he'd never allowed himself to love. He'd been in battle countless times, faced death, and caused it, and yet nothing caused him more fear than the thought that Alyce could—and would—turn him away.

But he wasn't a man to run from pain.

"Is it true you do not hate me for what happened to Cynwulf?" he asked, his voice hoarse.

She nodded as she pressed her lips together and furrowed her brow as though fighting to keep her composure.

He dared to step closer. "I did not want to do it. As hard as it is to believe, I did it to save both him and you from…."

"I know," she said, her voice hardly a whisper.

He stepped close enough to smell the fragrance of her hair and reached his hand up to cup her cheek. "Do you still love me?"

She stared at him through watery eyes for a long moment before he caught an almost imperceptible nod.

He held his breath, afraid to say another word lest he make a muck of this. "I should have told you the first night you came to me, because I knew it then." He framed her face in both of his hands. "I love you. I love you more than I ever knew a man could love a woman." He panicked when she closed her eyes and tears flowed over her cheeks and found himself babbling. But he didn't try to stop himself. "I love you beyond all measure. I love you so much that I convinced myself you were better without me because I didn't want to hurt you anymore. It felt like my heart was being ripped out of my chest every time I saw you on the parapets in the early mornings or the late nights. I wanted so badly to come to you, to wrap you in my arms and tell you I love you, but I thought you didn't want to see me."

"Stop," she sobbed, reaching her hands up to grab fistfuls of his shirt. "I missed you," she finally said in the faintest whisper.

That was all he needed. He pulled her into his embrace and buried his face in her hair. "I've missed *you*," he said, the words coming out more as a sob than he intended. "I was broken without you."

He kissed the strands of her hair, her ear, her forehead, his lips moving over her face as though he needed to touch every part of it to know she was real, that this wasn't a dream.

"I told you to come back to me, Hawk, but you didn't."

The sorrow in her voice nearly broke him again. "I was a goddamn fool," he said, his voice gruff with emotion. "But I will never make that mistake again."

"Tell me again that you love me."

He lost himself in her brilliant blue eyes that matched the color of the English summer sky. "I love you, Alyce, Lady of Hawkspur."

And then he was ravishing her mouth, claiming her with every ounce of his being, kissing her thoroughly, until both of their hearts were beating out of control. Hawk pressed his forehead to hers as their eyes locked on each other, neither willing to look away for even a second. "I give you my heart and my steadfast fidelity. If you will have me, I am yours."

"You are all I want, Hawk," she said, wrapping her arms tightly around his neck.

"I told you once that when I was back on my feet, I would give you my allegiance."

"And I told you I did not want you to bow to me."

Hawk pulled her arms from his neck and lowered himself to take a knee in front of her. "I will swear my allegiance to you in all things if you let me serve you for the rest of your life."

Alyce tugged at his arms, trying to pull him back to his feet. "I do not need another vassal, Hawk. I want you for my own. I want to sleep in your arms every night and wake up to you every day. I want you as my lover and my confidant, and I wish you to be my equal in all things."

"I will never be your equal." He put his hands on the curve of her waist as he looked up at her. "Lady Alyce, Mistress of

Hawkspur, I swear my undying love and the strength of my sword to you for as long as I live and breathe. I vow to love you and be at your command, to make love to you every night and kiss you every morning. I will be your protector and your ally in all things."

Alyce dropped her knees to face him. "You told me once you bow to no one but King Edward."

"I did," he agreed. "And now I bow to you. I will always bow to you."

"If we marry, you will be Lord of Hawkspur—"

Hawk shook his head and put his fingers to her lips to stop her from speaking. "I do not want to be lord of Hawkspur." He almost laughed at the hurt and confused look on her face. "I want you to be my wife, but I do not want Hawkspur for my own. All I want are barracks to house my men and a field to train them in."

"The king will never agree to such an arrangement," she protested.

"He already has," Hawk assured her. "You remain liege of Hawkspur, and I continue to serve the king by training an elite force of fighters ready to do his bidding. But only if this is agreeable to you, my lady."

"What of children, Hawk?" she asked, her eyes turning vulnerable. "Will you want a family?"

"*You* are my family," he said pulling her into his arms again. "I could never want for more. And when we die, we will leave what we have to the horses, or the dogs, or whomever you choose." He wished he knew what to say to assure her he cared nothing about leaving a legacy, but she would believe him with time.

She cocked her eyebrow and pinched her lips together as though considering it. "I want a family, Hawk. Children."

He tried to hide the sadness in his eyes that he could not give her what she wanted. "The people of Hawkspur will be our family."

She quirked a small smile at him. "Could you love a child and raise it as your own, even if he was not of your blood?"

"Of course," Hawk said, slanting his eyes at her, wondering what she was alluding to.

"Could you love Henry?"

"Henry?"

"His mother did not survive the last winter," Alyce explained. "And I am his closest relative. He calls me *Mama*, and he is growing so tall."

He didn't think he could love her any more than he did a few moments ago, but he was quite certain the feeling in his chest was his heart exploding.

"Edna calls him little Hawk," Alyce confessed with a grin. "But he needs a papa. If you will have me, then you must take him as well."

Hawk nodded. "It's perfect."

"I do not want him to be an only child, Hawk," Alyce continued. "There are other children in the village who have been orphaned."

"Let's have them all," he said with a laugh. He pushed to his feet and then held his hand out to her to haul him up next to her.

"I have one request," Alyce said.

"Anything."

"I was serious when I said I wanted an equal. You can train your forces and have free reign of the castle, but we rule Hawkspur together. *And* I want to be known as Lady Hawk," she added with a grin.

He shook his head. "Hawkspur is yours. I serve you."

"You said you would do as I command and accept your role as lord."

"No one can lord over Hawkspur better than you, my lady. I will not see it any other way."

"Then I will not marry you."

"That is your choice, but I will be sleeping in your bed, whether you marry me or not."

She gasped in mock astonishment. "Do you always get your prey, Lord Hawk?" she asked in a husky voice.

"Always."

"Good," she told him and kissed him thoroughly.

About the Author

Lois dreamed of becoming a writer since she was a child making up her own bedtime stories. She started writing after getting her master's degree in English literature, though the road to becoming a published author has been long and fraught with many of life's interruptions.

Medieval history, Great Britain, knights, and castles have been a passion of hers for as long as she can remember, but it wasn't until she was in her thirties that she became an avid reader of romances. After reading The Wedding by Julie Garwood, she was hooked on medieval romances and soon started writing her own. She loves writing about bold women, broody knights, and vexing Vikings.

She currently lives on the US West Coast with her husband and dog. They love traveling, visiting their son (also a writer!) in Los Angeles, and dreaming of living abroad.

Website – www.loistemplin.com
Instagram – instagram.com/lois.templin
TikTok – tiktok.com/@loistemplinauthor

www.ingramcontent.com/pod-product-compliance
Lightning Source LLC
Chambersburg PA
CBHW070520310726
48976CB00002BA/485